"Romance, revenge, redemption—and
a rock-music legend to die for."

Books by Tina Murray

Heston Demming Mysteries
A Chance to Say Yes
A Wild Dream of Love
A Big Fan of Yours

A Wild Dream of Love

SPEAKING VOLUMES, LLC
NAPLES, FLORIDA
2022

A Wild Dream of Love

Cover design by Hannah Linder

ISBN 978-1-64540-620-4

A Wild Dream of Love

Tina Murray

To S. L.

Acknowledgments

I am grateful to Kurt Mueller of Speaking Volumes LLC for publishing this reprint edition of A Wild Dream of Love. I am grateful to Erica Mueller for her willingness to assist in the editing and revising of the first edition. Furthermore, I thank both of them for having faith in the Heston Demming series. Thanks, also, to their staff members. I appreciate Hannah Linder, in particular, for her compelling cover design.

My thanks, as well, to the following people for their earlier contributions: Dak Alley, Shawn Bowling, Tinka Canfield, Chad Cornelius, Krista Derizeri, Joanna Gelinas, Robert Gelinas, Meredith Green, Gwendolyn Griffith, Mitch Johnson, Sandy Lender, Stephen Lifschitz, Gus Mendoza, Sonja Miller, Daniel Morris, John M. Murray, Debi Norton, Nancy B. Rugen, Drew Smith, Jane Kennedy Sutton, and Sue Torbin. Truly, I am obliged to my colleagues, friends, relatives, and gentle readers for years of unwavering support.

Tina Murray
February 2022

MANON
...Remember the intensity of our love!

DES GRIEUX
No! I wrote on sand
this wild dream of love
that Heaven sustained
for only an instant, for a day!

From: Act Three, Scene Two
Manon, an opera by Massenet
Libretto by Meilhac and Gille
English Translation
Source: opera-arias.com

Chapter One

"It's your choice, Poppy. Give up Heston or destroy him forever."

"Aren't you being melodramatic, Lennox?"

"Am I?"

In the lobby of the beachfront Fontainebleau Hotel, Poppy Demming stared into the shallow eyes of her ex-daughter-in-law, movie actress Lennox Cordova, whose hatred for her was obvious. Poppy watched as the petite sexpot's rubbery lips curled in contempt—as much as collagen could curl. Mercilessly, Lennox dragged Poppy into an unattended restroom.

Cornering her, Lennox sneered. "Heston Demming is mine by rights. I intend to have him. Give him a divorce, and I won't publish my mother's diary. I won't cry statutory rape. I won't drag your—rather, our—famous family through the mud. That is my final, and only, offer."

"In your dreams, dearie. How do I know your mother even kept a diary?" Poppy countered, playing for time, time to think. "Why should I believe anything you say?"

"Don't worry, Poppy," Lennox grinned, her once-fluid face now a twisted slab of lacquered plastic. "The diary exists. It's locked in my safe. I have a new penthouse in South Beach."

"Penthouse?"

"I've moved up."

"Bully for you. Now that you've bankrupted my son, you can afford it."

Lennox laughed. "Kipp still owes me child support for Shawnee."

Poppy bristled. "Leave my grandson out of this. How did you know I was here at the Fontainebleau? Our trip to Miami was spur-of-the-moment. I didn't even know we were coming until yesterday, when Banks Winston phoned us in Naples and invited us."

"The shallow eyes glittered. "Are you sure Shawnee is your *grandson*?" Lennox taunted, egging her on. "Not your *stepson*?"

Poppy regarded her in horror. "Meaning what?"

Languidly, Lennox hitched a hip, swiveled in disdain, and opened the restroom door. "Make up your mind, Mother-in-Law. Then phone me. You have 24 hours, or else I ship Mom's diary to the publisher. I'll be at home, waiting for your call." Tossing her mop of luxurious chestnut hair, a trademark of her image on film, Lennox sauntered away, expertly balanced atop stiletto heels. Heads turned.

Oblivious, Poppy followed her into the lobby, watching as she exited the main door.

Now what? Dazed, she sank into a chair in the hotel lobby and watched the guests pass by. In an instant, her world had collapsed. She had to decide if she would fight for her husband or not. Would she divorce him? Hand him over to Lennox? Or would she stand by and let him go to prison? Did he deserve to go to prison?

Had Heston really slept with Lennox two decades ago? Had Lennox's mother known? Sex with a minor was a serious crime. Was there a statute of limitations? Even worse, was he sleeping with Lennox now, as she had hinted?

Should I confront Heston? I can phone him at home.

But could she trust her husband? She thought he had confided all of his secrets during their eight years of marriage. He had always denied having a love affair with Lennox Cordova—to her, to the press, to everyone. He claimed a purely professional relationship with the starlet who had played leading lady to his leading man in five major motion pictures over the past two decades. *I believed you, Heston.*

And yet, if that were true, why had Heston become so upset when their son Kipp had married Lennox four years ago? And fathered a baby with her...supposedly...

She studied the bow-tie insets on the lobby floor.

Think, brain. What should I do now? Her life was unraveling around her in coils at her feet, and the coils were morphing into a python. Trembling, Poppy fingered the scarf at her throat. *I must do something to stop Lennox—and soon.*

Chapter Two

Paint brush in hand, mature superstar Heston Demming labored passionately on his latest self-portrait in oils. His silver-blue eyes gazed intently at a rectangular stretched canvas propped upright upon the wooden easel in front of him. The cool air drifting into the art studio in his Port Royal mansion was permeated by the mingled pungent odors of linseed oil and turpentine, a smell he had learned to love. It was a smell he suspected his wife of eight years, Poppy, and his children, Winner, Dakota, Sage, and Tegan, had learned to loathe. He didn't count Kipp anymore, not since the notorious row he and Kipp had had four years ago Thanksgiving.

On that day, he had banished his eldest son from the realm. *It doesn't bear thinking about. Think about the problem at hand.* Experimenting, he switched from brush to brush, first painting meticulously, now in sweeping swaths of vivid color. He furrowed his brow.

Will I be ready in time? His first public showing was only four weeks away. Six of his paintings would be on display for one week in the lobby gallery of The Naples Philharmonic. The week would culminate in a reception, given prior to his performance of songs and readings in "An Evening with Heston Demming." He was more nervous about the exhibition than the musical numbers. Theatre critics didn't faze him anymore. Art critics on the other hand...

His phone rang.

Damn and blast it. He grabbed for the small, offensive object but it was nowhere to be found. Fumbling through his pockets, he smeared his Tee-shirt and jeans with the cadmium red on his fingertips. The ringing stopped. Scowling, he glanced at his Rolex, which wasn't there because he had taken it off before painting. Cursing, he resumed his work.

Morning sunlight flooded silently into the studio through tall, open windows. Outside, the green fronds of the royal palm trees lining his waterfront estate swayed elegantly in the nippy January breeze blowing in from the Gulf of Mexico. Inside, only the distant hum of the gardener's lawn mower broke the stillness in the studio. His breaths came low and heavy.

Sitting back on the stool, he contemplated his own visage and sighed. He was dissatisfied. Frowning, he glared into the double-mirror set up on the table. Gazing into a mirror wasn't as gratifying as it used to be.

Twenty years ago, *he* might have seemed the most significant work of art in the room, apart from an original Gauguin self-portrait peering down on him from on high in the vaulted eaves. Yet, surely, the new silver wisps among the brown at his temples served only to heighten his appeal. He could still attract young women and girls—couldn't he?

His son's meteoric rise to fame as a rock star had hit him hard. It had underscored his mortality. The seeds of decay, in his own mind and in the press, had been sown. But he was still in the game.

He studied his physique. His still-tight derriere was parked atop a wooden stool. His Grecian form was balanced atop one long, lean leg, which was anchored, by one foot, to the floor. His other leg was bent at the knee, foot bracing the stool's top rung. His feet were shod in his favorite painting shoes: a pair of worn-out, paint-stained, brown-leather deck shoes.

Stretched tightly across his broad shoulders and trim torso, the front of his white Tee-shirt itself resembled an abstract painting of blue and green splotches. The brown and gray hairs on his muscular forearms were flecked with red and yellow ochre. Aged 47, he seemed the mature Poseidon, up for a breather to paint pictures. He tore his gaze away from the mirror and sighed. *Life's a bitch and then you die.*

Stepping down from the stool, he picked up a rag to clean his brush and discovered his missing phone. Grabbing the phone, he read the missed caller's name. *Poppy Demming.*

It can wait.

Three years earlier, he had won four major acting awards for his portrayal of the rebellious Post-Impressionist artist, Paul Gauguin, friend and associate of Vincent Van Gogh. His newly formed production company, Moon and Sixpence Productions, had made a mint on the film, *Decadent Virtue,* based upon Gauguin's life story—namely, the abandonment of his family in Paris and his flight to Tahiti, an island paradise in the South Pacific, and then his decline and burial in the Marquesas Islands. Now, at the peak of his career in films, Heston had become one of the most successful actors and producers in the history of motion pictures, rich beyond imagination.

As a thespian, he had nothing more to prove. As a painter, however, he was an insecure fledgling, eager to make his mark. To prepare for the role, he had studied painting with masters. Afterward, he had taken it up as a hobby. It had become an obsession. From the beginning, the role of Gauguin had threatened to wreak havoc on his personal life.

Uncomplaining, and with their young children in tow, pretty little Poppy had followed him to remote locations in the South Seas where he had shot the film. She had put up with his moodiness and bad tempers. When in character, his personality morphed, and his behavior toward his wife had regressed. He had been sullen, withdrawn, verbally cruel to her.

She had weathered the entire production like a trooper and a saint. She had seen to his every need. Never once had she denied him her bed.

He loved her deeply. He craved her understanding and support, which, until recently, she had supplied in abundance. He was unaccustomed to receiving resistance, but she was resisting him now, in new, subtle ways. He knew the reason, but this was a contest he must win.

Gauguin had let nothing, not even his wife and family, stand in the way of artistic expression.

Would he be forced to make the same choice? Could he bear to break his wife's heart? *Impossible.* Poppy *believed* in him. He would do *anything* to protect hearth and home. The misdeeds of his own father had damaged him too much to feel otherwise.

He daubed his palette and painted with fervor, hoping for a break-through—the right shape, line, tint, shade.

The phone rang. He knew the ringtone. "Hello, Red," he said irritably to his wife.

"Hello, darling," Poppy replied in a sweet, timid voice. "A-am I interrupting you? Are you p-painting?"

"Yes."

"I'm sorry."

Are you? Re-furrowing his brow, he daubed the canvas. "How's it going in Miami Beach? How's Winner getting along with her Uncle Banks?"

"She's smiling. They're having lunch right now. I've been gallery hopping."

"Find any bargains?" He glared at his painting. It returned the favor.

"I'm rather hard to deceive. I was an art dealer myself." She sighed. "Still, they will try."

Disengaged, he conversed mechanically. "When will you and Win be home?"

"Early tomorrow. I'm meeting my friends at *Curves*. We work out at 10 a.m. So you can paint your heart out until then without distraction."

He snorted a laugh. "If only!" He shifted the phone to his other ear. "I have a meeting with Ezra at 8 a.m." He chewed his bottom lip. "The kids miss you."

"Are they okay? Is Tegan still crying because we didn't bring her along?"

"No. Now Dakota is sulking. He wants golf lessons. The tennis pro is here for their *tennis* lessons. I made him go along. He threw a racket at Sage, so I grounded him."

"You did the right thing, darling. I'm sure Nanny Berry agrees."

Curling the left corner of his lips, he nodded insincerely. *Should I tell her now? "By the way, Brown Eyes, I fired the children's nanny this morning."* He kept mum. Better to tell her when she returns home. He and the housekeeper could hold Fort Demming for 24 hours. "How's your suite at the Fontainebleau?"

"Grand. Thank you, darling, for booking it for us. Wish you were here."

"Well, I'm not. I'm here in Naples, laboring like a fiend. Do you really feel I can have this last piece finished in time?" He attempted to chew a fingernail but spit out paint.

"Of course you can."

"I hope this 'Evening at The Phil' will rake in some needed coin for the Foundation."

"Have you eaten your lunch?" she asked.

He glanced at the table by the studio door. "Let's see. Lissette left me a tray with soup, apple, half a sandwich. To be washed down with keg of Jamaican ginger ale, apparently."

"Oh, Heston. Please do eat it. You need *some* nourishment. If the soup's cold, have Lissy microwave it for you."

"Later, maybe." Picking up a palette knife, he prodded a blob of crusted cerulean-blue paint on the tabletop. "Has Banks mentioned anything about Maude?"

"Winner's mom?" Poppy paused. "He claims he hasn't heard from his sister in years."

"Good. Did you tell him we thought we spotted her last summer at Forte dei Marme?"

Poppy coughed nervously. "Yes, but he let the subject drop. He's being careful not to upset Winner. He's good at handling people. He sizes them up rather quickly."

So do I, damn it. I'm an actor. Grunting, he jabbed the blob until it burst open and oozed blue. "It's his business. He's a criminal defense attorney. He certainly seems to have charmed you."

"Heston!" she cried. "Don't be ridiculous!"

He harrumphed. "I just don't want him to frighten my fragile 12-year-old daughter by speaking about her abusive mother. Winner has had no contact with Maude since our divorce. Not so much as a meager birthday card. Frankly, she's better off for it."

Poppy sighed in sympathy. "B-Banks Winston seems an honorable man," she observed.

"And we all know Brutus is an honorable man," he emoted spontaneously.

"What?"

"Shakespeare. *Julius Caesar.*" He glanced at his self-portrait. *Perhaps a toga?*

"Darling, I-I feel s-sorry for Banks. He has no family. His two brothers passed away."

"Leaving him filthy rich." *Scratch the toga.*

"Heston, you're no pauper," she admonished. "Banks just wants to get to know his only niece."

He rolled his eyes. "Trusting soul that you are *not*, Mrs. Demming, I find your defense of the defense attorney to be—indefensible."

"Meaning what?"

"Beware of snow jobs. Shady gallerists aren't the only ones peddling snake oil. Banks Winston has quite a rep as a ladies' man." He drew back and eyed his canvas. His wife remained silent. He could feel her squirming. "Just watch Winner carefully. How many times did she change outfits before appearing for lunch?"

"Three."

"Oh, good. Better."

"Heston..." Her voice trailed off.

"Speak up, Red."

"I-I..."

"Is our new bodyguard on his toes?"

"Y-young Mr. Kincaid is most attentive," Poppy said, a smile cropping up in her voice.

Now he squirmed. "Not to you only, I hope. I hired Ram to guard Winner."

The smile became a grin. "To both your daughter and me. Listen, Heston, somethi—"

"Listen here, Red, enough of your insolence. Get your sassy tush home, pronto," he growled, green as the lawn on his manicured estate. But he didn't sense her acquiescence.

The tension between them had been brewing ever since he had surprised her with the purchase of a private island in the Florida Keys two years ago. He'd given her the tropical cay as a Valentine's gift and built a mansion on it. He wanted to move there. She didn't. He craved freedom, the creative solitude of the artist. She wanted to stay in Naples among her friends.

He loved his wife. But did he now love painting more? Would she force him to choose?

"We're driving home tomorrow," Poppy said, a sudden edge to her voice. "Heston, one thing—K-Kipp's concert tonight—with Demonsong—in downtown Miami. It's s-sold out."

He felt a hot twinge of betrayal. "How do you know that, Poppy? Did you try to buy tickets?"

"Of course not, Heston! I-I heard it on the news."

"Why are you telling me this? Do you think I give a rat's posterior?"

"He's our son, Heston. It's been more than four years since you and he fought..."

Suddenly, he heard a muffling sound. Just as suddenly, Poppy's voice rang out distantly. "Oh, hello! How are you?" She spoke into the phone. "Heston, I've just seen Vivian Champlain. I wonder what she's doing in Miami Beach?"

"Slumming?"

Her thoughts were elsewhere. "Heston, I'll talk to you tomorrow—at home. Please give my love to the children." She rang off.

"Drive carefully, Red," he murmured uneasily, pocketing his phone. Why did he have an uneasy feeling she had been trying to ask him something but hadn't? Their mutual telepathy was strong. Still, she'd said nothing.

Selecting a clean brush, he merely toyed with it, twirling it between his fingers. His concentration had been broken. *Damnation, I never have a moment's peace. As soon as I get away...*

Again, the phone rang. He answered, irritably, without thinking.

"Poppy, please. I'm trying to work. I thought you said..."

"Go right ahead and work, Heston," said a frighteningly familiar female voice, one laced with jaded charm. "I'd model naked for you if you asked me to."

Rattled, he put down his brush. "Lennox?" he demanded, appalled.

"Yes, my heart."

"Don't call me that. I'm not your heart. Why are you phoning me? I have nothing to say to you."

Lennox uttered a perky laugh. "What? Not to me, your loving daughter-in-law? Oh, but I have something to say to you, Heston. I must see you today. We need to talk."

How he hated that phrase. "About what? If it's about Kipp..."

Lennox clicked her tongue prettily. "When I see you, my heart. Get ready for a shock."

His muscles tensed. His hackles rose. "What kind of shock?"

"Congratulate me! I got a book deal," she gurgled. "With a huge advance."

"Book deal? Who brokered it? Arlene Gold?"

"Absolutely not," Lennox spat. "You and I no longer share the same agent. I'm under new management."

"Since when?" Heston asked.

"For a while now."

"Who is the lucky devil?"

One beat, two beats. "Gabriel Cade."

Nerves unsteadied, Heston tried to keep an even keel. "The jerk who ripped off my son? Why am I not surprised?"

"Don't you want to hear about my book?" Lennox chided.

"What kind of book could you write?" he asked. "No offense."

Lennox uttered a guttural trill. "I didn't write it yet. It's based on Mom's diary."

Soundlessly, he echoed the word with his lips. "Diary? Handwritten?" he asked aloud.

"You know she couldn't type," Lennox cooed.

"I didn't know she could read."

"That's not nice," she said petulantly, betraying traces of an accent.

"I don't feel 'nice' when it comes to you and your mother," Heston sighed.

"Wait until you hear the rest. You'll really be mad. The publishers bought it sight unseen. Gabe sold them on *the idea.* They plan to make the diary part of a tell-all book—about you and me and Mom and—well, everybody! An expose."

He sprang to attention. "That's inconceivable!"

"Once I turn the diary over to the publisher, it will be, um, transcribed. Yes, that's it. Then I'll dictate my comments to a secretary."

"Lennox, you, you can't!" he sputtered, his face growing hot.

She clicked her tongue. "Too late, Heston. Now the whole world will know—and there is only *one thing* you can do to stop it. You do know what that is, don't you, Heston? I've never stopped loving you, in spite of everything."

His throat constricted.

"Heston, are you still there?"

"Yes." He wanted to kill her. Wiping oil paint from his free hand and searching his pockets for the keys to his newest Ferrari, he glanced at the time. He could drive to Miami right now and be back in time for dinner. He would put an end to Lennox's maniacal nonsense before it ever got started.

An image of heaving young breasts crossed his mind. He drove it down.

"I'll meet you at your place in two hours," he said, putting the call on speaker phone. Stealing one last look at his canvas, he wiped his brushes clean.

"Three. Kipp has a two-hour visitation with Shawnee today. He'll be here any minute."

"Where is here?"

"My new South Beach penthouse," she said. "Do you want the address?"

She was full of surprises. "Give it to me."

"Castle of the Sun, Tower One. End of Ocean Drive. 10th floor. You can't miss it. Twin spires, tall and tan, white roofs. Use the private elevator in the lobby."

Ten minutes later, showered and clad in clean gray jeans, a white ribbed pullover shirt, and a black sports jacket, he whisked through his primary home's immaculate kitchen. "Lissette, you're in charge of Dakota and the twins," he barked to the flabbergasted housekeeper on his way out to the eight-car garage. "I'll be home by nightfall."

Donning mirrored sun glasses, he dropped into the driver's seat of his Ferrari, fired the engine, passed through the automatic bronze and iron gate and turned east onto Galleon Drive. Turning north at the intersection, he sped northward along Gordon Drive, turning east on Fifth Avenue, and drove headlong toward Interstate-75, known as Alligator Alley.

You won't destroy me the way you've destroyed my son. This time, Lennox, I'll do whatever it takes to stop you. Speeding across the southern tip of Florida, he floored the gas pedal. Sun glinting from its chrome, the silver Ferrari streaked across the flat swampland of the Everglades.

Chapter Three

Ten hours later, on front-center stage in downtown Miami, 27-year-old Kipp Demming, lead singer of Demonsong, belted out the final bars of a deafening rock anthem, *Out into the Night.* It was the concert version of a popular old cut from Demonsong's first release and one of several hits Kipp had composed.

Out into the night, I go
Looking for you
Out into the night, I fly
Searching for you
Hoping in my heart
You're somewhere out there
Hoping in my heart
Taking the dare

Gyrating sensuously, Kipp, a scruffy stud with a shock of spiked, bleached hair, mesmerized the huge crowd of fans who packed the Arena to worship him. Behind him, on stage, each eccentric band member massaged an electrified instrument—lead guitar, bass guitar, electric keyboard, drums. Amplifiers ramped to the max blasted music excruciatingly loud.

Wild in an otherworldly trance, shaman Kipp danced in the zone. Dressed in tight black jeans and sleeveless leather vest, the tall, sinewy singer's overt sensuality and craggy face held his worshippers spellbound. Rippling across the bicep of his right arm was his famous tattoo—planets revolving in a solar system surrounded by stars. Singing, he was a worm-hole to the throbbing universe.

The anthem came to an abrupt halt, fizzling out in a sparkling light-show flurry. In the train-crash crescendo, Kipp thrust his pelvis repeatedly at the cheering crowd until their annihilation was accomplished and the cacophony ceased. Drained and spent, he dropped limply to his knees and bowed his head humbly to the crowd. He hated that song now. He was glad to be done with it. Breathing slowly in and out, he felt an ominous current moving through the crowd. Lulled by lust, the rapt onlookers threatened to erupt in thunderous, random excess.

He knew what they wanted. Dripping sweat, he was too exhausted to resist. He stared out at the yearning throng. Why should they be satisfied just to ogle his wiggling ass? If they tore him, limb from limb tonight, he would let them. He wanted them to.

Let's get this over with...

Springing to his feet, he bowed again, this time deeply, from the waist, and, rising in a flourish, bounded cavalierly across the stage, microphone in hand. A ripple of anticipation buoyed the crowd. They *knew.* As the final encore, he was about to sing his signature song, *Don't Die Wondering.* What they didn't know was that tonight would be the last time he would perform this, or any other song.

Readying his instrument, he drew deep breaths, his hand pressed to his sleek, gently rounded abdomen. Sober, but fatigued and titillated, he ran his jaundiced gaze across the volatile crowd swarming before him in the packed concert hall. Aroused, he willed his lean, muscular body to relax, but failed. Fans screamed as he pretended to unzip his black leather pants and massage his member. He grinned engagingly.

"You need to *calm down,*" he teased into the microphone. He leered seductively at the restless audience. Lecherous shouts rang out. One last time, he felt his power surge.

"I love you, Kipp!" shrieked a young tattooed woman shrilly from the sixth row. She was standing on her seat, waving her storied arms. "I want to have your babies!"

"We all want your babies, man!" a deep male voice boomed. The crowd roared.

Shaking his head in mock approval, Kipp laughed wickedly. Inside, he felt sick and demeaned. Instantly, his mind flew back to this afternoon's fiasco. He should never have doubled back to Lennox's penthouse after the monitored visitation with Shawnee.

Desperate, he coaxed himself. *One more song, man. Then it will all be over.*

Nervously, he popped the sweatband across his hot, wet forehead. Dry air felt cool on his damp skin. Straggles of hair fell damp and matted against the sweat of his neck. His arm muscles rippled beneath taut, bronzed skin. He eyed the lead guitarist, who gave him a "hold" sign. He had to play for time. The bass guitarist had ruptured a string.

What should he do? Colored lights began to swirl, splashing across myriad eager, young faces. The smoldering energy was electrifying. He shut his eyes, centering himself internally. He felt like screaming into the microphone. Was he screaming? He was.

"Kill me!" His voice rasped, guttural, bestial. He laughed maniacally.

The eager screams of his fans drowned out his own. Despairing he boggled at the sea of lecherous faces. He hated these people, but he desired them, needed them. Their hero worship turned him on. He wanted to ball them all into shrieking ecstasy. At the same time, he wanted to bludgeon them to death for screwing up his life. The only way he could do either was in song. Spitting phlegm, he spied his glass on the keyboard. Palming it, he raised it high.

"Sharkbite! Sharkbite!" the crowd chanted wildly.

Showman-like, he drained the sweet black tea, pretending with relish, for their sakes, that is was the syrupy rum, citrus, and grenadine cocktail he had made his special drink. Slurping, gargling, into the mic, his hoarse baritone voice reverberated throughout the arena.

"Thank you all," he breathed slowly, scanning the arena from floor to nose-bleed balcony. "For coming! Ye-ah!" He chortled.

"Thank you, Kipp!" they shouted, from every direction. "For making us come!" Enraptured, the raucous crowd of ten thousand cheered. Some screamed his name. Some sobbed hysterically. Others flung pieces of clothing, paper, flowers, relics onto the stage, along with pills and prescription drug bottles. Two girls tried to take the stage. Police escorted them away as lights dimmed. Seated fans rose, aroused their smart phones, and held them aloft. Tiny sparks of light began to emanate all around as darkness fell inside the arena.

A sole spotlight found him. Eyes welling, he turned away. Torn, he inhaled, fully alive, completely sober, in his last moments of glory. Odors of beer, marijuana smoke, and human perspiration permeated the highly charged air. The thought of his impending death hovered in his mind, but it quickly flittered up and into the rafters of the dome. A hawk on high, it watched down at him, a distant relative of the vulture.

"Here we go," the guitarist said from upstage. Nodding, Kipp stood to attention, clicking the heels of his high-top sneakers. Band members resumed their performance positions. Current surged through the mass of pulsating flesh that was his randy congregation. Isolated shrieks and howls sounded around the arena. Kipp's heart vibrated. The crowd smelled blood.

Countdown-ready, he heard the familiar blast of guitar chords, the opening riff of *Don't Die Wondering,* the major ditty these common folk had paid their hard-borrowed cash to hear. He could die proudly, knowing that the song he had written had debauched a generation.

In the spot's glaring icy-heat, he graced his worshippers with an impudent grin. Totally turned-on, they exploded in adulation. He contemplated them in astonishment.

What the hell do you all want from me?

He knew the answer. Union. The very thing he now wanted with his Maker. They were looking for the meaning of life, and they thought he embodied it. *What a joke.* His adorers lusted from afar, with a lust that would never be sated. In his darkest moments, he had sometimes wondered if what they really wanted was to consume his flesh in a beastly Bacchanal.

Let's find out.

It was time for the final finale. Tonight's performance had been the best of his life. He had balled their souls, and they were basking in afterglow. Now he would feed them his flesh. It would have to sustain them forever. *What a way to go.* What would Heston say? What had Heston said that day four long years ago?

You're a disgrace to this family, Kipp.

How can I be, Daddy? This family is beyond disgrace. You and grandfather saw to that.

He grabbed the mic. "The press hasn't labeled me a sex addict for nothing!" he shouted, glancing at the ascetic guitarist, who rolled glassy eyes and plucked his new guitar string vigorously with skeletal fingers. "Who wants the first bite?"

Running up to the stage, the young woman with the face tattoo tried to grasp his ankles. "Let me, Kipp! Let me!" She was led away, sobbing, by police.

Involuntarily, Kipp's lithe body found the rhythm, moving to Demonsong's beat. Slowly, deliberately, he peeled off his Tee-shirt and, revealing the golden hair of his underarms and the sleek musculature of his bronzed body, flung the shirt into the crowd. Unbuttoning his jeans, teasing the crowd, he finally slipped off the jeans and tossed them as well.

Pandemonium erupted. Instantly, the clothing disappeared, devoured beneath a surface swell of ravaging bodies. He now wore nothing save a leather codpiece thong. Laughing out loud, white teeth bared and gleaming, he pranced to center stage. Turning his face to the wall, he twitched his bare, bronzed butt at the crowd.

Gripping the mic, he teased the rattled crowd, "Do you want me?" Open-mouthed, he flicked his tongue repeatedly, scandalizing the rollicking crowd. Throwing his head back, he roared in decadent delight.

The opening riffs blasted from the amplifiers. The bulging veins in his muscular arms pulsed. *Four, three, two, one...*

On cue, he sang out, blasting open his lips, emitting the deepest breath he had yet drawn. His first word escaped into the frenzied ether. "Don't..."

A hush descended. Twenty thousand eyes focused in covetous awe on him alone. His glistening, exposed, sweat-soaked skin prickled as he absorbed the mountainous wave of unvoiced desire and poured it back through his pores, his chest, his microphone.

Closing his eyes, he stood spread-eagled, nearly naked, clenching his fists, he sang out in gutsy abandon, his soul-scraping baritone, warm and crusty with lust, buoyed by loud, raucous, relentless electric guitars, keyboards, drums, horns:

Don't die wondering
Don't hold back your love
Go out and find
That special kind
You've been craving
In your wicked mind.

He roared the obscene song, driving his thousands of virtual lovers to near mania. Over and over, he slammed the refrain:

Do it
Do it
Do it!
TAKE WHAT YOU WANT!

As the measures petered out, he spoke his final words. "Goodbye! And screw you all!"

Screaming fans surged around the stage like buzzards circling a carcass, shrieking ravenously for another encore, another speck of carrion. Breaking the police barrier, they surged over the stage. In the commotion, Kipp felt himself being lifted up and carried aloft by hundreds of hands, millions of fingers buoying him like a river current, the same fingers that would rip him to shreds. Now he felt his arms being pulled one way, his legs another. Fists clutched his hair. Hands, everywhere, groping, clawing, pinching his entire body, face, tongue. They were pulling him apart.

Kill me, please...

Sirens blared. Light flooded his eyes.

Dizzily, he descended from the heights. One by one, the hands slipped away. Within moments, he found himself cradling the concrete floor, abandoned, enmeshed in a forest of stampeding legs. Security swooped down. New hands, authoritative hands, tilted him upright. He leaned against a post, encircled by armed guards, as police cleared the arena haphazardly.

"Are you all right, man?" Roadies surrounded him like teammates in a huddle. One draped his shoulders with a jacket.

He tasted blood. "You should have let them kill me."

With hands on his hips, a roadie snorted. "Aw, man. You're stoned."

Ineffectually, Kipp shook his head. No one believed he was clean. It didn't matter now.

"Somebody get a doctor. His lip's bleeding." The huddle flurried. "Here's a towel."

Warm, wet terry cloth slapped across his face. Breathing heavily, he clutched the towel and wiped his cheek and jaw. The roadies lifted him to his feet.

"Great show tonight, man. You really had them going."

"They prosecuted Morrison for less," he muttered, dabbing blood. "Times have changed." Dazed and unsteady from maximum energy output, Kipp stumbled into the arms of his handlers, who rushed out from backstage to rescue him. Quickly, they groomed him, at the same time hustling him toward the rear of the arena. Clean, dry cotton fabric stuck to the skin of his wet, naked skin. Someone stuffed him in and zipped his jeans, giving him a little squeeze. In a muffled flurry, they whisked him outside the stage-door entrance.

Outside, red, green, and white street lights swirled, reflections in pond-like puddles on black tar. The scent of fresh rain eased his stress. Heavy, tobacco-ripe voices shouted instructions. "Quick! Here they come again!"

The handlers thrust him inside the waiting, black-windowed limo outside the stage-door entrance. One of the men buckled him into the back seat and tossed in his backpack. The car door slammed. The long car squealed away from the curb. Running alongside the car, screaming fans clamored to halt it. Morosely, he watched the mostly female crowd blur and disappear behind raindrops on a glass pane.

"Hope you win, Kipp!" a fan called. He had been nominated for a Grammy Award by The Recording Academy. He would never know if he had won. Too bad.

Quietly, he drew a .44-magnum from his backpack and slipped the hand gun into his jeans pocket. He didn't know which weapon he would use to commit suicide; the .44 or the loaded syringe. All he knew was that he was going to kill himself on the shore at South Beach, right in front of his ex-wife's new condo building. And he was going to do it tonight.

Chapter Four

One hundred miles west, an incensed Beryl Northgate—diminutive, chunky, fair skinned, and fiery-eyed—clutched her mobile phone to her ear. Distraught and angry, she stood alone, bathed in lamplight, at the far end of the Naples City Pier, a forgotten pair of horned-rimmed eyeglasses propped atop her head of cropped mousy-brown hair. Her loosely fitting Capri slacks flapped noisily in the sea wind, the fabric molded to her taut skin.

"He sacked me, Mum!" she cried, slapping the rough wooden rail of the pier as she leaned her body weight against it. "After eight years of faithful service, Heston Demming sacked me!" Around her, all was sea wind and blackness, save for the lights dotting the Naples shoreline. The stars overhead were obscured by cumulonimbus clouds.

"Just like that?"

"Yes! Oh, but he was so *oily* about it. He told me to take a week's leave to think about what I should do *with the rest of my life!* Then to come back and tell him, and *he'll help me reach my goals*—whatever *they* may be. He claims he's *concerned* about me. Oh, please, you pathetic Rembrandt-wannabe!" She shook a pale fist in the air. "Spare me!" Her high-pitched voice choked with tears. "Oh, Mum, I could just *kill* Heston Demming."

Mum's soothing cluck sounded in her ear. "How dreadful for you, luv. When did this happen?"

"Early this morning. He called me into his studio. I've been wandering around in a daze ever since. I don't even know where. One month's notice! That's all he gave me, Mum."

"Now, now, Berry. Remain calm," she placated patiently.

"He's such a worm. He waited until his wife was out of the picture. Then he pounced."

"Perhaps he was speaking for both of them, tactfully."

"Hah! I doubt it."

"Where is Poppy?"

"She drove to Miami yesterday morning with Win. Winner's Uncle Banks is in town. He requested an audience with his niece."

"Banks Winston? The prominent barrister?"

"One and the same. Banks has been trying a criminal case in Federal court in Miami. He won."

"Why didn't Heston go along?"

"Can't be bothered. All His Majesty wants to do is paint. He booked the girls a suite in the Fontainebleau in Miami Beach. Gave them carte blanche."

"Jolly nice."

Beryl rolled her eyes and groaned. "Self-centered, if you ask me. It's just that he's such a...a..." Searching for a word, she gripped the empty night air. "He's a...a..."

"Man?"

Beryl growled in fury.

"Sounds like male mid-life crisis to me," asserted Mum knowingly. "At 50, your Dad disappeared into the garage for two years and built a hot rod. Raced it, too, until he slammed that brickface in Buxton. That was *his* wake-up call."

She pondered. "Not seven-year itch?"

"Both," Mum concurred. "Still, I'm surprised Heston didn't safeguard his ladies."

"Oh, he sent Ram along."

"Who, or what, is Ram? A pit bull?"

Beryl sniffed. "Oh, no. Ram Kincaid. Winner's new bodyguard. This huge, hulking young body builder."

"How young?"

"Twenty-five-ish." Catching on, Beryl balked. "And before you even ask, no, he's not married. But he's scary-looking. Apparently, his hulking presence appeals to our resident control freak, Heston." Beryl inhaled sharply. "That's what he is, Mum. A control freak!"

"He is the man of the house, Beryl."

"Well, he's right in thinking Winner *needs* her own bodyguard, 24/7, while she's home. Ever since she modeled for that magazine layout last summer, she's had loonies after her."

Mum clucked. "Which proves Heston's judgment isn't perfect. That advert was too risqué for a young girl to do—especially a disturbed young girl. Show people have odd notions about what's appropriate. Oodles of charisma. No common sense."

Beryl sighed guiltily. "We all hoped it might improve Win's self-confidence, Mum."

"Perhaps you're well out of the whole business, Beryl. Why not fly home to England for a holiday? Dad would love to see you again. It's been two years."

"We had some laughs, didn't we?"

"A giggle a minute."

Beryl sighed plaintively. "Oh, Mum. It's just that..." She looked out across the shiny, black surface of the Gulf of Mexico as it dreamed beneath a brilliant moon. "It's so beautiful here in Southwest Florida. I don't want to leave. I've lived in that sumptuous winter palace of Heston's for the past eight years. I've weathered three new charges, four hurricanes, and two complete renovations—one of the house and one of *Windswept.*"

"Yes, you mentioned he had the yacht refitted last year."

26

"Mm-hmm."

"Daughter, you might enjoy a change of scene. Derbyshire might not do, I agree, but what's wrong with London?"

"Oh, Mum. I can't face a lonely flat in dreary London." Her voice cracked. "What about Winner? It's bad enough he's sent her off to boarding school. There's still Dakota and the twins. I'll miss them so much." She broke down, weeping.

"Dearest," crooned Mum. "Separating from your youthful charges goes with the territory. You're a well-paid *professional* nanny to the children of a big movie star. Not as big as he once was, but nevertheless...I know. I was a school teacher myself for thirty-three years."

"I know." Beryl sniffed.

"Do you? You can't get all whiny over leaving the kids. The end is implied by the beginning, luv. Oh, I've dreaded this day for you, Berry. I knew it would come eventually. You've made good money, but you've paid a price."

Beryl blew her pug nose into a tissue and shifted her specs back down over her eyes. Vision restored, she noticed a shape silhouetted against a backdrop of dark, silvery clouds—a pelican at roost on a piling. *Eavesdropper.* "So did I, Mum. It just caught me off guard."

"You have always been this way. It's your affectionate nature, dear. You've always cared too much for things that didn't return your affection, not to the same degree—stray cats, neighborhood dogs, bunny rabbits, friends at camp, substitute teachers, shop keepers, and arrogant, dallying young men. You become too attached to the transient in life."

"So shoot me. No one cares about me."

Mum sighed. "I care, luv. I don't mean to scold. Did Heston say what he plans to do?"

"Indeed. He's off acting but still wants to produce. He's aching to live the artistic life. But he's hampered by the kids. He's planning to send the children off to boarding schools."

"The twins are how old now?"

"Six. Dakota is seven. Old enough to take wing, Heston claims."

"Brrr, that's chilly. Of course, Winner is outgrowing a nanny..."

"But she needs me, Mum."

"Because her real mother abused her as a tot? She has a counselor."

Beryl's features twisted. "Yes. But she's still she's my little love; my fragile, fair-haired baby doll. Always will be. Even though she's already two inches taller than I am." She pressed her steamed-up glasses to the bridge of her nose.

Mum sighed. "Oh, Berry. If only you'd had a family of your own. It's not too late, dear. Perhaps this is a blessing in disguise. Isn't there some man you fancy?"

She gasped. "Why, no! Don't be absurd." She covered quickly. "Who'd want me, Mum? I'm short, dumpy, pig-headed, and near-sighted."

She heard a smile in Mum's voice. "Oh, you'd be surprised, dear. That's precisely what a lot of men are looking for, although perhaps not the arrogant lout you've set your cap for."

Beryl snorted. "What lout? I've said nothing to you."

"Forget whoever he is, luv. Settle for what you can get. Put yourself out there, where some eligible bloke can see you. They're not very bright, you know. You have to get their attention first. A little paint, a little powder..."

"And a stout, blinding whack with a two by four?" Despite her anguish, Beryl laughed.

28

"A home-cooked roast beef dinner would suffice," Mum urged. "That, sprinkled with a pinch of the affection you lavish so freely upon other people's children."

"Me be affectionate? With a man?" Beryl frowned. "It might work if there were any available men out there. There aren't enough to go round. Haven't you heard? Fifty million single women in this country alone."

"It didn't help that the men started wedding one another."

Beryl sighed. "It did leave us straight women in the lurch, didn't it?" She shrugged. "To each his own. All right, Mum. I'll call now and reserve a plane ticket. I'll ring you back with my arrival time at Heathrow."

"I'm glad you can't fly yourself across the Atlantic," observed Mum. "In your present state, you might pull an Amelia Earhart." Mom shuddered. "I hate it that you have a pilot's license, but perhaps some unsuspecting man will decide it's part of your pig-headed charm."

Beryl winced. "Not likely. Unless he's a better pilot than I am." She sighed. "I love you, Mum. And Dad, too."

"We love you, Berry, dear. Cheer up. It's not the end of the world. You'll see."

"Thanks for listening."

"Any time, luv. Can't wait to see you," said Mum, ringing off.

Alone at pier's end, Beryl stared out to sea. Beneath dark clouds, she scanned for a horizon line. She had left the most important name unspoken. Even Mum didn't realize her true attachment to the Demming clan.

What about Kipp? Will I ever see him again?

If she left the Demming family circle, she would lose all real-world connection to Kipp Demming. Not that he knew she was alive. Not that he even spoke to his family anymore—not since that fight with Heston at Thanksgiving four years ago. The well-publicized rift between father and son had never healed. The two handsome men had severed all ties.

Kipp had even dumped Arlene Gold as his agent and signed with sleazy Gabriel Cade for career management, a move Heston had correctly predicted would end in disaster for his son.

In anger, Kipp had even resigned his position as head of the Demming's family-run charity, The Franco Demming Trust, named for the son Heston had accidentally killed eight years earlier. Franco had been twelve. Franco's mother, Heston's second wife Inez, had been institutionalized for a time after the tragedy. After the disappearance of Inez's stepson, Danny Vega, she and her second husband, Rogelio, had moved away from Naples. *A sad case.*

Beryl wondered if Kipp now regretted his rash decision. Or did he even remember it? He was so drugged up back then. Of course, the tabloids claimed he was clean now. Regardless, he couldn't be happy. No one who did that much drugs and promiscuous sex could be happy— just driven relentlessly by a pain that refused to be acknowledged, much less healed. He'd been in and out of rehab many times. She wondered whether jail had changed him.

Oh, how she hated Lennox Cordova—that perennial glamour girl. Kipp had been young and naïve when he had met the conniving cat. He couldn't see past the violet eyes, the chestnut hair, the zoftig figure, the tiny stature. He couldn't see through her wiles. He couldn't fathom Lennox's true motives then. But she had. She had known all along. She knew with whom Lennox was really in love—and it wasn't Kipp. *Poor little Shawnee.*

In the chilly night sea wind, Beryl shuddered. She found herself staring bleakly into the homely face of Reality. She was a 30-year-old virgin, unmarried, unemployed, and unremarkable. What was she to do with the rest of her life?

On impulse, she found her mobile and rang Mum again.

"Mum? Berry. I've changed my mind. I'm not coming home for a holiday."

"Why, dear? What's happened?"

"I'm not sure. But I feel the need for a spot of 'me' time. I need to do some soul-searching, Mum—and not, at the mo', in jolly old England."

"Where, Beryl Anne? Out with it."

She crossed her fingers for luck. "I'm going to spend the week...on Heston's private island in The Florida Keys. It's south of here. It's quiet and luxurious, and it's a million miles from nowhere. Mum, are you still there?"

"Yes."

"He offered me free run of the place. I'm going to take him up on his offer. Tomorrow morning I'm going to fly myself down there—in Heston's Cessna, which he told me to take, and then, a seaplane—and spend a week basking and beach-combing and, well, getting to know the real me. Heston rarely uses that plane. These days he flies everywhere by corporate jet charter."

"All by yourself on a remote private island?" groused Mum.

"Look, it's not as though I'll be cut off from civilization. There's a MacDonald's not twenty minutes away by motorboat. And there's a caretaker—Robinson La Croix."

"Robinson Crusoe?"

"Not Crusoe! La Croix. Robinson doesn't reside on the island, but he drops by every few days to check on the place, make sure all's in working order."

"Beryl, I forbid it—"

Beryl stood her ground beneath the stars. White knuckles clenched, she spoke decisively into her phone. The lapping Gulf cheered her on. "I am flying to Heart of Fire Key, Mum. Look, it's what Heston wants. At first, I pooh-poohed the idea because I was livid. Now I feel I should take him up on it. He said I could bring friends. But I want to go alone."

"Alone?"

She ignored the outburst. "I know my way around. I've been there a number of times with the family."

"When?"

She heard angry clanking sounds and pouring water. "What are you doing, Mum?"

"Making tea. It's 05:00 here."

Beryl gasped. "Oh, I'm sorry. I'd forgotten the five-hour time difference."

"I do not recall your mentioning this island," Mum said.

"It's the property Heston gave to Poppy for Valentine's Day, two years ago."

"That's nice." Mum's words dripped with sarcasm as she shipped her cuppa.

"Isn't it, though?" Beryl giggled. This interchange was their own private joke, invoked whenever either felt envy. "Now Heston wants to move there permanently, but Poppy doesn't."

"What's he built on it—a grand hotel?"

"A big, new vacation home—a green-building marvel. It has almost as much charm as an old place, but it's all brand new. Dual staircases leading up to a wide veranda wrapping around the front and sides. Three Doric columns on either side of the front door. Three stories high. A pool. A green pitched roof crowned by a covered widow's walk,"

"Oh, my."

"The outside is painted ivory, but the trim is white. Swervy coconut palms practically swarm around it like stiffened vines.

Mum's tea cup slammed the table top. "Beryl Anne Northgate, however lovely it is, a mansion on a desolate tropical island is far too remote and dangerous for a girl alone."

"Oh, Mum! I'm a grown woman. Overgrown, really. I'll be fine. Do stop fussing."

"It's foolhardy, Beryl."

"It's an adventure, that's what it is. Mum, I'm a modern woman. I can fend for myself."

"But, Beryl..."

"Deaf ears, Mum." She hummed a tune to drown out the sounds of speech.

Resigned, Mum sighed. "What's the name again? I'm writing it down, just in case."

"Heston's private kingdom? Heart of Fire Key."

"How romantic."

"Romance doesn't exist, Mum."

"Beryl, you're daft. You live with romance every day—Poppy and Heston."

"Trust me, Mum, when I tell you there's trouble in paradise."

"Oh, really?"

"Yes, but I'm contractually forbidden to discuss it with you—or anyone else."

"But he bought her an island!"

"Ha! He bought himself an island and gave it to her for Valentine's Day. Clever, really. Heart of Fire Key is shaped like a heart—sort of. If you stand on the small hill in the center of it, and look out in all direction, you see it. Really, it's shaped like a paisley, but the round part of the paisley has cleavage—and a short right arm."

Mum would not be diverted. "Romance in real life may not be perfect. But it does exist, Beryl. True love does exist."

"Not for the likes of me, it doesn't."

"Love is where you find it, child. You won't find it alone on a barren cay. Can't you take a singles cruise?"

"Oh, do stop fussing!" She sighed longingly. "There's a ruined chapel. There's even an open-air mini-Greek theatre. It overlooks a grotto, a cove. Heston likes to direct his kids—and guests—in plays—whether they want to participate in them or not."

"Egad," emitted Mum, spoon clanging the teacup as she added more sugar. "Do you act?"

"Indeed not. I'm always the stage manager." As an afterthought, she added, "Heston calls it his Theatre on the Half-Shell."

"Half-baked, if you ask me."

"Silly. Heston built an art studio there, too, *a la Gauguin,* but he has his Van Gogh moods. Sometimes he paints plein-air, wearing a beat-up straw hat and an unbuttoned sports shirt, flapping in the breeze. If you want my opinion, he hasn't found himself as an artist yet."

There was a slight pause. "Maybe Dad and I should come and join you."

"No! I mean—I told you, Mum. I need to be alone."

"Will you build a fire with coconut hulls—to cook your daily catch?"

Beryl snickered. "Solar power, Mum. Ever heard of it? Propane for cooking? It's a modern world we live in—although there is a gigantic fire-place in the great room. Big enough to roast a wild boar."

Mum mulled. "Oh, I do seem to recall now. Heston won some type of green award thingy for the design, didn't he?"

"Luv, the place is smashing! It has received international acclaim."

Mum sighed. "My modern girl in her modern world."

" 'Fraid so, dearie. Mum, if you don't hear from me for a few days, don't be alarmed. I'll ring you when I'm ready to talk."

"Is this really what you want, Beryl?" Mum's voice was low and quiet.

What I really want I can never have. "Don't worry, Mum. I'm about to find out who I really am beneath this gaudy exterior."

Ringing off, she breathed a sigh of relief, resting her elbows on the pier's railing. Mum had to understand. She didn't want company now. She needed to be alone with her own soul.

Who was she really? She didn't know anymore. It wasn't about the money. Heston and Poppy had paid her a generous salary over the years. She was set financially for life.

What did she want now? That was the question. How was she going to spend the rest of her days? She determined to find out, starting bright and early tomorrow morning.

If she had known Heston was going to sack her today, she would have purchased tickets for the Demonsong concert in Miami tonight. Just to irritate him, of course. She didn't approve of them at all. Certainly not because she was aching to see Kipp's sensual performance on stage, up close, live in person.

She gazed longingly at the waxing moon. The tears began to fall. Was she doomed to a lifetime of virginity? What would it be like to be taken by a man? Base and bestial? Or fulfilling and sublime?

She remembered Demonsong's huge, vulgar hit *Don't Die Wondering*. Unfortunately, she knew she probably would die wondering—unless something extraordinary happened.

Oh, popsicles. How likely was that?

Chapter Five

"Momm-meeeeeeeeeeeee!"

Alone in the dark nursery, two-year-old Shawnee Demming wailed at the top of his small lungs. The digital clock on the dresser flashed 12:14 a.m. in red characters: *one, two, one, four.* Shawnee recognized each numeral. Again, he shrieked.

"Mom-mmmmeeeeeeeeeeeeeee!!!"

In the deathly stillness that followed, the curly-blonde toddler stood motionless, poised in his crib—waiting, listening, wondering. His pudgy hands clutched sporadically at the crib's wooden railing. From the big rooms of the penthouse apartment beyond his bedroom door, slightly ajar, there came no response.

Nothing.

Eerie silence settled once again. Shivering, Shawnee moaned aloud, inhaling and expelling the prickly, powder-scented air of his dark, lonely, air-conditioned bedroom. Fear gripped him. He grimaced in despair.

Mommy...?

He gazed upward. From on high, a beam of starlight filtered down, diffused by the stained-glass pane of the nursery's lone window. Cast in heavenly light, the tiny tot appeared lost, cast away, like an ethereal, glowing cherub who had fallen to earth by mistake, made a too-hard landing—who couldn't remember what had happened to cause his calamity.

Bowing his head, Shawnee sobbed. A halo of rainbow hues illuminated his blond curls, which shone brightly as angel hair. But his suffering was all too earthly.

"Mommy, come Shawnee," he whimpered fitfully into the vast emptiness, wiping the salty trickle from his cheeks. His strong, little hands, damp with tears, clasped the slippery rail. The pebble-sized toes of his tender feet, planted firmly in place beneath him, urgently kneaded the spongy mattress below. Fretting, he knitted his non-existent eyebrows.

Why didn't she come? She had never not-come before. Something was *wrong*.

He was hungry and thirsty. His bladder was full. He had just learned how to potty. He wanted to wait, to please Mommy, but the urge to pee-pee was strong. One final time, he sucked in a deep breath and bellowed out her name, sing-song into the cold, still, unrelenting darkness.

"Mah-ahh-ahhm-mmeeeeeeeeeeeeeeeeeeeeeeee!"

One last time, he cocked his head, ears scouring the night. He seemed to hear wind. The AC? He looked up at the vent. He stared at his bedroom door. Was it inching open? Was there light shining in?

Mommy?

Fear became frustration, then anger. Defiant, he pursed his lips. He would find out. Chin outthrust, he pulled his white Tee-shirt up to his cheek and wiped away wet residue. Corky was watching him. Poor Corky was scared. Reaching down, he grabbed the fuzzy stuffed blue dinosaur by its paw.

Shoulders back, dino in hand, Shawnee flung one chubby leg over the crib's railing, then the other. Climbing out of his crib was a big no-no, but he would do it anyway. He must find Mommy.

Mommy?

His foot slipped. Plummeting to the floor, he landed *feet* first, but toppled, with a plop, backwards onto his fanny. Stunned, he sat winded, eyelids blinking rapidly, in darkness on the soft, thick carpet. He still clutched Corky's paw.

Shawnee began to cry. After a moment, he stopped. No one was coming.

Rubbing his smarting backside, he hoisted himself onto his bare feet and trod unsteadily toward the nursery-room door. Groping the wall, he felt for the door. Mustering strength, he drew the door open with both hands. Brows knitted, parched lips parted, he peered down the brightening corridor. His arms tingled with goose flesh.

Where was the light coming from? Licking his lips, he stepped through the open door and out into the hallway. He bit down on his lower lip and thrust his right foot forward.

Toddling forward, he heard a roaring noise.

Fingertips grazing the wall, he toddled cautiously down the vaulted hallway, Corky's limp dino-form dangling from his free hand and dragging the floor. The light grew brighter as he approached the great room. Stepping into the great room, he caught his breath. The draperies fluttered. He could see the city at night. Warm wind rushed into the room.

The grand glass windows were wide open. A vast array of city lights glittered against the backdrop of midnight indigo. He clapped his hands in delight, but stopped abruptly.

He was not allowed near the glass door or on the balcony. Mommy said *no*. When Shawnee went near the glass doors, Mommy always took his hand in hers and slapped her own hand *no*.

Why were the doors open now? Warm ocean air swirled into the big room—windy, humid, restless. It gusted throughout the great room, swirling around Shawnee. Faint traffic noise reached his ears from ten stories below.

Obediently, he hugged the wall. He whispered softly.

"Mommy?"

Shadowy, shifting shapes danced around him menacingly. He could make out some objects in the room—chairs, tables, sofas, lamps. The big-screen TV was turned on, but the sound was muted. Images flashed across the screen. He stared.

Silence broke. He heard the familiar ring-tone of Mommy's mobile phone. He saw the red light flashing. The phone lay out on the floor of the balcony. Excited, he dashed forward without thinking. Tumbling over a large pointy object, he fell down in a lump.

He grimaced in pain but gained control. Lying flat on his belly, he put out his hand. He felt the pointy thing. It was a shoe heel. On a shoe. On a leg.

The phone kept ringing. The red light kept flashing. He forgot about it.

On his knees, he ran his small palm along the length of smooth calf stretched out on the dark floor in front of him. He looked down the length of the shapely limb. It was Mommy's leg. It was sticking out from beneath her shiny satin skirt. She was lying across the open door-way.

Mommy was lying, twisted, half in the room, half on the balcony. Her heel was up. Her face was down. Her shiny hair fell across her face and around her bare shoulders.

No wonder she hadn't come when he'd called. He shook Corky by the paw. Happily, Corky flopped up and down.

Corky, Mommy sleepy!!!

Crawling toward her face, Shawnee sat and cradled Mommy's head in his lap. He brushed back her hair. He recoiled. Her eyes were open. They stared without moving. One was swollen and purple. Her closed fist clenched a small, open plastic bottle. White pills lay strewn across the floor.

"Wakee, Mommy," he demanded. Mommy did not move. He shook her stiffening body. "Mommy, Shawnee!" Still, she did not rouse. "Mommy, Corky!" He dangled the toy in her face to no avail. Corky kissed Mommy on her owie. Then he realized.

She was sicky. Poor Mommy. Softly patting her hair and kissing her cheek, he stretched out along the length of her curvaceous torso, curling up against her lifeless ribs, beneath her generous breasts. For a few moments, he and Corky snuggled and dozed. But he was not sleepy.

Where is it? He rose and toddled around the great room. The tiny guitar was nowhere to be seen.

"Mommy. Gui-tah?"

Again, the phone rang. At once on his knees, he crawled back over Mommy and out onto the open balcony. He picked up the mobile phone and held it up to his face. Opening the phone, he saw it light up. He peered at the phone's keys and pondered.

"Dada," he said aloud to the Powers-That-Be. "Shawnee count."

He fingered the keys. Each key made a sound. He jiggled in glee. His eyes lit up as he heard Dada's voice. He babbled into the phone.

"Dada, come Shawnee. Mommee seepee. Dada, Momee sickee. No wakee." But Dada didn't answer. Only a beep sounded. He repeated his plea. Still, Dada did not answer.

Ringing off, he glanced down at Mommy. She did not smile. She did not move. He stared out the wide-open doors. There it was! He bounced in joy.

Leaning against the balcony wall, and partially hidden beneath a tarp, the toy guitar gleamed in the moonlight. It called to him. *Shawnee, come out and play a song like Dada.*

Phone in one hand, Corky in the other, Shawnee rose and stole a glance at sleeping Mommy. Sneaking, he toddled out onto the open penthouse balcony, ten stories above Ocean Drive on South Beach in

Miami. Dragging Corky behind him, Shawnee guiltily inched his way toward the unscreened balcony ledge.

Chapter Six

Meanwhile, ten floors directly below, Kipp Demming stood on the deserted shore of South Beach, his coppery eyes roaming the eastern horizon. A sinister storm was blowing in from the sea. The Caribbean, birthplace of Ska, reggae, and Bob Marley, and piracy, rum. shipwrecks, and American slavery. He himself was a modern-day pirate.

One never knew what to expect from the region. It could be warm and tranquil one day, raging and deadly as a hurricane the next, fickle and fascinating as a woman. Marissa Neville was out there, somewhere. Six months ago, he had searched on the Internet for his old college girlfriend. He had located her but hadn't contacted her. He'd lost his nerve.

Love and other horseshit fantasies.

Shivering, he zipped his scuffed black-leather jacket. He had the willies. Someone walking on his grave, his adoptive father Benjy McKendrick used to say. Was it the wind or was it the reverb from the amplifiers ringing in his ears? His tinnitus was driving him nuts.

Fingers trembling, he felt for the handgun. It lay hidden in his warm, fleecy jacket pocket. He fondled the unloaded firearm, nestled against a small plastic bag filled with bullets. In the other pocket, the lay his mobile phone and the syringe of painkiller purchased on the sly.

He had everything he needed to die—drugs to ease his pain, a gun to finish the job, and clues planted to flag his body for the authorities. After sun-up, some poor slob would find his carcass floating face-down in the Atlantic, his skull blown open and his brains hanging out.

His phone rang. He ignored it. No one on this side he wanted to talk to. Except maybe his birth mother. He knew Poppy would not phone him. Heston wouldn't let her.

He had mailed a letter of farewell—inside a box containing personal mementos, recordings, and notebooks—to her home address in Naples. She should receive it tomorrow. He would be dead by the time she read his letter.

By tomorrow night, he would be a rock-music legend. He could see the headlines now: KIPP DEMMING, NOTORIOUS LEAD SINGER OF ROCK BAND DEMONSONG, DEAD, AGED 27. MILLIONS MOURN WORLDWIDE.

He felt strangely alone. His fans had no idea he was bankrupt, debt-ridden, that his mansion on Star Island was being foreclosed, that he had lost everything, including his entourage. *Entourage?* What a laugh. When he'd run out of money, he'd run out of hangers-on. *Funny how that works.*

Even Demonsong had jilted him. Hours before the concert, they had voted him out of the band. Tomorrow his fans—and the rest of the world—would learn the truth about *everything*. He was glad he wouldn't be around.

In Davy Jones' locker, he wouldn't need his last $20-bill, now folded in the wallet in his back jeans pocket. He would take his paltry profit to his watery grave. Rest assured, Lennox would never *get* her hands on one last red cent of his, not even a cancelled credit card.

He rubbed his raw throat. Tonight he had screamed his last hurrah to his final audience of lunatics. Now he was face to face with his decision to die.

Just do it.

He drew the gun from his pocket and cradled it in his palm. Fumbling, he drew two bullets from the bag and loaded them into the barrel of the gun. Around him, the wind blustered.

Ozone filled his nostrils. The rainstorm was approaching rapidly. In the southeastern sky, he could discern a dark gray swath he knew was a curtain of precipitation. Again, he fondled the gun in his hand. Holding it aloft, he cocked it, aiming it out to sea.

Big waves crashed along the sand shoreline. He had bought the gun last year, the day after drunken fans had crashed a drug-orgy at his house on Star Island. He was going to use it for the first time tonight. But he couldn't screw up. Unless he did the job right, he could end up a vegetable for life. That's what worried him. Twisting off the cap of a bottle of Bacardi, he drank his first swig of sweet death.

He glanced down the deserted street. Tomorrow, after they had found his motorcycle, this place would become his shrine. He could hear the ruckus now: *It's Kipp Demming's Goldwing all right. Drove it here so he could off himself on the beach last night.* The reporters would gouge the grieving: *How did you FEEL when you heard Kipp was dead?*

He drank more Bacardi. In his mind, he heard the thunderous cries of thousands of fans. *Shark bite! Shark bite!* He grimaced. By walking into the Atlantic tonight, he would be risking a real shark attack. Zoned on booze, maybe he wouldn't feel the jaws of death as they snapped his leg in two. Maybe the fierce fish would strike after death, tearing him to shreds and swallowing the bits, leaving the shreds to quicksilver minnows.

He had scored painkillers illegally because of his previous conviction on drugs charges. If his visitation with Shawnee hadn't been monitored, he would have hit Lennox up for pain meds, maybe even given her the 20 bucks. She was the queen of prescription addiction.

He gathered his nerve. To the west, high above him, the bright, boat-shaped half-moon sailed the night sky, its glow reflected on the white-capped surface of the Atlantic Ocean. Like a lantern-laden junk, it beckoned him onward, lighting his journey into an afterlife of sorts, if not death itself as in pagan worship. Gun cocked and ready, he took his first step toward the sea.

He hated himself. He hated his life. The shame of being a debauched spawn of the dark side had become unbearable. He had earned his reputation as the King of Cock. In lusty revels, he had committed acts so heinous in their lusty abandon that he shuddered with shame as he recalled them.

And those were just the acts he could remember. Other acts, he had learned about from his companions in revelry. Some he had simply read about—or seen pictures of himself committing—on the Internet or in the press—maybe altered photos, maybe real. *Who knows?* His persona had overtaken his real life. His image had become more real than his true self. Stopping at water's edge, he raised the gun to his temple.

He cocked the gun. Panic seized him. Quickly, he lowered the gun and released the_ hammer. He resumed walking.

Soon people had started concocting false stories about him, crafting images to support the stories. He no longer knew where fiction ended and reality began. What had he actually done? What was bogus? It was all a cloud bank of innuendo, guilt, and shame. The drugs had helped him hide from his conscience. Sober, he was naked and vulnerable.

He trudged on, fleeing his past. The water of the waves lapped at his high-top sneakers.

Even now, alone under the moon and stars, beside the pounding impersonal surf, he blushed hotly. He was a beast, an abomination. He was, as Heston had asserted, a disgrace. This satyr he now was—this was not the person he had intended, as a boy, to become. How had this happened to him? Lennox had initiated his corruption.

She had invited him to her trailer that day, on the set of *Acapulco Moon,* when he was a naïve rascal, only 20 years old. There she had performed the first act of his downfall. He was hooked. It had been only a short step from randy frat boy to decadent sex-idol of the great unwashed. He stopped in his tracks, the gun dangling from his hand. He wept.

How mortified Poppy must have been when she'd first started reading about his escapades. Here he had been, her long-lost son, the football hero, the pre-med student, and suddenly he had descended into a licentious renegade, hell bent on self-destruction, out for self-aggrandizing pleasure—and all for what? He didn't know what.

Validation? Rebellion? Competition? *Why?*

Insecurity, Mommy. You abandoned me at birth. He had missed everything in life that was real. He ached in longing for the nurturing spirit of the Feminine. He raised his gaze skyward. Perhaps he would find it on his journey to the Moon herself.

He gulped another slug of rum. The howling wind whipped sand into the air. Tiny grains prickled his cheeks. He shielded his face with his gun hand and turned his back to the wind. His eyes stung. He wiped them with the back of his gun hand.

Where was the woman who would have loved him? He needed fluffing, pampering. He wanted his hash pipe and slippers. Did women do that anymore? Or did they all compete with their men now, and praise themselves as being smart in their unbridled slaughter of the Masculine? Heston had hit the jackpot in Poppy. *Shut up, you pervert.*

Heston—his arrogant father—had disowned him, that fateful day, four years ago. *If you marry Lennox Cordova, you're no son of mine! I don't want you anymore. Do you hear me? I forbid your marriage. She's using you, Kipp. Don't you see?"*

He had taken a swing at Heston. The rest was history. Belching, he chugged more rum. His eyes followed the moon boat's achingly slow but steady path across the heavens.

Woozy, he wondered if the drugs and alcohol in his system could affect a shark. *Would the shark get high after eating me? Jackass.* He belched. He felt righteous for the first time in a long time.

What would it feel like to die? Done right, he would feel no pain. Then he would blast into nothingness. Forever. Oblivion. That's all. He could handle that, assuming he didn't end up in Hell. But pirates go to Hell. He sure as hell wasn't headed for Heaven.

Lightheaded, he staggered backwards in the waves, dropping the rum bottle and landing on his butt. The gun did not fire. For a moment, he sat stunned. The liquid rushed down his throat and he swallowed, coughing. He was soaked. The bottle had emptied. Waves crashed around him, crests sparkling before him in the moonlight. Salty wind feathered his eyelashes.

He wondered how his mother would feel when she learned of his death. Tears welled in his eyes. After his fight with Heston, Poppy had rejected him a second time. The first time had been when she had bore him as a teenage unwed mother.

The once and future orphan. That's who he was. But he loved Poppy just the same. She was the only one who cared if he lived or died—except for the millions of deluded idiots who worshipped him for his legendary prowess. The fans didn't care about him, just his potency. *That's what they'll mourn. Not me.* He thumped his chest. *Not ME.*

But who the hell is me? The songs he had been writing in secret had gotten him laughed off stage by the boys in the band. They'd taken a vote and kicked him out of Demonsong. Even though the first song he'd written, *Out into the Night,* had been Demonsong's first huge hit. They'd called him a pussy when he'd showed them his latest stuff—which was why he'd sent it to his mother. *Does she know who I am inside?*

Did anyone know him? He'd only had one real friend—Ezra. You couldn't really blame Ezra for the choice he'd made. It had been a career move. Heston had tempted him.

He wiped his wet cheeks with the back of his hand. He blew his clogged nose. *Damn you, Daddy-O.*

What if Heston and Poppy had never found him? What if he had gone all the way through med school never knowing he was the grandson of a notorious medical criminal? He would be a heart surgeon now.

He *loved* hearts. Had his grandfather, Dr. Douglas Demming, loved medicine? How had Doug felt the night he'd hanged himself, 40 years ago? *Like me? Would I have had the guts to sling a noose around my neck and kick away the chair?*

His thoughts stumbled. What had he said today? Done? Something about a fiasco with Lennox. *Oh, yeah.* The Big News: Shawnee wasn't his son anymore.

He was his half-brother instead. *Nice of you to clue me in, you whoring slut.*

Irreverently, he belched. It was time.

He struggled to stand, but a powerful curl broke over him, submerging him. He lost the gun. *Shit.* Feeling along the bottom, he found it. Drenched, he stood, knee-deep in warm water. He waded southward, his legs sloshing through retreating water. He slogged on mindlessly until he stood in front of Tower One. He withdrew the syringe from his pocket. He toyed with it. Testing it, he squirted the contents. Abruptly, his mobile phone rang. *What the hell?*

He dropped the syringe. Fishing in the warm water, he could not find the thing. He came up empty-handed. His phone kept ringing, so he pulled it from his pocket.

Damn thing's still working. Focusing, he studied the caller's name. Lennox *again?* Was he hallucinating? She'd phoned twice in 20 minutes. Why? To apologize? He laughed as raindrops splotched his skin.

He toyed with the syringe. *At least hear the whoring slut out.*

"Hello?" he slurred into the phone.

It wasn't Lennox's voice. It was the babbling of a child. "Dada, Mommy sickee. No wakee. No lie down, Mommy! Wakee! Shawnee! Corky!" Weeping and howling, then distantly, grunts and groans, the child's hoarse voice begging, "Wakee, Mommeee!"

Lightning split the midnight sky. He stared up at Lennox's 10th-floor penthouse. The hair on the back of his neck rose. The windows were black. White draperies fluttered like dancing ghosts, in and out of the open balcony doorway.

Thunder boomed. The phone slipped from his hand. Instinct fired him like a bullet. In inebriated panic, he sloshed from the waves and stumbled up the sandy beach toward Tower One. Shawnee was alone up there, with a mother who wouldn't wake up. Raindrops pelted the slippery sand. Reaching the pavement he found his footing and ran.

What the hell happened to Lennox?

Chapter Seven

At 3:00 a.m., Ezra Gold lay naked in Vivian Champlain's queen-sized bed, swirling his agile tongue inside the shallow crevices of her warm, dainty ear. He tasted her salty-sweet flesh, his spittle hot and sticky. It made him quiver to his core. He could not stop. At last, she pulled away, sighing.

"Ezzie, stop. I can't stand any more. You'll be the death of me."

"I love the way you taste," he whispered, brushing his lips across her damp cheek, his fingers lost in strands of limp, wheat-colored hair.

"I know, my love. Give me your mouth." She threw her slender arms around his neck.

He crushed his lips to hers, his open mouth a gaping need, her open mouth a sanctuary as she let him enter her wet warmth. He lost himself there, searching and probing. Did she know how helpless he was? She could kill him with a sigh.

He loved this woman. He had loved her from the moment he met her two years ago. If he could, he would inhale her like cocaine. She was sickly and needy and yet defiant. Her waist was so small he could encircle it with two hands. He wanted to marry her. Too bad she was already married.

Fifteen years ago, when he had been a teenaged loser. Vivian Fairchild was already a successful art director, a rising talent with a number of films and magazine layouts to her credit. Then she had married the infamous corporate billionaire Truett Adair Champlain and had become stepmother to his two children, before leaving him—and the children—in an effort to save her own sanity and failing health. She had stopped working altogether. At an art exhibition, Poppy had introduced him to Vivian a few months after the separation.

Now he shared Vivian's bed. Reverently, he watched as she lay back and opened herself totally to him. He was on fire. He did not hesitate. Yet he remained mindful of her delicate physical health. Her heart condition was a serious consideration. He could never let himself go—totally. The expression of his passion was muted always. He tried to make up in intimate tenderness what he missed in rapacious rutting.

Later, as they lay sprawled beside one another on the bed, Ezra roused himself back to consciousness. "Vivian..."

"I'm here, my love." He felt the firm grasp of her strong, tapered fingers. Every long limb on Vivian's body tapered elegantly as graceful appendages of her compact hour-glass figure. He squeezed a loving response and dozed.

Moments later, she was sitting up, naked on the bed, her long, silky legs dangling as her feet found the hardwood floor. "Ezzie, I need to be alone tonight. You should go."

"Go? Why?" His breaths shortened. He stared at her elongated, elegant back. Her backbone protruded through her lean, flawless flesh. It reminded him of a fish's spine. A sleek mermaid would have a spine like that. Kneeling behind her on the rumpled mattress, he placed a gentle hand on her right shoulder. "I want to sleep with you tonight."

"Don't you have an early morning meeting with Heston?"

"Yes, but I also have the alarm set on my mobile. See? 7:00 a.m. I'm staying."

Halfway, she turned her wheat-blonde head, her blue eyes elusive. "No. Not tonight."

"What's wrong?"

"Feel dizzy. That's all. I need to take the new medicine and sleep."

"What new medicine?" He was worried. Her face looked drawn; the dark circles under her eyes, more pronounced. These were symptoms of hypertrophic cardiomyopathy, the medical condition that had afflicted her since birth.

At the beginning of their relationship, two years ago, her bouts with the heart condition had terrified him. Now that he knew more about it, he was better able to handle his emotions when her heart began to beat too quickly and her arteries began to constrict. He had her doctor on speed dial.

"Oh, it's nothing. Just some special sleeping tablets my doctor gave me. Here in the drawer." Opening the bedside table, she uncapped a prescription bottle, emptied pills into her palm, and swallowed them.

Watching her closely, he drew a cigarette from a silver holder, placed the filter tip between his lips, and lit a plump wooden match. Inhaling, he blew the smoke in a stream from his nostrils. Licking his lips, he blew out the match and placed it in an ashtray on the marble-topped bedside table. "I'm sorry if our lovemaking brought this on, Viv."

She sighed. "Ezzie, it didn't. I had a bad day today."

"Oh?"

"I overheard a private conversation—something unnerving. None of my business. But there it was. Now I don't know what to do"

"What? Where? In Miami?" He propped himself on one elbow and studied her. The color was returning to her cheeks.

"At the Fontainebleau. I was scouting a layout there. I ran into some old friends in the loo. I overheard something I shouldn't have. That's all. It made me feel ill. I felt ill all afternoon."

"Tell me."

"No." On impulse, she twisted her torso and planted an affectionate kiss just below his navel. Again, she turned away. "Go now, Ezzie. Please. I have a busy day tomorrow. A new photographer has flown in from Rio. We're doing a trial shoot."

Ezra bristled. "Why won't you ever confide in me, Vivian? Are you sure that's all it is?"

"Yes, love. Come. Sit beside me, here." She patted the edge of the mattress next to her. Her French nails were perfection—scarlet with ivory tips. Taking his hand in hers, she coaxed him into a sitting position beside her on the bed.

Bewildered, he sat dutifully. Something was wrong. He didn't know what. This was the first time she'd ever sent him home from her bed. He frowned.

"Tell me the truth," he said.

"I am telling you the truth, Ezzie. Oh, close enough. Go home now. I'll phone you tomorrow afternoon, after the morning light has gone. The contrast of light and shadow will be too stark by then."

"A magazine layout is more important to you than I am."

"If I'm going to make a comeback—as you've urged me to do—I need publicity."

He studied her narrow feet, which were planted on the floor next to his own wide feet. Her toenails were bare, free of polish—just as he liked them. Oh, how he craved her nearness. But he knew her too well to persist—and he did not want to upset her further. Too much stress and the consequences could be fatal.

"Maybe you shouldn't have taken the job with *Florida Fortunes* magazine."

"Don't be a child, Ezra. I know I'm fourteen years older than you, but it still surprises me sometimes when your responses seem so juvenile."

He was on his feet. If he waited longer or pushed harder, she would turn on him and savage him. By now, he knew her well. There was a bit of devil in her. Danger was the essence of her charm.

"Call me tomorrow," he said, wrapping himself in a scarlet-satin bed sheet and heading into the bathroom to dress. Turning on the gilded tap, he splashed cold water onto his face.

"Are you hungry?" Her throaty voice floated in through the bathroom door. "There's roasted chicken and decanted wine in the refrigerator. And some spinach-artichoke dip with crouton rounds. I thought you might have an appetite. You certainly earned one."

Turning off the spigot, he sponged himself briefly with a thick towel. "Yeah, I'll grab some on the way out," he said, dressing quickly. Reentering the bedroom, he was shocked to see Vivian doubled up in apparent pain.

He rushed to her side. "What the hell is going on?"

"I told you: nothing! Get out!" She tossed a pillow at his head.

Ducking, his ire flared. "I'll get out, all right! Hell if I'm staying her to be attacked. FU, baby." He stomped out the door and, grasping the knob, pulled the door half shut behind him. Pausing for a moment, he glanced back. "You're going to call me, right?"

"Yes, dammit!" A pillow flew through the air and bounced off the closing door.

"Let's do lunch," he shouted though the door.

"Go home, you fool!" He heard her giggling. Or was it whimpering?

What was she concealing? Undaunted, he decided to do some digging tomorrow on his own. He trotted down the hallway.

Standing over the kitchen sink—because Vivian would kill him if she found food on the floor—he bit with alacrity into a cold chicken leg and washed the spiced meat down with a glass of chilled sauvignon blanc.

If only she would agree to divorce His Moneyship. Not likely, since the old goofball was worth a couple of billion euros.

"Miss Greek Sorority. Miss Junior League. *Mazeltov, shikse!"* Chewing, he toasted the cool, vacant air around him. *Here's to schtooping.*

Thanks, Ma, for sending me to public school. His parents had become wealthy over the years, but they hadn't started out that way. Had he made the greatest mistake of his life by insisting his father sell the surgical supply business in Brooklyn? *Maybe not.*

He masticated the chicken flesh. *Good stuff.* He'd done all right. Graduated valedictorian. Earned a degree in communications from the University of Miami, with a minor in business. Nominated for top awards for directing his first feature film. *Thanks, Ma, you betcha. From your son, the hotshot movie director. Now to prove I wasn't a flash in the pan.*

"Ah, crap." In the excitement of receiving Heston's summons, he'd forgotten his mother's impending visit. She was arriving tomorrow, driving over from Aunt Edith's place. Edith wanted her sister to buy a retirement home on Florida's southeast coast, in Jupiter, Boca Raton, or West Palm.

He wanted her to settle in Naples—because that's where he was planning to be from now on—near Vivian. He could take care of his folks and be with his honey. It was a buyer's market. Ma wanted a deal—and she wanted a done deal before giving up the place near 63rd and Lexington in Manhattan.

Enough chicken. Go home. Get some shuteye.

Shuteye? Did people say that anymore? He'd seen too many old movies.

Tomorrow he would get to the bottom of whatever was eating Vivian. This was the *last* time he intended to be thrown out of any woman's bed, let alone Lady Vivi's.

Exiting through the garage door, he stepped into his Mercedes and opened the automatic garage door. The car had been a 30th-birthday gift from his mother. He popped a couple of antacid tablets. For a few luscious hours, he had managed to forget that his last two pictures had flopped. If Heston would give him one more stab, maybe he could impress Vivi enough to leave Truett Champlain.

Exiting onto the cul-de-sac at the end of Mermaid's Bight in Park Shore, he drove toward home. An hour before dawn, the night was dark and cloudy. It was just as well he sleep alone tonight. He needed to be rested when he met with Heston.

Maybe Kipp would forgive him someday for accepting Heston's offer to direct the Gauguin picture. He had heard Kipp was clean and sober now. Four years ago, drugs had made Kipp psychotic—*and scary.*

He wanted to touch base with Kipp, look him up. He still felt uneasy courting Heston behind Kipp's back, even though he hadn't seen or spoken to Kipp for four years.

But, lookit. Who could blame him for choosing a writing and directing credit with Heston over his friendship with Kipp? Kipp could, that's who.

Forget about it. He flipped on the headline news. Astonished by what he heard, he swerved to the curb on Crayton Drive and idled the Mercedes as he listened to the newscaster's words.

Chapter Eight

At dawn, Heston lay alone on his studio cot, a down pillow crushed beneath his head. Uncomfortable, he punched the pillow twice and tossed, frustrated. During his wife's absence, he had avoided the lonely master suite.

In semi-darkness, he appraised his half-painted self-portrait. He was anxious to continue his work, but, this morning, painting would have to wait.

He was meeting Ezra Gold for breakfast at Rainbow's on Fifth Avenue South in less than two hours. Cookie would hand him his customary cappuccino as soon as he walked in the door. The regulars at Cookie's no longer paid him any mind. Only the occasional tourist would gawk and awkwardly plead for an autograph or a group-shot photo. Irritated, he wrestled with the thin blanket that covered him completely—except for his frigid feet.

Unable to sleep, he had sought out the classic movie channel. He'd wanted to brush up to compete with Ezra, who was a movie-trivia nut. But the timing had been bad.

Tonight the channel had screened one of his own early films. *That* had made him feel old. He had become a classic. If they found out, his children would tease him about it.

He scowled at the unfinished canvas. Could he complete it in time for his first showing? His other canvases had not given him trouble. They were ready to hang.

Why was he painting his own portrait? Egomania? Or was he trying to find, somewhere inside this old relic, the man he used to be? The man he had suddenly become? The man he really was?

A ruthless man. An *old* man. Lennox had called him both yesterday. If only she hadn't...

He heard a scream. He bolted upright.

"Mr. Heston!" Lissette's cry emanated from the far side of the house. "Mr. Heston! Mr. Heston!"

Alarmed, he sprang from the cot and strode toward the studio doorway. Footsteps slapped down the hallway. Scanning for his slippers, he threw on his silver silk bathrobe and knotted the belt. Lissette burst into the studio.

"Heston, Mr. Heston! You must come! Quick! *Andele!*" the plump housekeeper shouted, anxiety stretching the skin of her round face like an inflated balloon. Her brown eyes goggled in their sockets. Forcefully, she yanked him by the arm, dragging him down the hallway.

"Why? What is it?" he demanded gravely.

"On TV! We just heard!"

"Heard what?"

"Pauvre cita! She is dead!"

"Who? Who in blazes is dead?"

Barefoot, he dogged Lissette's flat heels as she waddled down the hallway and into the kitchen. The TV mounted on the gleaming granite counter screamed the terrible news.

"The former sex kitten's body was found on the balcony lanai of her 10th-floor penthouse on South Beach less than an hour ago by a maid. No word yet as to the whereabouts of Shawnee Demming, Cordova's two-year-old son with her ex-husband, rocker Kipp Demming."

"See?" bleated Lissette, pointing to the TV.

"How...?" he whispered, unable to look away from the screen.

"Kipp Demming, as famous for his bawdy escapades as for his powerfully sensual music, performed a sold-out concert just last night in downtown Miami. According to spectators, Demming induced pandemo-

nium when he enticed the huge crowd to kill him at the end of his performance."

"For the love of..." Heston muttered, disbelieving.

"Kipp, who was saved by his security team, has not been reached for comment. His manager, Gabriel Cade, denies all knowledge of Kipp Demming's whereabouts. We will bring the latest developments as they happen."

Hypnotized, he beheld Lennox's familiar, once-flawless face flashing repeatedly across the screen—a montage of photos at least 15 years old. *Cleavage with a head attached,* one rag had dubbed her. *Don't think about it. It's too late now.*

"Oh, my dear ..."

Moved, he glanced at Lissette. Her eyes teared. He felt as if he'd been punched in the gut. Life as he had known it was over.

They would find out about him—his memories, his regrets, and his secrets. They would publish every word and deed. Dread inched from the depths of his being like a snake surfacing in a scummy pond.

"Miami-Dade police are combing the area in search of little Shawnee. The Missing Children's Network is now officially involved in the case."

"Oiye!" Lissette gnawed her knuckles.

Chewing the nail of his forefinger, he avoided her eyes and stared at the monitor.

"The cause of Cordova's death has yet to be determined. This just in—police are launching an all-out manhunt for the child and his father. Word is that this could be a murder-suicide."

"Funny, isn't it? Nobody bothered to inform me," he whispered, heartsick.

"They will, sir." Lissette breathed. "Sit down, Mr. Heston. I will make you a cappucino—unless you would prefer ginger ale?"

"Ginger ale. I'll pretend it's scotch and soda." Collapsing into a chair at the table, he palmed his face from forehead to chin. "It's times like these, Lissy, when I really hate being a recovered alcoholic."

"What about Mrs. Demming, sir? Shouldn't you phone her?"

"Yes." *But I don't want to.* He glanced at the oven clock. "Poppy and Winner should be on their way home from Miami. They were leaving early"

"Mrs. Demming had a workout date with old friends," Lissette said wanly. "At 10 a.m." She scrutinized him. He dialed his phone. "No answer," he said. "I'll leave a voice mail."

Lissette nodded.

"Poppy, it's Heston. Call me immediately. It's urgent." He rang off.

What would he say to his wife? Tormented, he brushed back the shock of hair hanging over his forehead. Elbows propped up on the table, he sat braced against the onslaught of personal carnage emanating from the broadcast.

"Pour one for yourself and have a seat," he told the housekeeper, pushing a chair out from under the table. It skidded across the floor. "Make it coffee, if you prefer."

"Espresso," she whispered, complying. "I am afraid for Shawnito!" Sitting, she stifled an explosion of sobs. *"Pauvre nino."*

"Cordova is rumored to have signed a multi-million-dollar book deal with a New York publishing house to publish her memoirs, based on the secret diary kept by her notorious stage mother, Lynne Cordova. According to manager, Gabriel Cade, however, the diary has yet to be located."

Lissette's brown eyes sought him out. "She was murdered for her mother's diary?"

"Shushh," said Heston, all ears.

"Older viewers will remember Lennox Cordova as the on-screen foil of Heston Demming. The cinematic duo, known for their romantic screwball comedies, were a major box-office draw 15 years ago. Cordova's surprise marriage to Heston's son Kipp is listed among the Top Ten Biggest Celebrity Shockers of the Decade."

Now his own face appeared on screen—smiling and years younger. It had begun—the publicity blitz from hell. *Where will it end?* How much about his and Lennox's early years could he keep secret? His marriage, his family, indeed his whole life, was at stake.

"I wonder how she died, sir," Lissette said, watching him closely.

She knows I was gone all yesterday afternoon.

Suddenly, his daughter Sage entered the far door. "Daddy, I thought I heard something." Half-awake, the six-year-old rubbed the sleep from her silver-blue eyes. She held up a book. "I had to finish my story first." Her thick, brown hair fell loose and uncombed. Sleepily, she hitched up the backside of her drooping pink jammies. Encircling his thighs, she leaned her head against him in sleep.

Remorse seized him. His first thought should have been for the safety of his children. Urgently, he pried the girl loose and crouched to her eye level. "Sage, where is Teggi?"

"Asleep."

"Your brother Dakota?"

"Listening to Kipp's music." She yawned. "He threw me out of his room. I told him I'd tell."

Relieved, he crushed the child to his breast. Releasing her, he rose to full height. He placed his hands on his daughter's shoulders and pushed her forward. "Lissette, take Sage back to bed. Then check on the other two."

The housekeeper nodded, round brown eyes agog. He could feel her suspicion.

Striding quickly away, he entered his studio, closed the door behind him, and stood, back to the wall. He needed to become numb and stay numb. He would have to present a strong front to his family.

He had to pull it together fast.

Spotting his slippers as they hid beneath the cot, he slipped them on, wiggling his toes for warmth. Slip-sliding before the easel, he contemplated his self-portrait.

"Why is this happening to me?" he murmured. *What if the truth comes out? What if Poppy learns about my relationship with...?*

Seizing his paint-loaded palette, he flung it at the unfinished canvas, fascinated as rivulets of paint bled down the imperfect likeness.

He heard a commotion. The door flew open. Lissette appeared. "They're home, Mr. Demming. Your wife and daughter —with Ram. Winner ran straight to her room. Your wife and Ram are glued to the kitchen TV."

Spared. "Tell Ram to stay. Scandal brings out the crazies. Tell Poppy I..."

His wife burst into the room. "Heston! Something terrible has happened to Lennox! They're saying she's dead. That Kipp killed her. And Shawnee, too. It's not true. I know it's not. Heston, come listen. It's on the news."

His wife was near hysteria. If he didn't do something fast, she would lose control. Clasping her firm upper arms, he pulled her up short, face to face with him, looking deep into her docile brown eyes, now mad with horror.

Ram Kincaid burst into the studio. Poppy gaped at the young stallion with the Fu Manchu moustache. Ram's hulking, muscular mass filled the entire door frame. A knotted red bandana wrapped the bristly dome of his head.

"Mr. Demming, sir," Ram said, unemotionally. "The satellite trucks are lining up outside the gates. It's a media feeding frenzy. How do you want to handle it?"

Chapter Nine

At the Naples Municipal Airport, Beryl Northgate trudged through the parking lot. She wore a sturdy backpack, toted a small cooler, and sipped a hot cup of brewed tea. Briskly, she entered the private aircraft terminal and scanned the bright, open waiting room. A few well-to-do people milled around her. Her digital watch read 9:08 a.m.

Her flight plan submitted, she stared mindlessly at the terminal's large television screen, which was tuned to a headline news channel. She watched video of the president's latest speech, minus the sound. Suddenly, the picture changed.

The glamorous face of Lennox Cordova slammed onto the screen. Beneath it ran the words Breaking News. What had Kipp's ex-wife been up to?

Disturbed, Beryl reached for her mobile phone. The headline on the mobile's screen stunned her. *Actress Lennox Cordova Found Dead in Miami. Kipp Demming and Son Missing.* She glanced back at the terminal's telly. A similar headline now appeared beneath a sexy head shot of Lennox: *Actress Found Dead; Rock Star and Toddler Gone Missing.*

Suddenly, the screen was flipping myriad images of Lennox, Kipp, Shawnee, and Heston. Mesmerized, she read the track running across the bottom of the screen. News of the gruesome discovery of Lennox's dead body had been released by the media. Dizzily, Beryl watched the kaleidoscopic images spin.

Tearing her eyes from the screen, she clutched her mobile. In disbelief, she read the article, batting her lids to clear her vision. The police had not ruled out a possible murder-suicide or murder-kidnapping. Bad blood between Kipp and Lennox. Money, sex, drugs, violence. Be on the lookout for Kipp Demming, tall, slender, blonde, hot, drug-addict, sex-addict...

The ugly words danced around her. A pretty girl's face appears on the TV screen. Reporter Cecily Hodges, the one who had broadcast the Demonsong's concert tour, the last person known to have spoken with Kipp before he disappeared.

"He kissed me," squealed Hodges. As photos of her lip-lock with Kipp hit the screen. "He told me something big was going to happen today. I had no idea he meant murder!" Gaping at the kissing couple, Beryl stood transfixed. The phone rang in her hand. Excitedly, she answered without noting the caller's name.

"Hello, Mum? Are you phoning about Kipp? I just heard!"

"Berry? Is that you?" growled a gravelly male baritone.

She gasped. "Ki—?"

"Shut up and listen!" the surly voice commanded.

"Is this...are you...?" she stammered uncertainly.

"Yeah!" Kipp rasped. "Zip it. Are you alone?"

"Indeed I am," she squeaked. Clearing her throat, she turned toward the wall and whispered. "I mean, no! I'm not with anyone, but I'm standing in the middle of the private air terminal in Naples. People are milling round. I'm flying down to the Keys for a week. Your dad gave me notice." She glanced over her shoulder.

"You're joking!" Kipp growled.

"I'm not. "

"It figures. The old man's still a control freak."

Anyone could be listening in, but she had to ask. "Oh, where in the world are you? What's going on?"

"I can't say—at the moment."

"Are you all right?"

"Yes."

"What about Sha—?"

"Don't say the name! I'll tell you when I see you. Can we meet up?"

"K—"

"Don't say it, Beryl! This is serious. I'm in real trouble this time."

She hunkered down and whispered. "I'll say you are. They think you murdered Len...your ex-." She paused, staggered by her blunder. "You know, don't you? She's dead."

"Yeah, I know. Man, do I know." His tone was eerily somber and pregnant with unspoken gory detail.

"It's all over the news. The telly is full of it. I'm watching it now. Your disappearance is breaking news."

"Beryl, I need help."

"I daresay."

"Beryl, I need *your* help. I need a friend. Meet me?"

"I—I don't know."

"Please! Please. It's urgent. Deadly serious."

She faltered. "I don't know when I can. I'm about to take off."

"He's letting you fly the Cessna? Even though you're canned?"

"Duh. It was his idea. So I'm taking advantage of him. Actually, I'm still his employee. He gave me a month's notice. Then he gave me a week off with pay to think about my future. Look, why did you phone me, of all people? It's been years since..."

"I'll explain when we meet up. Berry, please."

"Oh, all right. Where?"

"Dad's T-hangar."

"The T-hangar? That's a five-minute walk from here. Are you that close by?"

"Just do it, Berry. Stop questioning every damn thing I say. Be there in fifteen minutes. I'll find you." Abruptly, the phone went dead.

Guiltily, she glanced around the tiny, immaculate terminal. No one noticed her. Nothing unusual in that, unfortunately. Still, no one seemed the wiser. Nonchalantly, she tossed her coffee cup into a rubbish bin. Busily, she arranged the pack on her back. Still, no one minded her. No one guessed the secret knowledge she now carried.

Feigning *ennui,* she sauntered past the flight desk and out the glass doors. No one raised an eyebrow. They expected her to conduct a flight-check prior to departure. She *should* be on her way to the hangar. As she trotted out onto the airfield, she watched a small Lear jet taxing down the runway. As the Lear jet left earth, reason seized her. She stopped dead in her tracks.

What if Kipp *did* murder Lennox and Shawnee? Dimwit that she was, she had neglected to enquire. Not that he would have confessed. Her own life could be in danger now. Or it would be—if she had a life. She stifled a sad smile, then frowned.

What if he meant to murder her, too? The news had suggested a murder-suicide plot. Perhaps he planned to murder the whole Demming clan, including its nanny, and then kill himself.

She knew he was despondent. She knew he hated his life. Even if she hadn't known him personally since he was 19 and she, 21, it was all there in his music. Kipp's lyrics on Demonsong's new album dripped desolation and despair. And she knew by heart the lyrics to all his songs. For years, they had been the soundtrack to her own private internal drama.

She stared at the private T-hangar, a few hundred yards away. Odd that he would suggest it as a meeting place. It's where she was headed to begin with. It was the storage hangar for Heston's Cessna turboprop, the plane she soon would be piloting to the Keys. From there, she would fly a rented seaplane to Heart of Fire Key. If she lived. She had rented from that fixed-base operator before.

Am I to die by the hand of Kipp Demming? Only one way to find out...

On shaky legs, she ambled toward the small, T-shaped metal building far out on the dewy expanse of the flat airfield. Behind her, brittle eggshell clouds broke into yolk as the sun poured over the horizon. A chill in the air caused her to clutch together the open ends of her loosened collar. Stopping, she unzipped her bag and drew out a Swiss army knife. Weapon in hand, she proceeded cautiously toward the isolated T-hangar.

Why am I thinking about eggs? I ate breakfast. Oh, that's right. Kipp's favorite food was eggs. All his diehard fans knew that salient fact. *Rum and scrambled eggs.*

And what was she to the rock star but one of the great unwashed?

Chapter Ten

"Check all security systems, Ram," said Heston. "Do a head count of the kids."

"I copy, sir." The beefy bodyguard slammed the door to Heston's studio. Poppy flinched. He held on tightly to his wife's upper arms. She wrestled frantically for release.

He braced his wife by the shoulders. "Come here, Red. Sit down." Seating her gently on the only real chair in the room, he knelt before her taking her small hands in his. Softly, in a straightforward manner, he uttered the words. "The scandal mongers are wagging their tongues. They say our son Kipp killed Lennox and Shawnee. Either that, or he killed Lennox and kidnapped Shawnee. In either case, they don't know where Kipp is. He's fled the scene."

"No." Poppy shook her head. Her brown eyes were wide with denial.

Again, he took her by the shoulders. "Poppy, Kipp hasn't been himself for two or three years now. He's become deranged—sex, drugs, the trashy maniacs he cultivates."

"He wouldn't—He's clean now. He's sober." She faltered.

"Darling..."

"It-It's lies, Heston. K-Kipp wouldn't do that. He wouldn't! I'm his mother. I'm his real mother. I gave birth to him. I would know." Her fingers, interlaced with his, tried to escape. He held them in a fast grip. He sensed her hysteria rising.

Fiercely, he drew his wife into a standing position and cuddled her closely, whispering into her ear. He could feel the tremor of her body, a delicate machine he knew as well as his own. "You *must* steel yourself to the possibility that Kipp has committed this heinous act. I'm not saying he has. I'm saying it is a possibility. You have to face this thing head on, Red."

He could feel that she was about to short-circuit. Desperate, he sat her back down in the chair and squatted on his haunches, again taking her hands in his. He gazed into her eyes imploringly. *What the devil am I to do?*

"Listen to me." He shook her gently but firmly. "It could grow worse. No one has seen Kipp since his concert last night. He could be dead, too."

A hand touched his shoulder. He realized Lissette was still in the room. The plump housekeeper, sincere concern on her round face, knelt down onto the floor beside him. She placed a kindly hand on Poppy's freckled forearm. "It's what they're saying on the news, Poppy. They're saying maybe it is a murder, maybe a kidnapping, maybe a double murder-suicide. Nobody knows the truth yet. We have to wait and see." She patted Poppy's arm. "I'm sorry. So very, very sorry. I've always been so fond of Kipp. He was such a fine young man until..."

He shook his head in warning. Exchanging glances with him, Lissette nodded and pressed her cheek to Poppy's. Her round eyes brimmed with tears. Poppy did not respond. She stared at Lissette. Heston played his ace.

"Red, you must get hold of yourself. Our other children need your guidance now."

His comment had the effect of smelling salts. Suddenly, Poppy seemed to brace up. "You're right, Heston. I forgot about that."

Gratified, Lissette rose gracelessly to her feet. He offered her a hand, which she refused with the flick of a wrist. Dallying for a moment, she goggled at his ruined self-portrait.

"Don't ask."

"Sir, do you believe that Kipp...may have...been involved in this terrible thing?"

He avoided her eyes. "Anything is possible, at this stage, Lissette."

"Si."

He knew what she was thinking. Poppy had been in Miami last yesterday. *Not just me.*

Crossing herself, Lissette withdrew but returned in less than a minute, as he was walking his wife down the hall toward the study. "Mr. Heston, Ezra Gold is here to see you. He says you had an appointment. I buzzed him in."

Damn. "Yes, I did. In all this confusion, I forgot about it. Has he heard the news?"

"Yes, sir. That's why he came here from Rainbow's on Fifth."

He exhaled. "Tell him...Wait, Lissette. Ask Ezra to join the family in my study. He may as well hear this, too. At one time, he was Kipp's closest friend. He may have insight into Kipp's motives. Tell everyone We'll convene promptly at 10 a.m." Assuming Poppy's arm, Lissette guided her mistress down the hallway. Quickly, Heston doubled back to his studio and slammed the door shut behind him.

If anyone knew the dirt on this situation, if would be that swindler Gabe Cade, Kipp's parasitic personal manager. He didn't for a moment believe Gabe's statement to the press. Gabe Cade was a liar.

Every instinct in Heston's body told him Gabe Cade was at the center of this mess. What he didn't know was why. But ever since Gabe Cade had entered Kipp's orbit, Kipp's whole life had spiraled out of control. It was time to confront Cade about the diary. He dialed his agent's office in New York. Arlene's assistant answered. He told her he needed a phone number.

"Name?"

"Gabriel Cade." Selecting a piece of tangerine-colored chalk from his box of pastels, Heston wrote down the scoundrel's number on a piece of crinkled sketch paper. Meantime, the number was connected automatically. Gabe's phone began to ring.

Chapter Eleven

In the grandiose office aboard his mega-yacht *Angel Baby,* public-relations guru Gabriel Cade tossed down his magazine. The old man stood ruminating beside his splendid teakwood desk. Behind him, rows of framed gold and platinum records and CDs earned by his clients lined the burgundy-textured wall. Outside the windows, as the ship cruised the Caribbean. He tore a chaw and tucked it beneath his lip.

The desk phone rang. Reading the name of his caller, he sneered. *Almighty Heston Demming himself.* Expectorating into a spittoon, Cade did not bother to pick up the receiver.

Let him stew...

Shuddering, the dapper oldster crossed his arms and hugged his chest. He hated the damned AC. These days, you couldn't get away from it anywhere. It was his damned yacht. Why the hell was it so cold? His spit out the chaw, disgruntled.

On impulse, he hobbled to the French doors and threw them open. Noonday sunlight streamed in, along with warm, humid wind from the ocean. The solar heat penetrated his icy irritation. He longed for equatorial open sea. At the moment, *Angel Baby* was bound for Port Everglades, Florida, an American port of entry situated 30 miles north of Miami, on the Atlantic coast of Florida. In port, his crew would refuel.

That'll warm up this damned hold. He made a mental note: Instruct Chantal to turn up the air and keep it turned up—or else. She had messed with it, against his strict orders. He'd be glad when she came back. His arthritic bones ached as he squatted down behind his desk. Even as a young man growing up in Illinois, he had hated the cold. Now that he was old, it had become unbearable.

Morosely, he gazed at the abstract painting on the far wall. *A piece of shit if you asked me, but it's a genuine Cedric Spicer. Worth a bundle. That's my boy.*

Although recently painted, it was worth thousands of dollars already—because Cedric's early work had been bought up and hoarded away in storage by none other than *our old buddy, Heston.* That situation, too, would soon be fixed.

Not that he blamed Heston in this instance—after all, Cedric had broken The Unwritten Law. Still, in this dogfight, he would take his allies where he could find them—even fruitcakes with nuts. Even sons and grandsons. His empty stomach growled. *Dammee, I'm hungry.*

He was looking forward to a bowl of wonton soup. Chantal had gone to instruct the chef. She'd better remember a bottle of soy sauce and a sprinkle of those little green onions, too. And those crunchy, curly little fried suckers, when they didn't become lodged in his dentures. Screw his doctor's advice. He would suck down all the salt he wanted to. Soup was heat. Heat was life. He wasn't going to die yet because he wasn't ready to. His work wasn't done. And he was so close.

He slid a hand beneath his shirt. *Ticker's still working.* He took his own pulse. Satisfied, he contemplated the blood pressure machine in the corner. He'd just taken it. *Too soon.*

Grasping the arm of his leather-upholstered desk chair—while trying to pinpoint the wrenching back pain caused by his sciatica—he balanced himself and slid open a bottom drawer. His old bones were beginning to creak. He could almost hear them, groaning like a church organ out of tune. He had lived too long. But he couldn't die yet—not yet.

He needed patience and fortitude. In his conscious mind, he sought justice. In his heart of hearts, he craved *vengeance*—for himself and for those whose souls could not rest.

From the deep drawer, he exhumed a silver-framed photo. The familiar, faded black-and-white image of a fair-haired young woman smiled up at him. He held the treasured keepsake in his trembling, knobby fingers. Rising, he placed the framed photo on the desktop. Drawing a silk handkerchief from his pocket, he blew his dripping nose and, wiping his eyelashes, sat down in the chair. He stared at the comely young face, as he had done many times over the years.

He could view her with much less emotion now. Gradually, over many years, it had become easier, less painful, to contemplate her lovely face. He hardly remembered her at all anymore. And yet the wound stung, as though fresh. The wrong of it. The injustice. The need for reckoning.

"Angela," he whispered bitterly. "My once-upon-a-time wife. *'Long, long ago. Long ago.'* " Softly he hummed the old, old tune he had learned in childhood from his piano teacher.

A lonesome breeze stirred the draperies. The green fronds of the potted palm rustled despondently. He wondered what his life would have been like if his young wife had lived into old age alongside him. Would their son have turned out differently? The two grandchildren were a comfort—one in Naples, one in Miami. With luck and careful planning, they'd both be on board with him again soon.

"Forty-five years ago...." A very long time.

With infinite tenderness, he bent down and replaced the framed photo in its hiding place. Resolve renewed, he slid the drawer firmly shut.

Aloud, his aged voice crackled in the silence like an old phonograph record. "They will pay, my precious. That much I promise. I've been telling you that for a long time. Now it's happening. His descendants are going to reap the whirlwind. It took me years to set it up, but I've finally got 'em right where I want 'em."

Rising slowly from his chair, he stepped out the French doors onto the garden piazza, a welcome respite of greenery on the third floor of his 6,500 square foot, three-storied floating palace. Lighting a Lucky, he leaned against the ivory-painted door jam and watched tropical birds frolic in the frothing fountain. He released pale smoke from his lungs, watching, fascinated, as it drifted slowly across the courtyard, rising like a ghost toward the immense blue heavens, where it would merge with the clouds. He looked down again at the frisky birds, signs that new life had somehow found its way to this floating haven of rest.

Life goes on. For some. Despite his sour temper, he chuckled at the birds' antics. Snorting, he drew on his cigarette and, this time, belched pale smoke. He quelled his coughing fit. He felt the rattle inside his chest. His breathing was short. The main thing now was to not lose his aplomb. He needed *huevos* of cold, clanging steel.

He had never in his life desired any woman but Angela, his wife—that is, until the day, 25 years ago, when he had first beheld the beauty of six-year-old seductress Lennox Cordova. He had judged many child beauty pageants in those days. Little Lennox had been the most beautiful child on the circuit back then. Her mother had dolled her up in earrings, lipstick, and high heels. The girl could sing and dance like a professional even then. Movie stardom was sure to follow.

At the thought of Lennox and her tragic end, his fingers once again trembled. Fat ash, from the cigarette dangling between his fingertips, fell off and floated down onto the sienna-and-cobalt tiles of the floating piazza. Once more, he reached for his handkerchief. This time he dabbed sweat from beneath his shirt collar.

"Men sweat. Women perspire." Distracted by his own joke, he chuckled.

His desk phone rang again. Hobbling to his desk, Gabe read the name of his caller and picked up the receiver. "Cade here," he grumbled sociably. Listening for a moment, he replied, "Well done. I'm glad our plan is working. Keep me posted, my fine lad." He tossed the receiver back onto its base, a smile dallying upon his lips. *It has begun.*

He had tried every which way to infiltrate the Demming clan. It wasn't until he'd signed Kipp Demming to a Life's Rights deal that he'd struck pay dirt. Right now, Kipp was a wild card, but he would turn up sooner or later like that same bad, old penny.

Gabe's eyes rested on the magazine. It would all converge in the end, for he had found the key that would open the gates of Perdition. He picked up the magazine and gazed at the jeans ad. *What an exquisite beauty this Little Miss Demming is—but not for long.*

At last, his plan for revenge was unfolding.

Chapter Twelve

Away from the landing field, her shoes damp with dew, Beryl edged inside the T-shaped metal building that housed Heston's Cessna. Sliding the door closed, she crept cautiously, eyes searching the shadowy corners of the deserted airplane hangar. Her footsteps crunched on concrete. She took in her surroundings.

The tight space seemed neat and orderly. The lone airplane appeared well-maintained. Should she begin her pre-flight check? Stopping to ground herself, she placed her palm on the plane's clean fuselage. The cold metal stung her bare skin. Fear gripped her.

Will Kipp show up?

Rounding the propeller nose, she glanced behind her. If Kipp were a murderer, he could jump her from behind, stab her, and dump her body.

A strong hand wrenched her arm and whirled her around.

She screamed, but her scream died away. She stared up into the craggy young face that filled her lonely nights with longing. He was tall. Taller, even, than she recalled. But his natural golden fairness was obscured by a disheveled mop of platinum.

In his black-leather jacket—sleeves pushed to reveal supple and hairy, veiny arms—and tight black jeans, he looked scrawny, underfed, and tense. He was tense like a tomcat—taut, muscular, and hardened by the vicissitudes of alley life. She might get clawed if she got too close. Edging away, she got hold of her herself. "Kipp Demming, you scoundrel!"

Closing in, he hovered over her like a dark angel. "Hello, Berry." The low-rumbling growl was jagged as a broken bottle. The copper eyes darted nervously, settling on her eyes. "Are there cameras in here?"

His gaze unnerved her.

"I'm not sure. Heston's home is an armed media fortress. He might have installed some here. But he never uses those on the island." *Quit babbling, you idiot.*

He cast a quick look round. "Then let's make this quick, Nanny Northgate. Arms up."

"What?"

"I have to frisk you. You might be armed. I am." He waved a hand gun in her face.

Slowly, she raised her arms. Quickly, his free hand patted down her body. Her heart pumped furiously.

"What's this?" He pulled a Swiss Army knife from her front pocket.

"My protection from you."

He smiled, pocketing the knife. "Okay. That's done."

Even grizzled and dirty, he made her feel weak. Resolutely, she shook off her apprehension. Before she could take charge, he whistled sharply. The sound pierced her ears.

"Here's why I phoned you." Rounding the plane's tail, a tiny human figure toddled out from the shadows.

"Shawnee!" she gasped, gaping up at Kipp and back down at the boy.

Dropping to one knee, she beckoned to the lad. Opening her arms, she smiled welcomingly. "Hello, young man! Can you come to me? Pretty please? I'm Nanny Berry. Do you remember meeting me—when you last visited Poppa and Nana at the ski lodge?"

Reluctantly, the child shied away, hugging the plane's left wheel. His face was tear-streaked; his silver-blue eyes, red-rimmed; his blond curls, straggly; his Tee-shirt crumpled. He badly needed a change of clothing. But what a *gorgeous* child he was.

"When did he eat last? Does he need changing?" she asked Kipp, rising to her feet. Even at full height, she came up only to his chest. She looked up at his drawn face in concern. He was so handsome, he was hard to face squarely. Even in his skanky condition, his innate beauty was humbling.

Kipp shook his head. "He's potty trained."

She smiled at Shawnee. "Good for you!"

"On our moonlit ride across the Glades, around 4 a.m.—the kid and I—we grabbed a hot dog at the gas station—on the Miccosukee reservation," he said, watching the hovering child closely. "That's where I picked up these cool T-shirts." He unzipped his black-leather jacket and bared the words emblazoned on his chest.

"The Hippies Were Right?" Smirking, she looked down and read the writing on Shawnee's tiny chest. "Big Flirt in Training." She stifled a smile. "Very nice, indeed."

"You're just saying that," Kipp looked at her knowingly, "because it's true."

There was bite behind his grin. His scrutiny made her blush. She caught a whiff of the masculine scent she remembered from years ago: bergamot-cypress and athletic sweat.

"You drove your car?" she covered quickly.

He shook his head. "My Goldwing. Only wheels I could hide from the bank. The kid's life was in jeopardy. I had to get him out of there."

"What happened, Kipp?"

He scratched the stubble on his chin. "Kid phoned me on Lennox's mobile at midnight. He found her lying dead. Half-sprawled out on the balcony. Ten floors up. He thought she was sleeping. Then he cried, saying she was sick. He was trying to rouse her. Hard to take." Thrusting his hands into his pockets, he rose on tiptoe, and then settled flat.

"That's horrible." She watched the toddler.

"Damn straight. I rushed over, found him alone with her body out on the balcony. I freaked. I grabbed Little Buddy here and ran. Next thing I know, we're clear across the state."

"You left his mother lying there? Are you certain she was dead?" She eyed the gun dangling at his side.

"I studied enough medicine to know that much."

"Sooner or later, they'll connect you with her death."

"True enough. I'll be long gone by then."

"Will you? You're already Headline News, 24/7. You're up for a Grammy. The awards show is this week."

He placed his free hand on her shoulder. "That's why you've got to take pity on this kid. Help us out of this jam."

"This kid? Your son, Kipp! Your son needs sleep," she observed. "And nourishment. So do you, I daresay." She softened her scolding. She could sense the man's fatigue and desperation. She stifled an impulse to stroke his weary brow—*the brow of a murderer?*

"He's not my son."

She clicked her tongue. "You can hardly deny him, Kipp. He's a Demming if I've ever seen one—Oh, Great Scott!" His meaning sank in as she watched his eyebrows rise.

"Meet my little brother."

"I don't believe it. Heston detests Lennox."

"That's not what she told me yesterday. Look, Berry, I've got to get out of here. They're after my ass and I have—business to attend to." He glanced at Shawnee. "How you doing, Buddy?" he queried affectionately. The child did not reply but merely rubbed one eye with a fist. Kipp raised his eyes to hers. "I need to leave him with you. Take care of him. You can—better than anyone I know. He's in danger."

Beryl's eyebrows vaulted. "Danger?"

"Look, when I got to the penthouse he was teetering on the edge of the balcony. Trying to reach the guitar I had given him for his birthday, yesterday afternoon. Somebody—surely not Lennox—had placed it on the ledge."

Beryl's hand flew to her mouth. "How horrible!" She watched the child sit down on the cold, hard floor and yawn. She glared up at Kipp. "You swear you found her—already d-e-a-d? You didn't...?"

"K-i-l-l her? Hell, no!"

"Then how did she die, Kipp?"

"I thought it out on the ride over. Somebody murdered her or it was a simple OD. A bottle of pills was spilled out on the floor. Regardless, they're going to charge me, Beryl. If they can find me, which is where you come in. Take the kid."

"Tell them you're innocent!"

He laughed. "Lennox and I had a big fight yesterday afternoon. The doorman at Tower One heard us. People in the lobby heard us. Rest assured, we're on the lobby cam." He swiveled, glancing at the door. "Look, I've got something important to do. I won't be in touch."

"Kipp, I can't take Shawnee from you!" she cried.

He stopped. "Why not?" With sensuous grace, he sauntered toward her. "I thought you were my friend."

She stepped backward. "I am. Or I was. But it will make me complicit in a murder investigation. I can't show up out of nowhere with this child, and say I found him wandering the streets, now can I? Who would believe me? It's absurd."

Kipp exhaled. "The kid's safety trumps your cowardice, Beryl. He needs taking care of."

So do you. "Why can't you do it?"

"I'm...not long for this world."

"Meaning what? Do you have terminal cancer or something?"

"Or something."

"What will I tell the police, Kipp? They might accuse *me* of murder, charge *me* with child snatching."

"With what motive?"

"Ransom? What else? Grape popsicles!"

"Language, language," Kipp grinned irreverently, in spite of his fatigue and the seriousness of his predicament. His teeth were white and even. Translucent skin, like his half-sister Winner's, stretched tautly across his chiseled nose and cheekbones. His slim, sinewy body appeared gaunt in the fluorescent light of the hangar. "Take the kid for me, Berry. If not for my sake, then for his."

She wanted to run to the man, embrace him, caress his crown, kiss his brow, offer him nourishment, sustenance—her breasts? But she fought the feeling with everything she had. "Kipp, I will not take Shawnee. I can't."

"Why not? You said you were going down to Dad's island for a week. Who'd be the wiser? Take Shawnee, lie low, and..."

"And what, Kipp? Where will you go? What will you do?"

Kipp shifted his weight. "I'll finish the job I started last night."

"Which is?"

"It's The Eve of Destruction, baby," he sang into an imaginary microphone. "Sixties."

She blanched. "Suicide? Is that what you mean?"

An odd gleam formed in the copper eyes. "Take the boy for me, Beryl. One last favor."

Everything decent in her rebelled. "No," she said, backing away. "I refuse. I will not aid an act as cowardly as suicide."

"Cowardly? Hell, it takes more guts than you'll ever have, old maid."

"You're wrong. Suicide is the coward's way out." She was trembling so hard she feared he could hear her bones rattle. What should she do? What could she say to stop him from committing such a violent act? *Keep talking...*

"How can you do this to your fans?" Her armor slipped. "To me? I care about you—more than you know."

"Oh, yeah?" His eyelids blinked rapidly. "It's a done deal. I posted a suicide note to Poppy yesterday."

She gasped, hand to mouth. "You didn't!"

He flipped her fringe. "Did. I left evidence on the beach, too. They'll think I OD'd and drowned in the Atlantic. You'll be in the clear. They'll stop searching for me. Sooner or later. Deliver the kid to Heston. Shawnee is his problem now, anyhow."

"And tell him what?" she demanded.

"Hell, tell him the truth. Shawnee's his son, not his grandson. The old lech."

"Even if that were true, how am I supposed say I found him?"

Kipp bent down. "You'll think of something."

Outraged, she cried, "You think of something."

At their raised voices, Shawnee started to cry. He sat cross-legged on the hard concrete floor of the hangar.

"Dammit, I don't know what to do," Kipp muttered, plopping down on a metal bench.

"There, there. Shhh!" she crooned, lifting the child into her arms. "Are you hungry? Would you like something to eat?"

Dropping his stuffed toy to the floor, Shawnee rubbed his eyes and nodded. Clutching her suddenly, he laid his head upon her shoulder and stuck a thumb in his mouth. She cradled him gently, turning to face Kipp in disgust. "Well, son or brother, he deserves better than this from you," she declared rabidly.

Kipp hunched forward, elbows on his knees. His hands played in a small tool chest he'd found. He pointed a wrench at her for emphasis. "Want me to kill the kid, too? I'm the one who just saved his life. Don't forget that." He shook his head in sorrow. "I don't want to have to kill the kid."

She stood speechless.

"Know what this is?" He flung the wrench in her direction. It landed at her feet and skidded across the floor. "It's the damned monkey wrench that fell into my plans when I met Gabe Cade. I'm screwed, no matter what."

"So face your own mistakes. Turn yourself in," she steamed, tapping her foot. "That seems a most reasonable solution to me."

Kipp chuckled. "Woman, you are so naïve. I have a record. They won't believe a word I say. Hell, I'd rather die than go to prison for life."

Her mind was reeling. "So these are my choices? If I refuse, you'll kill yourself and Shawnee. If I take Shawnee, I'll go to prison for child snatching.

His hollow eyes echoed his fear. "Please, Beryl. I couldn't face one more night in the slam."

She heard his agony. "Why do you call it the slam?"

He poked around in the tool box. "Because when that door slams behind you, you know it's final. You know where you are. You know it's real. You are not going *anywhere*. You're theirs."

"How did they treat you in jail?" she asked softly. "The other inmates?"

"Okay. A lot of them were fans. My celebrity was the only thing that kept me from being punked. They respected my music."

"What's punked?"

Kipp eyed her, wolf-like. "Jailhouse whore. Men think I'm cute, too. You know?"

Beryl stared back at him, then lowered her eyes and turned away. "And the guards?"

Standing, Kipp propped one foot on the bench and considered his response. Hands on hips, he shook his head but didn't answer. His platinum locks shimmered in the ceiling light. Walking to the plane, he planted his palm on the fuselage. He avoided her eyes.

"That bad? Well, maybe they'll just put you in rehab."

"For murder one?" he scoffed. "Hell, I'm the one who'll be charged with kidnapping—the death penalty."

"You Yanks are so primitive."

He waved the hand gun. "My life sucks. I'm a total failure. *'Got no love, got no love, got no love.'*" Pretending the gun was a microphone, he mimicked his own recording.

"Stop it. Who has?" She recognized the lyrics. It was the title track from Demonsong's second album.

"Been a long time between dates, Nanny Northgate?"

"You arrogant lout."

"Don't call me names."

"Are you telling me the whole truth, nothing but the truth so help you?" She asked. His intensity seemed to fill the hangar. She felt it permeate her like a porous energy field.

"I swear it. On the soul of Nancy McKendrick, the Navy lieutenant who raised me." He stepped into shadow. The grave eyes were now pools of glimmering bronze.

Kipp fell silent. While he brooded, she completed her pre-flight check.

His eyes lit up. He pointed the gun at her and cocked it. "There's been a change in plan. We're both going with you, Beryl."

"Kipp, no!" She turned away to shield the babe in her arms.

He waved the gun, indicating the pilot's door. "Believe me, Berry. This is for the best. If I force you, you won't be considered an accomplice. You'll be a hostage, not a perpetrator."

She hugged Shawnee tightly. "But it will be one more capital charge brought against you."

"Not if I'm dead. My suicide plans are on hold, not defunct. Now, let's move out, shall we? As soon as you and the kid are safe on Heston's island, I'll disappear."

Horrified, she eyed Kipp's tortured face. She heard the whimpering of the unhappy child cradled at her breast. Swallowing, she gathered her strength. She was, after all, accustomed to handling the unexpected. At least she could play for time. Convinced, she retreated into her best defensive position, unperturbed bossiness.

She feigned indifference. "We may as well have a go. Get in the plane," she said, ambling over, babe in arms, and opening the door.

As she deposited Shawnee in the back seat of the Cessna, the toddler screamed and throttled her with his legs. "Mind yourself, child," she scolded while Kipp entered through the passenger door and sat down in the front passenger seat. "He's a Demming, all right. He behaves just like you lot."

"Sweet," muttered Kipp, watching her in fascination as he wielded the gun.

Humoring him, she strapped Shawnee into the back seat. "Strap yourself in," she said to Kipp, assuming the pilot seat and fastening her own safety belt. "I'll call the tower and tell them I've taken on two souls."

"Souls?"

"Duh? In case they need to do a body count."

"Great." He rubbed his eyes wearily and yawned. "You know how to fly this thing, right?"

"It'll be fine, Kipp."

"That's what they always tell musicians." Panic crossed his countenance. "This key's in the US, right? I can't use my real passport. They'll arrest me."

"We're not leaving the country."

Kipp exhaled, visibly relaxing. "I mean, I have fake ID. Plenty of it." Dipping into his pocket, he fished out his wallet. "See? I have at least twelve or fifteen different licenses—all in different names, different states."

She was aghast. "Why?"

"Duh?"

"Illegal gambling? Prostitution? Drug deals? Are you on drugs now? Roll up your sleeve." She grabbed for his wrist.

He pushed away her hand. "Prostitution, my ass. I don't pay for it. Hell, they offer me money."

"And do you take it?" She snorted in contempt.

Glancing at her, he balked. "Of course not." He shuffled through a stack of cards. "Maybe I should have. Who the hell knows? I'd be rich instead of bankrupt. Skip it, Beryl. Look, here's the license for Ben McKendrick, State of Florida. Neat, huh? My adopted father's name." He waved the card.

She tore it from his fingers and studied it briefly.

"Clean and legit, too. That old fox Gabe Cade knew which palms to grease, including his own."

She copped an attitude. "Oh, that's right. You're a celeb—like your dad. You need to ensure anonymity sometimes. On the road. To outwit your fawning fans."

Kipp rolled his eyes and grabbed the card away. "Damn, you're snarky. So what happens when we arrive in—where are we headed again?"

"Marathon Key. We store this plane. I've rented a seaplane. I'll fly it to the island."

"You can fly a seaplane?"

"Uh-huh. I earned my certification last year."

He rolled his eyes. "How many times have you flown one since then?"

Miffed, she sniffed. "Well, I haven't actually—"

"Great."

As the plane taxied, he settled back and shut his eyes. "Any volcanoes on this island I can throw myself into?"

Eyeing the gun, she suppressed a smile. "I'm afraid not. It's mostly a coral-rock and sand spit, with some wind-blown tropical shrubs clinging on for dear life."

"Heart of Fire Key, eh? My final gig. A hot meal and a shower sounds good. More likely, I'll be paddling my way down the river. I don't mean to jail, but I do mean the River Styx."

Her anger flared. "Blimey, you're a jackass."

Grabbing her roughly by the collar, he was in her face. "Don't talk that way to me. Ever. If you ever disrespect me again, I'll kill all three of us in a heartbeat. I'll shoot this plane down. Understood?"

"Y-Yes." She choked the word, barely audible. Her questions had been answered. Kipp was capable of anything. For all she knew, he *had* killed his ex-wife. What if he had psychotic flashbacks the way some drug addicts did?

"Good," he muttered, releasing her. "Now let's fly."

Her only hope of survival—and Shawnee's—was to play along with Kipp until she could alert the authorities, or Heston, whichever opportunity presented itself first. For the moment, she would play along. She contacted the tower for instructions and began to taxi.

Once airborne, the plane soared, leveling out in open sky. The plane could not be tracked. Beryl had turned off the transponder and opted out of Flight Aware, just as she would do on the second leg—if their luck held. She glanced at the gun. It was clutched tightly in Kipp's hand.

Who was this quibbling, defensive man at her side? What had happened to the strapping young American football prince she had first met eight years ago? What had brought Kipp to such a desperate state?

Chapter Thirteen

Should I do what Ram wants me to—or not?

Beautiful, 12-year-old Winner Demming was eager to learn. Her hot new bodyguard Ram Kincaid wanted to teach her. But hadn't she already gone too far with him? The thought of doing anything more scared—and excited—the pubescent girl. Ram was the first man who had ever offered to *teach* her.

At the Demming home on Galleon Drive, the delicate pre-teen beauty, tagged by the media as The Gossamer Girl, sat lost in thought, knees together, ankles apart, on the edge of the antique brass bed in her bedroom. Shivering in the AC, the long-limbed teenager draped her slender shoulders with a pale-pink gingham comforter. Perplexed, she furled and unfurled a strand of flaxen hair around her tapered index finger tipped with blue-glitter nail polish.

Beside the marble-topped vanity, a Louis Vuitton wardrobe trunk stood up-ended and opened, waiting, on the floor, to be unpacked. Her clothes obsession was evidenced by the trunk's overflowing drawers. On the far wall of the room, a collection of vintage dolls lined the shelves of a glass-enclosed case. The newest addition, a faceless Kachina, seemed to embody her own confusion.

What if Dad found out? Or Poppy or Berry? Or Lissette? Or that brat Dakota?

Behind her, at the head of the bed, lacy blue and white pillows were piled and fluffed. Travel-weary, she flopped back into the hill of pillows and stared at the vaulted ceiling of her bedroom, her hair now spread out around her head like shiny stalks of wheat flattened in a field. Like her worried thoughts, the white ceiling fan above her was spinning round and round.

Daddy would kill Ram if he knew what we've done so far. He might kill her, too. Her stepmother might help him. Poppy and she argued constantly now. Poppy was so skittish. If she knew, she might birth a cow—a funny expression coming from Uncle Banks.

Winner thought about her experience with Ram last night at the hotel suite. He had almost talked her into it then. She had never seen a man naked before, let alone...

Was she a woman now? Yes. Sort of. Almost. She was 12 years old. She felt strange, new urges. Men watched her in a strange, new way. Ram Kincaid had showed her why.

She was in love with her new bodyguard. Her bodyguard was 24 years old. She closed her eyes and drew a deep breath. She couldn't wait for their next encounter. His massive strength made her feel cherished and safe. She wanted to please him, to be everything he needed and wanted her to be—for him. She wanted to be his woman for life.

Blushing, she sat up. *It is wrong.* What Ram was asking her to do was wrong, and she knew it. She felt creepy—and sick.

Dashing into the bathroom, she vomited into the ceramic toilet. Wiping her mouth with a towel, she sat back down on the bed and stared at the pearl-white carpeting. But if she didn't do it, he wouldn't like her anymore.

She needed to talk to someone. If only Berry were here. She would listen. But Berry was no expert on guys. Who was? Her step-mother, Poppy? Out of the question. Felicia? Fe was less popular with guys than Berry. And yet?

Wouldn't Felicia understand how much she *adored* Ram? She wanted to marry Ram. How old did one have to be to get married? How had she lived for 12 years without knowing him? Until two weeks ago, when her father had hired Ram, on the basis of the best of references, she had been a child. *He has eyes like green sea-stars.*

She remembered walking into the living room and seeing Ram for the first time, standing there, at ease, work boots spread apart, wrists crossed. His cut muscles had bulged beneath his olive-drab sleeves. He had a tattoo of a skull on his neck. He had frightened her—until she'd peeked shyly into his eyes. She had known then. He was to be her teacher.

No one else had known. No one else could see. Love was born between the two of them. Last night had been their first and only opportunity to be alone together. Heart slamming in her chest, she had stolen to Ram's room and tapped lightly on his door.

"I'm afraid," she had lied. "I'm alone."

Noiselessly, Ram had vacated his own room, shutting the door gently, and followed her back down the length of the hallway to her room. Shutting the door to her room, he had stripped the flimsy nightgown from her body and gently engulfed her in his beefy arms, probing with eager fingers her most private places, his hot mouth scalding her skin. *No, stop!*

She sat up. She *had* to phone Felicia. She had to talk to someone about the volcanic eruption in her heart. She found her mobile phone and dialed.

"Felicia? What are you doing now?

"Napping...or I was...Winner? Is that you?"

"I'm not sure!" Winner squeaked into the phone.

"What do you mean?"

"I mean, I've changed. I'm different. I'm..."

"Changed how?" Felicia asked.

"Swear you won't tell?" Winner demanded.

"Cross my heart."

"I'm in love," Winner swooned.

"With who?"

"You'll never believe me...He *likes* me. He...he..."

"He who? What happened?" Felicia demanded.

"We sort of made out. Last night."

"No way!!"

"Way. Way, way, way..."

"Who????"

"You'll never believe me."

"I don't believe this whole conversation. Spill it, Winner!"

"Ram."

"Your bodyguard? No way."

"It was awesome, Felicia. Better than anything you've heard. I am SO in love."

"Oh, wow. What does it feel like? Is he a good kisser?"

"It's like...it's like being overwhelmed with this powerful feeling, so powerful you can't stop it. You don't want to stop it. You NEED it. It just takes you and uses you and amazes you and you just fall down and worship at the feet of this awesome being, this GUY who can make you feel this way. I don't know...it just makes you feel...adored. Like you're not this piece of garbage, but like you're someone who somebody CRAVES..." She growled ecstatically. "Oh, I'm CRAZY about him!"

"So you went all the way with this guy?"

"What? No. Not yet. But he wants me to."

"Does your dad know?"

"What? No way. And if you tell anyone, I'll kill you slowly and without mercy. Not a word to your mom, understand? Lissette would blab to Poppy, and Poppy would blab to Dad, just to get me in trouble."

"I won't tell, I guess. Are you going to do it?"

"I don't know. I don't know what to do. I don't know if or when I'll ever be alone with him again. Maybe I won't be."

"Get him to meet you somewhere," Felicia advised. "There's a dance at Cambier Park."

"A school dance? They'd never let him in. He's too old."

"Oh! Okay, that's out."

"I'd be doing the LOVE dance—with a real man."

Felicia moaned. "I think I'm insanely jealous, Win."

"Your turn will come, Fe."

"Yeah, but Ram is really cute."

"You'll meet someone cute."

"I don't know. I'm already 13, and I still don't have a boyfriend. My dad thinks I'm a wallflower. He calls me *'Flaca'* now. 'Hey, Flaca! Put on some lipstick. Put on that tight dress. Go outside. Shake it so the boys can see you.' "

"What does *Flaca* mean?" Winner asked.

"Skinny. It's a mean joke. He calls me skinny."

"No way."

"Way. They want me married and out of the house—yesterday."

"Your mom doesn't feel that way. Lissette wants you to go to college and study voice. She told me so."

"Her opinion doesn't count. It's what *Popi* wants that matters."

"Don't be like that," Winner said. "You should stand up to him."

"Like you're standing up to yours? You're practically crawling behind the woodwork."

Winner laughed guiltily. "Okay. I get the message. It's easy to preach. Oh, Felicia, I'm just so IN LOVE! I positively wither when he looks at me."

"Aren't you supposed to blossom? What about that other thing, Winner?"

"What other thing?"

"You know," Felicia nudged. "Are you still doing it?"

"Throwing up? Only sometimes. I ate some Oreos on the way to Miami. Once I was alone, I barfed them out. That's the only time lately. Except just a minute ago."

"You threw up?"

"I felt...nervous."

"You gotta stop this shit, Winner. Or I've got to start it. I don't know which."

"All I know is Ram loves my body. You wouldn't *believe* what he wants to do to me...And he gave me this stuff to snort..."

"What stuff? Drugs?"

"I don't know, but it's amazing."

"Save some for me, okay?" Felicia begged.

"Okay. Just keep quiet about it."

"Listen, how was your Uncle Banks? What happened with him?"

"We ate lunch. We talked. He made me nervous. He's intense. He's sophisticated. But he's old. He has thick white hair. He looks like my mother. On those old magazine covers. I haven't seen her in person since I was four. He...scared me, sort of. But I think he's nicer than my mom. He seemed interested in my life. He asked a lot of questions."

"Yeah?"

"Uncle Banks has a place on Fisher Island in Miami. He invited me to visit his ranch in California. I might like to go there."

"That sounds fun."

"Yeah. He owns horses. He makes wine. He collects Kachina dolls."

"He plays with dolls?" Felicia asked.

"No, they're artifacts. Poppy explained it to me...Hopi Indians used to..."

"Hold it, Win. I've got to go. That's my dad. He's going to break down the door. I have to cook his lunch. Oh, I dread this. He'll criticize everything I put on my plate. Later."

"Bye, Felicia."

Phone in hand, Winner flopped back on her bed and stared at the rotating ceiling fan. Would there be another secret rendezvous? How did Ram feel about her? Did he love her as much as she loved him? He had said nothing about love, but she could feel it. She wondered which bedroom in the house Poppy would assign to Ram. The guest room next door?

A knock at her bedroom door startled her. "Come in."

Lissette entered with tea and toast on a tray. "Eat this, Winnie. It might be some time before I serve a meal around here."

"Why?"

"Your father will explain. He wants to see you all in his study at 10 a.m. sharp. You got five minutes."

"Okay, Lissy," she said, sensing the housekeeper's distress. Winner toyed with her utensils until Lissette padded from the room. Furtively, she whisked the tea and toast from the tray and flushed them down the toilet in the adjacent bathroom. She was still all butterflies—because of the thing she *hadn't* confided to her best friend:

Ram asked me to sail away with him to the Caribbean—on his grandfather's yacht.

Chapter Fourteen

His Rolex read precisely 10 a.m.

Poised behind the desk in his study, Heston surveyed the eight somber faces before him. Seated around the room were his wife, four of his children, the new bodyguard, the housekeeper, and the family friend, Ezra Gold. A morose tension hung in the air. Everyone was apprehensive and confused. He knew they needed his guidance. He centered himself and took the stage.

"There has been a tragedy in our family," he began. "We must come together as a unit and help one another to deal with this sad situation."

He studied the faces of twins Sage and Tegan. Were they too young to be here? *Let them stay.* They needed to learn how to deal with the family's fame. He looked at his son. At eight, Dakota was old enough, but how strong was he? The boy was too sensitive. He lacked self-assurance. How would he handle the pain?

Say it.

"We've had some bad news," he continued. "Your brother Kipp's ex-wife Lennox, whom you all knew, has passed away."

Red-haired Tegan raised her hand. "What does that mean, Daddy?"

Dakota rolled his eyes. "It means she's dead, you ninny."

"She's in Heaven," Poppy asserted.

"Quiet, both of you." Training the room, his eyes found Poppy's and lingered there for a split-second. He couldn't do more. "Terrible as this news is, we have a further crisis on our hands. Little Shawnee has gone missing. So has Kipp."

"Daddy, what is 'missing'?" asked little Teggi, tilting her head to one side.

"It means Shawnee can't be found. No one knows where he is," he explained, raising a hand to silence Dakota.

"It means he's lost," said Sage, nimbly braiding a strand of her own brown hair.

"That's right," said Heston. From across the room, he could feel his wife's pain. Her eyes were red raw from crying. She held a tissue to her mouth and stared out the window.

"Is Kipp lost, too?" asked Tegan.

"Yes, he is." He drew a deep breath. "Now, you know that because Daddy is famous and rich, it means that we, as a family, have some special problems that other families don't share. So we have to be extra-strong to deal with our special problems."

"What special problems?" asked Tegan.

"People won't let us alone. They make fun of us," said her slightly intellectual older brother. Dakota sat slouched across the couch, elbow on the couch's arm, his head resting in his hand. "They chase after us and take our pictures and write mean stuff about us on the Internet. And they plaster our secrets all over the TV. They want our money and power."

"We have power?" asked Tegan, incredulous.

"Sit up straight, Dakota," said Heston, irritated. For a moment, the boy didn't move. Heston continued to stare at him, until the boy reluctantly sat up, putting ankles together, feet flat on the floor. "Now is not a time for whining. We need to be strong," Heston continued.

"What if we don't feel strong?" asked Winner, gazing at the floor.

"That's when we most need strength, isn't it?" said Poppy. "That's when we need each other." She patted Winner's knee affectionately. "Let's let Daddy speak, shall we?"

"Thank you, my love." He scanned the concerned faces. "Here's the thing," he hedged. "Because we don't yet know what has happened to

Kipp and Shawnee, we need to be extra careful." He saw both Ezra and Ram nod in agreement. Their silent support heartened him.

"Did bad people snatch Kipp and Shawnee?" chirped Tegan unexpectedly.

"She means were they kidnapped," said Sage.

"We don't know yet," he replied. "But it's possible."

"Are we going to be kidnapped? That's the question," said Dakota. "That's what you're trying to tell us, isn't it? Watch out for kidnappers? Don't take candy from strangers. Don't get into anyone's car."

"That's right. Don't." Voice exploding, Ezra shifted in his chair. "Your father is right to warn you, Dakota. Give him a break. This is a difficult situation for everyone." The subdued, masculine voice of the dark-bearded young director carried the weight of authority. Ezra panned the room, his brown eyes resting for a moment on Winner, who was draped along the window seat, staring out at the rain. Her long, straight flaxen hair gleamed in the filtered daylight. He looked back in concern at Heston. He lifted his chin in Winner's direction.

"Ladybug, come away from the window," Heston apprised his eldest daughter calmly. "Sit over here next to Ram."

Obeying, Winner rose and, glancing at the muscle-bound young bodyguard seated on the couch, eased her nubile body onto the empty cushion beside him. Sitting prettily, she tucked one long leg beneath her and rested her elbow on the back of the couch. Ram and Winner exchanged a brief glance. Both looked back at Heston, waiting for him to continue.

Tegan's features twisted in fear. "Daddy, are we going to be snatched?"

Poppy flagged Heston with a timid finger. "That's what Nanny Beryl calls it."

Sage rolled her eyes. "Don't be such a crybaby, Teggi." She thrust her hands to Tegan's side, tickling her. "Watch out! The Boogie Man will get you!"

"Sage, stop teasing your sister!" Heston rounded the desk and took Sage by the arm. "This is a dangerous situation. You need to take it seriously."

Sage's face fell. Jerking her arm from his grasp, she frowned and crossed her arms at her chest. As he strode back behind the desk, she glared at him, her silver-blue eyes hostile.

Gently, Poppy wrapped her arm around Tegan, drawing the small girl near. "It's natural to feel fear, Teggi. At this moment, we all feel it. What we have to do is help each other be brave, not scare each other. Listen to your father." Poppy's tears had ceased, although her brown eyes remained glassy. On impulse, she reached over and squeezed Sage's hand.

Gratefully, Heston cleared his throat. "What we need right now is a plan of action. I have devised one. Here it is: For the next twenty-four hours, no one leaves this house, with the exception of Ezra. Ram, this includes you. You will be required here indefinitely."

"At your service, Mr. Demming," Ram replied loudly, tapping his feet on the floor to release pent-up tension. Thin sprigs of blond hair arranged atop his prematurely balding pate gave the only hint of possible vulnerability. The red bandana was now tied around his thick neck.

"Thank you, Ram. I'm sure we all feel more secure thanks to your presence." Heston leaned against his desk. "Do not, I repeat, do not talk to anyone other than the people seated in this room. Is that understood? Anyone else on the property is a trespasser, not to be trusted. No matter who they say they are."

"Yeah, they'll lie to you," said Dakota to Tegan, his lips curled in a cynical smile. "They act like they know your parents, and then they tie you up and hold you for ransom—if you're lucky. If you're not, they'll torture you and..."

Tegan wailed.

"Shut up, Dakota," cried Winner. "Leave her alone."

"They won't hurt me," declared Sage, arms still crossed in defiance. "I'll bite them." She clacked her pearly whites together for effect. Terrified, Tegan buried her face in her mother's abdomen.

"Don't tell me to shut up, Winner," said Dakota, face flushing.

"Stop it, all of you! At once!" Heston snarled. A swift silence descended in the room.

"Heston," piped Poppy, all of a sudden. "Where is Nanny Northgate?"

He improvised. "I gave Berry the week off. She's flown home to England."

"Of all times to..." Poppy glowered, cradling Tegan and stroking her forehead.

"Just so." He looked at the housekeeper. "Lissette, get Beryl on the phone. Tell her we need her. Explain the situation. Tell her to please..."

"Get her fat ass back here on the double," murmured Dakota to the carpet.

Heston glared at his 8-year-old son. "Ask her to return to Port Royal immediately. I'll make it worth her while." As Lissette left the study, Heston shook his head in disgust. "The idea of being cooped up here with you bunch is about as inviting as..."

"Heston!" Poppy bleated before he could finish. "Everyone, listen. This is quite serious. There has been a tragedy in our family. Your brother and his son may be in danger. We have to be..."

The intercom buzzed. Everyone froze.

"...careful," Poppy whispered, clutching Tegan closely.

"Shall I?" asked Ezra, half-rising.

"Better let me," said Ram, jumping up.

Heston showed his palm. "No. Lissette will answer it. Anyway, I believe I know who our callers are. I've been expecting them."

"I just hope they are who they say they are, sir. If they ain't, it could get messy," Ram offered, limbs twitching with excitement. "It wouldn't be the first time bad guys pretended to be good guys to get in." His eyes darted to Winner, who looked away.

Meeting Ezra's gaze, she looked down and studied the chipped blue-glitter lacquer on her nails.

"The intercom buzzed from the gate, sir," Lissette said, entering.

"Fine. Answer it." Heston swallowed back his apprehension. If ever he needed a poker face, this was the time. He flashed back to the time he had played Doc Holiday in a western feature. He would be drawing on the homework he'd done when he played the notorious gambler. He held a bad hand, but he knew a gambler's trade was to bluff successfully.

"Demming residence," they heard Lissette say. As they waited, she listened on the receiver, then covered the mouthpiece and spoke to Heston. "The police are here. One's from the FBI. Outside the gates. They want to come in. They have questions to ask you, sir."

"Wait," cried Ezra. "Let me phone their headquarters. Let's *make sure* they are who they say they are," he said, phoning while giving a heads up to Ram.

"Buzz them in, Lissette," Heston said. "I'll deal with the police. Have them meet me in my studio. The rest of you scoot—discreetly. And *no one but Ezra* is to leave the house without permission. Is that clear?

Eight heads bobbled in silence. Unnerved, the group of people roused and stood.

"And no TV news for the twins, Poppy," Heston added. "Diversion only."

Nodding, Poppy escorted the two little girls from the study. The others filed out after them. He would have no further opportunity to speak with his wife alone before the police came.

Just as well, perhaps.

Draining his glass, he rose and stood tall to face, once again, the half-forgotten refrain of violent death and loves long lost. He had faced death and loss often enough. But this time—this was different. This time he would have to lie to protect the ones he loved.

This time was murder. He *knew.* Knowing Lennox, how could it have been otherwise?

And the one thing he never, ever wanted his wife Poppy to suspect was the truth. Nor did he ever want his son Kipp to learn the truth. The truth had plunged them all into this mess in the first place.

Damn me for a coward. Striding into the art studio, Heston took some deep breaths and listened for Lissette's steps leading strangers through his home. When they entered the studio, he extended his hand in friendship. One was a tall, gray-haired African-American man in his mid-fifties. The other was a swarthy, dark-haired man with pointed white teeth and spindly bow legs.

As Lissette closed the door, she whispered to him. "Sir, I tried to reach Nanny Beryl. She didn't answer. I left a message. I asked her to return to work."

"Keep trying," said Heston, before giving his attention to two forbidding officers of the law.

Chapter Fifteen

Skimming the ocean's surface, Beryl's seaplane was a shining bird. An expanse of iridescent turquoise sea shimmered beneath her as she flew. Now on the second leg of their journey, the trio had survived the plane switch at the Marathon Key airport. They were bound for their final destination in the Lower Keys, Heart of Fire Key.

Beryl's two intrepid passengers had dozed off. Chancing a glance at Kipp's chiseled profile, she wanted to grasp the gun in his hand. Despite her fear, she felt a surge of power as she gazed out upon the boundless depth of brightness—above her, below her, around her. Could she slip the gun from his grasp without waking him?

Though Kipp was the star, he was in her realm now. This portion of the universe belonged to her. It was her possession. She was mistress of the cloud canyons of Heaven.

In the seat next to her, Kipp stirred. The symmetry of his features took her breath away. Suddenly, she heard the word she had dreaded to hear.

"Mommy," croaked Shawnee from his seat. "Dada...?" He reached his small arms in Kipp's direction. "Mommy?"

"I know, buddy. I know," Kipp said, reaching back to smooth the boy's hair.

For a time they flew in silence. Shawnee whimpered until falling asleep again.

At length, Kipp shifted to sit up properly. His eyebrows met in disapproval.

"What's up, Beryl? You look happy. How can you be enjoying this?"

"I love flying," she said, pulling back on the yoke and sending the plane into an unexpected ascent. "Whee!! Ha ha ha..."

"Stop this shit!" Kipp groaned, doubling over. "You think this is funny? You've got another think coming, little mama."

"I beg your pardon," she said huffily.

Shawnee stirred from the motion and raised voices.

Leveling out the plane, Beryl blew a kiss to Master Shawnee. The child was rested and clear-eyed.

"Meaning that I have serious concerns about your sanity." Kipp placed a finely formed hand on the yoke. His nails were clean and filed.

"Well, that makes us even. I have serious concerns about yours." She patted his hand. "Don't, Kipp. Please! It's too dangerous," she scolded, trying to pry his hand free. His pliant flesh felt warm and vibrant. His fingertips were callused.

"Yeah? Tough." He placed his other hand, which held the steely pistol, on her shoulder and drew close. "I hate flying. Don't take risks. Is that understood?"

She understood. He, not she, was in control. The gun was his scepter of power. He was close enough now for her to see the flecks of gold dust encircling the black pupils of his eyes. His thick golden lashes curled at their tips. His skin was alabaster swathed in Coppertone.

For a moment, awed by his proximity, she felt weightless, suspended in an ancient fantasy, as though the Cessna was the sun-chariot, being driven by Helios himself. She felt as though he were capturing her and spiriting her off to Mount Olympus or Valhalla, or wherever it was that mythical deities lived at the top of the world. Her fingertips feathered the back of his hand. The plane dived.

"Bloody hell, Beryl!"

"I'm sorry," she gasped, quickly righting her chariot. Relinquishing the yoke, he eased back into the seat next to hers. Relieved, he sighed. "Watch the damn road."

"Did you have a good nap?" she asked brightly.

"I wasn't asleep."

"Oh."

He was antsy. "Do you have any chips back there?" He indicated the stuff in the back seat. "Abject terror gives me an appetite."

"Uh, yes," she said, preoccupied with flying. "In the basket. Grab some wipes and clean his hands."

"Hang on, buddy," he said to Shawnee. He leaned over the top of the seat and fished inside the basket. Grasping his treasure, he sank back down into his seat. "Want a chip, honey?"

"No, thank you."

He glared at her. "I was talking to my...to Shawnee. Here, buddy. Give me your little paws."

Holding out his hands, Shawnee crinkled his nose. Cleaning the boy's hands, Kipp crinkled in return. Shawnee giggled and glanced at her.

"It feels good to be clean, doesn't it?" she smiled. Shawnee nodded once, decisively.

Popping open the chips bag, Kipp shared the crunchy fare with Shawnee. The two chewed with gusto. The odor of potato chips permeated the air in the cabin.

"You were hungry, weren't you?" she cooed, smiling back at Shawnee, who handed her a chip.

"Thank you," she said, accepting his gift and popping it into her mouth. She wasn't hungry, but she wanted to earn the boy's trust. She might need it.

Kipp crunched a mouthful of chips. "Maybe I shouldn't commit suicide," he said.

Her heart leapt. "No?"

"I mean, I want to *be* dead. I'm just not so sure I need to actually *die.*"

"Is this a pop quiz?" She turned her gaze back to the mountainous clouds floating past. These fleecy, fat, flat-bottomed giants were laced with gray. Rain in the forecast.

Kipp munched. "Everybody thinks I'm dead. Fine. Let 'em. I want to start fresh."

"You mean *fake* your own death?"

He offered her the open bag of chips. She shook her head. He returned the bag to his lap.

"Why not? I want to lose the rocker lifestyle. I want...something else. Got any napkins?" He wiped his hands on his pants, and then used a wet wipe.

"They think you're dead now," she said. "It won't take long for them to realize you absconded with Shawnee. It will be on the building's security cams."

"Yeah, but..." Pausing, he stared out the window at the endless expanse of aquamarine sea below. "How beautiful. Do you remember Marissa Neville?"

"What?" She hadn't heard that name for at least seven years, not since Kipp had dumped his old pre-med school girlfriend to marry movie-star Lennox. "Your old girlfriend from college?"

Her fantasy dissolved. Raindrops splattered the windshield. Rivulets of water streamed upward on the glass. The drone of the engine steadied her.

Limbs twitching, Kipp stared straight ahead. She guessed the weather was making him nervous. He played it cool. "So, do you have a boyfriend?"

She jolted. "Why do you ask?"

"I don't know." He stared out the window. "Last week I found a blog entry about Marissa on the Internet. It was about a year old, but it said she was in the Dominican Republic, working for an international health organization. She's an obstetrician. She gives free pre-natal care and delivers babies for indigent women there." He chewed a chip.

"We're almost there. We'll have to fly into the rain. Can you handle it?"

"Sure. Do what you have to. Just don't screw up."

"I won't. I'm fully aware of the precious cargo on board—and I don't mean you."

Reaching back, she groped for and found a beach towel. Quickly, she covered Shawnee with it. It made a fine impromptu blanket, the only suitable covering she could find inside the cabin.

To the west, a bolt of lightning exploded in the sky. A gigantic boom ensued, rocking their world.

"Shit!" Kipp yelped. Shawnee started. Frightened by the blast, the boy began to wail.

"Take him, Kipp," said Beryl, her whole being focused on escaping the storm. "Pick him up. Hold him. Comfort him, for Heaven's sake!"

"All right. All right. Shut up a minute, and let me think."

"Dada!" whimpered Shawnee, his arms outstretched.

"I'm not your...Oh, come here," sighed Kipp, enfolding the boy into his arms and snuggling him.

"Kipp!" cried Beryl, as another lightning bolt streaked the dark sky.

"What, Beryl?" he cried sarcastically, cringing as the loud boom sounded.

"The gun! Shawnee is in your lap! Move it!"

"Oh, yeah. Okay. Done," he said. Rearranging himself and Shawnee, he placed the gun on the cockpit floor. "It's okay, buddy. Relax."

"Okay? Are you mad?" *Oh, yes. That's right. You are mad.*

To their east, the sky was clear. She maneuvered the plane straight into the heart of clear skies and recited a small prayer of thanks under her breath. As the skies around them cleared, so did her thoughts.

"We'll be landing in ten minutes, Kipp. What do you want to do about dinner?"

"I generally like to eat mine," he said, playing peek-a-boo with Shawnee.

"Me, too. I brought enough fresh food for myself—for one week. There's frozen food at the house—and tinned. Fruit trees, if they're in season. *What* do you like to eat?" she huffed, irritated by his insolence.

"Anything. Eggs. You bring eggs?"

"Oddly enough, I did. Organic, free-range. One carton. I was going to make a soufflé one night—to treat myself."

"Why is it odd?"

"Just coincidence, I suppose."

"You still hungry, buddy?" he asked the boy affectionately. Shawnee nodded decisively.

"Fine," she said. "What does Shawnee like to eat?"

"I don't know," Kipp said.

"Well, you should. You were allowed visitations, weren't you?"

"Monitored. It's not like we went to the food court at the mall." He sat pensively, and then looked her way. "He gobbled down that chili dog at the Miccosukee station."

"Wieners are not healthful."

"Depends upon the wiener, doesn't it? Sometimes a wiener's just what the doctor ordered."

She tossed him a withering glance. His eyes were dancing. She blushed to her toes. "Oh, stop it, you!" She watched as he made a balloon of the empty potato chip bag.

With vigor, Kipp sealed off the bag, and popped it. The loud bang delighted Shawnee, who crinkled his nose and clapped in glee.

Suddenly, she realized who Shawnee reminded her of—Heston. And Winner. Both crinkled their perfect noses in the same adorable way. The thought disturbed her.

She wondered if Zeus had ever joked to Hera about the Greek version of wieners. She realized Kipp was watching her as Shawnee entertained himself by slapping the empty crisp bag.

"Lighten up. Don't you want to know how I like *my* eggs?" Kipp queried flirtatiously.

"How?" She could feel the blood flooding her cheeks.

"Soft scrambled. But right now, I'd eat anything."

"A roast beef dinner, no doubt," she replied smugly.

"So you cook?" he queried.

"I can, but usually, I live on yogurt," she retorted.

Suddenly spotting the floating island in the distance, she pointed excitedly. "There's our island. See it? Heart of Fire Key." She began the plane's descent.

"Marissa's not in the Dominican Republic anymore," Kipp said, hoisting Shawnee into the back seat and buckling him in. "She's back in the States. I think she's somewhere in The Keys. She works at a clinic for indigent mothers. I admire the hell out of her."

Her blood pressure sky-rocketed. "Is that the real reason you wanted to come to The Keys? To find Marissa?"

"Bloody hell!" he cried suddenly, as the plane plummeted angrily toward earth.

Chapter Sixteen

"You have my sympathy, Mr. Demming," said the middle-aged African-American officer of the law, the taller of the two men Lissette had ushered into his studio. "I'm Special Agent Nicholas Townsend, FBI." He presented a badge. "I've been assigned to this case because of its high-profile nature and your son's inter-state record." He offered his hand. "I'm a big fan."

"Very generous, Mr. Townsend. Please come in." Mask on straight, Heston shook hands with both officers. Townsend had grainy hands; the other, shorter officer had clammy, damp hands. He followed behind Townsend and appeared to be of Hispanic origin and in his early thirties. He smelled of spearmint.

Heston cleared his throat. "We've had a shock, my family and I."

Townsend coughed. "It's part of our job to inform you officially. Since you already know—"

"I'm Jorge Betancourt," said the shorter officer, eyes predatory. He was wiry, with a feathery black moustache and slab-like white teeth set in skin of oiled pastry-sheets. "Miami-Dade Homicide. In cooperation with your local authorities, we've been assigned to investigate the death of Lennox Cordova Demming—and the disappearance of Shawn Demming."

"And Kipp, too?" he asked doubtfully.

"We're not sure he's missing. We're looking for him. He's a person of interest in this case." Betancourt placed his hands on his hips. "My office received a tip from a local informant. Your son's been buying drugs again. If he's using, he's most likely dealing. Drugs may figure into Lennox Cordova's death."

"If he's high—or in withdrawal—he may be out of control," Townsend noted, quietly taking in his surroundings.

"It's possible. That degenerate son of mine is capable of..."

"Anything? Is that what you were going to say, Mr. Demming?" asked burly, gray-haired Townsend.

"Well, I..."

"We've just come from the victim's penthouse on South Beach." Townsend appeared less than comfortable in his synthetic blue suit, cotton shirt, and tie.

Heston glanced from face to face. "Was she murdered?"

Townsend shrugged. "We won't know until the toxicology report comes in."

"Looks like an accidental OD," said Betancourt, lolling a mint on his tongue. "Looks can be deceiving."

Townsend skewered Heston. "Mr. Demming knows that, Jorge. He's an actor."

Like a dog from a rival pack, Heston sized up the two lawmen. He had portrayed enough cops in movies to know they set you up to take you down. He continued to play Doc Holiday.

"Thank you for conducting an investigation," he said, with just the right air of affable gravity. "As you can well imagine, I'm anxious for the welfare of my grandson—and my son, of course. Any help we receive in locating them will be greatly appreciated. How can I help you?"

Betancourt peered out the window. It overlooked a stand of royal palms and, beyond, *Windswept,* sails furled, moored at his dock in Naples Bay. "Sir, are you aware that a crowd of reporters and fans are massing outside the gates of your home?" Betancourt wheeled around. "Local police are being called in to manage them."

"Yes. I'm aware of the media's interest. Every minute of my so-called life."

Betancourt exchanged a look with Townsend.

"Won't you have a seat, gentlemen?" He indicated his stool and the studio's one stuffed chair.

"No thanks, sir. We'll stand."

Heston shrugged. "As you prefer."

Betancourt spoke directly. "Mr. Demming, you had a professional relationship with your son's ex-wife, is that right?"

"Many years ago. Not anymore." He heard the crack in his own voice.

"You two made a great team," observed Townsend unexpectedly, eyes darting and lighting on the damaged self-portrait.

"Thank you. It was a long time ago."

"Eight years. The good old days, eh?" Betancourt crushed the mint between his back teeth. "Not all that long—since your last movie with Lennox."

Heston counterthrust. "My family and I learned the details from TV news. A heads-up phone call from you fellows would have been appreciated."

His visitors, although polite, poised on point. They were his adversaries, not on his side, not on anybody's side. They wanted a collar.

"Somebody leaked the news of Ms. Cordova's death to the press, sir. Regrettable, but it happens," observed Betancourt. His eyes, too, scanned the shadowy room for clues.

"I know all about the press, gentlemen." His knees buckled, threatening to give way. He beat back the panic. "Mind if I sit?" He parked his lean frame on the tall stool in front of his splattered self-portrait. The two officers stood facing him.

"Mr. Demming, sir, why don't you tell us what else you know. That way, we won't waste your time sharing useless details."

"Well, I can't think of anything..."

"Try," said Townsend. His voice, demeanor, the cut of his jib, were all noncommittal.

Heston wobbled. To steady his balance, he placed one foot on a rung of the stool. "Men, I'm deeply concerned. We must act quickly to find my son and grandson. What's being done?"

"Our people are all over this case, Mr. Demming," said Betancourt. "We've notified the Missing Children's Network. They're on nationwide alert. They're posting contact information and pictures of Shawnee and Kipp on their websites."

"Excellent. Do they get results?"

"Oftentimes." Townsend cocked his head. "Sir, the two most important questions we have to ask you are these: *Numero uno:* Have you had anyone contact you demanding ransom for your son or grandson?"

"No."

"Are you certain?"

"I swear it, Townsend. I've heard from no one."

"Not yet," Townsend muttered, exploring the room, fondling objects here and there. He looked up. "Gauguin?" he smiled, pointing.

"Yes. An original."

"Impressive."

"My wife's an art dealer. She surprised me with it on my birthday—a couple of years ago."

"When things weren't so rocky between you?"

He stared at Townsend, aghast.

Betancourt was in his face. "Be aware, sir. We're being issued a warrant, to monitor your phone and intercept your emails. If anyone—including your son—tries to contact you, we'll soon know about it."

Townsend stepped between him and Betancourt. "Are you prepared to pay a ransom, Mr. Demming?"

He blew hotly. "Of course I am!" Cover blown, he regained his composure.

Townsend forged on. "It's your duty to advise us, should an attempt be made through another venue. Second question, do you know the whereabouts of your son or grandson? Remember that harboring a fugitive is a crime in and of itself, that will prosecute to the fullest extent of the law."

His mouth went dry. "Man, I have no idea where my son is. Don't you read the tabloids? He and I don't communicate. Not since our blow-out four years ago."

"Tabloids? No, sir. I read the sporting news."

"Well, Officer Betancourt—"

"Detective."

"Detective, it's common knowledge that my relationship with Kipp tanked a few years ago."

"And your grandson, Shawnee?"

"I rarely see my grandson. Our family relations have been...strained over the past few years. Shawnee seems a fine boy—a normal, healthy child. My wife adores him."

"I know about the fight," inserted Townsend. "Heston, are you aware that your son induced a near riot last night at his concert in Miami? He begged the crowd to kill him. They tried to. Roadies stopped them just in time from tearing Kipp limb from limb."

He twitched. "Idiot. Yes, I heard. They would have done it, too. All in the name of love."

"No offense, sir, but fans pay your bills. They gave you all this." Contemptuously, Betancourt swept his hand around the room.

"I earned all this, Detective."

"From poor slobs like me who idolize you like a..."

"Jorge, stop it." Townsend turned to him. "What about the victim?"

"What about her?" Now his voice sounded distant.

"How close were you to Lennox Cordova? Personally, I mean."

"I-I... We...weren't 'close.' "

The officers exchanged glances. Townsend's mobile phone rang. He answered, moving away. "Yo, what's up? Check. We're inside the house. Heston claims to have no knowledge of the perp's whereabouts. The kid either. No ransom demands, FYI."

Perpetrator? Shaken to his core, Heston sank onto the stool in front of his easel. His fingers grasped a dry paintbrush, a big flat, one of his favorites. Blindsided, trying to absorb the news, he fanned the dried bristles.

Townsend's back stiffened. "When?" he said into his phone. Turning, he arched a brow at Betancourt. "I see," he said into the phone. "Yes, I copy. I'll tell him. Thanks. Out." The officer rang off.

"What is it?" asked Betancourt.

Townsend avoided his eyes. "Lennox Cordova's body is now with the medical examiner. Her next of kin hasn't been located. We need permission to proceed with an autopsy. It may take some time for the official time of death to be made public."

"She has no next of kin," Heston murmured. "Her mother died a few years ago. Her mother was unmarried. Lennox never knew her father— or who he was."

"They say her old lady threw wild Hollywood parties." Betancourt flicked his brows up and down. "Go to any of those in the good old days, Mr. Demming?"

He dropped his voice an octave. "See here—"

"Can it, Jorge." Townsend toyed with the knot of his unruly tie. "Sir, there's been another development." He cast a glance at Betancourt before squaring Heston in his sights. "On our way over, we got a call. About an hour ago, some of your son's effects were found on the shore at South Beach—right in front of his ex-wife's condo."

He felt battered. "Effects?"

"Kipp's state-issued ID card was found on a soggy Demonsong beach towel. Next to an empty liquor bottle. A used syringe and Kipp's portable phone were found in shallow water at low tide. A man's foot-prints led straight from the towel into the Atlantic surf."

Heston felt sick. He clutched the seat of the stool beneath him with both hands. It couldn't be true. "You think that Kipp...?"

"The signs point to it. The rest of his stuff is still in the hotel room he had rented the previous night. But he didn't pay for a second night. And he never checked out this morning. Our men are on the scene now, speaking with the hotel manager."

"Kipp *killed* himself last night?"

Townsend eyed him. "He never made it to the rock-tour wrap-party. Gave the driver the slip. Asked him to stop so he could use the men's room at a shop'n rob. *No one* has seen your son since."

"Whoa," said Betancourt, rising on tiptoe.

Townsend continued. "Did you know Kipp is bankrupt? While he was on tour, his home on Star Island was foreclosed."

It was too much to bear, too much to take in. He sat still, listening to the men drone like dual outboard motors on a fishing skiff. Betancourt sidled up too close.

"So, the question is—did Kipp drown himself before or after the death of his ex-wife and the disappearance of his son?" Betancourt crossed his arms. "Both your parents committed suicide, sir—according to the work up."

Touché. "According to the tabloids, you mean."

Shaking his head, Townsend sighed. "Sorry, Mr. Demming. Part of our jobs."

"Heston, please. Was there any sign of my grandson—on the beach?"

"No. Heston, it's possible that Kipp took Shawnee with him—into the deep."

Cold, clean, practiced. Like a swift fist in the gut.

"We hope the security tapes from Sun Tower will give us some new leads."

"You mean the comings and goings of...murder suspects?" he breathed unevenly.

"Uh-huh. If it *was* murder. And the movements of the deceased herself."

"Obviously, Kipp is your prime suspect."

"We have others," said Betancourt. Pausing, he added, "Whoever took the kid down the elevator, it'll show up on security monitors."

Townsend shifted uncomfortably in his loafers. "Sometimes, Heston, in family disputes, when one member of the family kills another, the remaining family members are in grave danger from the lone killer. We don't know yet what type of situation we're dealing with. Kipp may still be alive and at large. We want to place you and your family under our protection. Will you agree to that?"

His heart stopped. *They think Kipp...*

"Sir?"

He attended. "Of course. I will do everything possible to protect my family. Even from one of its own."

"We'll need to question your wife now, sir."

"Yes. Naturally." He reached for his phone.

"Your name's on these paintings, Mr. Demming." Betancourt injected, sliding finished canvases from their rack along the wall. "Your hobby?"

"My passion. Ever since *Decadent Virtue*."

"I like action movies," Betancourt shrugged. "And sci-fi."

"I saw it. Great flick." Townsend twisted his head to the right and studied Heston's damaged self-portrait. "What happened here?"

"Angst?" he bluffed, phone in hand.

Unannounced, Lissette cruised discreetly into the studio and sidled up to him. On tiptoe, she whispered in his ear, her hand shielding excited eyes. Her breath was warm. "Heston, excuse me. A package has just arrived for Mrs. Demming. It's from Kipp. I put it on your desk."

"What's up, sir?" asked antsy Betancourt loudly. "Anything we should know about?"

Chapter Seventeen

The seaplane splashed down into the waves just off the northern shore of Heart of Fire Key. Inside the plane's cabin, Kipp clenched Shawnee tightly in his arms as Beryl held the plane steady in the crashing surf. Washing ashore, the seaplane spun around and shimmied to a halt amid coral rock formations on the island's sandy beach.

For a moment, the three travelers sat in awkward suspension, riveted in tense disbelief. The air inside the cabin was close and moist. Kipp struggled to catch his breath.

"Thank Heaven," Beryl pronounced, dropping her forehead to the yoke.

Livid, Kipp exploded. "Beryl, you scared the living shit out of...Shawnee! Don't ever do that to me again!"

"Do what? Save your life?" she retorted.

"Lose control of a plane that me and the kid are flyin' in! You almost got us killed up there! You lost it!" He felt claustrophobic.

"I recovered in time. You're overreacting," she counterthrust primly.

"We almost died!" he bellowed.

Miffed, she sneered. "So what? I recovered in time. Besides, I thought you wanted to be dead."

Stunned as if struck, he gaped at her, speechless. "But not to die. I told you." He wanted to kill her.

Her face fell. "I'm sorry," she said immediately in a small voice. "I didn't mean that."

Shawnee's face wrinkled into a bawl. The tension in the small cab was too heavy for his little nerves to bear. "Mommee!" His hoarse cry was heart-wrenching.

"Now see what you've done?" she accused, once again playing offense.

"What I've done?" he retorted. Cuddling the small boy, he crooned in his ear. "Take it easy, buddy. We're here. We made it. Everything's cool. You'll see." After a few moments, Kipp's own muscles relaxed. The downpour was so thick it obscured any view of their surroundings. The raindrops pelted the plane's metal exterior like thousands of tiny amplified drumbeats. He felt like a steamed shellfish dinner.

"Are you sure we're in the right place?" he demanded above the din.

Beryl, mouthing a prayer, released the controls and collapsed back into her seat, exhaling and shutting her eyes. She opened them again. "Of course we are." She glared at him, her baby face pinched in disapproval.

"I'm only asking," he said, dawdling Shawnee on his knee. "The ocean's a big place. With lots of islands. How do you know this is the right one?"

"Because I saw it. I recognized the shape. I've been here before. Okay?"

"Okay." He looked at her askance. "So what do we do now? I'm not stepping out into this rain. The kid could catch cold, couldn't he?"

She sighed heavily. "Fine. We'll sit here and wait for it to end." She settled back and shut her eyes, attempting to rest.

He scoffed at her cavalier attitude. "And then what? I can't see a damn thing."

He watched as she removed her eyeglasses and let her hands fall to her side. She was cute. Damned cute. This was something he hadn't bargained on. He intended to bonk her just on principle—but he hadn't planned on her being cute.

"You said Heston had a house here." He was beginning to shiver, even in the warm tropical climate.

"He does, Kipp. Up there. On the highest point of the island." Sitting up, she donned her glasses, and pointed to the right of the plane's nose. "There's a path leading to the house. Right over there's a shed with an electric cart, but we'd have to make a run for it, which you don't want to do, apparently. Heaven forbid you should get wet."

"All right, all right. Take it easy." He squinted out the window through the white sheet of water. Thick rivulets drained from the plane's wings. "You could be right. I think I see the shed."

"I could be? Thank you."

"How can he have electric carts? Where does he get his power?"

Again, Beryl pointed. "The solar panels. They're up there, a huge array, on the top of the hill beyond the shed, just behind the row of arecas."

"Oh." His mouth felt dry. He felt feverish. Fear had made him queasy.

"You know, arecas—those huge tall, palmy plants. Can you see them?" She leaned across him to peer out his window. Her upper arm pressed against his chest. Soft and warm, her fine brown hair smelled fresh as the rain itself. Lilies of the field? Was that it? As she peered out the foggy window, her smooth skin glowed, luminescent in the pale light of rainy afternoon. Her black-rimmed glasses, which framed sky blue eyes, were a stark contrast to the paleness of her fine, toned skin. Her plump pink lips, beneath the pug nose, parted as she peered.

"Yeah. Maybe." He felt her presence, the warmth of her body and breath as she huddled against him and embraced Shawnee in a tender hug. Responding, Shawnee threw his small arms around her neck. The nearness of woman and child troubled him. *Move.*

He squirmed. "Maybe we should get out. The rain is letting up." He flipped open the door handle on his side of the plane.

"That's how these tropical storms are. They come with a flourish, but they die just as quickly. Are you game?" she asked, opening the pilot-side door. "We can run up the walkway to the house. It's a few hundred yards. We don't have to use the carts. It'll be faster. We can find some dry clothes."

"Clothes?" He needed shelter. He needed to lie down.

"The house is fully equipped. What's more, we'll have plenty of supplies. We'll want for nothing—until they find us."

"Let's risk it—trek up to the house. I can't stay here. I'm feeling...yuck." He licked his lips. "Take the kid," he told Beryl.

She looked at him, askance. "Come to Berry, luv," she said, taking Shawnee into her arms. The rain had slowed to a trickle as the weary pilgrims alighted from the aircraft.

"Leave the stuff," said Kipp, shoulders hunched, hands in his pockets. "I'll come back for it later."

"Corky?" croaked Shawnee, in Beryl's arms. The tot looked around, craning his neck in search of the stuffed toy.

"Corky?" Kipp frowned, going back to the plane and quickly scouring the interior. "Hey, buddy, where is Corky, huh?"

"You had him at the T-hangar," Beryl said, brows knitted. "I saw him in Shawnee's hand. Correction: I saw him fall from Shawnee's hand."

"Well, he's gone now." Kipp slammed the plane door.

"Corky!" Shawnee whined, restless in Beryl's arms.

"Don't worry, young man. We'll find him." But her eyes met Kipp's as they exchanged a silent thought. The stuffed blue dinosaur had been left in Heston's private hangar in Naples. Sooner or later it would be found—and noted.

"I'm afraid—well, it's a bit like Hansel and Gretel leaving a trail of breadcrumbs, isn't it?" she confided.

He picked up the gun. "Indeed it is, Nanny Northgate. Indeed it is." They exchanged glances.

"You can dispense with the gun, Kipp. You won't need it here."

He waved the firearm at her. "You're not going to rat me out?"

She suppressed a smile. "No. I've developed Stockholm syndrome."

"What?"

"I won't rat you out. I promise. Come along," Berry said. "The main house is this way."

He couldn't live without sleep. He would have to trust her, no matter what. He secured the gun in his belt.

"Here, give him to me," said Kipp as they began to trudge the uphill path.

"Are you sure?"

"I'm sure."

She handed the boy into his arms. Shawnee rested his head on his shoulder.

"How far is it?" he enquired of Beryl as they traversed the wooden-slat walkway winding through dense tropical foliage. He heard the crunch of their footfall and the caws of distant seabirds.

"Only a few hundred yards. Look," she said, as they came into a clearing. "There's the main house."

He and Shawnee looked in the direction she indicated. "It's not what I expected," he said, as they contemplated the grand plantation-style vacation home. Three stories tall, the ivory-colored house with it pitched green roof crowned a grassy promontory overlooking the vast turquoise sea that encased the small pearl of an island.

"What were you expecting?" she queried, as though insulted.

"I don't know—a castle, maybe a fort. Some antebellum-nostalgia-gingerbread monstrosity. This is classy." The house was ringed by a bevy of swaying coconut palm trees, their fronds floating gently on the mellow sea breezes. The languid scene made his growing discomfort all the more difficult to bear. Beryl stopped to pick a sprig of gardenia blossoms.

"I adore it," she said smugly. Inhaling, she placed the sprig beneath his and Shawnee's noses. Shawnee pushed it away. Rubbing his nose, he frowned.

"It's girly," Kipp mimicked.

"Look, Shawnee!" Beryl poked the boy in his arms. "That's where we're going." Shawnee twisted and turned his small body, searching for the house. Spying it, he smiled and pointed and looked from him to Beryl and back again. He laughed engagingly, making Beryl laugh. Her two front bunny teeth turned him on, or would have, if he weren't feeling so weak—and hungry.

"Makes me crave a bowl of Fruit Loops," he joked, glancing again at the nearby orchard.

"Fwuit Loops," echoed Shawnee, nodding vigorously.

"You'll eat real fruit here and like it," she smiled, again prodding Shawnee's round tummy with her stubby forefinger. Shawnee giggled in glee. This was a soft side of Nanny Northgate, the charming, tender part that made the little Napoleon part bearable. He liked this woman. He always had. He marveled. She had the tiniest fingernails he had ever seen on an adult human being. Her fingers were half the length of his own slender digits.

"Let's move on," he said quietly, pushing past the leaves of a loaded banana tree. "I need to...lie down." He felt the sweat draining down him, mixed with the warm moisture of the remnants of the tropical rain. His drenched clothes clung to his skin.

"Certainly. Let's," agreed his companion in crime, snagging a bunch of bananas from the tree. "There are orange and lemon trees behind the house," she noted. Pushing on, they resumed their upward trek, leaving behind the lush vegetation as the path worked its way across an expanse of green lawn.

"Any grapefruit?" he asked, panting as he trudged. "I like grapefruit." He blotted his brow with the tail of his shirt.

"There's grapefruit," she said noncommittally, now lagging behind him and Shawnee.

As they approached the house, it seemed to grow larger with each step. It was not, as he had first imagined, an antique dwelling. It was, rather—and much more characteristic of his father—a new home built to look old. This became apparent as they climbed the steps of the left staircase to the front porch, a long veranda lined with wicker rocking chairs.

"It's open. Walk right in," said Beryl.

He tested the door knob. The door eased inward. "No security?" he asked, astonished.

"Yes," she said, pushing past him. "When no one's here. Your father turns it off. He wants this to be a place of total privacy for him and the family."

"Don't you believe it. Ego-Man probably ringed this key with secret live video cams. He's spying on us now."

"You turn off the cameras here." Pointing, she cast a worried eye upon him. "I'll do it."

He knew he looked wretched. "Here, honey. Get down," he said to Shawnee, dropping the boy to his feet. He heard his own stomach growl.

Taking the toddler by the hand, Beryl announced, "Welcome to your new—if temporary—home, Mr. Demming and Master Demming." Throwing open the front door of the private island mansion, she entered the foyer.

"Please wipe your feet," he heard her say as he crossed the threshold. The moment he entered the vaulted open space of the elegant cottage, he felt at home. In the expansive living area, Beryl deposited Shawnee onto the parquet floor. The boy toddled directly to the wall of sliding glass and pressed his tiny palms to the panes.

Beryl followed him, and the two of them stood gazing out at the panoramic view. Kipp followed her. The whole house, with its southern exposure, opened onto a long lanai. Steps lead down to the sea. A long, L-shaped wooden dock jutted out into deep, open waters. An open motor-boat and a covered catamaran clung by a mooring line to its pilings.

"This is beautiful," he said, beholding the tropical vista—gardens giving way to lavish growth and the horizon of sea beyond. Nothing but wide, empty ocean as far as the eye could see. "We're safe here. For the moment."

Nonchalantly, he eased up and stood behind Beryl, whose small palm also was plastered to the glass. Pressing himself to her back, he placed his right hand above hers on the glass and leaned in. He felt her body electrify.

He stared down at the crown of her head. The childlike wisps of brown hair begged to be fondled. He inhaled the fragrance. Its seductive power astonished him. He couldn't give it a name—a mix of vanilla and lilacs and the earthy promise of unexplored woman.

Tenderly, he placed his left hand on the back of her neck and kneaded the firm, white skin.

"Where do we sleep?" he whispered, nuzzling her neck.

Chapter Eighteen

"Here's the package, gentlemen," said Heston, standing behind the desk in his study. An 18- by 12-inch box wrapped in brown paper and tape sat on his desk top.

Poppy—to whom the package was addressed—sat apart from Townsend, Betancourt, and Lissette. Sad but serene, she waited, unmoving, in a chair near the window of the study, ankles crossed, her dainty hands resting, palms upward, in her small lap.

"It does appear to be from Kipp," said Townsend, examining the box. Eagerly, he turned toward the window. "Will you open it, Mrs. Demming?"

Heston found a letter opener. "Let's go, Poppy," he said. "Open it up."

Angrily, she rose and walked to the desk. Ripping the opener from his hand, she tore into the box, severing the clear, plastic tape at lid's edge. "There," she said, tossing the opener onto the desk. She lifted the lid and sorted through the contents. He followed suit.

"What is it?" demanded Betancourt. "Looks like CDs, recordings, sheets of music."

"It appears to be a body of work," Heston said to the lawmen. "Here's a letter addressed to you," he added, carrying the letter over to his wife, who had resumed her seat near the window. He looked from Townsend to Poppy, and then back at Townsend.

Townsend turned to Poppy, ensconced near the window. Madonnalike, she was a picture of sorrow bathed in soft light. "Mrs. Demming? Please. It's important."

Heston felt lost in a morass of deception. He would give his life to shield her from the blow. He looked down at the letter still in his hand. "I'll read it," he offered.

Poppy's eyes remained downcast, but her empty hand found his. "It's all right, Heston," she said softly, squeezing his hand and dropping it. "I'll read it."

So he did the only thing he knew how to do. He retrieved the opener and stood beside her while she sliced open the envelope and extracted from it a single sheet of paper. Silently, she read Kipp's note. A tear drained down her cheek. She pressed her face into the letter and bent forward.

In an agony of helplessness, he drew her up from the chair and folded her in his arms and held her fast. The letter fluttered from her hand to the hardwood floor. Hitching his trousers, Townsend bent and picked it up.

"Read it aloud," Heston said to Townsend, his shoulder damp with his wife's tears. Rising to his feet, Townsend drew a pair of bifocals from his pocket, unfolded them and donned them. He held the letter up to the window. He read aloud:

> *Dearest Mother,*
>
> *Thank you for giving me life. Forgive me for destroying the gift you gave me. Please don't remember me as the world will. Remember me as I am in my heart, in these songs and poems. Don't let Gabe get his hands on these. Give all proceeds to Franco's foundation. This is the real me, my true self, my only hope for redemption in your eyes and in the afterlife. I cannot go on in my shame. Please forgive me. Ask Father to forgive me.*
>
> *I love you.*

Your son,
Kipp (crossed out)
Noel

In his arms, Poppy's slight shoulders heaved. His arms tightened around her waist. Pressed against him, her small body shuddered. He heard Lissette cough behind him.

"Noel?" said Townsend, looking at him quizzically over the bifocals.

"My wife's original name for Kipp. Before giving him up for adoption as an infant."

"Oh," mouthed Townsend soundlessly.

Betancourt stepped into the sunlight. "You know, we'll have to confiscate the box and its contents, including the letter. It's all evidence."

Tearing free, Poppy raged. "No! You can't have it! He sent it to me. He's my son." Her brown eyes shined, red-rimmed and fierce.

"Lissette, come here." Remaining calm, Heston motioned his housekeeper forward. "Escort my wife to her sitting room."

Flaring, Poppy turned on him. "Heston, you can't let them!"

"Brown Eyes..." he whispered, heart ripped from his chest by the necessity of his lies.

"You can't let them steal our son's legacy."

Townsend took her hands as Lissette laced a plump arm around her waist. "Mrs. Demming," he said kindly. "We're not positive that your son is dead. The evidence may give us some clues. You want us to find him—if he's alive—don't you?"

She stamped her foot. "What more do you need? I've just read you his suicide note!"

"Sometimes the obvious—isn't," said Townsend quietly. "This material may lead us to your grandson. We have no time to waste. Every minute matters."

"I-I..." Poppy stuttered, flustered and struggling.

"Come on, honey," urged Lissette, shepherding her mistress toward the door.

Betancourt stepped across their path. "Mrs. Demming..."

Townsend raised a hand. "Jorge..."

Betancourt ignored him. "When did you last see your son Kipp alive?"

Heston moved in protectively. "Detective, my wife is not up to your interrogation."

"Sir, do you want to recover your grandson?"

"What do you think?" He appealed to Townsend. "But I'd prefer not to shatter my wife in the process."

"Jorge is right. We need answers, Mrs. Demming. When did you last see Kipp alive? And where were you yesterday?"

Poppy glanced at Heston. She licked her lips. "I-I...l-last s-saw my s-son at Thanksgiving—n-nearly f-four years ago. Here, in this house."

Betancourt looked at Heston. "That's the day you two fought?"

He nodded.

"I-I spent yesterday on Miami Beach," Poppy said, wincing as if to ward off a blow.

"Really?" said Betancourt with irony impossible to miss.

"At the Fontainebleau."

He stepped in to explain. "My wife and eldest daughter drove across state to visit with my daughter's uncle—on her mother's side—criminal attorney Banks Winston."

"*Oye,*" muttered Betancourt under his breath.

Townsend nodded. "I read about his case in *The Herald.* He argued—and won—in Federal Court."

"As usual," Heston said. "Banks always represents the 'haves,' never the 'have nots.' He upholds the traditions of his old California monied roots—on his father's side."

Betancourt cornered Poppy, eyeing her from top to bottom. "You were at the hotel all day?"

Poppy cringed. "N-no. I went gallery hopping. For a few hours, while Winner and Ram lunched with Banks."

"Who's Ram?"

"A bodyguard. I just hired him. Young man, great references, name of Ram Kincaid. Raymond, really, but a huge, burly guy, so he goes by Ram. He asked not to be addressed as Raymond. Therefore, I do not address him as Raymond, and I suggest you follow suit." He raised an eyebrow for emphasis. "Ram is a martial artist, a black belt. Early on, he was a professional wrestler. Of late, he served as a marine."

Brows up, Betancourt popped a spearmint into his mouth and crunched down. The odor made Poppy sneeze.

"Bless you," crunched Betancourt, obviously taken with her.

"Why are you asking me all these questions?" she demanded. "Do you know your job? Get out there and find my grandson," she cried, agitated. "If you can't find him, my husband can. Heston can afford to hire the best."

"Take it easy, Mrs. Demming," Townsend placated, countenance immobile. "We need this information first, so we can do our jobs effectively. Heston, where were you yesterday?"

Heston blinked. "Me?"

"You."

"Uh...here. Most of the day. I took a drive midday."

"Alone?"

"Totally," Heston answered.

"Where to?"

His mind tried to race—like the wheels of his Ferrari mired in sand. "Nowhere in particular. I did legwork for a new project I'm developing. I left my housekeeper with the children. Last night I was here alone with my younger son and twin daughters. The nanny is...on vacation."

Betancourt whistled. "Nanny? We'll need to know more about the nanny." His nimble fingers crumbled a cellophane wrapper. "What's her name?"

"Beryl Northgate. She's a British national."

"You two get along?" Betancourt asked Poppy.

"Very well." She glared at Townsend.

Townsend stared at him. "Any other domestics? Office help?"

Palms up, he shook his head. "Not here yesterday. My wife has acted as my personal assistant since our marriage. My former PA moved to The Bahamas."

Townsend took a deep breath. "We're going to need formal statements." He pursed his lips and looked at Poppy. "From all of you."

Betancourt swept Kipp's package under one arm. "We'll need the letter, too, Mrs. Demming." Nodding, he indicated the missive in Townsend's hands.

Uncertain, his wife looked his way for reassurance. In the flicker of an eye, he denied it.

"Take it," he said.

"Heston, no!" Poppy screamed.

He took her by the shoulders. "There's no time for your sentimentality. Shawnee could be dying." He crushed her to him. "We must cooperate."

He nodded to Townsend, who tucked it safely into an evidence envelope. Tearing herself free, Poppy glared at him. His heart sank.

I'll have hell to pay tonight.

Townsend shook his hand. "If you don't mind, we'll be in touch." He and Betancourt started for the door.

"Would it matter if I minded?"

"No, sir." Betancourt sneered. He leered at Poppy. "Aren't you curious to know how Lennox died?"

Heston looked at his wife.

Ignoring Heston, Poppy faltered. "I...heard it on the TV."

Was she lying? Heston addressed Betancourt. "No blood? No violence?"

"None, sir."

"Had she been...?"

"Raped? No sign of it, although she may've had recent sexual intercourse. Forensics will give us answers. But that takes time."

"Thank you, Mrs. Demming," said Townsend cordially. Distraught, Poppy fled the room, followed by Lissette.

The two lawmen strode down the hallway to the front door. He followed them, stopping in the foyer as they exited. Beyond the tall box hedgerows and bronzed gates, the world was waiting, watching, salivating.

Say it.

"Gentlemen, for your edification—the man who fomented this fiasco is Kipp's manager, Gabriel Cade—an A-list scoundrel."

Townsend nodded. "He's next on our list."

"Good luck finding him."

"They say he's out to sea," Townsend said.

"He is that."

Betancourt paused, shifting the weight of the box. "If you don't mind my saying so, your wife is a knockout. I'm a sucker for a redhead with freckles."

Heston wrestled with his own ire. "Say anything you like, Detective. Only, don't touch." He felt like clawing the clod's face but, instead, remained outwardly calm. It was that or jail. Jail would come soon enough.

Grinning, Betancourt walked out the door. Following, Townsend waved dismissively. He tarried on the door step. "One more thing I need to ascertain, sir."

"Shoot."

"You and this Nanny Northgate—any hanky panky there?"

"Heaven forbid."

Townsend laughed engagingly.

"I'd sooner molest my Great Aunt Tillie—if I had a Great Aunt Tillie."

"Understood." Descending the steps, Townsend stopped near the tiered fountain. His eyes swept the manicured estate. "Ever do any fishing off your boat?" he inquired.

"Yes, I do." He thrust his hands into his pockets. "You fish?"

Townsend nodded. "Yep." Turning, he followed Betancourt to the car. "I'll let you know who turns up on video," he called, sinking into the driver's seat. As the gate opened and the white sedan pulled out, a crowd of reporters and photographers swarmed the vehicle.

Diving back inside, Heston leaned his full weight against the closed front door of his mansion. He broke into a sweat.

I already know—I have top billing. But what about Poppy?

Chapter Nineteen

Opening her eyes, Beryl gasped and bolted upright. *Is he going to murder me, too?*

Looming over her bed, Kipp, half-naked, belt in hand, stood watching her. Had he been watching her while she slept? Quickly, she felt for the slumbering Shawnee. He was there, nestled by her side.

Disheveled and unkempt, Kipp appeared every inch the raucous rock star. He was shirtless. His lean muscles rippled, his arms, shoulders, and torso, a toned, sculpted mass of early morning light and shadow. Yet something had changed. He looked *different.*

In the jacaranda trees outside the bedroom window, morning birds twittered. In the eastern sky, the tangerine sun broke through a drifting cloud bank. Kipp's eyes caught the golden glint of its heat as he deftly slipped the belt through the loops of his low-cut jeans and fastened the buckle.

"Where's the coffee?" he asked her matter-of-factly.

Was he angry? Forgiving? Remorseful? She had rebuffed his advances the night before and taken Shawnee into bed with her in a guest bedroom upstairs. She had left the master suite across the hall for Kipp's future use.

Shifting her seat, she dislodged the child sleeping at her side. "In the freezer," she whispered so as not to wake him. Protectively, she drew the blanket over Shawnee, whose eyelids opened, fluttered, and closed again.

Kipp watched her with impudent eyes. "No wonder I couldn't find it. You're not supposed to freeze coffee. It dries out the oils or something."

"Silly me," she sighed, reclining as he sauntered toward the door. A pungent fragrance of bergamot Cyprus tinged with citrus lingered on the air. He had not yet showered. She watched him saunter out, musculature in sync like a finely tuned machine.

"You cut your hair!" she cried, immediately cupping her hand across her mouth and glancing down at Shawnee. "No more platinum spikes," she whispered to Kipp, pointing at her head.

Turning, he stood framed in the doorway. Reaching up with both hands, he latched onto the top of the door frame and raised himself off the floor in a display of athletic prowess and underarm cornsilk. "Thanks for noticing," he said, veins popping. He lowered himself to the ground. "What do you think? I've decided to go natural. Part of my new disguise." Leaning against the door frame, he scoured the three-day growth of beard on his chin.

"I like it," she pronounced. "Your natural coloring is so..."

"What?"

"Nice." *Glorious.*

"Get your ass out of bed, Berry." Slapping the door frame, he clattered down the grand staircase.

Last night, after inhaling a meager meal of yogurt and oatmeal cookies, Kipp had fallen asleep where he lay—on a sofa of the great room. She had been unable to drag him, so she had covered him with a comforter and placed a pillow beneath his head. She had unlaced and tugged the sneakers from his feet. He was wearing them now.

Shawnee, too, had been content with a small, impromptu supper, a smoothie made from bananas and yogurt, along with a cup of cinnamon apple sauce. Exhausted and fussy, the frightened tot had clung to her afterwards so that she felt to separate from him would break his little heart. He had whined for his mother until he had fallen asleep. He couldn't understand why Mommy had abandoned him. How would she be able to make him understand? Suddenly, she smelled coffee.

Her face flushed. *Had Kipp been watching me? Or simply craving caffeine? Beryl, get a grip.*

Last night she had sung Shawnee a lullaby. Her attempt had made him fussier. She knew she had no singing voice. What she needed was a storybook. She would search the library downstairs.

She gazed out the window. *What am I doing on an island with Kipp Demming?*

The sun was rising in the sky. A bath for all three of them was the first order of business. Shawnee's should have come last night, but the child was so exhausted, she had let him sleep.

"Can you scramble eggs?" Kipp called from downstairs.

"Of course," she muttered. "Of course!" she called a bit more loudly. Shawnee stirred.

"Then do it," he ordered. "I'm starving."

"You brought in my things from the plane?" she called, sitting upright and cradling Shawnee, who was now wide awake and rubbing his bleary eyes.

"Yeah."

"Thank you."

"I'm passing out from hunger down here."

"Have you ever heard the word 'please'? Or doesn't the word exist in the rock and roll vernacular?"

"Lexicon. I forgot. Please," he shouted up from the foot of the stairwell.

"Would you please put your shirt on?" she called, swinging to her feet and scooping Shawnee into her arms. "Goodness, you need bathing, don't you?" she said to the child. "So do I, I daresay."

"Why?" Kipp yelled.

"Why what?"

"Why do you want me to put my shirt on?"

"On second thought, don't. Let me launder it first. I'll do it while you take a shower."

"I don't want to take a shower. I want breakfast. I want scrambled eggs and toast."

"Fine. Keep your shirt...off." She waved a dismissive hand. "I'm going to change your son's apparel after his bath." With Shawnee balanced on one arm, she clutched the mahogany banister and advanced carefully down the staircase. Kipp was waiting, arms crossed, toes tapping.

"Excuse me," she said, pushing by him into the kitchen.

"You're not excused," he said, not moving, instead standing his ground.

"Dada," said Shawnee, reaching for Kipp.

"Morning, buddy. How you doing?"

"I'd like to pass," she said. "Unless you'd like to help him potty?"

Towering above her, Kipp bent down and met her belligerent glare head on. "What's the magic word?" he prompted, eyes glittering.

Her heart raced. Her face flushed, more deeply this time. His nose was two inches from hers.

"Pwease," Shawnee replied cheerfully.

"Good boy! Be my guest," Kipp smiled cordially, flinging the door wide and stepping aside to let her and the kid pass.

"You're my guest," she huffed futilely, breezing past him and heading through the kitchen and into the bathroom. "You crashed my vacation."

"Such as it is," Kipp countered from the kitchen. "Don't you have any friends?" She heard the screen door slam. "I'd be partying in a place like this."

A few minutes later, as she ran the bath water for Shawnee, Kipp appeared in the bathroom doorway, a steaming cup in each hand. "Coffee?" he asked, in a gesture of appeasement.

"Creamer and sugar?" she asked, lowering Shawnee into the tub of tepid water.

"In there."

Soaping a washcloth, she chanced a smile. "Thanks. Set it down there." With a nod of her head, she indicated the vanity counter.

"You scramble some eggs. I'll clean the kid," he said.

"Do you know how?"

"Eggs," he said, nodding toward the kitchen. "Please." He was leaning against the door jam, sipping coffee from a cup of his own. "I checked out the premises," he reported.

"And?" She lathered the washcloth vigorously for Shawnee. If she kept busy, she could avoid looking at Kipp's bare chest.

"Impressive. Secluded. Pretty cool to have your own private lagoon."

"Well, it's a cove, really. But not deep enough to accommodate *Windswept.* That's why there's a dock out to sea."

"I checked the news earlier." He watched her every move. "No one knows we're here, Berry."

"Mum knows I'm here," she corrected. "Heston doesn't. No one knows you and Shawnee are with me. Hand me the shampoo, please?"

"I can wash his hair." Lifting the travel-size shampoo bottle, he moved toward the tub.

"Wash his hair, will you? Be careful; it's not for little ones." She scooted past him carefully so as not to touch him and washed her hands in the lavatory sink and dried them with a clean towel from the linen cupboard. Picking up her cup of coffee, she took a sip. "Um. Heavenly," she smiled. "I might keep you around."

"Really?"

"Um," she confirmed, heading for the kitchen. "Scrambled hard or soft?"

"Soft," she heard him say. "Soft," she heard Shawnee echo. Then she nearly dropped her coffee cup—Kipp was *singing*. And it was a song she had never seen on any of the playlists.

"Do you love me as I love you? A brook meandering..."

What would Cecily Hodges give to be in her shoes right now? "Soft it is," she mumbled under her breath. "I hope you like strawberry jam—because it's all I brought." She opened the refrigerator door. Removing the carton of eggs and a box of milk from the fridge, she looked up to see Kipp emerging from the bathroom with a clean and shiny Shawnee dripping in his arms.

"You two fellows look good together." She smiled and pointed. "You'll want a towel."

"That's the first time I've ever seen him take a bath." Kipp scrubbed the tot dry.

"You didn't bathe him when he visited you? After the divorce?"

"I visited him. I told you. Monitored visitation. That's all I got. Two hours max, once a month. The judge was a prick. Lennox sold me out. She told him I was unstable."

"Weren't you?" Cracking eggs into a bowl, she felt him bristle. *Be careful, Beryl.*

"Then. Not now. I went through rehab."

"You're clean, but are you stable? Aren't you the man who forced me to fly at gunpoint?" She poured a small glass of juice and handed it to him. "Help him drink this, will you? There are sippy cups here somewhere, but I haven't found them yet."

He scowled at the glass in his hand. "Damn it, you're bossy."

She blinked. "Professional hazard. Sorry."

Accepting her apology, Kipp lifted the glass to Shawnee's lips. "I'm clean now. I told you. My head is clear."

The boy's small hands cupped around the juice glass as he drank. "Hey, buddy! How do you like that? Good stuff, eh?"

After draining the glass, Shawnee smacked his lips and burped.

"Outstanding," Kipp praised, setting down the glass.

"Pour yourself a glass if you'd like—I mean, if you want to." As butter melted in the pan, she whisked the eggs.

Kipp shook his head. "I should check the news again."

She nodded. "TV's in the den. Remote's on top."

"Okay. What the hell." Balancing Shawnee on one hip, Kipp sauntered from the kitchen. She heard one newscaster's voice, and then another, as Kipp flipped through the satellite channels.

Setting the table, she stood to attention. *"Authorities have now verified that Kipp Demming did remove his son from the penthouse home of his dead ex-wife, Lennox Cordova Demming. Security footage from the building elevator shows Kipp arriving at the condo and leaving with his son at around 1 a.m. on the night in question. Although Demming's and his son's whereabouts are still unknown, investigators speculate that the pair have either died in a murder-suicide committed that same night, or that they are currently alive and at large. Meanwhile, facts about Kipp's dire financial straits are coming to light. The investigation is ongoing. We will keep you up to date..."*

Suddenly, there was silence. Kipp and Shawnee reentered the room. Kipp's eyes met hers.

"Breakfast is ready," she breathed softly. "Nothing like a fortifying English breakfast—minus the kippers and kidneys, mind you."

"Praise be for small favors." He was crestfallen.

She clicked her tongue. "Hand him to me—if you don't mind. I'll feed him. You sit down and eat your eggs while they're hot."

This time he didn't argue. Straddling a chair at the kitchen table, he fell upon the meal, wolfing down the steaming food in great mouthfuls.

Washing it down with juice, he kept his eyes on his plate. He belched politely and regarded her earnestly. His eyes moved to the window. "Let's go outside. It's a beautiful day."

Unstraddling the chair, he carried his steaming plate out the back door and onto the immense deck overlooking the crystal-blue pool. He sat down at a table and continued eating. She followed with Shawnee, who shaded his eyes against the sun's glare. Kipp pushed away his empty plate and looked her in the eye. "I was hoping to explore the island with you."

"We still can," she said.

"I can't stay here, Beryl."

"Why not? We're all doing so well together. I want to hear all about your life. What drove you to this?"

"There is no we," he assured her, gun suddenly lolling in his hand. "I'm taking the speedboat to Big Pine Key." He spun the revolving cartridge.

"What? Why?"

"While you were asleep, I used the PC in the library—to search for Marissa."

Her heart thumped. "Marissa's on Big Pine Key?"

"She works at a free clinic there."

She sank into a chair. "When will you go?" *Don't go.*

"Right now."

"Shawnee is your responsibility, Kipp."

"Then I'm doing right by him. He's in good hands."

"Have it your way," she acquiesced, conflicted. Was he still suicidal or not?

"My little take-charge woman." He rose, gun in hand, and stretched. "Thanks for the breakfast. I'll take that clean shirt now. I'll shower upstairs."

Moments later, she heard the same song, above running water, booming from the shower. *"Do you love me?"*

Discreetly, she hung the clean shirt on the bathroom doorknob.

Chapter Twenty

Ezra felt dirty creeping around, but he tailed Vivi anyway. All he needed was a fedora and a .45, and he'd feel like gumshoe Dick Powell in *Murder, My Sweet*—except that this was no old movie, and he was tailing the woman he loved, not some film *noir* dame. His worst suspicions were confirmed as he watched Vivian enter a nondescript medical building and walk directly into the office of a heavy-duty heart surgeon. *Something is very, very wrong.*

Driving home in his Mercedes, he had chewed a gap in his moustache—and hadn't even realized it until he thrust his personal key into Vivian's lock.

Now, alone inside her home, he had to act quickly. He needed to find something, some scrap of paper, some computer record, some straggling phone number, that would give him even the slightest clue to what was afoot in the life of his married mistress. *No use confronting her head on. I tried that. She won't give.* He made tracks for her private office.

He *hated* sneaking behind her back, but he had to know—and she wasn't talking. Damn it, he had a right to know. He loved Vivian. Her health was his concern as well as hers.

He wanted to share her burden. He wanted her to confide in him. He needed her vulnerability so that he could be strong for her when she most needed strength—like now.

He pulled open the drawers of her desk, rifling through them and slamming them shut. *Nothing here.* He jabbed the computer keys. *Locked. To keep out jerks like me.* Exhaling in frustration, he scanned the room for clues. Where would Vivian keep—keep *what?* He didn't even know what he was looking for.

The cabinets? Opening and shutting various doors, he found magazines, linens, tchotchkes, stemware—but no date books, no calendars, no nothing.

Something brushed his ankles. He jumped, cursing as he realized it was her stupid cat. The Burmese longhair ignored his rebuff, hopping atop a neutral-floral upholstered footstool in front of the overstuffed armchair. Curling up on the cushioned stool, the cat proceeded to ignore him.

Peeved, he walloped the footstool with the side of his athletic shoe— and the lid popped off along with the cat. The top of the upholstered footstool was simply a cushioned lid. Beneath the lid, now lying upside down on the floor, the inside of the footstool was hollow.

And inside was...? He peered in. *An old scrapbook.*

Diving into the hollow, he extracted the heavy book. He sat down on the couch and placed the unopened scrapbook on his knees, contemplating it. *Did Vivian hide this scrapbook from me on purpose? Or does she just think the footstool is a good place for storage?*

What was in it?

Leafing through the pages, he saw that most of the photographs in the scrapbook had been taken 20 or 25 years ago. Pictures of Vivian's life before he'd entered it. He shuddered involuntarily. He couldn't stand to admit that Vivian existed before he'd met her. But she had. Here was proof. Her early days in Hollyweird.

Aw, man. Here she was, stunningly beautiful in her early twenties, standing beside that elegant jackass who'd become her husband a few years later, cut-throat billionaire Truett Champlain. He flipped the pages in disgust. Here she was with her step kids, Hailey and Adair The Fourth, when they were just sprouts. Before Truett had blackmailed their mom into giving them up.

Poor 'Viv. She must have thought she'd met Prince Charming. What a cruel joke Fate had played on her. *Miss Vivian Fairchild and her esteemed fiancé, Truett A. Champlain III, at Lincoln Center...blah, blah, blah...*

The cat was back, wrapping itself around his ankles. "Not on your life, Jojo," he whispered, patting its head. "You'll get no treats out of me, you mewling, simpering little snob, you secret son of an alley cat. Papers, my ass." But he stroked the cuddling cat as he turned the pages of the scrap-book. So breathtaking Vivian had been. She reminded him of someone.

He inhaled sharply. *Winner.* In youth, Vivian had had the same type of ethereal beauty as Heston's pubescent daughter had now. He turned the page and chewed his moustache fervently. What he didn't need right now was a woody.

And then he noticed the snapshot. Four people on New Year's Eve. Twenty-one years ago. He recognized three of them: Lennox, Vivian, and Heston, all bright young things, all in party hats, all looking stewed to the max. Vivian had known Heston back then? She had never mentioned it. Neither had he.

But who was this fourth woman? The grown-up holding hands with young Heston?

He didn't recognize her, but she was a striking female, very comely in a middle-aged, athletic, boozy sort of way, which was okay with him because he dug fast older women. So, apparently, had our boy Heston. *Who was this broad?*

Slowly, he thumbed the pages. Whoever she was, she had been important to Lennox. At least ten photos of her graced the pages that followed. In some photos, she was alone. In others, she was with Vivian or Lennox or Heston or a combination. He turned the page.

He gasped. Here was a black-and-white art shot, an 8 x 10 of the same woman, with Vivian in a clutch. *An erotic embrace.*

He slammed the book shut. The cat dashed from the room.

Quickly, he crammed the scrapbook back into its hole. Reaching down, he grabbed the cushioned lid and pounded it back into its place atop the footstool. For a moment, he stood motionless in the silent, empty study of the woman he thought he had known intimately.

That'll teach you to snoop, you sly son of a bitch. No offense, Ma.

The overhead light came on. Vivian stood in the office doorway. "Looking for something?" she asked snidely. Her skin was pale; her tone, deadly.

"Hell, no," he cried defiantly. Unsure, he pivoted on one leg. "Hell, yes," he admitted, confronting her. "I saw you go into the surgeon's office. I want the truth, Vivian."

Sadly, she tossed her designer bag onto the desktop and lowered her slender body into the chair behind her desk. "Then you shall have it, my love." She sighed resignedly, as the pushy Burmese leaped into her lap, purring like a souped-up Maserati.

All of it? He wondered, but did not ask aloud.

She chucked the cat's chin. "Ezra, I need a heart operation. The doctors—the specialists—want me to have it. It's a very dangerous procedure. I have to make a decision soon. Without it, I may die anyway." She hid her eyes with the back of her hand. "Oh, my love. I didn't want to burden you."

Chapter Twenty-One

Kipp was angry again. She hadn't been able to leave it alone.

"Stop correcting me, Beryl." Showered and changed, he banged out the front door.

She followed, boat keys dangling from her fingers. "You'll need these. Do you know how to drive a boat?" Fascinated, Shawnee grabbed the keys from her hands and shook them playfully. She let him, as she jogged to catch up with Kipp, dogging his steps.

"What if she turns you in, Kipp?" The sun was hot and beating down on her face. Shawnee needs a hat. So will Kipp.

"She won't."

"How can you be certain? She's a respectable member of society."

"And I'm what—a derelict?"

"Indeed you are, to her way to thinking—a drug addict and an ex-con, a sex deviant—"

"I'm not deviant. I'm promiscuous."

"That is deviant."

"What do you know, Virgin Queen? Hey, what's that?" He quipped, pointing to her hand. "The key to your chastity belt?"

She huffed, jogging to keep up. "Don't start that again. For all Marissa knows, you're a murderer and a kidnapper. For all I know!"

"Come on."

"You're the object of an international manhunt. Dr. Neville will..."

"Dr. Neville," he mocked. As she jogged, Shawnee sang an elongated, bumpy "Aaahhhhh" The length of Kipp's stride was twice hers.

"Dr. Neville will feel obligated to turn you in, for your own good, if for no other reason. One of those sorts of things," she panted.

"Shit." Kipp clattered down the steps leading to the long, extended dock and dropped with a thud onto its wooden planks. He made a beeline for the speed boat, *Ladybug*. Huffing, she was right behind him, with Shawnee clasping her neck for dear life.

Nearing the boat, Kipp hopped down into it and found the controls.

"Give me the key," he ordered. Wresting them from Shawnee's grasp, she obliged.

"Pwease," admonished Shawnee.

Fuming, Kipp ripped the cord on the outboard engine. The motor roared to life. At the loud racket, Shawnee jumped in her arms.

"It's all right, luv," she voiced calmly into the child's soft ear. "Dada thinks he's doing something important. We must be patient with him."

Kipp shouted above the engine's roar. "The tank is full, topped off, even. We can make it there and back easy."

"We?" she barked loudly.

"Get in," he yelled. His golden beard glistened in the sunlight. His face glowed, mirroring the sunlight—or was he lit from within? For the first time, he looked purposeful. She hadn't seen that expression on his face since he was college-age. He seemed almost radiant.

"You're sure? You want us to go with you?" she cried from the dock.

"Both of you. Get in the boat."

Shawnee kicked his legs in delight.

"Just like that?" Faucets are off. Stove is off. Coffee pot, unplugged. Dryer, on. "Maybe I should stay here. I'll keep Shawnee. You go. We'll be fine until your return."

The copper-penny eyes held new determination. "I can't leave you two here alone. It's not safe. Hell, you could be raided by pirates."

"Kipp," she objected, half-laughing. "This is Heart of Fire Key, not Treasure Island." Around her the wavelets lapped. Gulls danced in the sea breeze. He was the loveliest man she had ever seen. She felt herself melting, as if she might dissolve into a puddle and ooze through the cracks between the planks at her feet. As if reading her thoughts, he smiled warmly. Her heart sank, along with all its defenses.

"Beryl, please get in the boat. Before I come up there and throw you in bodily."

Her eyes locked his. The Golden Fleece couldn't have shined as brightly to Jason, that other hunky, erstwhile sailor and adventurer who wouldn't listen to reason. The thought of touching Kipp's beard was as heady as the thought of running her fingers through a cache of coin and jewels. She felt faint. She fanned her face with her hand.

I need a drink of water.

"All right," she acquiesced. Handing Shawnee down into Kipp's outstretched arms, she squatted down onto the dock, and—unladylike, she knew—climbed down onto the small deck of the speed boat. Clutching Shawnee's waist, Kipp steadied her by the arm. His flesh felt hot and rough; his grip, strong and reliable.

As she found her footing on deck, Kipp handed Shawnee back to her. Rifling beneath a vinyl seat cushion, he located three life vests and threw two of them her way.

"Put on the jackets," he commanded, donning his. "No ifs, ands or buts."

She did as she was told. She put Shawnee's on first, buckling his in place. Hers could wait.

"Now sit," Kipp told Shawnee.

Suddenly, the engine died. "What the...?"

Scowling, he ripped the engine cord again. The engine sputtered and died. "Who needs this shit?" he griped. Again, he ripped. Again, the engine sputtered and died.

"Kipp! Listen!" she said, hand on his arm. In the distant, a boat engine sounded. The boat was headed their way.

Alarmed, Kipp scanned the island at the end of the dock. Grabbing Shawnee, he tossed the boy onto the dock and pushed Beryl up the short ladder. "Take him! Run!"

Scooping Shawnee into her arms, she bounded down the dock toward the island.

"Hide!" he yelled after her. The engine sound grew louder.

On solid ground, she dove into the foliage. Ducking down, she pressed her finger to Shawnee's lips. "Shhh!" breathed Shawnee, enjoying the excitement. Covertly, Beryl searched. *Where's Kipp? He should be right behind me.*

She saw him. He was hobbling quickly up the dock toward them, a plastic box in his hand.

The engine grew louder. Kipp reached solid ground and limped in their direction.

"Here!" she cried, yanking him down into the foliage.

He panted rapidly. His foot was bleeding. "Stepped on a damned fish hook." He shook the first aid kit in her face. "Apply direct pressure. I can clean and patch the wound. But I'm past due for a tetanus shot."

"Oh, Kipp." She clasped his ankle and staunched the bleeding gash with gauze.

"Shhh!" The three fugitives dipped down behind coral rocks sheltered by palmettos. A hydroplane appeared in the distance, heading straight for the dock.

Peeking through fronds, they watched in apprehension. The boat's engine died as the driver, a middle-aged black man with a magnificent physique, approached the dock, alighted from the hydroplane, and secured the mooring line. He wore a shirt, shorts, and sunglasses.

Ambling up the dock, he spotted something on the wooden planks of the dock.

Abruptly, he stopped and squatted down, examining the curious spots. Rising to his feet, he doubled back and peered inside the *Ladybug*. Slowly, he did a 360-degree scan of island and sea. Swiftly, he trod back to his hydroplane and slung a rifle over his shoulder. Gingerly, he trooped back up the dock toward them.

"Da—" Shawnee started.

Brusquely, Kipp yanked Shawnee into his arms and placed a hand over his mouth. The angry child struggled, but to no avail.

"It's the caretaker, Robinson LaCroix," Beryl whispered. "What should we do now?"

Stopping, La Croix looked down at the plank walkway, which ended in a grassy overgrowth. Ten feet away, he stared directly into the bushes. Shaking his head, he turned and proceeded up the walkway toward the front door of the house.

"He saw my blood," Kipp whispered. "The question is—did he see us?"

Chapter Twenty-Two

Five minutes later, a wild-eyed Beryl crept furtively among the jut-ting branches, silently following Kipp, who toted a gurgling, flailing Shawnee under one arm. Stalking clandestinely through treacherous terrain, he emerged on the island's ocean shore and followed it around to the hidden cove. Hunkering down at water's edge, he signaled for Beryl to drop to the ground. Gratefully, she did.

Sweating, he deposited Shawnee onto clear, sandy ground. Breath-less, he peered out from the swampy bower, anticipating any sign that the caretaker had departed the island in his hydroplane. He could see the far end of the dock.

"His boat is still here," he whispered. "Which means he is, too. He's somewhere on the island."

Collapsing to the ground, he caught his breath. Lying beside him, she caught hers. Their hands brushed accidentally.

Kipp sat up, elbows on knees. Stone-faced, he ripped off his sneaker and examined the bottom of his foot. The gash had stopped bleeding. He tossed the plastic box to Beryl. "Open the first aid kit."

"I know how to bandage a cut," she countered. Sitting up, she as-sumed a cross-legged seat on the sand. Her hands were shaking. She was thirsty. Shawnee would need water soon.

"It's worse than a cut," he croaked, steadying his foot and thrusting it into her lap. "Hurry." Receiving no response, he spoke again low and succinctly. "The hook went deep. If it becomes infected, it won't matter if I get tetanus. Either way, I'm a goner."

"I'm hurrying." She sent up a silent prayer. He was talking like a man who wanted to live.

Steadying herself, she cracked open the box. She tossed a glance at Shawnee, who lay on the ground behind her. The tot was playing with his own feet, waving them in the air, and singing softly to himself.

Restless and in pain, Kipp exhaled impatiently.

"Don't move. I'm working."

"It's about time. Clean your hands first. Scrub with alcohol wipes. Any gloves?"

"Yes. Hush, or I'll find another use for this gauze."

He mimicked her words. "Just do it. In this jungle climate, you can't be too careful. Clean the wound. Be thorough."

Meticulously, she cleaned as directed.

He winced. "Ever heard the joke about the patient who ran into a busy doctor's office and cried, 'Doctor, I'm shrinking!'?"

"No." She cleaned the wound, absorbed.

"The nurse told him to take a seat. 'You'll just have to be a little patient,' she said."

Beryl giggled. He giggled stoically. She prodded deeply. He inhaled sharply.

"Sorry," she said, tearing gauze for the bandage.

"No problem."

Tearing strips of tape, she sat back on her haunches and admired her work. "You'll need to stay off of it."

He craned his sinewy neck to discern Shawnee behind her. "Do you boss the kids around this way? Do they rebel?"

"Not in my universe." She reconsidered. "Dakota does. He leaves me notes."

She tried to ignore her front-row view of the wide breadth of his golden shoulders, the glistening skin of his naked, taut torso, and the sinuous muscles of his arms and shoulders.

How much more intimate could she be with a man than cleaning his wounded flesh? Her gaze caressed his thighs, flitting discretely over the disturbing bump. Covered by cloth, in between. She didn't know...

She trembled at the thought.

"See anything you like?"

"No."

"The girls don't leave you notes, eh?"

"Winner's been known to draw pictures of me when she's angry. The twins..."

"They're not old enough to write."

"You've been gone four years, Kipp. The twins are past the scribble stage." She could sense the heat of his pulsating body, so close to hers. She felt his warm breath on her shoulder.

"The what?" he asked blankly, watching the deft movements of her small hands.

"The scribble stage," she sighed, finishing her task. Patting the bandage into final place, she sat back as Kipp sat up and faced her. She raised her gaze to Kipp's face. The look of adoration she saw there sent shockwaves throughout her system. She felt herself flush from forehead to knees. Her eyes darted here, there, anywhere to avoid his eyes. Rocking to her feet, she busied herself by peeling away the latex gloves and again scrubbing her still-trembling hands, her back now to Kipp so that he could not witness her confusion.

"Who cares?" he asked, suddenly in intimate proximity.

Startled, she caught her breath. He had moved in close behind her. She felt his strong presence, heard his deep, tender voice. Her stomach flip-flopped. She didn't turn around. Her muscles tensed. She couldn't move. She tried to speak but squeaked instead. Mortified, she cleared her throat. She felt too vulnerable. *Any closer and he may...*

"I do." Moving away, she turned to face him. Assuming a condescending air, she answered his question.

"You care about the scribble stage?" He traced the hairline at her temple. She felt hot and short of breath.

"Indeed, I do. The scribble stage occurs at a specific time in a young child's development. It precedes the writing stage. Of course, there are sub-stages within the scribble stage." She nodded knowingly, dislodging his fingertips from her hairline. She stepped back.

"You don't say," he uttered, golden gaze sweeping her body head to toe.

Her breath shortened. "Sage and Tegan have entered the writing stage," she rambled on, hideously aware of her own discomfort.

"Really?" he observed. She heard the mockery in his voice. He was teasing her now. He was teasing her unmercifully. *I hate this man!*

"How do you know all this?" he mocked, standing his ground, eyes dancing.

"Because I earned a degree in child development from The University of Miami," she baited haughtily, edging away. "I—unlike some people I know—did not drop out of college to pursue a degenerate lifestyle of sex, drugs, and popular music. I studied hard. I worked hard. I found a real job."

His eyes narrowed. He contemplated her in silence for a moment. He attempted neither to restrain her, nor to draw her near. "So now you're a children's nanny, a servant who knows slightly more than how to make a mean P,B & J, or kiss away a boo-boo."

Outraged, she postured. "I can bandage a gash. It doesn't take three years of pre-med to know how to do that," she scoffed, clawing him away. She couldn't surrender to him. If she did, she would be forever lost to herself.

Kipp grinned now, but not happily. His copper eyes glinted as sunlight penetrated the branches.

"Are you surprised?" she queried.

"Sort of. I knew you were educated. I didn't know in what field." The earthy odor of damp permeated the air.

"Now you know."

"I know that you know about child development. I know you can fly an airplane, and bandage a wound, and bathe a baby. What I don't know is what else you are educated in, or not?"

Hands clenching at her sides, she chided him abruptly. "Don't take that tone with me!"

Moving toward her, he suddenly towered over her. "What tone?"

His scent overwhelmed her. His smirk infuriated her. She stomped her foot. "Treating me as though I'm a...a..."

"A what?" he teased.

"A whore!"

"A what?" He laughed out loud. Quickly, he placed a forefinger to his lips and lowered it. "Don't you mean a virgin?"

She gaped, dumbfounded. She couldn't tear her gaze from his parting lips.

"Well, aren't you?" Gently, his warm grasp encircled her upper arm.

"How dare you?" she peeped. Breaking free, she ran down the path leading into deep forest. She had to get away, far, far away...but he was following her.

"If you weren't still a virgin, you wouldn't be so angry," she heard his deep voice behind her. He limped, keeping pace. "Tell the truth. At least I'm not afraid to face the truth about myself. I don't hide my desire from the world. That's more than I can say for you, Nanny Northgate."

Her heart pounded with the rhythm of her running footsteps. Minutes later, along the darkening pathway, she stopped for breath. Every cell in her body quivered. In awe she shook her head.

How dare he? The cheek of him! Oh, how I despise him...

How dare he see through to the very core of her being? Collapsing onto a nearby coral boulder, she wept in despair—until she heard heavy footfall on the pathway behind her. *Has he followed me?*

Indeed, he had. Panting, sweating, the virile, menacing young lion emerged from behind a palm frond. His unbuttoned shirt flapped open, the golden hairs on his broad chest exposed. Sweat dripped down his body and seeped through his cotton clothes. He limped forward defiantly, steps crunching the sand. Latching onto her wrists, he dragged her into his arms.

She formed a semi-fist with one hand, but her will to resist subsided as Kipp's mouth found hers. His ardor made her weak. She slumped in his arms, face pressed to his breast.

She kissed his hot, wet flesh. For the briefest moment she let herself taste him. She tasted the strength of him. She tasted his need of her. She tasted his power—and his vulnerability.

"Kipp." She struggled between her desire for him and her fear. "Kipp," she nuzzled breathlessly, nearly catatonic. Ashamed, she pushed away, drooping like a spent fern, arms limp at her sides. His arms enveloped her, holding her fast. He kissed the crown of her head.

"What?" he asked tenderly. Taking her firmly by the shoulders and standing her upright, he cradled her chin in his hand. "If it weren't for the kid..."

She froze. "Shawnee! Where on earth is Shawnee?"

Instantly, the strong hands relinquished her. "Oh, crap! You left him in the clearing, didn't you?"

"*I* left him? Ooooh!" she muttered, struggling to her feet. *"Men!"*

She stormed back down the path. As she ran, Kipp pushed past her and sprinted, pain forgotten, quickly beyond her. Rays of sunlight pierced the dense growth through the trees.

"He's gone," she heard Kipp groan as she approached the clearing. Running smack into his back, she collected herself and scanned the empty clearing. Shawnee was nowhere to be seen.

"Where the hell is he?" growled Kipp.

"Kipp, look!" Joining her, he looked to where she pointed. Shawnee was lying sprawled on the ground at the edge of the lagoon. He had slid down the embankment. He wasn't moving.

"Shit!" Kipp cried, horrified. But he stopped in his tracks. Standing at the base of the tiny Greek theatre on the high side of the lagoon, stood Rob LaCroix, phone to his ear. From his perch, Rob couldn't see Shawnee, who lay behind an outgrowth of cypress trees. Across the lagoon, she heard Rob LaCroix's voice.

"Heston, Rob LaCroix on Heart of Fire Key. Sir, is someone visiting the Key this week? If yes, I was not informed. If no, you got squatters, sir. You got your hands full, this I know. But I must tell you. It's my job. Call me back, sir." Rob pocketed the phone, and moved away, down the back side of the hill. In seconds, they saw him walking on the shore, headed for the dock.

"Watch him," commanded Kipp. "I'm going for Shawnee."

Crouching under cover, she watched LaCroix stride up the shore, glancing several times over his shoulder. As the shore rounded, he disappeared from view.

Kipp appeared at her side. Shawnee was lying limply in his arms. "Kid's out cold. His leg twisted. It's sprained, I think, not broken. But he needs help."

She swallowed hard.

"Where's LaCroix?"

She turned. "There." She pointed to the far end of the dock. Rob was now aboard his hydroplane. In seconds, the engine fired, and the craft flew away across the waves like a jet.

"Come on," said Kipp. "We're taking Shawnee to the clinic."

No sooner had she lowered her bum onto the seat cushion of the *Ladybug,* than the speedboat roared away from the dock at Heart of Fire Key, leaving a churning, white wake and making for open sea. Kipp was at the helm. To her delight, Shawnee stirred on the seat cushions beside her. "Kipp, he's awake!" she cried amidst the din.

As the warm wind rushed around him, the injured child sobbed in pain. His curls tossed wildly. Clutching him, she grabbed onto the nearest railing and clung to both in desperation.

Astride at the helm, Kipp, unfazed, steered the boat into open water. Unable to keep her eyes off him, she swallowed back her fears. *I hope you know where you're going, Kipp Demming. Our lives are in your hands.*

Only then did the obvious occur to her. Marissa might believe she was Kipp's partner in crime. She might turn her over to authorities, too.

She contemplated Kipp's agile body. Maybe it was worth the risk. If she was going to prison, she wasn't going as a virgin. But would she ever be alone with him again?

It doesn't matter, fool. Nothing matters but Shawnee's survival.

Chapter Twenty-Three

At home in Naples, Tegan Demming was snooping again, despite her nanny's repeated warnings. The headstrong six-year-old had sneaked into her mother's walk-in closet. Once upon a time, she had sneaked into her mother's closet often, borrowing small things here and there. Not even her know-it-all twin, Sage, knew how often—until Berry had found her out.

Berry had caught her red-handed with a beaded evening bag. Furious, Berry had punished her and told her father. After that, she hadn't loved Berry as much.

"No pilfering!" Berry had scolded her. "Or else." She didn't know what "else" was and she hadn't wanted to find out. So she had stopped snooping.

"Now I know what happened to that mauve cap of Winner's," Berry had said, causing her cheeks to burn, even as she denied the theft. She had put all the other things in a safe place.

But now Berry was gone. Tegan was free to do as she liked. She loved to go through her mother's things. Boxes of beads, bangles, and bracelets made her heart flutter with excitement. Scarves, petticoats, and high-heeled shoes—what more could a girl ask for?

She knew all her mom's belongings by heart. So she was surprised to find a small locked box in the bottom drawer of the closet's built-in bureau. The box was hidden beneath a flouncy mound of yellow, green, and teal silk scarves, outdated and forgotten. Turning the box over in her hand, Sage wondered about the possible contents. Pursing her lips, she tried to force the gold clasp—and it sprang open. She gasped in surprise as the lid rose.

What had she expected to find? Certainly not this. She scowled, lifting out a raggedy cloth-covered book. Sitting back on her heels, she sighed in disgust.

She had hoped the mystery box would contain jewels—emeralds, rubies, sapphires, pearls. Instead, it was nothing more than old, yellowed pages with purple marks on them. Thumbing the dog-eared pages of the book, she could not make head or tails of it. She wasn't good at cursive writing. She couldn't read it. Sage might be able to, but not she. Sage loved to read and write.

Curious, she examined the first page. A name was printed on it. Here was a word she recognized! She knew it was a name because the second word was her own last name: Demming. And she had learned a few phonics. She sounded out the first name: L-Y-N-N- She recognized the whole name now. The book belonged to Lennox Demming, that bosomy old cat—their relative who had just been killed, the one who smelled like potpourri.

She flung the book from her hands. Terrified, she scooted away from the tome and hugged the wall. She was scared now. She was afraid of ghosts.

Why had Mommy hidden Lennox's book at the bottom of her closet? Why had she locked the box? She wished she had never entered the closet. From outside the door, a rap sounded. Tegan screamed. The noise ceased abruptly. The knob of the closet door rattled angrily.

"Who's in there?" barked the no-nonsense voice of Lissette Garcia.

Oh, popsicles! Huddled, quivering, Tegan remained silent.

"Tegan, is that you in there?" Lissette demanded. She rattled the door handle. "Open the door this minute."

"I can't!" Tegan cried out.

"Why not?"

"I'm scared!"

"That's ridiculous. Open the door at once."

Distracted, Tegan caught sight of an old photograph. It had fallen from between the leaves of the book and had fluttered to the closet floor. She picked up the old photo. She recognized the man in the picture. It looked like Daddy. But he seemed far too young. The girl looked like Lennox. But she, too, seemed too young.

Lissette's firm hand pounded the closet door. "Open this door at once, or I will call your father!"

"Daddy's not home. He's in Miami today," Tegan retorted, gathering the photo and the book. Quickly, she shoved them into the roomy pocket of her pink chenille robe and fastened the cord clasp. Rifling through the soft mound of scarves, she thrust the empty box beneath it, closing the drawer just as a key turned in the lock of the closet door.

"I would take you straight to your mother, but she's busy in the gym with her personal trainer," scolded Lissette, as she dragged her by the hand from the closet and into the master bedroom.

"I won't do it again, Lissy. I promise," she said, looking up into the round brown eyes of her housekeeper. Tegan batted her eyelashes. "I'm sorry. Truly, Lissy. I am."

"You deserve a good paddling, *nina,*" Lissette frowned.

Tegan wrapped her arms around Lissette's broad thighs and hugged her close. "Oh, please, Lissy. Don't tell. I won't do it again—ever. I promise."

Lissette clucked in consternation. "Well, I..."

"Oh, please." Tegan squeezed the plump thighs more tightly.

"All right, *nina.* But this is the last time. Do it again, and I'm telling. Do you hear me?"

"Yes. Yes, Lissy, I hear you. Thank you. Thank you ever so much." She hugged Lissette fast until the tidy woman pried her loose. "What's for dinner, Lissy?"

Lissette rolled her eyes. "Your father's favorite: creamy curried shrimp over saffron basmati rice. I made it special to cheer him up."

Tegan crinkled her nose. "Daddy's not home. Let's have hot fudge sundaes, instead."

"He'll be home later tonight. I'll save him a portion," she sighed. "Shrimp curry was your Berry's favorite, too. I hope she's all right, wherever she is." Instinctively, she made the sign of the cross.

"Well, I'm plucking out the cauliflower," Tegan exclaimed.

Lissette threw up her hands. "Your twin sister likes cauliflower."

Tegan frowned. "Sage likes a lot of things I don't. She likes to read. And to ride horseback. And she likes the colors green and yellow. I hate green and yellow. I want to wear hot pink!"

Lissette pulled affectionately on Tegan's auburn pigtails. "Teggi, your mother has explained to you, over and over, that redheads don't wear pink well."

"I do," she asserted hotly. "Mommy bought me this robe and pajama set—and a whole pink ski outfit last year. You remember?"

"Only because, in front of a shop full of sales clerks, you nagged her plenty good."

Tegan crossed her arms at her chest. "I don't care what other people think. I'll wear what I want to. Let go!" Abruptly, she jerked her pigtail from Lissette's fond grasp.

"Oye, what a child. How come I'm so crazy about you, hun?" Hands on hips, Lissette stared down at her.

"You have good taste," Tegan reflected earnestly, tossing her head haughtily.

"Silly goose that I am," Lissette shook her head knowingly, watching as Tegan bounced exuberantly out of the room. "I'm a fool for freckles and a turned-up nose and a brazen spirit. And I have been since the day you were born, *nina pelirroja loca."*

On impulse, Tegan spun around to face the housekeeper. "Lissy?" she enquired. "Do you believe in ghosts? Sage doesn't believe in ghosts, but I do."

Lissette pursed her lips and considered the question. "I believe that some poor souls can't rest in peace. If that's believing in ghosts, then, yes—I believe."

"Me, too!" Tegan cried, skipping down the hallway to her room, her small, pale, freckled hand clutching a bulging pocket at the far side of her pink robe. "I want a caramel sundae for dinner, Lissy!" She rounded the corner and ran.

"And I want a gold mine in South America." Lissette busied herself, straightening Poppy's closet. "Ain't gonna happen, *chiquita.*"

Chapter Twenty-Four

"So tell me, Ezzie. What happened that day?" Vivian shielded her pale blue eyes beneath a cute, little red and white-striped visor that matched her bikini. "I don't understand. How did things go so wrong between Heston and Kipp?"

"Which day, Vivi?" Worried, Ezra sat, upright, on the pool deck of Vivian's waterfront home on Mermaid's Bight. He contemplated the *Lady V,* a gleaming cabin cruiser, lying docked in docile Venetian Bay. The Venetian Villas, Italianate townhouses built over the bay waters, lay directly west of Vivian's outdoor pool deck, and beyond it, the row of sedate condominiums along Park Shore Beach. This scene of serenity, for which daily sunsets provided breathtaking backdrops, surely must be deceiving. What went on inside those hundreds of abodes?

"The day Heston and Kipp had their famous quarrel."

"Oh. That day. Thanksgiving Day—four years ago—at Heston's place in Port Royal."

"Yes." Vivian's skin seemed as white as a hospital pillowcase. He squeezed her hand. She squeezed his in return. "I'd like to know." She arched her brows, pleading. "It will take my mind off the surgery."

He knew she was nervous. Who wouldn't be? They were waiting to hear from her doctor. He would phone soon with the results of her recent medical tests. "Yeah. Okay, babe." His fear was worse than hers. They both needed a diversion.

Settling into a comfortable position, he drew a deep breath. He thought back to the day he had wrecked his own friendship with Kipp.

"It was a typical Thanksgiving Day, Demming style. Mom and I were seated at the table with the Demming family. My dad had died three months earlier. Heston had invited my mom because he knew the holidays would be tough for her. Me, too, I guess. She was shaky then, breaking down at odd moments. That day she seemed nervous.

"Heston carved the turkey. The table groaned with lo-cal vegetable dishes. Everyone was pigging out, kids included, except Winner, I noticed. She pushed her food around on her plate to make it look like she'd eaten.

"The conversation was light and airy, but hardly carefree. Everyone was tense, trying to ignore the fact that Kipp was loaded out of his mind, embarrassing everybody, making an ass of himself."

"Loaded? On what?" Vivian's interest was piqued.

"Probably everything. Prescription painkillers, pot, the works. He was a mess back then. This was before rehab, before jail. He was riding the crest of new success back then. *Demon Menace* was about to be released. He'd just become hot, commercially speaking. He was so out of it—and he didn't even realize it.

"Everyone else did. Poppy looked sick. The kids kept eyeing each other around the dining table. Kipp was oblivious. He was yammering about some nonsense. *Oh, that's right—surfing...*

***

"I've been in Costa Rica for a few months," Kipp said, between mouthfuls of mashed yams and marshmallows. He was s-o-o-o stoned. He had the appetite of an elephant. "Me and the boys recorded our second album in a private studio in Costa Rica. Some great tunes coming down. Release is next month."

Dakota asked him, "Where's Costa Rica? "The twins were babies then, but Dacks was old enough to—want to be included. Tegan's mouth was full, her cheeks puffed out like a chipmunk's filled with nuts. She giggled, covered her eyes. Sage was listening, so precocious.

Kipp said, "Central America," like the big, bloated expert.

"Will you show me on the globe?" Dakota asked him. He was poking his fingers in his stuffing. He was three or four then.

"You bet." Kipp's eyes were glittery and bloodshot.

Dakota jumped up, on his way to his father's study.

"After dinner," Beryl forced a smile. "Eat your stuffing. Don't play with it."

***

"The nanny was at table?" Vivian asked, pale blue eyes wide. "Children, too?"

"Sure," he said. "Berry's like one of the family. She has the world's greatest nanny job. They pay her a mint. Can't do without her. Kids adore her."

"Wow."

"She has free run of everything—even Heston's boats and planes."

"Not my style, but they are *noveau riche.*"

Her comment took him aback, but only for a moment. It was who she was. She couldn't help it. In fact, her privileged attitude was part of the prize package he coveted. He kissed the back of her privileged hand and continued.

***

So Kipp applauded. "Good girl! Yeah, I was there for about seven months. My buddies and I stayed about 20 minutes from the beach—on the way are waterfalls, rivers, mountains. There's a place called Jaco— spelled with a 'J' but pronounced like an 'H.' Jaco has one of the biggest surfing conferences in the world—in July. The waves are so big, they break the boards."

"Boards?" asked freckle-nosed Dakota. He was in awe.

"Yeah, man, the surfboards. People come from all over the world come."

Lissette approached, and I dropped more green beans onto my plate. I was all set, until...

Ma asked Kipp, "Is that where you and Lennox got engaged? Isn't Lennox from Costa Rica? Her folks are dead, but she told me she liked it there. She bought a place on the Pacific Coast last year."

***

"Your mom dropped the bomb?" Vivian asked, clutching his hand tightly.

"Basically." He nodded. "Heston's reaction was bizarre."

***

Heston dropped his fork—it clanged onto the china, chipping the dinner plate's rim. He glared at me, then Kipp, then back at me, then back at Kipp.

Kipp scowled at me, bloodshot eyes all glittery. "Nice work, Ezra." He nodded toward Mom.

"Kipp, I only mentioned..."

Alarmed, Poppy, such a pretty little hostess, sat back and scanned the faces around her dinner table. She goes, "Heston?" He ignored her.

"What's wrong, Daddy? Are you okay?" Winner was seven or eight—stunning even then, so beautiful and blossoming, I could hardly

keep my eyes off her. She placed her hand on Heston's forearm, but he shrugged her off.

"He pounced on his eldest son like a rabid fox. "You got engaged to Lennox?" he said to Kipp. Then his crazy eyes found me. "Do you mean Lennox Cordova? What do you mean engaged?"

"It usually means to be married," Ma told him.

"Heston." Poppy half-rose.

"Sit down," he told her. She sat back down and kept silent.

"I didn't mean to..." I said, stumbling over my own lie. "I—I—"

Kipp put down his fork and stared squarely at his father. "Screw it, Ezra," he said to me. "The cat's out of the bag. Daddy Dearest here had to learn about it sometime. Ain't it a gas?" He started singing—you know that one song of his—'Life is short. Party naked...' "

Ma cried out, "Kipp, forgive me. I wasn't thinking!" She covered her mouth with both hands, as if to say she'd been a bad girl.

"About what?" asked Winner.

"What's the big deal?" asked Dakota. He was puny—stabbing a slice of gravy-drenched turkey. Elbow propped on the table, he was on Kipp's side, resting his head on his hand.

"Hush, Dakota," Poppy said, real soft. "Sit up straight."

Heston and Kipp locked eyes in a staring battle. Heston jumped up. He threw his napkin down on his broken plate. "Kipp, I'd like to see you in my study."

"Here we go!" said Kipp, also rising.

"Heston, don't!" my mom said suddenly. I started to rise, but she caught me by the coattail and yanked me back down. "Stay out of it," she whispered in my ear. "The damage is done. It had to be done, and I did it."

"What are you talking about?" I whispered into her ear. "Yes, Kipp swore me to secrecy, but I only told you..."

172

With a quick flap of her hand, she shushed me. She was listening. The argument between Heston and Kipp was escalating. She leaned close to me, said, 'Take Heston's side. He wants you to direct his new picture.' I was astounded.

"You have no right to object to our marriage!" Kipp yelled at Heston. "There was no romance between you and Lennox! She told me so. I don't have to ask your permission for a damned thing! She was your on-screen paramour. So what? That shit is just acting."

"Then why were you hiding it, Kipp?" Beryl asks him, all innocence.

Heston orders, "Beryl, be silent," He points a rigid forefinger at the floor. "Come into my study, boy!"

"I won't!" shouted Kipp, stoned and losing control. "I'm not the help. You can't order me around!" He turned to Nanny Beryl. "I was hiding it because I had a bad feeling. I knew this old man was going to overreact." He turned back to Heston. "Because of the age difference! Lennox told me he would. She was right. She's a very intelligent woman."

"Oh, for the love of...!" Heston cried. "You can't be serious."

"Poppy, we should take the children out of here." Beryl slid her chair away from the table and stood up and said, "Come on, I'll help you.."

"Yes, all right, Berry. Into the kitchen, everybody. Bring your plates." Rising, Poppy waved Sage and Tegan into the kitchen. Beryl grabbed Dakota by the arm, dragging him, kicking and flailing, into the kitchen as well.

"Go with her, Dakota," I said, grabbing the kid's scrawny arm. "You too, Winner."

"Win goes, "But, Ezra, they're about to—" She points at the two enraged men. They were confronting each other—alongside the dining table"

"Go on, Win," I said. I lifted her from the chair and patted her back-side. "Scoot." The Demmings' plump brown bean of a housekeeper is Lissette, a real gem. Lissette scuttled in and ushered the young girl out.

"Winner!" Poppy beckoned her from the kitchen doorway. Winner complied, but she kept glancing backwards, as Lissette dragged her off, in case she should miss any of the action between her father and half-brother.

The kitchen door swung shut. Mom and I were suddenly alone now with Heston and Kipp, who had begun circling one another like tense dogs in a fight for dominance.

"You will NOT marry Lennox Cordova," Heston growled from his gut.

"Too late, Big Daddy." Kipp freaked us all out then. He climbed up on the dining table and caught hold of the chandelier. Hanging by his arms, he was swinging to and fro, balanced by the balls of his feet on the tabletop. He was beginning the war dance.

Heston sucked air. "What do you mean, too late?"

Kipp leered. He dropped to the floor. "It's a done deal." He drew a gold band from his pocket, and he slid it onto the ring finger of his left hand and wiggled his fingers. "Congratulate me, Heston. Lennox and I were married two weeks ago in Paris." Suddenly, he let loose, hopping back onto the table and grabbing the chandelier.

I was staggered by his comments, his behavior. So was Ma. Even we didn't know that Kipp and Lennox had already tied the knot. I did know Lennox was taping a reality show in Paris that week. I also knew she wasn't an American and didn't celebrate Thanksgiving. These kind of disjointed thoughts were running through my mind. I had wondered why Lennox wasn't here today—when Kipp was.

"Mom whispers, "Oh, Kipp, no!" She starts to wobble. She grabbed the back of a chair. I helped her sit down.

*"Heston was breathing low and hard. He said, "Boy, you're a fool."
He was barely audible. He grabbed for Kipp's ankles.*

*"Well, hell, I had to marry her, Daddi-O. Not that she held a shot-
gun on me or anything. But, hey—the baby's mine. And I love Lennie to
pieces."*

*Even I gaped, now. Ma was speechless, a rare event. I thought I
heard her making a weird, moaning sound, but I paid no attention. I
didn't have time.*

*"Idiot!" cried Heston, latching onto his son. "Don't you know why
she married you? Can't you guess?" With a terrific jerk, he brought
Kipp crashing down onto the dining table.*

*Kipp lay on his back. He was covered in sweet potatoes. "What,
you? You think it's about you, Heston? Damn it! Your ego is like a black
hole. It sucks in and destroys everything around it. Lennox married me
because she loves me, and our love has nothing to do with you or your
frigging ego. Got that? Do you have that? Do I make myself clear?"*

*Suddenly, he rolled off the table and onto his feet. Father and son
circled one another like rabid feral beasts. Kipp was bopping he was so
excited.*

*I burst to the kitchen. "Poppy, is there security around? Call them.
Do you have any guards in house?"*

She was on her mobile in a flash. I ran back into the dining room.

*"You naïve infant," Heston snarled. "Lennox is not just too old for
you. She's too worldly for you."*

"Keep pumping, old man!"

"She's an expert gamesman. You have no idea what you're in for."

"Fourteen years isn't that much of a difference."

"Is that what she told you? To trap you into marriage?"

"She didn't trap me."

"You bloody sot! You're so drugged up, you've lost all good sense. You were putty in her hands."

"If I didn't know better, I'd think you were hot for Lennox yourself!"

The dining room crackled with electricity. My mother swooned. At the same time, the two men lunged at one another. As they collided, three security officers thundered into the dining room like buffaloes with a purpose. Between the four of us, we pulled father and son apart. We all did the best we could to restrain the pair. They were still enraged.

The security guards, who had abandoned their vehicle at the gate, were followed by two neighbor ladies who had been out walking their breed dogs on Galleon Drive. In the commotion, nobody noticed that one of them was taking pictures—and sending them off—with her phone. Their shitsus were yapping. Hearing the hullabaloo, the kids came rushing in from the kitchen.

Running in behind them, Poppy went to my mother. She was patting her hand and held a glass of water to her lips. My mother fanned her away, then drew her back and drank the water. I watched this scene out of the corner of my eye—while I was securing Kipp's knees in a choke-hold. Kipp and Heston were both bleeding and bruised and panting.

I looked up at Kipp. "I'm sorry, man," I said sincerely. "This was all my fault."

Kipp nodded, head lolling. "Yes, it was. You broke faith with me, man. I will never trust you again, as long as I live. Our party is over, Ezzie."

Heston snarled, straining to free himself from his captors. "Ezra, you knew about this and didn't tell me?" It was then I realized my career hung in the balance. I had to choose a side. I chose Heston's."

***

Vivian squeezed his hands. She was holding both now.

"It was only later that I realized my mother had spilled the beans on purpose. She was trying to warn Heston and protect Kipp. If she'd known Kipp and Lennox were already hitched, she never would have said a word that day. She told me so later."

"I wonder," mused Vivian. She sat up suddenly as the phone rang. "Ezra, it's time," she said, embracing him gently. She whispered in his ear. "I love you so much, Ezra."

Preparing himself for the worst, Ezra answered Vivian's phone.

Chapter Twenty-Five

Kipp recognized Marissa instantly as he entered the clinic on Big Pine Key. She greeted him at the doorway of the small, remote free clinic. What caught him off guard was...

"Hello, I'm Dr. Marissa," said the beautiful expectant mother in the white lab coat. "Please put your child down here." Kipp did as she asked. Beryl lingered behind, shadowed by the door frame, her blue eyes never leaving Shawnee.

Quickly, a short, gray-haired, middle-aged man in a white lab coat took charge of the small, meager but clean examination room. He appeared to be Latino. "What happened?" he asked, taking Shawnee's vital signs.

Kipp removed his dark glasses. "He fell. Hit his head. Sprained his ankle. Lost consciousness." At the sound of his voice, Marissa turned to gape at him.

"Aloha, Marissa," he said quietly.

"Aloha, Kipp," she whispered.

Sunglasses in hand, he indicated her swollen abdomen. "Congratulations," he said, heart sinking. He was too late. He had lost her to someone else. Shyly, he studied her. She had matured into a lovely woman. Her long hair was tied back in a loose ponytail. A plain, gold wedding band adorned her left hand.

"How long was he unconscious?" the male doctor asked.

"Maybe 20 minutes."

Marissa stepped toward him, waving her hand. "Kipp, this is my new husband, Dr. Perfecto Logue. Perfecto, this is Kipp Demming and...?" She indicated Beryl, who was hanging back, still lodged in the open doorway.

"This is my friend, Beryl." He avoided Beryl's eyes.

"Hello, Beryl. Haven't we met?"

"Hello. Will Shawnee be all right?"

Hovering over the examination table, Perfecto spoke up. "The leg is sprained. He has some abrasions. I'd like you to leave him overnight. We'll watch him."

"Overnight?" said Beryl, eyes flying to him.

"That's impossible," Kipp said to Marissa, whose eyes had never left him.

Slowly she turned to her husband; she placed a gentle hand on his bicep. "Perfecto, Kipp is my old friend—the one I told you about yesterday."

Perfecto snapped to attention. "The fugitive?" he demanded.

"Yes." Kipp nodded.

Perfecto scrutinized him. "They say you murdered your wife and son." He looked down at Shawnee and then back at Kipp. "This is your son. You did not murder him. You kidnapped him—and beat him, perhaps?"

"No! He rescued him," asserted Beryl, stepping into the room and standing beside him. "Shawnee fell. It was an accident—my fault. I'm a nanny. I was negligent. You can't blame Kipp. He loves the boy. He's saved his life twice now—once when he removed him from a crime scene, and once not an hour ago on the island. He risked his own safety to bring him here."

"What island?" asked Marissa intently.

"Quiet," he said to Beryl, who had been about to divulge their hide-away. He turned to Marissa. "I found Lennox dead on the floor. I took Shawnee to safety." He walked past her and watched Perfecto wrapping the child's sprain. "Or so I thought."

"Why are you limping?" Marissa asked, turning to face him.

Beryl spoke up. "He stepped on a fish hook."

"You'll need a tetanus shot," said Perfecto. Absorbed in his task. "Unless you've had one recently."

Kipp shook his head. "Not since freshman year at Vandy." He smiled at Marissa. "Remember?"

She laughed lightly. "Yes." She moved to the wall cabinets. "I'll do it," she said, preparing for the injection.

"So you are the big rock and roller?" said Perfecto, finishing his work and brushing Shawnee's curls affectionately.

"I was. I admire the hell out of your clinic."

"Roll up your sleeve," said Marissa, brandishing a hypodermic needle. She swabbed his upper arm with alcohol. He steeled himself. She inserted the needle. He didn't flinch.

"There," said Marissa, removing and disposing of the empty syringe. "No lockjaw in your future."

"Thanks, Rissa."

Dr. Perfecto Logue stood holding Shawnee, who was sucking a cherry lollipop. "You understand, Kipp. Even if you are innocent—of which I am not certain—we must contact the police."

"Perfecto, I told you when we heard the news reports yesterday—Kipp is no killer. He is a healer. In all the years we dated, he never raised a hand to me. He would have made a wonderful heart surgeon." Marissa's eyes flooded, but the flood receded. "When he was a boy—I saw him treat and nurture animals and birds back to health."

Perfecto looked skeptical. "Men change, Marissa. Life changes them."

"I tell you, Perfecto. Kipp did not kill his ex-wife. I don't believe it."

Beryl intervened. "Your wife is right, Dr. Logue. It's all a big mistake."

"Were you a witness?"

"No, but..." Beryl sighed, exasperated. "I know Kipp, too. Not as well as you, Marissa, but well enough to believe him if he says he didn't do it. He loves Shawnee. He dotes on his son. He took him from the scene to protect him. He believed Shawnee was in danger. He brought him to me and asked me to protect the child. Kipp was going to take his own life, not his son's."

All eyes found him. "Is this true, Kipp?" asked Marissa, concerned.

"It was a weird coincidence," he muttered, ashamed.

Perfecto pursed his lips, considering the circumstances. "There are no coincidences," he said. He indicated with a nod. "Is that why you have a gun in your pocket?"

"Yes. No. I—forced Beryl at gunpoint. She's not involved in this."

Perfecto looked from Kipp to Beryl to Shawnee. "You want to go to your Popi?" he asked Shawnee.

"Dada" Shawnee gurgled, opening his arms to Kipp, cherry lollipop waving happily.

"Take your son, Kipp," Perfecto said, handing the boy over. The sticky lollipop found its way to Kipp's beard. "I'll rescind my own orders. You can watch him. If there is any change, bring him back."

"We don't need to stay overnight?" Beryl asked, relief in her voice.

"No," said Perfecto. "Kipp will tend him. But you should stay to lunch. Eh, Marissa? I have never before dined with a rock star."

She looked at her husband. She turned to Beryl. "Yes, please do. We have a small cottage just up the beach."

Then Marissa frowned. "Please understand. We could both lose our medical licenses for aiding a fugitive." She glanced at her husband. "I'm willing to take the risk—to save you, Kipp—but I'm not willing to involve my husband. His work here is too important."

Loosening his stance, Perfecto moved to his wife's side, sliding an arm around her shoulders. "The decision is not yours to make, Marissa.

It's mine." He turned to Beryl. "You truly believe in your man's innocence?"

"My man?" Beryl nodded, blushing. "With all my heart. He needs a chance to prove it. Right now, he's sick with guilt and worry. He needs your help. Please, help us now. The rest can be worked out in time."

"All right." Perfecto went to the sink and scrubbed his hands. "But here's my deal—48 hours and no more. If, after 48 hours, Kipp has not turned himself in to the authorities—I will do it for him."

"Deal," he said. *By that time, I'll be out of everybody's hair.*

Chapter Twenty-Six

Mid-afternoon, on the following day, Heston found himself standing on the shady balcony of Lennox's penthouse in South Beach. He'd driven all morning, straight into the glare of sunrise, to get here when Townsend requested. He stared east at the churning gray Atlantic Ocean. Strong, warm gusts ruffled his hair.

From his perch, he could see the shore of South Beach, 10 stories below. A growing crowd was gathering in the sand as fans arrived to pay reverent homage to the memory of his eldest son. A figure in the distance was talking to a camera. Obviously, she was a reporter, probably that cute girl Cecily Hodges, who followed Kipp's career. She'd been reporting the story on television for two solid days now. He marveled at the throng surrounding her.

Did they believe Kipp to be dead, drowned in the deep two nights ago, having walked into the ocean, with Shawnee in his arms, from that very spot and taken his own life and the boy's? Or were they holding a vigil—for a safe return? What compelled them to this?

A blossoming mound of flowers, mementoes, and photos of Kipp, Lennox, and Shawnee grew as each new arrival offered a token of esteem. Could he be witnessing the birth of a media legend? Was Kipp the latest 27-year-old rock-music icon to become immortalized by tragic death? That the revered idol was his own son was remarkable. He couldn't take it in.

This can't be real.

"Thanks for ID-ing the body and for facilitating the autopsy," offered Townsend, who stood beside him, adjusting his tie and sucking smoke from a cigarette. "Thanks for making the drive from Naples. As you can see, your son is popular."

"Even when they think he murdered his wife and child?"

Townsend shrugged diplomatically. "Fame covers a lot of sins."

"I hope it will cover mine." *What will happen when I kick the bucket?*

"It might. You deities can get away with stuff we mere mortals only dream about."

Cloaked by dark shadow, Heston turned to the special agent. In contrast, the G-man stood ablaze against the backdrop of shimmering sea. Stark light poured over him as the sun descended slowly behind the building, in the western sky.

"Thank you for allowing me to see the crime scene," he replied.

"I hope I'm not speaking out of turn," Townsend commented. "But I know what it's like to lose a son. I lost one myself. Last year—in Iraq."

Startled, Heston glanced at him quickly and again stared down at Kipp's impromptu memorial. "A tremendous sacrifice," he mumbled selfconsciously. Morosely, he turned and shuffled inside, into the great room, his conceit diminished, his outlook anxious.

"Not officially a crime yet," said Betancourt, sitting inside on a barstool and sucking on spearmint. "Cooler in here," he commented, as Heston's eyes adjusted to interior light.

"Where's Cade?" he asked Betancourt, glancing at his Rolex.

"Late." Betancourt clinked wine glasses together, improving a tune.

"You said he was at sea."

"He was. His yacht, the *Angel Baby,* docked in Port Everglades for refueling—two days ago. He flew down here on his own private chopper—at my request."

Following Heston inside, Townsend moved close and spoke in his ear. "Heston, I have an ulterior motive for inviting you here today. There is something I need to show you later—after the others have gone."

Not yet numbed, he nodded, watching as Townsend returned, trailed by pungent wisps of gray smoke, to the balcony to finish his cigarette. Still sickened by the bleak sight of Lennox's gruesome, pathetic body, with its surgical scars and distended breasts, he waited just inside the open sliding glass doors, on the very spot where it had been found by the maid 36 hours earlier. He pressed the butt of his hand to his forehead and shut his eyes.

Oh, honey, how horrible for you.

He opened them and faced it. A taped outline of the slight yet voluptuous figure was visible at his feet. The fleeting image of her cold, hard corpse lying on an icy slab in the morgue pierced his mind's defenses. He wanted to vomit. He had vowed never to revisit the memory willingly. He fortified his intestines and resumed the mask.

"Everything in the apartment is just as she left it?" he asked dubiously. His drive to Miami at 6 a.m. had left him groggy and dispirited. From here they would be going to the beach, a short walk away, across Ocean Drive. He had promised Poppy he would investigate the site where Kipp's effects had been found, the spot from which it was believed their son may have walked into the sea, babe in arms.

Betancourt nodded and blew a smoke cloud from his nose. He was squinting in the afternoon sunlight. "An officer has been on duty at the scene, round the clock. Your party is the first to enter, other than law enforcement officials. Now that the crime unit has completed its work, it's no big deal."

Seated on the sofa were his companions, Ezra Gold and Ezra's mother, Arlene Gold. Arlene, his longtime New York theatrical agent had flown down yesterday at the first sign of trouble. He felt gratitude. She had been his rock over the years. He needed her no-nonsense point of view now, more than ever before. Her son Ezra was along for the ride, even though it was he who drove her in the Mercedes.

"Who owns this condo, Townsend?" Heston asked. The answer was deferred, as the elevator door opened and an arthritic knuckle thumped on the adjacent wall.

"May I come in?" the old man asked pleasantly.

Leaving his cigarette stub in an outdoor ashtray, Townsend entered the great room and ambled to the front door. "Come in. Mr. Cade, I presume. We've been waiting for you."

"Thank you, young man," said Gabriel Cade. The oldster was stoop-shouldered, but not yet immobile. He walked not with a cane, but with a long, black umbrella, which doubled as a cane. His suit was Saville Row. His thick salt and pepper hair was arranged in steely, pomaded waves in a spiral do around his bald spot.

"Greetings, Heston," he said, smiling diplomatically. He assessed the others. "Arlene, nice to see you." He looked quizzically at Ezra.

Ezra rose to his feet and held out his hand, which Cade pumped. "I'm Ezra Gold, Arlene's son. We've met. I was a friend of Kipp's at one time."

Cade's eyes grew shady. "Ah, yes. I remember you. The *Wunderkind* director. How's business now that you're all grown up? Heard you took some hard knocks at the box office."

"I have some irons in the fire." Ezra glanced at Heston. Heston watched Gabe Cade like a creature of prey, poised to make its kill.

"My son is an artist," Arlene asserted proudly. "He need not justify himself to you."

"Spoken like a true mother," Gade nodded approvingly.

"Don't think I don't remember you, old man," snapped Arlene, rising. Her sophisticated garb and rail-thin figure belied her 60-plus years. A diamond watch band glittered on her wrist. "You're the vermin who stole Kipp Demming away from my agency. You promised him the moon, and then destroyed him financially. You stole him blind..."

"Classy trimmings but the soul of a street fighter," Gabe Cade observed, taking umbrage. "Madam, I assure you—"

"Save it, you old goat. I know who you are, and I know what you did to that naïve boy."

"I made that boy into the greatest music icon of his generation. Am I to be blamed for giving him immortality—now that he's dead?"

On her feet, Arlene lunged. "You are to be blamed for setting him up and bleeding him dry. You are to be blamed for working him to death, stripping him of every cent, and then encouraging him to do himself in with drugs, while you lived it up in the lap of luxury, you old shmuck. Bah!" She whipped her hands in the air.

"Ma, relax." Ezra gently clasped his hand around her forearm. "Please."

"I did no such thing." Cade stared her down ingenuously. "Certainly, I understand that his defection from your firm caused you great financial loss. That, however, is the wages of business, and business, as we all know, is war—to quote a very successful entrepreneur. I have no regrets. Kipp's choice to end his life was his own."

Ezra bridled. "And what about Lennox? And Shawnee?" His mother shook her arm free. "What about their choices?"

Cade's mouth twisted in irony. "What about them? Regrettable, but not my doing. Their fate, too, was in Kipp's hands. He made his own choices."

"Choices you pushed him into," Ezra said raggedly.

"I am not responsible—legally or morally—for Kipp's decision to murder his wife and child."

"That's strictly surmise, Cade," corrected Townsend. "The m-word hasn't been used."

"I surmise nothing, sir. Everyone knows Kipp had a troubled history. In high school on Oahu, he was a handsome star athlete prone to impulsive violence. In college, he became a spoiled hot-head with a chip on his shoulder."

"What chip?" asked Heston.

Ezra added, "Kipp wasn't violent, just *mashugennah*." He tapped his temple.

"He learned he'd been an orphan—your offspring, not that of the Navy man he'd called 'Dad.' "

"It didn't make him a hot-head."

Gabe scoffed and turned to Townsend. "Kipp beat his own father in front of witnesses."

"That was *after* you'd hooked him on drugs, Cade," snorted Ezra. "I was there."

Cade postured nobly. "Special Agent Townsend, I *heard* Kipp Demming make death threats against poor Lennox, on more than one occasion."

"You lie," spat Arlene. "Now that he's not here to defend himself."

Ezra shouted. "Cade, if he did, it's because you destroyed his sense of decency. You encouraged him to sell out. He was a pure soul until you corrupted him. He wanted to practice medicine, not ball the hordes of strung-out groupies you funneled backstage."

Gabe Cade chuckled. "Kipp wanted to be a star. He became *The* Star. Don't believe me? This morning, sales of Demonsong's latest album is now outselling today's second, third, and fourth most popular albums combined. Kipp is a bigger star in death than in life. Ten years from now, he'll be bigger still, in twenty years, even bigger. Wherever he is— hell or heaven—I'm certain he feels vindicated in his course of action. Face it, Mrs. Gold. Could you ever have done as much for Kipp as I did?"

"Ma! No!" Ezra grabbed his mother before she could strike the old man.

"And you just happen to own his Life Rights!" Arlene struggled, fist balled. "I ask you, Agent Townsend. Who had a better motive for doing away with Kipp Demming and his family than this *schmuck?*"

Townsend interceded. "Where do you really think he is, Cade?"

"Why, at the bottom of the Atlantic, of course. I heard this morning that his mobile phone had been found on the ocean floor, about a few feet off shore. Sooner or later, his remains will surface. I have no doubt of it. Our Kipp is swimming with the fishes."

"Do you give a damn?" Disgusted by the image, Heston hissed through bared teeth. "How much was your life insurance policy on him?"

Gabe's brown eyes glowered beneath bushy gray eyebrows. "Of course I give a damn. I loved that boy. He was like a son to me—once you disowned him. I gave him everything I had."

"You mean you took everything he had, you old bloodsucker! I'm sorry, Townsend. I can't be in the same room with this foul beast. If you need me, I'm going to the Four Seasons on Brickell." Arlene handed Townsend a business card. "I'll be happy to answer any questions, but I'm not soiling myself any longer in the presence of this charlatan."

Townsend rose. "Very well, Mrs. Gold. Thank you for coming today. I'll be in touch." Nimbly, he guided the agitated celebrity agent to the elevator door of the penthouse. "We may have further inquiries about Lennox Cordova's business dealings."

"So call me. I'll talk."

"Your mother doesn't like me very much," Gabe said confidentially to Ezra.

"Who does?" replied Ezra, following his mother and Betancourt to the elevator.

"I'll meet you in the lobby," Arlene said to her son. "I can't breathe up here."

He kissed her powdery cheek. "All right, Ma. Take it easy. I'll be down in a minute."

As the elevator door closed on Arlene, Ezra, and Betancourt, Townsend turned to face the three men who remained in the penthouse.

"So what's the real beef?" Townsend asked Cade. "Why is she still so angry at you?"

"Perhaps you should ask Mrs. Gold," replied Cade smoothly.

"I have a hunch, Townsend," Heston chimed in. "Arlene hinted as much. A couple of months ago. Cade here lured Lennox herself away from The Gold Group."

"You stole a second client?" Townsend confronted Cade head on. "Of many years standing? Tsk, tsk." He shook a forefinger in Cade's face. "That explains a lot."

"A nasty rumor, I assure you, sir." Gabe Cade grinned. "No papers were signed."

"No fair using that old hedge," Heston taunted the codger. At his side, Ezra listened intently, hands in his pockets, eyes alert and watching.

"You had a gentlemen's agreement with the lady?" Townsend posed.

"Iron-clad," Cade conceded affably.

"So it's conceivable that you were acting as Cordova's agent?"

"Conceivable, yes. True, yes." Cade postured regret and shook his grizzled head.

"Why were you so eager to come here today, Mr. Cade?" Townsend asked.

"Well, you see, I was hoping to find something—something I was promised by Lennox herself—contractually."

"And what would that be, Gabe?" Heston taunted, incredulous. The coot had gall. He'd made his way on it.

"Must I answer, Mr. Townsend?" Cade asked disingenuously.

"Might as well. If you don't, I'll have to subpoena you to testify about it."

"Out with it," Heston insisted, moving up next to the dapper old marketer.

"Well, it was a manuscript, of sorts."

"A manuscript?" Townsend parroted.

Recovering himself, Heston asked nonchalantly. "What type of manuscript?"

The corners of Cade's mouth twitched in merriment. "More along the lines of an...autobiography. To be precise, a diary."

"Whose?" Betancourt asked quietly.

"Why, Lennox's mother's. Lynne Cordova had written down her life story. Lennox gave me the sole rights to her book." Cade snickered happily.

"What about her book?" Townsend asked.

Heston barely breathed.

"Yes. I was acting as her literary agent."

Townsend butted in. "I thought you said..."

"I was not acting as her theatrical agent. That is Mr. Gold's job and always has been. I had negotiated a huge book deal for Lennox—as her literary agent. I obtained an advance—for her alone—of a million dollars plus from a major publishing house. I had absolutely no interest in her film career. It was *kaput.*"

"Had you read this *manuscript?*" Townsend fired quickly, moustache bristling.

"No," Cade replied. He ogled Heston. "But I know what was in it."

"What was in it?" Townsend demanded patiently, fists balled in his pockets.

"Everything," smiled Cade meaningfully. "Simply everything. The whole sordid story of her daughter Lennox's girlhood deflowering, the

unrequited love of her life, her rise to fame to gratify this man's ego."
Tilting his head, he cast a sidelong glance Heston's way. "All the juicy
details about her other lovers, too—male and female—along the way."

"Which lovers?" Townsend demanded. "Who?"

"Oh, I daren't name names," balked Cade sleazily. "Not prior to pub-
lication. Buy the book."

"Name names here, or name them on the stand. The choice is yours."

Amused, Gabe Cade eyed Heston coyly. "I'll see you in the witness
box, Mr. Townsend," he grinned. Tottering toward the elevator, his
umbrella supporting his steps like a cane, Cade stopped to ask one more
question. "Am I to assume the police have found no such diary among
Lennox's belongings?"

Townsend stonewalled. "No book here. If it's on her computer
somewhere, we'll find it."

Cade hacked a laugh. "You won't find the diary on any computer,
Townsend. Lynne Cordova died before computers became common-
place. Her daughter was barely literate. The idiot girl read children's
books. But little ole Lynne was a business mind *par excellence.* Her
journal was no child's diary, all frivolous pining and misspelled words.
Lynne's was a tawdry tale, and she bore all. Best of luck to you in your
hunt, I might add. Just remember, I own the rights to everything that's in
the diary—tearstain splotches and all."

Townsend looked askance. "I thought you said Lennox hadn't signed
any papers."

The elevator door opened slowly. The old man stepped inside. "We
didn't—about acting. She did, however, sign a binding contract giving
me exclusive life rights to her story. You see, gentlemen, I now OWN
the life story of Lennox Cordova—and Kipp Demming's, by the way. I
can publish it without her—what I know of it. She and I had become
very good friends of late."

"You and Lennox hung out?" Ezra gawked in disbelief. "No offense."

Gabe Cade sucked his teeth. He contemplated Ezra. "Miss Lennox and I were social acquaintances long before we became business partners. A charming woman. Not so lovely as in her prime." His gaze flew like a knife. "Don't you agree, Heston? You knew her then, quite well, did you not? Intimately, no doubt?"

"We made five pictures together," Heston whispered vehemently.

Ezra cocked his head of thick brown hair. "You're a debonair old dude, Gabe. Maybe—with the right pitch—you could have scored with Lennox. It's hard to tell about women—what they go for." Ezra scrutinized the old man solemnly. "You're loaded. That can work wonders."

"Thank you, Mr. Gold," Gabe Cade said charmingly, with a genteel thrust of his umbrella cane. "Good afternoon, Heston!" Cade guffawed, despite a congested cough, as he pointed his umbrella at the elevator buttons.

Townsend bolted forward. "One more question, Cade. Do you own this penthouse?"

"Au contraire." He pushed a button. "I can't wait to find out who does. It will make an exciting final chapter. As will the cause of Lennox's death—if it's murder."

Unconsciously, Townsend rose up and down on the balls of his feet. "We know this place is owned by a corporation. Who comprises that corporation—that's what our people are looking into."

Gabe Cade cackled. "Best of luck to your people. But I guarantee. You won't find my name on any list of corporate officers or stockholders. Lennox was my lunch-table companion. I didn't pay her rent. Little Miss Chantal DuBois is my current paramour." The elevator door closed and the elevator began its descent to the condo lobby.

"What do you make of that?" said Townsend snidely, resuming a flatfoot stance. Disturbed, he turned to Heston.

"Cade's as slippery as seaweed," Heston murmured.

The three men were now alone in the great room. The ghost of Lennox Cordova hovered heavily in the highly charged atmosphere.

"Is Cade implying what I think he's implying?" Ezra asked Heston, unabashed.

"I plead the Fifth," mumbled Heston, glancing at Townsend. He felt as if the world had stopped revolving suddenly and was now about to toss him into space.

"Guess I'll be seeing you on the stand, too, Demming," Townsend glowered.

So he has seen my image on the condo's security footage.

Admitting nothing, he eyed his surroundings. "If you were a light-weight former femme fatale, Townsend, where would you hide your mother's memoirs?"

"Under the mattress?" Ezra smirked, striding to the elevator as it returned to the penthouse floor. "That's probably where they belonged."

"Too bad they didn't stay there," Heston whispered, appalled by his new dilemma.

"They never do," observed Townsend assiduously. " 'Never write down anything you'd be ashamed to see printed on the front page of the New York Times.' That's what Pop used to tell us kids. Change that to the Internet, and it still makes good sense."

"I suppose so. Seeing as how I've led a totally crass life, I can't speak to it." As he turned to join Ezra in the elevator, Townsend blocked his path.

"Go on ahead, Mr. Gold. I have unfinished business with Heston."

"Now there's a cryptic comment if I've ever heard one," said Ezra, pushing the elevator button for the ground floor. The door closed, and the elevator descended.

"We're alone now, Townsend. What gives?" he inquired cautiously.

"There's something else you need to see."

Nausea flooded him like seawater in a damaged wheelhouse. "What is it?" he asked quietly. But he knew instinctively. He could feel what was coming next.

Chapter Twenty-Seven

"So, where is it, Townsend—this thing you want me to see?" Reluctantly, Heston followed the big man through the great room of Lennox's penthouse and down the hall.

Stopping, Townsend turned. "Hold it. We know you visited Lennox on the day of her death. Why?"

Startled, Heston stopped abruptly. "She phoned me. Asked me to come over."

"Why?"

"I don't know. By the time I arrived, she had changed her mind."

Townsend sighed in mock disgust. "Heston, come on. Was it about the diary?"

"Could have been."

"Sheesh." Townsend turned around and proceeded down the hall.

Following, Heston dabbed his own sweat with a silk handkerchief. At the far end, the door to Shawnee's vacant nursery stood ajar. He glimpsed hanging mobiles and shelves bulging with unused toy cars, trucks, airplanes, books, and computer toys. Large letters and numbers were pasted on the wall above the vacant crib. A sense of foreboding twisted his gut.

Leading the way, Townsend stopped halfway down the hall and explained. "There's a room—meant to be a spare bedroom. Locked. My men forced the door open this morning. You need to see what's inside."

I already know. "If you insist."

"In here," said Townsend, leading him into a sitting room with a small desk. Preparing as though for a performance, he stared at the floor, and then lifted his eyes to confront the inevitable.

His own image was everywhere—his and Lennox's. The room was wallpapered with his and her portraits, images of him and Lennox as a loving couple—black and white photographs, movie posters, snapshots, digital images in frames, still shots from all five films he and she had starred in together. Sexual images of them in bed together dominated the others. He recognized them all. They had done a nude scene for *Acapulco Moon.* Here they were, exposed in all their glory.

"This is pathetic," he mustered, embarrassed.

"Your daughter-in-law was obsessed with you, Heston," Townsend stated quietly. Looking around, with a sweep of his hand, he added, "This room is a shrine to you—to your partnership."

"I'm speechless, man. I really don't know what to say."

How did he feel? Humiliated? Flattered? Terrified? He was no stranger to the obsession of fans. But Lennox had been no simple fan. Her obsession had run deeper, her heart a tainted aquifer of jilted passion, emotion that had been rising and swelling for years, like lava in a volcano's cone. She had stalked him for years, indirectly. She had infiltrated every area of his life—on purpose.

"Obviously, she thought of you two as a couple." Townsend faced him squarely. "Do I need to ask? Were you and your son's wife lovers—in real life?"

"Damn it, Townsend." He choked on the words. He could not utter them.

Townsend fingered a brass incense burner. It contained a half-charred stick of cherry-pomegranate. "You asked me earlier if Lennox had been raped. The official answer is no. However—preliminary reports on Lennox's body suggest that she was pregnant."

He inhaled sharply. "Townsend, I assure you, I swear to you, Lennox Cordova was not pregnant with my child." *Not this time.* "Not when she died."

"She was infatuated with you."

"She with me—not I with her. For crying out loud!"

"Relax, buddy. I have to get to the bottom of this. You know that."

"Granted, Lennox had feelings for me, but I never..." he idled, glancing at the photographic images of his visage, his own young eyes staring back at him from every wall, accusingly. *Liar. Guilty. I am NOT guilty!* He caught sight of bulging scrapbooks on shelves above the little desk. "Did you search for it here?"

"For Lennox's diary?" Opening a drawer, he drew out a jewelry box and flipped the lid. A rectangular impression was imprinted on lavender velvet. "We think she kept it in this box. Hid it in the wall safe. Whoever fed her the overdose—if that's what happened—may have stolen her diary. We'll know more once the data comes in."

"When will that be?"

"No way to know. We've asked them to speed it up—due to the high-profile nature of the case. I'm waiting for the results by phone." He pointed to a scrapbook lying open on the desk. "Take a look at this," he ordered. "We found it like this, lying open to this page."

Reluctantly, he viewed the photograph. He remembered that night well. *The four of us at Dan Tana's. The night before we sailed for Catalina Island.*

Townsend leaned against the desk. "I recognize you, Lennox, and this woman..."

"Lennox's mother, Lynne."

"Who's this fourth person? This blonde fox here." He tapped the pretty figure.

He shrugged. "I can't recall. Some wannabe actress, perhaps."

"You might as well tell me, Heston. My men will identify her eventually."

"Then why ask me?" Heston demanded.

"Have it your way, my man."

"May we leave this space, please?" Claustrophobia was descending upon him like a cloud of perfumed smog. It was the pervasive scent of Lennox herself. *Escape.*

"Everything in this room is evidence," Townsend noted, as he nimbly led him out and shut the door behind him.

"Of what?" Queasy, he broke a sweat.

"Of Lennox's state of mind at the time of her death. Of who might have had a motive for her murder." Townsend trod back down the hallway.

He followed briskly. "Meaning me? That's absurd. I knew nothing about this." *Bloody liar.*

"Meaning you—or someone who was jealous of you—or of Lennox. Someone who did know about this room. Gabe Cade said Lennox had many lovers. Was one of them jealous? Was Kipp? Did your son know his wife was infatuated with his father? Or was it more than infatuation? Was it love? Were you in love with your son's wife?"

"Damn it, I told you no!"

As they entered the great room and approached the elevator, Townsend stopped mid-stride, whirling around, face to face. "Talk to me, Heston."

Exasperated, he ran his hand through his mussed hair and blew a soundless whistle through puckered lips. "To the best of my knowledge, Kipp knew nothing about Lennox's obsession with me. No one knew— about *this.* " He pointed toward the secret room. "She kept her feeling hidden—from everyone except me. Oh, she played Kipp so well, the young fool."

"How?"

"Shortly after Kipp re-entered our lives—eight years ago, when he was 19, I hired a PI, who found him enrolled in pre-med at Vanderbilt

University—Poppy and I married. We took Kipp and Win—who was four at the time—with us to the set of *Acapulco Moon* in Mexico."

"Yeah, Lennox was hot in that one. I liked the car chase at the end."

Heston's lip curled. "You liked it because I played a smart cop."

Townsend's dark eyes roamed, half-lidded. "Go on with your story."

Collecting his thoughts, he proceeded. "Lennox was an expert at managing men. She'd learned it from her mother, Lynne. Once she'd conceived the idea of marrying my son..."

"Which she did because...?"

"Who knows? To make me jealous? To make me pay?"

"For what?"

Startled, he became cautious. "For shunning her advances?"

"A babe like that? It stretches the imagination, Heston. You have quite a rep as a heartbreaker, but not many men would turn her down."

"That's why they pay me the big bucks, Townsend. I have *that* many options."

"More likely she married Kipp to be near you."

In fear, he squelched his rising fury.

"Tell the truth. Heston. Did you jilt Lennox—for Poppy?"

"Absolutely not!" *If only the Academy could see this performance.*

"Easy, easy." Townsend placed a firm hand on his shoulder.

Brushing it off, he stepped away. "Lennox caught my college-aged son the way a sport fisherman hooks and reels in a tarpon. Once he'd been netted, his life went downhill—thanks to her toxic influence. She insisted Kipp enter show business. Insisted he sign with Gabriel Cade. Refused to marry him, otherwise. He only did it to impress Lennox. I wanted to kill..." He stopped short.

Townsend shifted his weight. "All to attract your attention. Was that it? Catch you in her trap? Be part of your life in the only way possible?"

He threw up his hands. "One assumes." He nodded at the wall. "She was twisted inside."

"Why didn't you get a restraining order against Lennox?"

Think fast. "She never threatened me. Just tantrums—and covert declarations of love."

Crossing his arms at his chest, Townsend shook his head. "Actors." His smile slowly faded. "You're very convincing, Heston. I almost believe you."

"Screw you, Townsend."

"Ah, ah, ah!" The big man wagged a finger. "Don't forget. I can have you arrested at the drop of a hat."

"For what?"

"Suspicion of murder."

The blow below the belt. It had begun. He absorbed the blow in silence.

Townsend paced the floor. He stopped near the balcony doorway, near the outline of Lennox's body. "I get it. Kipp felt competitive with his new movie-star Daddy? Oedipus resurrected?"

"How would I know?" His tone was subdued.

Spreading his feet, Townsend placed his hands on his hips. "Heston, come on. This is real life, man."

He averted his eyes. "Have it your way. You won't believe me, no matter what I say."

"I will believe what the facts bear out. Nothing more, nothing less."

He narrowed his eyes at Townsend. "I can see I'm going to need a lawyer."

"Your decision, not mine."

"I just made it."

Townsend shrugged. "Lucky you. You're related by marriage to the best in the business." He adjusted his clip-on necktie.

"So I am."

"Come on." Townsend strode to the elevator. "Are you ready to visit the site where your son allegedly walked into the Atlantic?"

"I reckon." Dismal, he jabbed the elevator button repeatedly without mercy. He could feel Townsend eyeing him, searching him out, creeping around inside the hollows of his soul like a spider in a dusty attic.

"Must be quite a revelation," the big man opined, coming alongside.

"What is?"

"The power of youth. You are no longer the world's most popular Demming."

"Am I not?"

"No. You saw that crowd of Kipp's young fans. Wait 'til you're among them. It's pretty intense—a human zoo. Sure you don't want to wait?"

In his mind, a picture formed—poor Poppy, lying in their bed last night, angry and inconsolable. He nodded firmly. "I promised my wife I'd lay a wreath at our son's memorial," he replied earnestly, as the elevator door opened and the two men stepped in. "Dead or not. Nothing else matters." *Except keeping her from learning the truth.*

"Are you going to arrest me?"

"Not yet. Not without proof."

The door closed. The elevator descended. After lunch, he would pay a little visit—alone—to Gabe Cade aboard the *Angel Baby*. Docked in Fort Lauderdale, it would be a mere detour on his drive back home to Naples.

Driving the Ferrari north on I-95, he fretted over the old photograph Townsend had showed him. With his teeth, he tore off a leather driving glove and chewed the buffed nail of his forefinger. What would Townsend do—once he discovered that the mature version of the young beauty in the snapshot was Ezra Gold's current lady love, Vivian Fairchild Champlain?

Where would it all lead? He felt as if he were sinking into Glades quicksand.

Chapter Twenty-Eight

In the waiting area of the clinic on Big Pine Key, Kipp gave silent thanks that the two doctors, husband and wife, had cooperated and not turned him in.

"Come on. Let's chat before you leave," said Marissa, leading him out the door. He followed her onto the beach. "I want to hear your side of things."

He was still appalled at the unexpected developments in his reunion with Marissa. His ex-fiancée was now pregnant and married to a middle-aged Dominican doctor. He had watched in envy as Perfecto had embraced and kissed her possessively, even reverently. He felt P.O.'d.

His own hopes for reunion with Marissa had been dashed. But her husband had done well by Shawnee, who now was sitting beneath a patio umbrella, under Beryl's watchful eye. For a few moments, he could stroll the solitary island beach with Marissa. They had not been alone together for seven years.

"He's afraid I'll hurt you," Kipp observed, staring back down the long, solitary beach where, in the distance, Perfecto had come outside and stood chatting with Beryl. But he was watching his wife stroll up the lonely beach. "That's why he won't let you out of his sight."

"It's true. Perfecto doesn't want me to be alone with you. But he's also concerned for your welfare. I told him that you and I need to talk. He agreed to keep his distance, but he wants you to stay off your injured foot. You're still his patient, legal or not."

"They're following us," he said irritably.

"My husband is protective of me," she acknowledged. "For that I am grateful. Especially when—"

"When you may be in the company of a homicidal maniac? Like me?"

Marissa flashed but subdued a smile. "I don't know what my husband thinks, Kipp. But I don't think you murdered your ex-wife. I don't think you could murder anyone. Not even yourself."

"I tried to. I was going to."

"No. Else you would have succeeded. You wouldn't have dropped everything to rescue your son when you thought he was in danger."

"Beryl told you everything?"

"Yes."

"You know me well," he admitted.

She rested her palms atop her pregnant belly as they walked up the sandy beach. "I know you well enough to know one thing: you don't like the man you have become."

He stopped and pivoted. Grasping her bare arms, he faced her squarely. "I want to be a doctor, Marissa. I want to help the helpless, the sick, the injured. Instead, I became one of them, a druggie freak show. Look, I know I made a huge mistake—bowing out, giving up my dream because of—the past."

"Because of your grandfather's mistake?"

"Yes. I should have faced his crime like a man—and done my own thing, screw the consequences. I didn't. I let Lennox talk me into show business." Cringing, he slapped his palms to his temples. "Damn it! How could I have been so flipping stupid?"

With loving hands, she pried his palms away and rested his arms at his side. "You weren't stupid. You were young and foolish. Naïve. Green. Call it what you will. We all make mistakes when we're young."

"You didn't."

"Didn't I?"

205

She faltered, turning away. "Let's just say that—after you left me—I made some mistakes of my own. Perfecto found me." She looked into his eyes. "He bought back my soul—and he returned it to me—no strings attached."

He didn't feel well. He was still weak. "I'm sure you're exaggerating, Marissa."

"No." She extended an arm towards him, turning the palm of her hand to the sky.

He stopped to breathe. For the first time, he noticed the scar.

"I worshipped you, Kipp. I was mad for you. I had planned my whole life based on our being together. When you dumped me—it was in magazines, on television, on all the big websites, all the social networks—I was humiliated, publicly scorned." Covering her eyes, she shuddered in the hot sun. "Then you married the movie star—and had a son. I, too, contemplated suicide. Unlike you, I nearly made it."

"Is that how...?" Gently, he cradled her hand and examined the scar on her inner wrists. He pressed her wrist to his cheek. She pulled away. "Yes, and it's how I met Perfecto. He saved my life. After my internship, I was too ashamed to return home to Oahu. I couldn't face family and friends. I took a cruise in the Western Caribbean. It made me so homesick for the islands that I-I... He was a passenger on the same ship. That night, he..."

"Staunched the bleeding."

"Yes. He's a G.P. He was very kind. He'd studied medicine in Havana. He was on his way to the Dominican Republic to open a free clinic. I told him about my studies. He invited me to apply. I did. He accepted me." She said the words again for emphasis. "He accepted me, Kipp."

"I hear you."

"I sincerely hope you do."

He gnashed his teeth. "I ruined my life."

"Not so, Kipp. You may have a rough go, but you can begin again."

"How, Marissa? Can I save lives? I can't go back to med school. I couldn't get in. I have a rap sheet—a police record. Even now, I'm violating probation." Spotting a piece of driftwood, he lifted it and hurled it into the ocean. Hands on his hips, he watched it sail and splash. *Anything to avoid her eyes.*

She stood behind him. "You don't have to be a physician to save lives, Kipp. We have a number of volunteers at the free clinic. And we need donors—money, medical supplies, equipment. We need things all the time. What we really need right now, is a new building, a new home for the clinic we founded in the Dominican Republic. We're being evicted."

"Forget about it. I'm bankrupt, Marissa. Worse. I'm in debt up to my ying-yang."

"We'll find something for you to do, Kipp—once this mess is cleared up. You can work with Perfecto and me. Your celebrity could draw attention to our needs. But you will help us, even without it—if you wanted to be—what do you call it—incognito. Don't give up so easily."

Awed and in pain, he contemplated Marissa's Madonna-like form, as she idled against the backdrop of hibiscus and seashore. Her slender figure, with its round protruding belly, exuded an aura of peace and grace. Had he not been envious and jealous of her new husband, he might have absorbed some of her quietude. As he limped along the shore, he twitched, agitated and angry. "You could have waited for me," he chided suddenly.

"Waited for you?" she uttered, flabbergasted. "Kipp, I never once heard from you—not in seven years. Have you forgotten? You married someone else."

"How could I forget? She destroyed my life."

"Kipp..."

"She wanted to do my father. Not me. I was the next best thing. Go figure."

"Kipp, please..."

"Lennox used me—to be near him. I did everything she asked—dropped out of school, changed careers, dumped my agent, signed my finances over to Gabe Cade, did drugs—I even styled my hair—all because she batted her spider-lashes and pouted, 'Pretty please, Kipp-man.' " In mockery, thrust his lower lip forward. "Then she'd poke me with her pointy-bra."

Marissa's long brown hair floated on the breeze, as did the loose fabric of her ankle-length mu-mu. "Why did you do as she asked, Kipp?

"What'd you mean *why?* Because I loved her, obviously—or thought I did."

Marissa captured her floating locks and twisted them into place. A ponytail draped down over one shoulder. It reached almost to what once had been her waist. "Did you?"

"Well, Duh. What do you think? Nobody stops to think how I felt, when she told me she was hot for my dad."

She stopped and turned to him. She looked into his eyes. "I think you loved yourself more."

He, too, stopped and confronted her gaze. "Why's that?"

She resumed strolling. "If you had loved Lennox more than yourself, your own needs and desires wouldn't have mattered to you. Her happiness would have been your only concern."

"You're wicked crazy," he joked, limping forward to walk alongside her.

"No. You did what she asked in order to win her over. You wanted her approval."

"I wanted in her bed. I wanted up her panties."

Marissa stopped and dug her toes into the sand. "Same difference. You wanted what you wanted. You manipulated her to get it."

Stopping beside her, he placed a hand on his hip. He swiveled his head, taking in the view. "Well, maybe. But it was because I lusted for her body. I did love her."

Close-lipped, Marissa smiled. With her toe, she toyed with a sand dollar half-buried in the sand. "Kipp, may I tell you something?"

"Sure." He gave her his attention.

She continued to toy with the shell. "When you dumped me that summer, seven years ago, I was so heart-broken I wanted to die."

"And I'm sorry about that," he mumbled. He stared down at the sand dollar and watched as she moved it around in the sand.

"But, you see, I'm glad you did it—now."

"You are?"

She nodded and smiled again, close-lipped and serene. Her eyes searched his.

He was puzzled. "Why?" He pointed to her abdomen. "Because of that?"

She giggled. "Because of Perfecto. If you hadn't dumped me for Lennox Cordova, I never would have met the love of my life. I owe you a debt of gratitude."

He winced. Glancing behind them, he spotted Perfecto and Beryl standing a few hundred feet behind them down the shore. "That old guy is the love of your life?"

"That old guy is my husband, Kipp. Yes, I love Perfecto dearly. He's a great man, the best I've ever known. He loves people. He *serves* them."

"Yeah, right."

"He does. He loves everyone, not just me. I don't believe I could adore him this much—if he loved only me, I mean. Often—quite often—I'm last on his list. But he gets around to me, eventually." Baring even teeth, she patted her distended belly.

He felt wobbly—hot and weak. Was he going to be sick?

"Here, Kipp. Sit down in the sand." Bracing his arms with her strong hands, she helped him lower himself to the ground.

"Stupid of me." Giving way, his knees bent.

"Watch yourself."

His rump hit the sand.

"You're stressed," she said, settling down beside him in the sand, her feet tucked beneath her posterior. The loud mu-mu encircled her like a circus tent.

"Thank you for coming over to help me out, Marissa." He lay back, propped on his elbows. "This Perfecto-thing sort of took me by surprise—I have to admit. I was kind of hoping you and I might—"

"Reconnect?"

"Well, yeah. The thought had occurred to me."

"Too late, old friend," she said. "It wasn't meant to be. Your fate lies elsewhere."

"The hell you say. Where, pray tell?"

She laughed gaily. "Where one's fate usually lies—right in front of your nose."

"Meaning what?"

She rolled with laughter. "Oh, Kipp, really. Don't you know?"

He laughed at her laughing. "What the hell are you talking about, Marissa?"

Filled with glee, she lay back in the sand. "You'll figure it out," she laughed, rollicking. "The only thing I can't figure out is—how the heck are we both going to get up?"

He burst into laughter beside her. Propped on both elbows, he watched his flat belly quiver. He didn't understand what she was hinting at, but it felt good to join in her joy. It felt comfortable. He felt okay with it.

Suddenly, he realized a truth. He didn't begrudge his old girlfriend her new life. *I am happy for her.* Instantly, he realized a second truth. *Marissa has forgiven me.*

"What's all this silliness?" Perfecto's voice boomed as the spindly physician sprinted rapidly up the beach. He was dogged by Beryl, whose legs were half the length of his. At the sight of Perfecto and Beryl together—one loping like a Great Dane and the other scurrying like a dachshund—he and Marissa broke into riotous peals of laughter. For the first time in years, his sides ached from levity. Marissa laughed so hard it was difficult for the old man to hoist her to her feet. Beryl had to assist, propping her up by the backside.

Chapter Twenty-Nine

Where is the blessed diary? I KNOW I hid it under my scarves, in the bottom drawer. I know I did! Now, it's gone...

Frantically, Poppy tore through her undergarments, searching for the missing journal. In desperation, she had ransacked her closet—and in vain. The diary was missing.

Someone must have stolen it. The empty box in the bottom drawer of her bureau gaped like an open wound. *Who could have taken it?*

No one else on earth knew she had the diary in her possession. Who had been in her closet? She dare not ask anyone—it would be a tip-off that she had buried treasure. Certainly, she couldn't ask the only two people who had regular access to her possessions—her husband and her housekeeper.

Was it one of the kids? Which one? Tegan, most likely, although it could be Dakota or even Sage. She *dare* not ask them.

She shuddered in terror. *If Heston stumbled upon it...*

Shaking her head in denial, she clamped her eyelids shut. Clasping herself in a tight embrace, she rocked rhythmically on her haunches. No matter what, she was in serious trouble.

Maybe I have just misplaced it. Deep down, she knew that was impossible. *If only I'd had time to rent my own safety deposit box...*

Her phone rang. She jumped on it. "Hello? Kipp? Is that you?"

"I'm sorry, Poppy. No, it's I. Banks Winston. I'm sorry to disappoint you."

"Banks?" Her mind clawed its way out of the bleeding hole.

"Surely you remember...?"

The sickening-yellow mist lifted from her mind. "Of course I remember. Banks. I was just—um, preoccupied."

His smooth tone soothed her frayed nerves. "Considering all you have on your plate at the moment, that's perfectly understandable."

She relaxed slightly. "How nice to hear from you. It's just that I was so...I am so..."

"Distraught, no doubt."

"I was going to say frazzled. I have so much to contend with."

"It's a devilish circumstance you find yourself in since last we met. In fact, that's why I phoned you." His voice was easy, confident, cultured, and well-modulated. "I want to offer my assistance to you and Winner and Heston."

He sounds just the way he looks—too well-groomed to be real and too suave to be trusted. Heston had called him a debonair Lothario.

It takes one to know one.

Yet Banks' concern sounded genuine.

"We're having an awful time, Banks," she admitted. "I'm glad Winner had a few happy hours with you before this madness about Kipp began."

"Any word?" he asked.

"Nothing. The FBI is on the case. But, so far, Kipp and Shawnee seem to have fallen off the face of the earth." She sobbed suddenly, unable to stop herself. "I'm sorry, Banks."

She dabbed her eyes with a hanky from the bureau. "It's been hellish—not just for me. Especially for Heston. He knew Lennox so well, you see...in the past. Banks, I..."

He interrupted. "Pretty little Poppy. I know how difficult this situation is for you. And I want to volunteer my services—to you personally, not just to you as Winner's stepmother or Kipp's long-suffering birth mother."

"B-Banks, I..."

"But as a beautiful woman in need of aid. I am at your service, Poppy. Know this."

"I do. Thank you, Banks."

"If anything dire occurs, if you need me in any way, do not hesitate to call upon me. I am at your disposal in this matter."

"I will. Honestly."

"Good. Well, I won't keep you."

"Banks, it was g-good of you to phone."

"My dear lady, call upon me—for anything at any time, day or night."

"Thank you. Goodnight."

"Pleasant dreams. Try not to worry."

She turned off the phone. That's all she needed—a come on from the most attractive man she'd encountered in years. He was no Heston, but then, who was?

No! She mustn't let herself succumb to the need for emotional massage. No matter how much of a rat he seemed to be, she was still Heston's wife. Her job—her only job at the moment—was to locate the lost diary. Then she would have the luxury to decide if Heston was worth protecting or not. What would she do with the diary once she'd found it?

By destroying the diary, she could protect Heston from being charged with statutory rape in the international press—and maybe from a charge of murder. Not that he deserved protecting. He had been betraying her behind her back for the past eleven years—if Lynne Cordova's written words were to be believed.

So far, she had no reason to doubt them. But, in the wrong hands, Lynne's written confession could prove to be Heston's undoing—and not just Heston. *Others* were named, too.

For the first time in her life, she let herself admit the truth—she hated fame and everything that went with it. She wished Heston had never become a celebrity. She wished she weren't a movie star's wife. And yet, her sex life with Heston Demming had been the best part of her life. It had been worth the price.

So far.

Chapter Thirty

Aboard Gabe Cade's ostentatious mega-yacht, in a seagoing mausoleum of an office, Heston stared at the painting on the wall. To be allowed to board, by Gabe's goons, he'd had to display a civility he did not feel. Once aboard, the ruse hadn't lasted long.

"Cade, that painting behind you—on your office wall—it's signed Cedric Spicer," he indicated with a slight nod forward. "And it's dated for last year."

Glancing behind his desk, Gabe Cade frowned, tugging at his ear lobe. "Damn, so it is!"

He stood immobile, hands jammed into his pants pockets. "Where did you get it?"

"Well, I don't rightly know," Gabe said. "Guess my dealer picked it up somewhere."

"Do you know Spicer personally?"

Gabe shuffled his feet. "Ain't he some kind of AC/DC fruit cup?"

"Cut the crap, Cade. You know very well I own the body of Cedric's early work—and that I've been warehousing it for the past eight years. It's common knowledge, in art circles."

The old man stroked his chin. "Heard something about it. Cedric canoodled your second wife, didn't he? That cold-blooded supermodel. What was her name?"

"You know very well. Maude."

"That's it: Maude Winston." Gabe's humor evaporated. "Little Winner's sadistic mama." His two bushy white eyebrows drew together. "Just what do you intend to do with Cedric's work, Heston?"

"Got a match?"

"You wouldn't dare," Gabe said.

"The hell I wouldn't."

"It's worth a fortune," Gabe baited him.

"Not to me."

"Do it. See what happens."

"I see your threat, and I double it," Heston smirked.

"Don't threaten me, you pansy actor."

"You can't con me, you old windbag, the way you conned my son. I'm on to your tricks. I have been from the get-go. I know you bribed the label's A&R man."

Cade's cool was turning to heat along with Heston's. "What are you going to do, actor? Scratch my eyes out? I'd call you pretty boy, but you ain't one no more. Kipp's the pretty boy now. How does it feel to be old? Welcome to the club."

Heston felt his own lips curling. His anger was base; his breaths, quick and shallow. His eyes seized upon the artful old codger who leered up at him from behind the immense desk. The old man's head was a skull, his eye sockets, windows to hell.

"Cade, if anything has happened to my son or my grandson—because of you or for any other reason—you'll pay—one way or another."

Gabriel Cade stood and faced him, his spindly form still spry enough to react to Heston's raw ire.

"Demming, I allowed you onto my ship and into my office as a professional courtesy. Now I am inviting you to leave. Post haste." He pressed the intercom button. "Miss DuBois, come in here immediately and escort Heston Demming from my ship." His leer became a grin. His sly eyes slipped by Heston to find the woman entering the office door.

"Yes, sir?" The frosted beehive hairdo of Cade's secretary popped through the opening, followed by her short, curvaceous form, adorned, as it was, in a sleeveless, rose-colored mini-dress cinched at the waist with a metallic belt. Black fishnet stockings completed her ensemble.

Not bad. Heston assessed her fleetingly, out of habit. *But no class.* The heavy layers of black mascara around her eyes masked her small features. Something about her made him cringe and oddly evoked a feeling of *déjà vu.*

"Chantal, get him out of here." Gabe thumbed toward the door.

"Please come with me, Mr. Demming," said Chantal DuBois. She stood in the open doorway, one hand on the doorknob, the other extended toward the outer office. "I'll see you to the gangplank."

"My pleasure, Miss DuBois." Raising his arms, he encircled the expanse of Cade's sumptuous office. "When I see all this largesse, Cade, all this booty, all this geld and glitter, I know where it came from. It came from the sweat of my son, Kipp, and his hard-working band mates, the naïve chumps you stole it from—the trusting souls you bilked out of millions in earnings over the years, the ones you led to ruin through your lies and misrepresentations."

Gabe Cade snorted. "You don't know shit, Heston. Get your fairy-actor carcass out of my office," Cade sneered, a grin of pleasure rippling the deep-tan wrinkles in his face. "If you don't, I'll call the cops."

Baiting the old man, Heston stood his ground.

"Chantal, make the call." Gabe nodded at his secretary, who made a move toward the phone.

Heston grabbed her arm. "Don't."

Gasping, she stopped in her tracks, her arm encircled by his curling fingers. He flung her onto the leather couch and glared at Cade across the desktop. "Give me one bit of trouble, Gabe, and I'll beat the old out of you. Do you hear me? You set out to ruin my son, and you did it. When I find out how and why, I'll be back for your hide."

Cade simmered, apoplectic, in spite of his cool words. "Like I said, you're no spring chicken anymore, Heston. Look in a damn mirror. Really see yourself. But do it somewhere else. I hate to watch a grown man cry. Now vacate my office. Get the hell off the *Angel Baby.*"

"For now," he said, ego sliced and bleeding but determination intact.

Cade leaned forward for the kill. "I don't have to answer to you or anyone else. Your son's a bum. You're a lousy father. None of it's my fault. It's all yours, Heston. You killed one son, and now you've destroyed another one. You're a weakling like your father. Why not hang yourself like he did?"

"I'll see you in hell, Cade." Stunned, it was all he could manage to utter. Shaken but unharmed, the secretary fell across the couch. He gave her a passing glance on his way out the door, but he was startled by a dive-bombing green parrot, who whizzed by his head. Settling, the bird perched beside Chantal on the couch back.

"Haw, haw," Gabe guffawed.

"Freaking shrike!"

Masking his hurt pride, Heston strode out the office doors and made his way down to the main deck of the white behemoth that Gabriel Cade called home. Nimbly, he negotiated the gangplank, hand sliding along the damp railing. He disembarked, panting, and strode to the parking lot beyond the marina, his heart pounding.

Seated inside his Ferrari, he caught his breath. His head was spinning. Something was afoot here, but he didn't know what. Why did the secretary seem so familiar? Had he ever met this short, buxom woman named Chantal DuBois?

Leave it to Cade to keep such a woman on his payroll. *The horny old bastard.* In what pole-dancing establishment had he picked up this trollop?

And yet...

He *knew* he had met Chantal DuBois—somewhere, at some time, in his past. But when? Where?

Worse yet, he had a bad feeling about it. Whatever the connection was, it wasn't good.

Was she a forgotten lover from his youth? She may have been lovely and innocent once upon a time. His keen aesthetic sense had kept him from anything more than a few dalliances with hardened women, and those were in the distant past—the days of his youth, when his sexual tension sometimes had become unbearable.

Was she a fan of his? He could have met her at some premier or some fan club meeting. He had met so many fawning women in his life. He could not place her—yet. But he would, if he let his subconscious go to work.

An odd tingling sensation crept up his spine. Why had Cade mentioned his father's suicide? *As though he had been waiting, hoping, for an opportunity to mention it.*

And what was Cade's connection with his old nemesis Cedric Spicer? Too many questions. None of it made sense.

From the safe distance of the parking lot, his eyes roamed Cade's enormous white yacht, all 115 feet of her. Not his vision of a seafaring vessel. He preferred his own agile 54-foot sailing yacht, *Windswept.* He needed the grace of wind and sails, Still, the seaman in him couldn't help admiring the seaworthiness of such a lavish ship as the—what was called it again?

The yacht's name was emblazoned in golden block letters across its broad stern: *Angel Baby.* His heart skipped a beat.

Who was Angel Baby?

Had Gabe named his ship after someone? Surely not Chantal DuBois. She wasn't boat-naming material. Was *Angel Baby* a ghost from the old man's past? What did he—or anyone else—know about Gabriel Cade's history? *Nothing.*

Igniting the Ferrari's engine, he felt a new surge of hope. As he shifted gears and floored the accelerator, the precision sports car careened out of the harbor parking lot. Inspired, he veered the Ferrari west on I-5, stopping only to pay the toll on Alligator Alley. He glanced at the Rolex. He had invited Arlene and Ezra to dinner at the yacht club. Accelerating, the car roared off.

Gabriel Cade—like everyone else—had a past. Old Gabe's was longer than most. Perhaps he could dig up some information to use in his fight against the crooked manager. Perhaps Cade's knowledge of the Demmings was a clue to his destructive behavior toward Kipp. *Toward us.*

The first step: Find out who the angel-baby was—or is—in Gabe Cade's life. The best way to do that? Hire a private eye.

He had toyed with doing that anyway—to find Shawnee and Kipp. Last time he'd hired one was eight years ago. Now he needed a sophisticated professional, not that yokel from East Naples. What was his name—Rick Something...

Rick *DuBois.*

The alarm bells clanged inside his brain.

Chapter Thirty-One

At twilight, *Windswept* lay moored in Naples Bay behind the Demming home on Galleon Drive. Below deck, Winner lay snuggled in Ram's arms on a cabin bed. In the quiet darkness, she steeped happily, infatuated with her muscleman. She could stay this way forever—feeling one another, bodies close, hearts beating in tandem. For the first time in her life, she felt safe with a man other than her father.

"You *want* to go away with me. Right, Win?" Ram massaged her backside with his massive hands.

"Mmmm. I *want* to go with you, Ram," Winner said dreamily, "But..."

His grip intensified. "But what, sweet girl?"

"Ouch," she yipped, pulling away. Or had she said it out loud? She wasn't sure. But the nightmare sear of pain was unmistakable.

She looked up at him. She looked quickly away. Had he seen it in her eyes?

Once again, he drew her in. "That's not hurting you." He wrenched her arm behind her back. *"This* is hurting you."

Pain shot through her arm and shoulder. She yelped, this time aloud.

"Quiet!" he laughed. "I'm only playing."

She was stunned by the pain. Sense memories flooded her psyche. "Ram, no! Please."

He loosed her. She jumped from the bed, her bare feet slapping the cold floor. Tossing aside the woolen blanket, he joined her.

"Don't let me catch you making that mistake again, girl," he laughed, spinning her around and hugging her to his tree-trunk torso.

You won't. This time she was sure. Easing away, she abruptly dashed toward the cabin door. It was locked.

She looked back. His hulking silhouette was inching toward her. Shrinking bodily, she backed into the nearest corner.

"Don't be upset, baby. I was just funning you."

"I'm not upset," she heard herself lie.

" 'Fraid I might throw you overboard to the gators?" He snapped his jaws repeatedly and laughed. Darkness was closing in. She could feel his hot breath on her cheek. She rattled the door handle.

"Let me out." She should never have told him. Now he knew her greatest fear. She had thought she could trust him.

Never trust anyone who tries to hurt you. That's what Dr. Fishburne had told her in therapy, over and over. *Tell someone, Winner. Tell your father, your step-mother, your nanny. Tell me, tell your teacher, your school counselor. Don't be a passive victim. Your mother is gone— physically and legally. She can't hurt you ever again. Except in your own mind.*

Ram's hand caught the scruff of her neck. Panic blinded her. She screamed, but his other hand muffled the sound. She felt his erection pressed against her.

"Take it easy, Winner." His hot breath brushed he forehead. "I ain't throwing you to the gators."

Not yet.

"I know you hate them. What animals do you like?" Giant hands roamed her body. She could breathe again, but she felt sick and giddy.

"What kind?" he urged, teeth clenched as he concentrated.

Play for time. "Manatees. I like manatees."

"Those fat cabbage-eaters? I seen them at Sea World."

She caught her breath as he explored. "They're gentle. They're vegetarians."

"They're prey for meat-eaters," he whispered ominously, stroking her skin. "That's this life," he whispered. "The weak get devoured."

"Winner? Where are you?"

Miraculously, she heard Lissette calling from outside on the dock. "Are you out here? Come back in the house before your father gets home!"

Suddenly, Ram withdrew, cold as he had been hot moments earlier. He unlocked the cabin door.

"Get out there, Winner. Cover for me, baby girl, or I will throw you to the gators." His smile, once appealing, was now menacing. "Just remember. Cross me, and I can hurt your whole family—not just you." He grabbed her wrist. "We'll talk about this later, baby. Have your bag packed. We're leaving tonight."

In the twilight, she looked through his eyes into his dark soul. She had seen that place before. She still saw it in her nightmares. She tore her wrist free.

"Here!" she shrieked, clamoring onto the deck.

"Winner?" Lissette came running, relieved.

On deck, the warm winter wind blew her clean. She rushed into the housekeeper's open arms.

"Winston Demming, you scared the life out of me." Lissette embraced her. "I thought you were missing, too. Isn't Ram with you?"

"He went diving," she lied. "I helped him."

"He's supposed to be here guarding you. If only Berry was here. I've left half a dozen messages on her voice mail. She doesn't call me back. She would handle him. Me, I'm telling your father when he gets home."

"No!" Panic seized Winner. Her teeth chattered.

She couldn't lie to her father. But she couldn't tell him the truth, either. He would know she had been sneaking out with Ram. He would kill her. If Ram didn't kill her, her father would.

"Please, Lissette. Let it go. Ram got antsy. You know how guys are. He'll be back soon."

"You're shivering, *nina*. Let's get you inside the house." Lissette wrapped a plump arm around her waist and guided her up the walkway toward the house.

Compliant, Winner allowed herself to be led. She knew she should tell Lissette the truth. Dr. Fishburne had told her to.

But she couldn't tell the truth to anyone. If she did, Ram would do the unspeakable. Or would he? Could he, if she told the truth? She didn't know what to do.

She, too, wished Nanny Berry were here. Berry always did what was right—especially when one had been "naughty," as Berry said. But Winner knew she had gone beyond the boundaries of naughty. What she had done with Ram was vile.

Stopping along the pebbled walkway, Winner vomited into the grass. Holding back strands of flaxen hair, Lissette watched in dismay.

"Did you say anything to Poppy?" Winner asked, wiping her mouth. Lissette tidied her with her apron, and then encircled her waist again with an arm.

Resuming their walk, Lissette shook her head. "I was afraid to tell your stepmother. She's headed for a breakdown as it is."

Chapter Thirty-Two

Outside the clinic on Big Pine Key, under cloudy afternoon skies, Beryl and Marissa stood waiting on the seawall near the seaplane. Kipp had left them discussing babies and motherhood like the pros they both were. Now sitting at the foot of a bed, he was deep in conversation with Dr. Perfecto Logue, who stood cleaning his pipe, making ready to depart the clinic on a routine house call. The physician's packed medical kit sat ready on a nearby stool. He captured Kipp with an earnest stare.

"Many people envy your fame, young man. Why do most people want fame—or money, cars, homes, fancy clothes? What are they actually seeking, in your opinion?"

Kipp thought a minute. "Power? Happiness?"

Perfecto tilted his head. "They are seeking joy. And what is joy but love?"

"I hate being famous. Fame caused all my problems."

"You don't have 'problems' in the plural, Kipp. You have only one problem." The sun peeked through the parted window blinds. Its light reflected on Perfecto's balding pate. "You don't understand what love is."

Kipp snorted. "Hey, I'm all about love, Doc. I loved everybody." He grinned valiantly, but he knew he was in too deep. "Every chance I got. Hell, I've had the STDs to prove it."

Perfecto scoffed. "So you said. Man, *lust* is not *love!* Lust is a form of human greed—like gluttony, covetousness, addictions of all types. Insatiable greed, man. Nothing matters but *my* pleasure, man, *my* consumption. 'Wham, bam, thank you, ma'am.' I'm using you to slake my desire." Steamed, Perfecto chewed the stem of his empty pipe. "Or to calm my fear."

Kipp sat forward, his brow furrowed. "So what? You're saying love is the opposite of greed?"

"Precisely." Perfecto removed the pipe from his mouth. For emphasis, he pointed the stem at Kipp. "All sins are forms of greed. That's what "sin" means—well, it means 'to miss the mark'—but it involves unbridled excess, in one form or another, that leads to a man's downfall—and destruction."

"Such as...?"

"Gluttony, sloth, envy, wrath..."

"Envy?"

Shrugging, Perfecto stared at him. "What's envy, except an excess of self-care? It's a lack of love. It's not being able to allow others to have when you don't have—bringing evil upon them because they have what you want. Not being able to wish them well and move on."

"Me-first."

"Bravo, nino. Wrath, for example, is unbridled anger. Someone ends up maimed or dead. In war, it's many someones."

"Mass murder."

"Take sloth. Sloth is an excess of laziness, an inability to discipline oneself to work—basically—to take care of one's self, one's need for cleanliness. Cleanliness and survival go hand in hand. If you can't get your hind-end out of a chair to wash the dinner dishes, you'll contract disease—eventually, if your excess is unbridled."

" 'The wages of sin is death,' " Kipp uttered slowly, in realization.

"Bright fellow."

"So, what's love?"

"Love is the opposite of Me-First."

"Yeah. I get it. I think."

Perfecto pointed a finger at him. "You first. Not me, but you first." He poked Kipp's chest with the pipe stem. "Your needs matter more to me than my own needs do. That's what love is. That's what doctoring is. That's your true nature, man."

The truth of Perfecto's words swept through him. "Do you think I can find it again? Reclaim it?"

"Of course, you can!"

"In spite of everything?"

"Unquestionably."

"How?"

Perfecto rose and brushed imaginary ash from his trouser lap. "Ah, now, that is something you must come to on your own." His brown eyes shone softly. "But I can tell you this—it starts with that bossy little woman who's following you around like a lost pup. Your answer lies there—the beginnings of it, anyway."

Kipp glowered. "With Nanny Northgate? The chipmunk?"

Smiling mischievously, Perfecto slipped the pipe into his coat pocket. "I have to make ready. My patient awaits." He laughed, a deep and hearty rumble. Inhaling, he opened his mouth to offer one more comment but, thinking better of it, pursed his lips. Tucking one hand into his pocket, he picked up his medical bag with the other. He cocked his head. "You'll be all right," he promised, the smile lingering on his full lips. Turning on a heel, he strode purposefully out the front door and up the stone path.

Alone in the clinic, Kipp sat in silence on the stump and contemplated the doctor's shocking words. He looked around at the environment that should have been his.

"And that," he whispered to himself at last, "is why Marissa married you and not me."

He jumped up and dashed out the front door. Perfecto was halfway down the stone path. "How can I find it?" he called from the front porch.

Turning to look back at him, Perfecto tapped his heart. "Look here." He pointed to Beryl and Shawnee. "Look there." He extended his arms outward. "Look everywhere. It's all around you, Kipp. It's inside you, *corazon*. It is you—and it's everything else, too."

As truth flowed into his soul from his departing mentor, Kipp slowly began to spin in circles, arms outstretched, foot pain forgotten, his whole being encompassing sky and sea. Feeling a hand on his shoulder, he turned. Perfecto had trotted back for one last word.

"You have to love and forgive yourself before you can love and forgive others. Never forget, Kipp," he said assuredly. "Those who are the hardest to love are the ones who need it the most."

Chapter Thirty-Three

"Thank goodness that's behind us." Arlene Gold gulped half her martini. "I feel bad for Lennox, but I never want to visit another crime scene."

"Me either," said Ezra, pocketing his mobile. "Heston, Vivian said to thank you for the dinner invitation. But she begged off. She's under the weather." He scowled.

"Too bad." Heston was checking his messages. He had several, including one from Rob LaCroix. He would listen to it after dinner. He pocketed his phone. "Poppy refused to join us. She's angry—at me," he announced to Ezra and Arlene.

"Sorry to hear it, boys," said Arlene. "But it keeps me from being a fifth wheel. Unless you two want to head on home?"

He looked at her, chagrined. "We've got to eat." *I'd rather face her on a full stomach.*

Clinking his spoon against the side of his glass, Ezra stirred sugar into his iced tea. "So, what was it you wanted to see me about, Heston? We never had our meeting." Ezra exchanged a glance with his mother.

Heston drummed his fingers on the white tablecloth. "That's right. I'd forgotten. Fact is, I secured the rights to a bestseller, *Overboard Express*. It's an epic adventure tale. Heard of it?"

Ezra beamed. "Read it. Loved it." He sipped his tea.

Heston sat back and folded his hands. "Want to direct it?"

Arlene, poised at attention, looked at her son.

Ezra's eyes were on him. "What do you think?"

"Moron," said Arlene, slapping her forehead.

"Ma, I've got to play hard to get." He shuffled his feet beneath the table. "Yes!" He grinned. "Try and stop me."

"Mazeltov." Arlene downed the rest of her martini and picked up a menu.

Heston sipped his ginger ale. "You'll direct, Ezra. There's a part for Winner—the princess."

"Works for me," agreed Ezra, eyes alight.

"We'll hire the same casting firm we used on Gauguin to cast the principals."

"What about you?" Ezra asked.

"I'm going to produce—and do a cameo. Probably the professor."

Ezra stiffened. "You aren't playing the lead?"

Heston regarded the young man across the table. "I'm too old for the lead, Ezra. He's in his twenties. Jack's a swashbuckling action-hero."

"Are you sure, Heston?" Ezra sipped tea. "This is like John Barrymore in *Dinner at Eight.*"

Heston smiled. "How's that?"

"Dinner at Eight. Directed by George Cukor. Starred Jean Harlow and everybody who was anybody in Hollywood in the 1930s. John Barrymore plays this big-ass actor on Broadway. He thinks he's going to be cast as the lead in the next Broadway play. The producer—or is it the director?—comes to his hotel room and offers him a bit part. Naturally, Barrymore is crushed."

"Naturally. Well, Ezra, on this picture, I'm playing both the producer and John Barrymore. As producer, I'm demoting myself to character roles—before the industry does it for me."

Sympathetically, Ezra pursed his lips. He glanced at his mother.

Behind the menu, Arlene shrugged. "He's right."

Heston sighed. "It's only a matter of time, my boy."

Ezra sat forward. "Whatever you want to do, Heston, I'm in."

He patted Ezra's forearm. "Good. That's settled. If only the rest of my life were as easy." He looked around. His party was one of the few dining at the yacht club this evening. Tables were empty. It was early yet. He took in the vista from their table on the terrace.

Like a Rococo seascape, a softly spectacular pastel portrait was unfolding in pale baby blues and pinks in the western sky, a gentle backdrop to scattered luminous, cottony tufts of white cloud. Below, a darkening sea reflected the dimming palette of the skies. Boats bobbed in the water, their masts shifting aimlessly. Circling seabirds fished for dinner.

"I wonder where Kipp is tonight," he said. "Alive or dead."

"It's Shawnee I'm worried about," Arlene said, putting down the menu. "Heston, you've got to do something. You can't expect law enforcement to find them. The world is too big. Use your influence."

"I have done something. On the road, I phoned my attorney. I'm hiring a private investigation firm. I'm sick of not knowing. I need answers." He signaled the waiter. "Another martini for the lady, please. More tea, Ezra?"

Ezra nodded. "Please." He handed his glass to the server, who filled it from a pitcher.

"You did the right thing, Heston," Arlene said.

"I've got a question," Ezra announced. "Why didn't Kipp become a doctor—if that's what he wanted to be?" he asked sincerely, dark eyes boring through Heston's hesitancy, straight into his reluctance.

"You've never discussed it with him? Your best friend?" Heston cast a skeptical look at the lad, who shook his head.

Although thirty years old, Ezra Gold still had the feel of a creative kid about him. His enthusiasm for film and the process was contagious. He had something special, that indefinable something that separates the artist from the hack. His shaggy, mahogany-brown mane and careless dress added an artsy-drifter ambience to his persona. One half-expected Ezra to pull out a guitar case, to begin plucking the strings of a battered instrument, while humming a sensitive, home-made ditty in a haunting minor key. Then he would charm you with an off-color quip. He was great at handling actors.

"Talk to me, Heston," Ezra urged, blatantly curious. "I want to know. Maybe there's a clue to Kipp's recent behavior here, buried beneath the pain of his past." Before taking the helm of the Gauguin picture, Ezra had directed two outstanding music videos for Demonsong. He and Kipp had been pals back then.

The server returned with Arlene's drink.

"Not his past. My father's past," Heston blurted out as the server departed. "Can I trust the two of you—with a family secret?" He felt desperate to unburden his heart. His wife had shut him out emotionally.

Arlene exchanged a glance with her son. "Proceed."

"My father was damaged goods. He was in hiding. Disgraced. Ashamed. Fearful. Guilty. Volatile." He stared at his half-empty glass, rotating it with the fingers of one hand.

"Your father? Hiding from what? Guilty of what?" Ezra demanded, sitting forward, forearms on knees, sensitive hands dangling loosely between his legs. He eyed Heston earnestly. "And what does it have to do with Kipp?"

Rolling his eyes, Heston sighed and looked away. "Everything. Years ago, my father was a highly regarded neurologist and psychiatrist in Chicago. He was a professor, but he also had a private practice. Home in the suburbs. Doting wife. Loving son—that would be yours truly." He drew a deep breath. "But he blew it. Big time."

He pursed his lips and swallowed hard. He glanced at Ezra, eyes searching. His voice quavered. "I once had an acting teacher who told us students, 'If you're going to blow it, blow it big.' He meant on stage, during a scene."

Sipping slowly, Arlene shook her head. "Meaning what?"

"I get it," Ezra chimed in. "If you make a mistake, play it for all it's worth—to the audience."

"Bingo." Grinning, he returned his gaze to the rug. The grin receded. "That's what Dad did. Blew it *big*. In his medical practice. Resigned his seat at the university. Tremendous scandal, although very hush-hush. He got out by the skin of his teeth."

"Thank you, Thornton Wilder," injected Ezra.

"But he never recovered."

Arlene mused. "He didn't play to the audience."

"What kind of scandal?" Ezra asked.

"A scandal of professional ethics resulting in death. Three deaths." Heston steadied his voice and hands. He knew how. He was a showman, after all. He stole a glance at his companion. "Malpractice."

"A professional disgrace," Ezra observed, eyes tolerant yet shrewd.

"A potentially criminal disgrace."

Ezra put his fingertips together. "Potentially?"

He nodded. "The case never got to court—nor into the public eye. It was hushed-up because some of the players were wealthy and well-connected in the pharmaceutical industry. But the specter of disaster hovered over my father's head, every day of his life from then on."

Ezra cocked his shaggy head. "So, your father committed a medical crime? One that cost some lives. And he was in hiding because of it."

He licked his lips. "Yes. My father violated his Hippocratic oath, to put it mildly. He also violated the laws of the land—and common decency. He was a self-centered egotist. He cared about no one but himself. I inherited my narcissism. So did Kipp."

Embarrassed, Heston rose, and then dropped back down into his seat. "No, that's not true. That's my old adolescent-self talking. My father had begun his career as a promising medical researcher. By the time of my childhood, he had become a pathetic and tortured failure. He lived in a constant state of guilt, fear, and remorse. I know that now. I didn't know it as a kid. All I knew was the vicious, erratic bully he had become. Now I believe he was afraid of...revenge. And he couldn't handle his fear. Which is why he hanged himself when I was a teenager."

Leaning forward, Ezra clasped his hands together, elbows resting on his knees. "What happened, Heston? How old were you at the time?"

Heston stared at the carpet. Then he turned the silver-blues full force on Ezra, revving up the intensity. "I've paid a lot of money to certain people to keep this matter quiet. I'm counting on you, Ezra, Arlene," he nodded respectively, "to honor my privacy. I don't want my wife and daughters harmed. Nor my first-born son—if he's still alive. He's a jackass, but he's my jackass."

Ezra sat up straight. "My word of honor, Heston. I won't tell a soul, unless you give me leave to."

Arlene nodded. "Me, either."

Heston was unconvinced. He knew human nature too well. But he needed emotional release. He needed shoulders to lean on. He needed help to carry the heavy load. The cumulative weight of years of subterfuge was crushing him. "I tell you this only because I need your help to find Kipp—in more ways than one."

"I hear that."

He eyed the eager, young closet-intellectual. He would accept the risk. He needed a male friend, young, strong, and able. *Is that why I stole Kipp's?*

"I was five years old when we left Chicago and moved to Miami. We moved to Naples the following year. It was...more remote. Back then, Naples, Florida, was the end of the world, a jungle outpost, almost, with a few palm-shrouded mansions tucked away from prying *eyes.*

"Still that way, only now they're in gated communities," nodded Ezra.

Heston raised and lowered his brow in agreement. "I started school here. At Lake Park Elementary. I sat behind Poppy in assembly. If I close my eyes, I can still picture those two bouncing red ponytails, those slight, pretty little shoulders. Her last name was Craft. My name was Demming. Of course, you know that. We were seated alphabetically. For a time, we were also neighbors. She and her parents lived down the block. Before the fatal crash that took her parents' lives. Before she moved to The Moorings to live with her crusty Uncle Melvin."

"Obviously, your dad didn't work as a doctor here. What did he do for a living?"

"Odd jobs. He couldn't support us. He...drank."

"An alcoholic." Arlene set down her glass.

Heston sensed Ezra was treading softly over the subject. He nodded. "And he practiced what we now term 'substance abuse.' "

"Drugs, too? Yeah, that fits. A doctor could procure them. Legal and illegal."

"My father could create them. In a laboratory."

"What? Man, that does complicate things. What kind of drugs?"

He narrowed his eyes. "Hallucinogens, among other things."

Ezra gaped. "Your old man made LSD? Did he sell it? Is that how your family got by?"

Heston's mind receded into the past. "I don't know everything about my father. Only that he grew more and more derelict. My mother worked as a nurse. I mowed lawns in our neighborhood. When I turned 14, I got a job as a bag boy after school. At a local supermarket. Kept a blue-green-polyester shirt in my locker. I rode my bike every day from Gulf View Middle School. On my 16th birthday, I bought a used motor-bike. Later on, after I'd landed the job crewing with Captain Mackay, a beat-up van."

"Whoa. Freedom. Peace and love, man."

"Yeah. I played at surfing for a while. But sailing stole my heart." He gazed out over the shadowy boatyard. The sun had disappeared. Gray darkness was descending. "I still love it so."

"What was your mother's name?"

"Kay. MacCormack was her maiden name." Again, his voice quavered.

"Your dad?"

"Sean Douglas Demming." He uttered each word precisely.

"Shawnee," whispered Arlene, chin resting on her hand.

"So where'd they get 'Heston' from? Or did they? Is it a stage name?"

He glared at Ezra coldly. "It's my real name. I'm Sean Heston Demming." Relenting, he stifled a smile. "My mom loved the movies. When I was small, she took me with her to the movies all the time. Nearly every day-off she had. Dad wouldn't—or couldn't go. There was only one movie theater in town. It was this old Army Quonset hut, like a metal cylinder sliced in half and laid out on its flat side. Down on Third Street South. Where exclusive shops are now."

"You're joshing me."

"Long, and deep and dark inside. Two long aisles snaking past row after row of seats. I could barely see over them. Sticky floor that curved down to the big screen on the far wall. Place reeked of buttered popcorn. In some ancient dream." He sniffed. "Mom named me after my dad and her favorite movie star. Dad let her. She was very diplomatic. Not an explosive jerk like he..."

Ezra nodded, non-committal. "I get the picture." He shifted his position. "The hippie pater, Doug—he was abusive. To you? To her?"

He swallowed solemnly. Words wouldn't form.

"Heston..."

"I can't..."

"Forget I asked. Just tell me what Doug was running away from, okay? Who wanted to exact revenge upon him? And why?" Ezra connected the dots. Light dawned in his brown eyes. "Did he give hallucinogens to his patients? Was that his crime?"

Exhaling loudly, Heston nodded his head in disgust. He clasped his hands behind his neck and raised his head slowly, stretching, as though by controlling his movements he might control his deep-seated anger. "Yes, as I understand it. Without their knowledge or consent—or the knowledge and consent of their families or guardians. He'd lost his judgment. He thought he was helping them. He conducted his own private anecdotal experiments on his mentally disturbed patients. There are laws regarding the use of human subjects in experiments, but he ignored them. He had to. Because he wanted to experiment with illegal drugs—I guess."

"How do you know this? Did he tell you?"

Lowering his hands, he shook his head. "No. I roughed out this sketch myself. After his death. After Mom's."

"He must have been psychotic himself. He must have been using."

Heston shrugged. "He was a son of the Sixties. He'd studied medicine in San Francisco. I was born there. In Chicago, he played it straight...deceived everyone. For a while."

"Until...? Something very bad happened, didn't it?

"Yes."

"No shit. Somebody died. Right?

"Three died. One middle-aged man, a scion of wealth; one rich, old lady; and one young mother. For a while, no one connected the deaths. Eventually, they were traced back to Dad, to his practice. He was the common denominator in the lives of the victims. Others suffered lesser effects—some, devastating, unfortunately. Incurable insanity."

"Oh, man. I am sorry." Ezra looked appalled.

Arlene patted his hand.

He nodded in acknowledgment. He squeezed Arlene's soft, warm hand.

"So you don't remember much about the scandal itself?" she asked.

"No. I remember only the repercussions. I remember what happened to our lives."

"What happened? No, wait. Finish telling me about the case." Ezra pressed his thumbs together patiently.

"Dad's protégé, his young female research assistant, fled the country. Dad's medical license was quietly revoked. I found the old newspaper clippings about his resigning his position after my mother died. Both my parents...died when I was a teen."

"Did Kay die by her own hand, too?"

He crumpled. "I can't..."

"Forget about it. Do you still have the clippings?"

"Yes. But it may be on the Internet now."

Suddenly, Ezra sat back in his chair. "Oh, wait. I get it now—the Kipp connection."

Arlene gasped, putting hand to mouth.

Heston looked at Ezra's bright face. "Before Kipp knew who his real family was, he was a free agent. He was studying to become a doctor. Once his true ancestry was revealed to him—once *I* revealed it to him, he had to make...choices."

"He dropped out of college?"

"Yes. But it wasn't all about his career path. Actually, he dropped out right after meeting my co-star Lennox for the first time. I guess it was the combination of things. He simply abandoned his old life. Threw himself headlong into show business. To be near her."

"How did Kipp and Lennox meet? Did you introduce them?"

He nodded. "On the set of *Acapulco Moon.* I took Kipp and Poppy and Winner with me to Mexico. I was so...proud of him. At that time, Lennox and I were still a cinematic 'team.' "

Ezra poked the tablecloth. "You were in good company, along the lines of Gable and Lombard, Fred and Ginger, Bogie and Bacall."

"Well, it was our last film together." Heston's voice broke. "Eight years ago, this was."

"Acapulco Moon is a classic screwball comedy. It's a riot," Ezra grinned encouragingly. "You and Lennox did some great work together."

"Yes, we did," nodded Heston wanly, his vanity fluffed in spite of his gloom. "I can't believe Len's dead. That Kipp's dead. That little Shawnee..." He clapped a hand over his face. "Damn, this is too hard!" he shouted, leaping from his chair and pacing the floor angrily. "Where the hell is my son? And my grandson? They can't be dead! And who the hell killed poor, pitiful little Lennie?"

"Don't ask," growled Arlene, *voce sotto.* "Unless you really want to know, Heston. Truth can be an ugly bugger—as you well know."

Ezra picked up a menu. "But, Ma, you're wrong about the authorities. I guarantee you one thing. If anyone can root it out, that Townsend guy can. He's the man."

"You may be right," mused Heston worriedly. He signaled the server to take their order as sun set over the yacht club terrace. "Let's eat. I need to get home. I'm worried about my wife and kids." He decided not to mention his interview with Gabe or his suspicions about Chantal DuBois. He would not speak—or make a move—until he had the facts.

Chapter Thirty-Four

"Dinner, men." Buoyant as a balloon, Beryl breezed out onto the veranda of the house on Heart of Fire Key. "What's all this?" she exclaimed, pressing her palms together, kindergarten fashion. "Music lesson? You're a lucky young man, Shawnee Demming. Not all fathers want their sons to play the drums." She smiled, exchanging a glance with Kipp.

Beating bongo drums, Shawnee was sitting atop a cushion on the tiles. Kipp himself sat on a nearby footstool, a pair of makeshift drums between his knees. Patiently, he was teaching his son rhythm and technique. Shawnee was eating it up like mashed bananas.

"Show her, man." Kipp smiled at Shawnee, who, grinning, worked the rhythm with Kipp. "A Native American beat. *One,* two. *One,* two. *One,* two. *One,* two..." Shawnee kept up with Kipp's lead. As their stint ended, Kipp applauded. "Give it up for the small fry."

Beryl applauded with gusto. "Good job, Shawnee!" She looked his way. "You're a good teacher."

He flushed. "Thanks, babe." He did a double-take. She looked slinky, showing skin. "Nice threads. Didn't know you had it in you."

She looked disconcerted—hurt and sad, yet oddly encouraged. "It's a sari. The shawl came with it. I bought it last year in Trinidad Tobago."

Don't lay it on too thick, man. She's breakable.

"Kipp, if you'll wash Master Shawnee's talented hands, dinner is served."

"I'm starving." Rising, he scooped Shawnee, giggling, from the cushion and headed for the guest half-bath. Within minutes, he and Shawnee had shed the grime and reappeared at the dining table, where

Beryl had assembled a tropical meal of baked plantains, black beans and rice, quenepe fruit, and coconut milk.

"Such as it is," she smiled, with a sweep of her hand. "We're out of *eggs*."

"A high chair?" Kipp marveled, dipping Shawnee in. "And coconut milk in a sippee cup. All the comforts of home."

"It was nice of Marissa to give us plantains and black beans."

"Hang on," said Kipp. He was silent, eyes closed. His eyes opened. "Let's eat."

"Wet's eat," seconded Shawnee, chubby legs swinging.

"What were you doing?" she asked, spooning rice into Kipp's plate.

"Giving thanks."

"For what?"

He shrugged. "I feel comfortable with you, Berry."

"Then help yourself." She handed him the plate.

Accepting it, he grinned. "I will."

Flushed, she adjusted her eyeglasses. "Look, I didn't mean—"

Standing, he heaped food onto his plate. "I'm a boor. What can I say?"

"Manners, Kipp!" She slapped his wrist.

Astonished, he frowned and then laughed and popped her back. Shawnee laughed.

"You like it when I put you in your place." She grinned, self-conscious about her teeth.

"No, I don't. Not really. If I weren't so hungry, I'd paddle your fanny. Later."

As Kipp resumed his seat and chowed down, she fixed a small plate for Shawnee and placed it before the tot. Dipping a baby spoon, she fed him skillfully.

"I was raised by a woman just like you."

"Your adoptive parents?"

He nodded. "Benjy and Nancy McKendrick. They named me Kieran Jacob McKendrick. That was my name growing up."

"She was US Navy. Was he?"

"Yeah, both of them. She retired an ensign. When she married Benjy. He was a machinist—a lifer. They opened a bicycle shop."

"You think I'm like your Navy mum?"

"An exact replica—little, bossy, prudish, efficient, fearless—and when you're sweet, it's so unexpected, it catches a man off guard."

"Is Nancy still running the shop?"

"She died—last year—on the Big Island. She always pushed me to be my best. Funny—I was desperate to get away from her. When she died, I was destroyed. Why is that, Beryl?"

"I don't know. You loved her, I suppose. More than you realized."

"Yeah."

"I suppose your family lived all over the world."

"Yeah, we did. The last place was Oahu. It was rough because I wasn't a native Hawaiian. I got in fights. I loved the place, Hawaii—the North Shore. Huge, crashing waves. What I remember most about it was surfing—and the smells. Kind of like here, only more redolent."

"Redolent? That's a big word."

"Believe it or not, Little Miss Efficiency, I can read and write."

"Do you read a lot?" she asked.

"I did—during rehab, and afterwards. I read a lot of—esoteric stuff."

"What kind of esoteric stuff?"

"Philosophy. Religion. Do you know what theosophy is? Occult stuff, too. When I shed the drugs, I was searching for a way to calm myself." He paused. "Correction: I was searching for inner peace. Obviously, I didn't find it. I seemed to circle all around the truth—I made stabs at it, but I never penetrated the heart of it. You know? Finally, I stopped trying."

"You gave up?" she asked.

"My life fell apart. What was the point?"

She considered for a moment. "Maybe that is the point."

He took a sip of coconut milk. "What do you mean?"

She adjusted the shawl around her shoulders. "Well, anyone can find peace of mind when things are going well. The whole point is to find inner peace when things aren't going well. That's when one needs it most."

He studied her closely. "Needs it most?"

"Uh-huh."

"Beryl, do you what synchronicity is?"

"Sounds familiar, but..."

"It's when two or more seemingly unrelated events occur in such way as to seem meaningful," he said. "Like a coincidence that seems like a sign. You know?"

"Two occurrences coming together in a meaningful way? But not really accidentally."

"Who really knows?" he asked. "Seems so. Ever read Carl Jung?"

"Not since university." She regarded him with heightened interest.

"You look fetching this evening, Miss Northgate. That's a good Olde English word, isn't it." He mimicked her accent. "Fetch-ing."

"Indeed." She cast her eyes downward. Shawnee mashed his plantains with a spoon.

"Do you go out with men? Hey, pass the coco milk—what's the word, buddy?"

"Pwease," chirped Shawnee, mouth full.

"I have in the past," she answered. "Not too much lately."

"But you didn't sleep with them. You don't approve of me, do you?"

"I know you better now, Kipp. I do care about—what happens to you."

"My lifestyle offends you, doesn't it?"

"I never understood it."

"I could tell you stories," he said with a sigh.

"Tell me stories. Please. I want to understand you. What drove you to consider suicide, Kipp? Tell me about your life. I can only imagine what you must have endured—everyone pulling at you, using you."

"Ripping me off."

"They all want a piece of you, no doubt. All that temptation..."

He smirked. "All that degradation?"

"You're not doomed, Kipp. You can begin again."

"Frankly, I was hoping to start again with Marissa."

She said nothing.

"What's the matter?" he asked.

"Nothing."

"I don't know how to find another Marissa. I'll never be able to find someone like her."

"Maybe—maybe you aren't supposed to be with someone like her," Beryl suggested.

"No? Who then?"

"I don't know," Beryl said, avoiding his eyes.

"You don't know much, do you?"

"Are you finished?"

"I haven't started good yet. Oh, you mean eating? Uh-huh."

"I know you ate enough for two men." Rising she began clearing the table. Smoothly, he ran his hand up the back of her thigh. His hand slipped inside the slit in her skirt and roamed expertly between her legs. For the briefest moment, she let him...

"Stop it, Kipp!" Pulling away, she glanced at Shawnee. "Maybe you are too far gone."

Annoyed, he tossed his napkin on the table and stood up behind her. Leaning over her, he kissed her one bare shoulder. "You can run, Beryl, but you can't hide from your own nature. Nature always wins."

Plates in hand, she drew away. She walked to the kitchen door, pushing it open with her back. Stopping, she looked at him, bottom lip quivering.

"It's not true that I'm fearless, Kipp. There is one thing I'm afraid of."

He hitched his thumbs in his belt loop. "Men? Me?"

Her eyes locked his. *Wide, blue yonder.*

He seized his opportunity. "Beryl, I'm sorry I made a pass." He reconsidered. "I'm sorry I touched you inappropriately. It's a bad habit. I need to break it. I don't actually know how to approach a woman in any kind of mature, real—um, meaningful way."

Calm, she licked her lips and balanced the empty plates. "I believe flowers and candy have been working for centuries on."

He laughed, trying not to. "Yeah. A good suggestion. Would you settle for a song? I'm sort of—writing one for you."

More wide blue yonder.

She sniffed. "Tomorrow you can catch us a fish to eat." Dignified, she pushed the door open with her backside and disappeared into the kitchen. The door swung shut behind her.

"Ha!" he exclaimed, throwing up his hands. He slumped down in the chair next to Shawnee. "Okay, buddy. You heard the whole thing. What would you do if you were in my shoes, eh?" He stared at the swinging door. "The strange thing is—I'm as afraid of her as she is of me. Don't tell her I said so, okay?"

Troubled, he tousled the toddler's blonde curls. Rising, he strode around the high-chair and pushed open the swinging door. She was standing at the sink.

"Beryl, that's just it, see? I can't catch you a fish. I won't be here tomorrow. I'm clearing out. That way, you and the kid will be out of danger." He moved toward her. He stroked her hair. She was crying. "If I thought I could make love to you—without hurting you, I..."

The house phone rang. Neither one moved to answer it. The recorder engaged. They listened to the message. "Beryl, this is Heston. Are you on Heart of Fire Key? Your mother seems to think so. Rob will check on you in the morning. He thinks you're there with a man. Call me. I need you ASAP. You haven't answered my other messages. Maybe you'll answer this one."

Click.

"I can't wait until morning," Kipp murmured. "I've got to clear out now."

Dishcloth in hand, Beryl blocked the doorway. "If you leave tonight, Shawnee and I are coming with you."

Chapter Thirty-Five

At 3:00 a.m., Heston, seated on the bed he had shared with Poppy for the past eight years, regarded his wife intently. Neither of them could sleep. He was stalling for time.

"Poppy," he asked, "Whatever became of that bosomy little brunette friend of yours—the caterer. The one who tried to steal your first husband?

"You mean Sasha Bassett?" Poppy said. "She's not my friend. I haven't seen her in years. Someone saw her working as a clerk or something in a big-box store, ages ago. Why?"

"I thought I saw her today."

"Where?" Poppy asked.

"On Gabe Cade's monstrous yacht."

"What were you doing there?"

"Demanding answers," he quipped.

"Did you get any?"

"I'm not sure yet." Quickly, he changed the subject. "You should have joined us for dinner at the club," he scolded.

Ruffled, she inhaled cigarette smoked deeply and exhaled it through her pretty nose.

"Dinner, Heston? Our son is dead. Our grandson is missing, probably dead. You gave away Kipp's legacy to the police, including his last words to me. Lennox is dead, a woman you knew for 20 years, and our son is suspected of killing her. Our other children could be in grave danger—and you're upset because I wouldn't go out to dinner? Take a hike."

Stubbing a butt into a cut-crystal ashtray, she returned his gaze nervously, her wide-set brown eyes searching for something hidden. He was being carried by the current of her anger and defiance as it coursed like a river. His allowing the authorities to take Kipp's belongings without a subpoena had dealt the final blow to his wife's compliance. Now she was demanding answers.

"I'm not going to ask you a third time, Heston," she stated emphatically. She licked her lips in anticipation. She reached for her purse and fumbled for her vanity case, extracting a gold-mirrored lipstick. "What was between you and Lennox?"

He hadn't seen her smoke for years. "Surely you knew Lennox was off her rocker," he began slowly. "At first, I thought it was a joke. When I realized Kipp was serious about her, I was horrified. I knew the truth—an ugly truth that Kipp *didn't* know."

Poppy searched for a tissue. "What truth?"

"Red, think back. Lennox was obsessed with *me*. She wanted to be near *me*. She didn't want Kipp's children. She wanted to bear *my grandchildren* because I refused to give her my children."

"You conceited..." she muttered.

"She *told* me so," he declared. "She tried to seduce me even then. Not long after Shawnee was born."

"It's possible." She applied orange lipstick and blotted her lips with the tissue.

"It's a fact. Lennox knew I would never tell Kipp the truth. It would hurt the boy too much. It would hurt *you* too much." He brushed his right hand along the top of his head. He paced the floor. "But, in retrospect, I should have told him right away, when he first became engaged to her. But I didn't..." He stood still. He looked pleadingly at his wife.

"Because of me," she whispered, eyes red and raw. Her small face was haggard with woe. She shredded the tissue in her hands. "Because you would have had to tell me that you and Lennox had been lovers."

"No!" he hopped to his feet. "Never."

"But you said..."

"I said Kipp didn't know the truth. That wasn't the truth. Lennox and I were never lovers."

"Then what is the truth?"

He eased down beside her on the divan. "At the time Lennox was a young girl breaking into films, I was a young rake." He felt as though he was driving a knife into his wife's tender heart and into her love for him. He was standing in the dock, a place he had dreaded for so long. If this wasn't Hell, it was close enough.

"I want details, Heston," she said, wrath smoldering beneath her pain. Coughing softly, she held the tissue to her lips.

Reluctantly, he cleared his throat. "Yes. All right. You deserve that." He glanced at her. "Are you sure, Poppy? Do you really want to know? Once it's been said..."

"Tell me!" Head in hands, she held the tissue to her closed eyes.

"Oh, Poppy Sue." He shook his head. He wasn't certain now which of them was in greater pain. "All right. Here goes.

"I first met Lennox Cordova when she was a teenager. She was 15, pretending to be 18. Her mother, Lynne, was a true piranha, an aggressive Hollywood mother of the old school. She would have killed or slept with anyone or anything to help her daughter's career."

"I seem to recall that. Wasn't Lennox on the baby beauty queen circuit?"

"Lynne meant business. Brilliant young directors quaked when leggy Lynne strode onto their sets. She had been a gymnast in her youth. She was slick with sheen and muscular, a tad taller than Lennox. There was an air of the circus performer about her—something perverse."

Eyes averted, Poppy mused coldly. "I never met Lynne Cordova. She had died by the time I met Lennox, eight years ago in Acapulco."

Heston nodded. "Right after you and I were married. I remember the meeting well. You met Lennox on the set. I introduced you as my bride. What you don't know is that Lennox took me aside later that day and threw a violent temper tantrum in her trailer." He was leaning close to her now, touching her body with his.

"Did she? You never told me that, Heston. You never t-told me anything about this whole affair," Poppy cried. "Why should I believe you now?"

"Because I'm telling you the truth now, Poppy. If you'll let me."

Guiltily, she nodded, outburst subsiding. "All right."

He sighed. Images, sounds, smells, all flooded his mind. "It all happened such a long time ago. Lennox was so young, so fresh, so stunning then. The girl was staggeringly, blindingly beautiful in her youth. She had creamy skin with the muscle tone of an athlete like her mother. Luscious lips, breasts the size of juicy melons on her small, slender frame, dazzling shapely legs with perfectly formed knees, feet, and ankles. She always wore an anklet, even then. She was exquisite."

Poppy opened her eyes. "And you fell madly in lust with her the moment you saw her. I think I'm in hell."

"No. I never fell for Lennox."

"Then what?" Poppy asked, barely audible.

"How do I say this?" He lowered his eyes. "That first summer I worked with director Ivan Lukasy. On the set of *Daredevil Alley.*"

"Of course. Your first picture with Lennox."

"Yes. Her mother Lynne had bartered Lennox to that lecher, bartered her for a leading role in his racy little racing film."

"At fifteen?"

Heston nodded.

"How old were you?"

"Twenty-six," Heston admitted grudgingly. "I'll never forget the first time I saw my future co-star. It was one of the great aesthetic moments of my life. Lennox made a dramatic entrance onto the set on Lukasy's arm. She came down a flower-strewn flight of steps surrounded by a gawking cast and crew. She didn't appear to walk beside Ivan. It was more as if she floated in on a white mist. She was dressed in a filmy white gown with a flowing full skirt. It was like seeing a voluptuous angel drift down from heaven—like a sparkly marshmallow inviting you to eat it."

"Lennox was no angel," Poppy murmured. "And no marshmallow."

He shrugged in agreement. "Then I found out she was to play my wife in the film. I was playing a race car driver. We had our first love scene. I was supercharged. She fell for me from the beginning. Sparks flew—from her plugs, anyway. Which was why we made such a marvelous cinematic team back then.

"She followed me around the set incessantly. She wouldn't leave me alone. She brought me cappuccino the way I like it. She pressed against me, asked me questions about acting, sought my guidance, her deep cleavage looming like a secret cavern, begging to be explored. I was interested for a while. Do you really want to hear this?"

Poppy sniffed. "Y-you're admitting it was g-good between you."

He sighed. "Only as flirtation. Love affairs are like scotch. Most are rough, but the best ones are smooth. Young Lennox was rough. True, I admired her luscious body. But I never actually fell for her."

"Oh, Heston! Do you take me for a fool?"

"You didn't let me finish. I'm trying to tell you the truth. You asked me to."

"Then go on."

"Already once-divorced—from Inez Greco—I was no callow youth. I wasn't bereft of my senses. Lennox was underage. I was a grown man.

Actually, I was a young idiot. True, I wanted her badly. But I was old enough to know better."

"Heston, if you never made love to Lennox, then what's the problem? What's the truth?"

"The truth is—Damn it, Poppy! I was seduced by her mother, Lynne."

Poppy leaped to her feet. "Her mother?"

Fondling her wrist, he pulled her back down beside him on the divan. "The first time Lynne Cordova came on to me was at the home I'd rented in Malibu that summer, on the advice of my publicist. Star digs to give myself star status. Lennox was still a child, unsure, clumsy, but passionate and giving when we made love on screen. But her stage mother Lynne—she was an old pro. I was hungry and so was Lynne. I let Lynne have her way with me—off the set."

Poppy rested her chin on his shoulder. "Did you...love her?"

"Hell, no. At that time, I thought I was in love with Montserrat Flynn. If Montsey was a fluffy mousse, Lynne Cordova was meat and potatoes."

Poppy flinched.

"I'm sorry, my love. That was callous of me."

Poppy studied the tissue, now balled in her hands. "How long were you and Lynne lovers?"

"For about six weeks. Lynne was—insatiable. She began treating me like a blue-ribbon stud at the county fair. She wanted to sire me out."

"What?"

"To share her swinging lifestyle. I didn't want to. I believed it would hurt my career down the line. In my own way, I'm something of a prig, I suppose."

"You mean orgies?"

He smiled at her innocence. "Well, yes. Multiple partners, indecent acts. That sort of thing. I don't know why I attract the sicko gals."

"You attract all the gals, sicko or no."

He broke a smile. His shoulders bobbed in amusement. But her demeanor remained serious.

"So you broke it off?" she asked.

"So I broke it off. Lynne was furious. Lennox didn't know about us at that point—or so we thought. Lennox was hurt when I stopped coming round to their place in the Hollywood hills. I felt bad for her, but all I wanted was escape from her mother's claws."

"Then why did you make four more movies with Lennox?"

He took her face in his hands. "Because I was contractually obligated to do so." Squeezing, he let her go. "Blast it." He rubbed the back of his neck in frustration. "By our third picture, I realized that every time I turned around, Lennox was underfoot."

Poppy inhaled sharply. "She started stalking you?"

He gave her a big hug. "Yes. That's what I've been trying to tell you—or to conceal from you—oh, I don't know. All I know is I couldn't get away from that nut case. Do you understand? And then, lo and behold, she up and marries my son."

"Did you ever file for a restraining order?"

He shook his head. "No. I couldn't. She never did anything overt. She never threatened me. She was just always *there*—somewhere, in the foreground, in the background, or right in the middle of everything I did. It took a while for me to grasp what was going on."

"Why would she have stalked you?" She eyed him slyly. "I have a feeling you haven't told me everything, Heston."

He avoided her gaze.

She moved in for the closing. "You ended things. How did Lynne take it?"

He paced feverishly. "Lynne was hard core—with a large circle of acquaintances. She told no one of our trysts. I wanted it that way. I was afraid of blackmail, or of being charged for services rendered. Lynne was a tiger. One time Lennox let it slip that her mother had rented her out during adolescence to at least two billionaires. I was appalled, but I didn't really care. I wasn't planning to marry into the Cordova family, only to take my erotic exercise with Lynne the gymnast, and then move on."

She tossed the balled tissue into a trash basket. "Do you hear yourself? How can you men be so unfeeling?"

"I don't know. We are what we are, Poppy. I am what I am. I'm leveling here with you as best I can. Do you want the truth from me or not?"

"Finish it," she whispered scratchily. Her nasal breaths were short rasps of air.

Again, he sighed. "Fate had other ideas. One night—one drunken night—I was wildly horny. I drove over to Lynne's. Lennox caught me off guard. She told me her mom was already in bed. It was dark. The lights were out. I entered Lynne's bedroom and climbed into bed. By the time I realized it wasn't Lynne, *but Lennox* who was heaving and moaning beneath me, it was too late. I had succumbed to her charms—drunken sot that I was."

"Lennox tricked you into bed?"

"Uh—yes."

"A 15-year-old girl? Heston..." Her features twisted in suspicion.

He raised his right hand. *"That* is the truth. But it gets worse. Despite her protests, I zipped up my knickers and bolted like lightning.

"Not long after I'd put the kibosh on that action, Lennox came to me, frightened, in tears. She told me that she was pregnant with my child. I laughed it off. Too cagey to fall for *that* old ruse. I refused to be hoodwinked. I accused her of trying to trap me into marriage. I truly did not believe her, Poppy."

"No?"

"After only one time? Come on."

"One time is all it takes, Heston," she said plaintively. "You know that as well as I do."

He blanched. "Yeah. I do. Now. That night I said it must be Lukasy's kid—or one of his billionaire buddies. She began to cry. She swore she was telling the truth. She said Ivan had had a vasectomy. I was the only other man she'd been within four months."

He shut his eyes in shame. "I howled with laughter. I humiliated her. I raged at her. I told her I was way too savvy to fall for the trick she was trying to pull. She ran out crying, demeaned and devastated."

"Oh, Heston."

"I was freakin' drunk, Poppy. I congratulated myself on my shrewd knowledge of women. Then I passed out. That night Lennox had a miscarriage. Fifteen years old, and she miscarried my baby. She refused to tell anyone who the father was. She never got over the miscarriage or me." Glancing at Poppy, he met a blank stare.

"Lennox miscarried your child? You mean your first child with her?"

"What?"

"Are you denying that Shawnee is your son?"

"Of course I deny it! Ludicrous. Not even worth discussing. Where did you ever get that idea?" He sensed sub-surface pressure building. He could feel her pain. "I'm talking about the child she lost many years ago that she claimed was mine." He hung his head. "Now I believe she was telling me the truth." He picked at stray lint on his trousers.

"And that's why..."

"That's why I didn't want my son to marry her."

A light appeared in Poppy's eyes. "But it's also why she wanted to marry your son."

"Yes." The word itself was a sigh of relief for him.

"She wanted *you*."

"Yes."

"She didn't want Kipp. She wanted you."

"Yes, Poppy. Lennox used Kipp to be near me." He felt her hand stroking his neck.

Poppy shuddered. "It's grotesque, Heston. You mean to say that if Lennox couldn't have your baby..."

"She would have my grandbaby. Which she did."

"Shawnee!" Poppy looked aghast. "S-She even..."

He dropped down beside her on the steps. "Named him after me? Yes. She just changed the spelling, probably to throw Kipp—and you—off the scent."

Poppy gasped in realization. "Kipp still doesn't know. Or never knew? Oh, my poor darling!"

"Him or me?" Heart bruised, he felt Poppy's small, warm hand on his arm. He felt her soft, moist lips brush his cheek. His loins flamed.

"Oh, my love." He nestled his face between her sweet breasts. Cuddling him closely, she stroked his hair. Suddenly, she moved away from him. "But it still doesn't explain..."

"Poppy, you are the love of my life," he rasped. "Lynne, Lennox—these women meant nothing to me—except turmoil. Lennox was a thorn in my side and a threat to my family's happiness."

"How much of a threat, Heston?" she asked.

He sat upright. "You mean, did I kill her?"

"Well, did you?"

"No. But, in the interest of full disclosure, here's something you deserve to know. I did go to visit Lennox the day she died."

Her eyes widened. "Why?"

"She phoned me here. She told me she was publishing Lynne's diary—unless I left you and took up with her. I drove to South Beach to steal the diary."

Poppy's wide eyes riveted him. "And did you—steal the diary?"

"No. I couldn't find it." He flushed. "I tore her place apart. I yelled at her. I threatened to kill her. She reveled in it. Kept trying to undress me. I didn't know about the secret room."

She tensed. "What secret room?"

"Townsend showed it to me today. It was kept locked. It was a kind of a shrine to me."

"Wow." She covered her mouth with her hand.

"Poppy—I think you should know. They're going to arrest me. They have me on the security videos."

She turned. "As long as we're confessing things, there's something you should know."

"What?" He stopped breathing.

"I stole the diary from Lennox."

He inhaled. "Where is it?"

She backed away. "I was hoping you had it. I can't find it. I hid it in my dressing room closet. It was gone the next day. I haven't seen it since."

"Who the hell has it?"

"I don't know, Heston. And it terrifies me. You see, I read it, every word—that night in Fontainebleau, while Winner slept. I couldn't put it down."

"Then you already knew—"

"Everything about Lynne. Nothing about Lennox. And I know about the others."

"Then, Red, you understand why we must find that diary—before the law does." He scratched his brain. "Was it one of the kids? Who knew it was there? Did Lennox see you take it? Did she give it to you?"

"Too many questions." She pressed her palms to her temples. Her panic was rising.

"Poppy, how did you know about the diary?"

"Lennox told me. In the bathroom. At the Fontainebleau. I ran into her that morning."

"Ran into Lennox? Too pat."

Her face contorted. "She told me to leave you—or she'd publish the diary—and ruin you and destroy our family." She inched toward the bedroom door. "Heston, I—"

He followed. "Did you kill her?"

She ran for the door, but it flew open as she approached. She stumbled backwards into the room. Detective Betancourt sauntered in after her. "Need a ride to headquarters?" he asked, unsmiling.

Without fanfare and with a quiet precision born of practice, Agent Townsend entered behind him, papers in hand. Two policemen followed him. He directed them.

"Master baths—his and hers. You know what to look for." He turned to face them. "Good evening, Heston. Mrs. Demming." He thumped the papers. "We have a warrant to search the premises."

"For what?" he asked, disbelieving. He stepped in to shield his wife.

"Anything and everything." A police officer entered from the bathroom. Betancourt stepped around him. "Mrs. Demming, you're under arrest."

"For what?" Heston breathed.

"Suspicion of murder." Stone-faced, Townsend addressed Poppy. "Your fingerprints turned up on a bottle of pills found at the scene of Lennox Cordova's death and on a wine bottle. You appear on the security videos visiting her condo the day she died. You also have a motive."

"What motive?"

"Jealousy and financial gain. We believe you may be in league with your son Kipp to gain control over Lennox Cordova's money. In her will, she left everything to Shawnee."

Heston stepped back. "In league with Kipp?"

"H-Heston, it's not t-true!" Poppy stammered.

He stepped in. "Townsend, arrest me! I was there, too. You know I was. I had access to these pills. My wife isn't capable of..."

"Easy, Heston. We aren't charging her with the crime—yet. We're taking her in for questioning. You can come along for the ride." He turned to Poppy. "Your wife stole the diary. It was in her hand when she entered the elevator. She crammed it into her purse before reaching the lobby. Where is the diary, Mrs. Demming?"

He was livid. "You were eavesdropping. Didn't you hear? She doesn't know."

"If the diary is in this house," Townsend assured him, "my men will find it. Let's go, Jorge. Mrs. Demming, if you please." He stood aside, allowing them to pass.

Helplessly, he watched, as Betancourt placed handcuffs around Poppy's tender wrists. Sneering, Betancourt offered her candy from a roll of spearmints as police led her away.

Contrite, Ram appeared in the hallway, followed by Lissette, in a bathrobe. "Sorry, Mr. Demming. He ordered us not to let on they were here."

Chapter Thirty-Six

The sun was rising. Tired from lack of sleep, Ezra quaffed his caramel macchiato. "Ever since Heston bought his own island, he thinks he's Errol Flynn in *Captain Blood*."

Seated beside him at the outdoor table, Arlene cracked a smile. "He's got the tush for it." Napkin in hand, she dabbed milk foam from his moustache. Her diamond rings reflected the morning sun's rays.

"Ma, please." He waved her away.

Arlene tossed the napkin onto his lap. "I'm just saying."

"What? Don't tell me you were in love with him, too? All these years?"

"Were?" She smiled from the corner of her eye. Don't underestimate Heston. I've known him 25 years, ever since he was a bit player on the New York stage, a hick from Florida. The first time I took him to a dairy deli, he ordered a cheese omelet. He couldn't understand why the waitress kept yelling, 'We're kosher!' He was so good looking she forgave him. A nightingale with balls, that's what he was. A regular Adonis in those days. He could dance like a dream. He learned from his mistakes. He fought his way to the top. Ezra. If you're smart, you'll do what he does—learn! Fight! Don't write him off as a has-been."

Ezra frowned. "I never said he was a has-been. Hell, he's my boss."

Arlene poked his shoulder. "And he never dropped me, even when times were tough. I've lasted through all three of his wives. He likes me a little, you can be sure."

"I am sure."

Arlene deflated. "And the deaths of two sons. I only hope this current mess doesn't kill him."

Ezra craned his neck, searching up and down Fifth Avenue South in Naples, the downtown street lined with sleek shops and eateries. The sun beat down hotter every minute on their outdoor table at Rainbow's. Soon they would need to open the umbrella.

"Vivian should be here any minute," he said. "She promised me she'd join us for breakfast."

Arlene checked her diamond-encrusted wristwatch. "It's nearly lunch time now."

Annoyed, he sipped. "I've got to tell you, Ma. I was right about her health."

"Yeah?"

"Yeah. I confronted her. She needs surgery. I'm worried sick. I really love her."

"Are you going to eat that cookie? Don't eat it." Arlene pointed to the white-chocolate chip and macadamia confection lying on his plate. "You know, Ezra, your sweet tooth is going to kill you. Diabetes runs in your father's family."

"Take it."

His mother reached for the cookie and dropped it, uneaten, onto her own plate.

"Did someone say 'cookie'?" asked the coffee-shop's owner and hostess, approaching their table, a coffee pot in her hand. Her short, blonde curls bounced merrily. "Good morning, Ezra. Where's Vivian?"

"On her way. Cookie, my mother, Arlene Gold. Ma, Cookie Talbot. She's married to Poppy's ex-husband. My mother's visiting from New York."

"Then you're Heston's agent," Cookie smiled, filling Arlene's empty coffee cup. "Welcome."

"You're married to Poppy's ex?" Arlene marveled, brushing crumbs from her hands and reaching for her lipstick-rimmed cup.

"Sure. Poppy and I stayed friends, even after she hit the big time. We still work out at *Curves,* up on Creech Road. Our kids have play dates together. How's she doing, Ezra? This business about Kipp is awful. It was all over the morning shows. Nobody knows where he is, or poor little Shawnee either. Poppy must be a wreck."

Arlene nodded. "She is. We stopped by their home last night—in Port Royal? I took the kids some gifts. Poppy's wretched."

Cookie looked concerned. "How 'bout the kids?"

Ezra stirred. "Kids are okay. Winner seems shell shocked. She's more sensitive than the others." He waved and stood. "Here's Vivi!"

"Hey, don't knock 'em." Arlene pointed a red nail at her son. "I love those kids. I can say what I want to about them, but nobody else. Granted, Dakota's moody, and Teggi's a wimp. But that Sage." She patted her purse. "That Sage is a smart...well, cookie."

Cookie laughed and put a hand on Arlene's shoulder as Vivian Champlain sat down in the chair Ezra had drawn for her. Pushing Vivian's chair in, he resumed his seat at the table.

"Good morning, Vivi," beamed Cookie. "Decaf, as usual?"

"Nothing for me, thanks," said Vivian, looking bedraggled. She changed her mind. "Oh, why not?"

"Back in a jiffy," Cookie said, heading inside her café.

"Aren't you feeling well?" asked Arlene, placing a hand on Vivian's forearm.

Vivian patted her hand. "Didn't Ezzie tell you?"

"I told her."

"It will all work out," Arlene told her.

"I hope so."

Running, Cookie returned with a cup of steaming decaf and set it down before Vivian. "I just heard the news—they think Lennox was murdered! The police arrested Poppy!"

"Seriously?" Ezra asked.

Vivian put her cup down. "I thought Lennox overdosed—pills and booze."

Cookie looked smug. "The pills she took weren't her prescription. They were switched."

"How ghastly." Vivian looked to Ezra for reassurance. Dark circles rimmed her blue eyes.

"We'll find out from Heston," he said. He wanted to cry. *She looks bad.* "Check, please, Cookie." The hostess looked frantic. "Hey," he said, pulling her apron. "Don't worry about Poppy. It'll work out. It must be a mistake."

"I don't want to see Heston," Vivian declared outright. "I'm not going with you."

He glared helplessly. It was damned disturbing. "How come you always avoid Heston? It was embarrassing last night at dinner. Your attitude didn't matter before, but, once production begins, I'll be working with him 24/7. Get used to it, Vivian."

Biting her lip, Cookie dropped the check onto the table. As he reached for his wallet, his mother edged closer to Vivian.

"Vivian, bubbie, you and I need to talk," Arlene whispered confidentially, clutching her handbag with both diamond-cluttered hands.

Chapter Thirty-Seven

Agent Townsend nudged Heston awake. "Follow me, please." He led him into a small room off the main office. "We're using the County's facilities," he noted. Heston looked at his watch. It was 9:32 a.m.

"Sit down, Heston," Townsend ordered, sidling up to a small table and pulling out a rickety chair. His shirtsleeves were rolled up, his tie loosened and hanging limp. "You look like shit. Bet you don't hear that too often."

"I've been waiting all night, Townsend." Wearily, he complied, seating himself at a square metal table. The middle-aged agent took a seat across from him. The two men were alone in the room, but Heston knew he was under surveillance. He nodded cordially toward the large mirror.

"Eyes front, Heston."

"Sorry, Chief. Just saying howdy." It was his best James Cagney impression. He shifted his shoulders and stroked his chin contemplatively. "Ah ha." He smiled wanly. "No?"

"We know how Lennox died," Townsend said, face immobile, his skin tinged green under the fluorescent lights of the stark interrogation room.

"How?" he demanded, on edge.

"Take it easy." Townsend held up a sheet of paper. "Because this is a high-profile case, the Coroner has issued a preliminary report. To soothe the savage press."

"What does it say?" He leaned across the table and grabbed for the sheet, missing it, as Townsend pulled it away.

"Easy, Heston." The agent placed the sheet flat on the table and clasped his hands on top of it. "It says this: the deceased consumed a lethal amount of prescription narcotics, which she unwisely topped off with a bottle of wine. She died from the toxic mixture of alcohol and painkillers. We doubt she knew she was pregnant."

Heston rubbed his face with his hands. "Oh, Lennie," he moaned softly.

"Do you have any idea who would have wanted to injure your former daughter-in-law?"

"Injure? Injure means a bitchy comment, a dig in the press, a forgotten invitation. This was violence, murder."

"Of the passive-aggressive sort."

"The only people I know who have had cause to murder Lennox are—oh, never mind." He palmed his eyelids shut.

"I have to mind, sir. It's my job. You were going to say—perhaps—your son Kipp—and yourself?"

His lids popped open. "Me? Why me? Why would I want to commit such a horrendous act?"

Townsend's arms dropped to his sides. "Speaking of acting..."

"I wasn't."

"No, but you were doing it. Good, too." He smiled irreverently. "That's why they pay you the big bucks, sir."

"Can it, Nick. What are you implying?"

"We know, Heston."

"You know what?" Hopping to his feet, he flung the chair under the table.

"That you have Lynne Cordova's diary."

"I don't," Heston said, thankful to know the detectives were fishing. "Who does?"

"Search me. Now can we..."

"Not so fast," grunted Townsend.

"Let's have it," said Heston, sweat beading his upper lip.

"We think someone else may have aided and abetted Kipp."

"Me?" Heston asked.

"The security cam that day shows four other visitors besides Kipp."

"Really?" This news surprised Heston.

"Really."

"Who, for instance?" He reseated himself at the little table.

Townsend leaned forward, eyes pointed like knives. "For instance—you."

"Oh?" He crossed his legs and adjusted his shirttail. He suppressed the urge to chew the nail of his forefinger. He clasped his hands in his lap.

"Why didn't you tell us you'd visited Lennox's penthouse on the day of her death? You must have known we'd find out eventually."

Pressing his lips together, he returned Townsend's stare. He shrugged. "Earn your keep."

"Stall's over, Heston. What were you doing there?"

He pressed his lips tightly. He studied the table top. "I wanted to see my grandson."

"We know Lennox phoned you that morning. We have her phone records."

Heston glanced at the mirror. "She wanted to know what time I'd arrive."

Townsend growled. "Look at me. Was she alive when you arrived?"

"Of course; Yes. She buzzed me in."

"Was she alive when you left?" Townsend asked.

"Yes. Everything was—"

"What?"

"Fine," Heston assured him.

Townsend exhaled in frustration, drumming his fingers. "Would you like to know who *else* visited her penthouse that day? Besides you and your wife?"

He sat to attention. Eyeing Townsend, he raised his brow.

"Over the course of the day in question, five individuals rode the private elevator up to Lennox's floor: Kipp; yourself; a woman identified by building security as Vivian Champlain; your wife; and Gabe Cade's secretary, one Chantal DuBois, in that order. And then Kipp once again, after midnight. And the next morning, the daily maid who couldn't get buzzed in and who rode up with the daytime doorman. Together, they found the body."

Chantal DuBois? Heston inched forward in the chair. "What about Kipp? What was he doing there?"

Townsend explained. "On the condo's security video, we can see Kipp keying in a generic security code. How he got it, we don't know. Then we see him running through the empty lobby, then ascending in the private elevator to Lennox's penthouse. We see him descending, ten minutes later, with Shawnee in his arms. He flees down the street out of the building cam's range."

"You don't know where they went?" Heston asked.

"Not yet. We're working on it."

"Have you told my wife any of this?"

"We'll talk to her, in the presence of her attorney." Townsend nodded at the bleak plaster partition. "She's on ice in the next room."

"Right now?" he gaped. "Is she all right?"

"Of course." Townsend nodded smugly. "Any idea why Poppy would visit Lennox—other than to steal the diary?"

"No, they h—"

"Hated each other? Is that what you were going to say? Enough to kill?"

"That's absurd. Family squabbles, nothing more." He gulped dryly. "What about the security cameras inside the penthouse? What do they show?"

Townsend cocked his head. "Nothing. They were turned off. The daily maid said Lennox kept them shut off. Apparently, Lennox had a new boyfriend, a mystery man she didn't want recorded in compromising situations."

"Bedroom sex?" Heston relaxed in his seat. "Was this mystery man paying for the penthouse?"

Someone knocked at the door.

"Enter," bellowed Townsend.

Betancourt eased into the room, clutching in his hands a clear plastic bag containing a blue stuffed animal. "My men found this."

A distant alarm rang in Heston's mind. He had seen the little dinosaur before—but where? Realization engulfed him. *Oh, no...*

"We think it belongs to Shawnee Demming," said Betancourt, scouring Heston's face.

Townsend glanced from Heston to Betancourt. "Have the lab work it up. Where'd you find it?"

Betancourt grinned sourly. "In Heston's T-hangar at the Naples airport. On the floor, right where his missing airplane should be."

"My plane isn't missing." He rubbed the heavy morning growth on his chin.

"Where is it?"

"Being serviced?"

"Where?"

"You'll have to ask my mechanics."

"We will. Anyone else have permission to use it?"

"No one." He inhaled sharply. "Only Nanny Northgate. She's a first-rate pilot. One of her job perks is *carte blanche* to fly my Cessna. But she's supposed to be on holiday with her parents in England."

Betancourt grinned, exhaling peppermint breath. "The nanny's not in England." He looked at Townsend. "We checked."

"Do her folks know where she is?"

"Spoke to her mom, Alba Northgate, not an hour ago. The mom said Beryl phoned her, told her she was going to fly Heston's plane to The Keys—to spend a week alone on Heston's private island. Something about a seaplane. Claims she phoned you about it last night."

"When was this?" Townsend asked.

"Three days ago." Betancourt sneered at Heston. "That's why we checked out your hangar, bright boy." He looked back at Townsend. "What better place to rendezvous with the help, eh? On your own private island in The Keys." He winked at Heston. "When were you planning to join her?"

"You've got this all wrong, you imbecile," Heston said.

"Man, you sure as hell live up to your reputation." Betancourt grinned, shaking his head. "How were you going to get to your shack-up? On your little sailboat?"

Heston leapt to his feet. "You moron. I'm not going to rendezvous with the nanny. I fired her smart ass."

Townsend blinked. "Fired her? I thought you said she went on vacation."

Heston sighed, pacing. "I said that because I didn't want to upset my wife. While Poppy was in Miami, I gave Berry a month's notice, but I gave her the first week off with pay. To think about her future. She told me she was going to the UK." He shoved his hands in his pocket. "The news about Kipp and Shawnee was bad enough. Poppy was near hysteria. I had to fudge."

Townsend twirled a pen between his fingers. "So you lied under pressure."

Betancourt grinned from the corners of his eyes. "That's right. Your wife was near hysterics when she returned from Miami."

Heston balked. "Yes. Because she feared the worst about our son and grandson."

"Because she'd just done away with her biggest rival for your affection."

"No!" Heston thundered.

Townsend leaned back in his chair. He clasped his hands behind his head. "If she had just murdered Lennox, and then aided and abetted Shawnee's kidnapper, your son..."

"What?" He backed away.

"Come on. I'll bet you know, too. Where's Kipp hiding the kid?" Betancourt posed. "Did the nanny take him? Are you all in cahoots?"

"Will I need a criminal attorney of my own?" he asked.

"Your wife has Banks Winston sewn up. He's arriving from Miami this morning."

"Nothing like keeping it all in the family," jeered Betancourt, offering him a stick of spearmint gum. "Yeah, Banxy showed up five minutes ago. He's in there, right now, getting the low-down from your sexy little wife."

"I'll wipe the floor with you, little man."

Townsend cast Betancourt a disparaging look. "Jorge, get out of here and get to work. Follow up on Kipp's movements. See if you can place him in the hours after he left Lennox's penthouse with Shawnee."

"Sure thing." Betancourt popped his gum. "See you later, movie star," he called, double-slapping the wall on his way out the door.

"There's a coffee shop in the middle of the complex, Heston. Why don't you grab yourself a cup," Townsend suggested. "You're going to need it."

Chapter Thirty-Eight

That afternoon, in the lobby of the beachfront Ritz-Carlton Hotel in Naples, Ezra approached the concierge. "I wonder if you would help me, please."

"Certainly, sir. How may I assist you?"

Ezra spoke in a low voice. "I seem to have misplaced my mother. She's a guest here. I can't seem to raise her. I've phoned. I've knocked on her door. I'm becoming alarmed. I wonder if you could have someone check her room."

"She left no message for you at the desk, sir?"

"No, nothing. We had a date for early cocktails at The Starfish Grille. She isn't there, either. I've phoned a couple of times to check. I thought maybe our plans got tangled. Please, just have someone check the room. I have a bad feeling about this." He handed the man a bill.

"I'll be happy to do it myself, sir. Allow me to obtain a pass key. We'll go right up. I'll meet you at the elevator." He pointed.

"Thank you."

Several minutes later, he found himself in a corridor on the third floor. The concierge bent over the doorknob and inserted the electronic key, removing it quickly. A green light appeared. "After you, Mr. Gold."

Nodding, Ezra entered the dark suite of rooms. He found and flipped on the first light switch he saw. The room appeared empty.

Then he heard a moan.

"Beyond the bed, sir!" The concierge ran past him. Ezra stumbled, stopping abruptly behind the concierge, who crouched down over Arlene's inert body. The concierge found his radio. "Call an ambulance immediately," he commanded. "Room 310."

Ezra crouched down beside him. "Ma." He took her wrist. He felt a low pulse.

"Don't move her, sir. The paramedics will know what to do. I'll ask them to take her to North Naples Hospital, unless you have some other preference."

"No, none. That will be fine." Sitting down cross-legged on the carpet, he held his mother's hand in a loose, supportive grip. In less than a minute, he heard the sirens approaching down Vanderbilt Beach Road.

Waiting anxiously, he noticed that his mother's handbag was lying open on the bed, its contents strewn across the bed and the floor.

"It looks like robbery," the pacing concierge observed.

"What happened, Ma?" Ezra asked the prone woman. "Who did this to you?"

She whispered, but he didn't catch the word.

"Say again?" He leaned over her, his ears close to her lips.

"Vivian," his mother whispered, as paramedics burst into the hotel room, a stretcher in tow. "She stole the diary..."

"Ma! Ma!" He massaged her hands as paramedics pushed him aside. His mother had lapsed into unconsciousness.

Chapter Thirty-Nine

In the close private room, Banks Winston stretched out his long legs under the table.

"I'm glad you called me, Poppy. I'll do everything I can in your defense. I believe in your innocence. But we have our work cut out for us."

She stared into the steely gray eyes of the dapper, snowy-haired lawyer seated across from her at the table in the interrogation room. Banks clasped her hand, his caressing fingers warm and strong. He smelled vaguely of aromatic tobacco, woodsy-cherry, and manly aftershave. She felt reassured.

He glanced at the matron waiting outside the door. "Poppy, before they take you back to your cell, I need to ask you to do something for me."

"What, Banks?" she asked, dazed and confused by the nightmare that had enveloped her.

"Think about leaving your husband," he replied, pressing the back of her knuckles to his dry lips. "When this is all over."

Unsettled, she withdrew her hand and rested it on top of her thigh. "Leave Heston? Why?"

"Surely that's obvious." Sighing, he gazed at her. "Do I need to spell it out?"

"I guess so."

"Are you happy with Heston?"

"I love Heston."

"But are you happy with him? I can make you very happy, Poppy." Her gaze fell to the floor.

"What kind of a protector is he?" Banks pushed his chair away from the table and stood to his full height. He was tall, elegant, and undeniably attractive. "Think about it," he said, fastening his briefcase. He signaled and the matron opened the door for him to leave.

As he exited, Poppy thought back to the conversation she'd had with her stepdaughter on the previous day. On the indoor pool deck.

She'd cast a sideways glance at Winner. "Men are like swimming pools," she'd told the girl. "All men have shallow sides, honey. They each have a deep side, too. A deeper nature, but not all have equal depths." Gazing across the lanai, she extended her arm. "The best ones have the greatest depths. If they're deep enough, dive right in. If they're too shallow—you'll break your neck when your head hits bottom. Most are fit for wading and nothing more."

Shuddering, Winner winced, teeth bared. "What's Daddy? Is he good for diving?"

Poppy grew sad. "He was. One of the best ever." She chewed her bottom lip. "He's lost a little water down the drain lately."

"Hmm." Winner nodded. "Can't he be refilled?"

Poppy smiled. "Maybe. If he's willing to pay the water bill."

Winner laughed. Poppy joined in. "Well, you get what I mean, anyway, even if I don't say it very well."

"You're funny," Winner tittered, shoulders bobbing. She crinkled her perfect nose the same way Heston crinkled his. But her smile faded. "You mean Daddy's changing."

Shading her eyes from the morning sun, Poppy tried to hide her sadness. This had been the first time in days that she and the pubescent Winner had had a moment of contact. Now, arms folded on the table, she collapsed her head in grief.

What will happen to my kids if I'm convicted? What will happen to Heston? Do I care what happens to him? Roughly seizing her elbow, the matron jerked her to her feet and marched her back to her jail cell.

Chapter Forty

That afternoon, Heston's digestion was acting up. He grimaced, placing a fist on his solar plexus. He was about to return to Townsend when Banks Winston accosted him.

"Hang on, Heston," called Banks, approaching from the county jail.

Tired, he shook hands with Banks. The attorney seemed weary and preoccupied.

"Let me grab a coffee," said Banks, a briefcase strapped to his wrist. "Be right back."

The complex of county buildings surrounded the coffee shop. He was seated at an outdoor cement table beneath the shade of oak trees. Banks returned with a half-spilled coffee cup and set it down on the table's pink and turquoise mosaic. Placing the briefcase on the concrete bench next to him, he flung spilled coffee from his fingers into the monkey grass lining the patio.

"I know we talked on the phone, Heston," he said, taking a sip of what remained. "But there have been some developments since then."

"How is she?" Heston asked.

"You can imagine."

"They told me I can see her soon."

"Right now, they're only interested in gathering information. They aren't sure she's guilty. The big money's still on Kipp. But they can't keep her more than twenty-four hours without charging her. I'm stalling until tonight so we can take her home."

"What a freaking mess." Heston chewed a nail. His hands were quivering from nerves and fatigue. "What new developments?"

"That's what I wanted to speak to you about—they're on Kipp's trail." Banks's thick, white hair and Brooks Brothers suit gave him an air of formality. Or was it authority?

"I know they found Shawnee's toy. Is that what you mean?" Heston asked.

"There's more," Banks said. "They located Kipp's Goldwing in the long-term parking lot at the Naples airport. GPS showed that Kipp rode the bike from a storage facility on South Beach to I-95 and across Alligator Alley to Naples, arriving here around 5 a.m. They checked the gas station on the Indian reservation, halfway across the Alley. Kipp purchased gas, food, drinks, and shirts. He paid cash."

"Shawnee was still with him?"

"Yes. The boy is in all the videos. Apparently well and unharmed. Lennox would have birthed a cow. She never let the boy eat junk food." Banks yawned and sipped his coffee.

Heston covered his eyes with his fists. *How the hell did you know that?*

"You look as though you need a night's sleep." Coldly, Banks stared at passersby going about their business. "Once upon a time, Naples was old money. That bird has flown." He examined Heston. "Brace up, man. This situation will become worse before it becomes better—if it does."

He lowered his fists to the table. He eyed the blue-blooded attorney. "It's your job to see that it does—become better, Banks."

"For the time being, Heston, I'll let bygones be bygones. My concern is for Poppy's welfare."

Watch your tone. "As is mine. She's *my* wife."

"Speaking frankly, old man, your concern has landed her where she is now," Banks said.

Truth is an ugly bugger. Isn't that what Arlene had said?

"Do you want to hear the rest about Kipp?" Banks asked.

277

"Obviously, I do."

"When Kipp exited I-75, he drove up US 41 to Tin City. There he used a pay phone to call your nanny. From there, he drove to the airport. Law enforcement has verified his movements via the security cameras at the Alligator Alley toll booth. Kipp paid the toll to cross at 3:04 a.m."

Alarmed, Heston listened in silence. Banks continued.

"Security cameras inside the Naples private air terminal reveal that Beryl took Kipp's phone call while she was inside the terminal building. She then walked out to your T-hangar and boarded your Cessna. Taxing onto the airfield, she radioed to say she had taken on two more 'souls.' "

"Her flight to where?" he demanded.

"The airport at Marathon Key," said Banks, pouring out the remnants of cold coffee from his cup. "Authorities are working to trace her movements from there." Banks' eyes left him. Someone was approaching from behind.

He turned. It was Townsend, who plopped down on the third bench at the circular table.

"I was hoping I would find you here," he said. "Heston, it's about your agent."

"Arlene?" Heston said. "What about her?"

Townsend nodded. "I'm sorry. She was found unconscious this afternoon, lying on the floor of her hotel room at the Ritz. We believe the woman seen leaving her room on the security cam was Vivian Champlain, the same woman seen visiting Lennox's penthouse the day of the murder. We're going to pick her up for questioning."

He had to find Vivian before the cops did. He had to warn her.

"Bad luck, old son." Rising, Banks put a hand on his shoulder and tossed his cup into a nearby receptacle. "I'll phone you later."

"Thought you'd want to know," said Townsend, entering the coffee shop door.

Alone for the moment, Heston dashed into the parking lot and located his car. Leaning against the hood, he dialed his phone.

"Hello?"

"Ezra? Heston here. How's Arlene?"

"Alive, but unconscious."

"Ezra, is Vivian with you?"

"No."

"Do you know where she is? I don't have her number."

"She's here," said Ezra. His voice was monotone.

"Where's here? The hospital?"

"Yes. They just brought her in. Her heart condition has flared. They're taking her into emergency surgery. Heston, there's something I need to tell you about—"

"Save it, Ezra. I'll be there in 20 minutes." He ended the call and made another one.

"Hello, Mr. Demming. Rob LaCroix, at your service, sir."

"Rob, I'm sorry I didn't return your phone call yesterday. Things have been—hectic."

"I understand perfectly, sir. You received my messages?"

"Yes. Squatters on Heart of Fire Key."

"What would you like me to do, sir?"

He covered his mouth with his hand and spoke in a low tone. "Find out who's there, Rob. And report directly back to me. *Capeesh?*"

"Yes."

"Don't call the police or the Coast Guard or anyone else, until you speak to me first. Got that?"

"Yes, sir. It's Miss Beryl for certain. The others, I'm not sure. Friends of yours, sir? Relatives, perhaps?"

"Whoever it is, Rob, it's our little secret. Now do it, and get back to me. I've got to go."

279

"Right away, Mr. Demming. My sympathies for..."

"Yes, yes. Thank you, Rob." He rang off. Belching, he used his phone to unlock the doors of the Ferrari. Banks Winston rolled up in his BMW, stopping behind the Ferrari. He lowered the driver's seat window.

"Heston, one more thing. We should speak in person, not over the phone. I heard Betancourt say that they're now monitoring your phone calls."

Chapter Forty-One

At the hospital, Heston avoided Arlene's double room and slipped stealthily into Vivian Champlain's private room. A nurse was just leaving. "Be quick about it," the nurse said. "We're taking her to pre-op in a couple of minutes. She closed the door behind her, where a policeman stood sentry in the corridor.

"Thank you," Heston said, eyes on the frail woman lying in the room's only bed. A small lamp on the nightstand gave off the only light.

"Heston?" Vivian asked weakly, surprised.

"Vivian, listen to me. The police are right behind me. Tell me! I need to know. Did you kill Lennox that day?"

She squeezed his hand and answered weakly. "No, Heston. I swear it."

He tried to release his hand, but she held it fast. "But, Heston—Lennox died while I was in her penthouse. She hid me in her secret room."

"That awful shrine to me? Why did you hide?"

"Because your wife came to see her, while I was there. Lennox had the diary on her desk. She taunted me with it. And when I came out of the room, Poppy was gone. The diary was gone, and Lennox was dead. The balcony..."

"What about the balcony, Vivian?"

"When I went into the room, the balcony doors were closed as when I arrived. When I came out of the room, they were wide open—everything was, windows, everything. Poppy must have opened them. Why did she?"

He shook her hand in anger. "That can't be true, Vivian. It can't!"

"Oh, Heston. I'm sorry. If I die, tell Ezzie I'm sorry. He was just here.

He left his key." She glanced at the nightstand. Her tears trickled. Her voice was weak and broken by shallow breaths. "He asked me if I'd stolen the diary from Arlene."

He hunched over her. "Arlene—?"

"Arlene got it from your daughter, Sage. Sage got it from her twin. Tegan found it in Poppy's closet. I wanted it! I wanted to burn it, but Arlene wouldn't give it to me. She'd read it. She knew what was in it. She was going to tell Ezra—so he'd drop me. I'm too old. She wants grandchildren. I love Ezra. I pushed her. I took the diary from her purse and ran out. But I lied to Ezzie. I told him I hadn't. If I die during surgery—"

He cupped her hands. "I'll tell him. I swear it. Vivian, where is the diary?" He sat erect. He heard noise coming down the corridor—men's deep voices and pounding footsteps.

"Vivian, where did you put Lynne's diary?"

"Come closer," she motioned. He leaned in as she whispered. Listening, he took the key from the night stand and put it in his pocket.

Police burst into the room, followed by Detective Betancourt, who tore him away from Vivian's side. A local officer read Vivian her rights.

"Vivian Champlain, you are under arrest for the attempted murder of Arlene Gold. You have the right to remain silent—"

"She's about to have heart surgery, you bloody fools!" cried Heston as policemen pushed him out the doorway.

"We'll post a guard," sniffed Betancourt. "By the way, Demming— thanks for tipping us off. Now get the hell out of here before I arrest your butt."

"Bless you, Vivi," he called, loud enough for the sick woman to hear. Then he walked briskly down the hall to the service elevator. Mermaid's Bight in Park Shore was only a 15-minute drive to the north, up Gulfshore Boulevard to Crayton Drive.

He prayed the police weren't tailing him yet. If they weren't, it was only a matter of time. He'd cope with his feelings about Arlene later.

Chapter Forty-Two

On the indoor pool deck of the Demming mansion in Naples, Ram pinned Winner to the outside wall. She couldn't escape, even if she wanted to—but she was afraid to cross him. His rock-hard, pulsating body was so close to her, she could feel the current, alive and surging, as if a boulder had come to life.

"It's time, Winner," he said. A gold chain sparkled around his thick neck.

"Time for what?"

"Action. I overheard your father talking on the phone. Did you know? He's hired a private investigator."

"Why?" she asked, scarcely breathing.

"Do you know anything about your Grandfather Doug?"

"Like what?"

"Your grandfather killed himself. Across the US 41 over there. Your dad was a teenager. Found him hanging. You didn't know?"

"No."

"Your grandmother died soon after. Left pretty little Heston all alone in the world."

"Dad did all right for himself."

Ram snorted. "Your granddad didn't. He died in disgrace. He experimented on his patients without telling them. Very unscrupulous. Some died."

"I don't believe you."

He pushed his weight against her, squeezing her to the wall. "Think I'd lie to you? Now your dad's hired someone to check the facts in Chicago. What do you think he'll find?"

She couldn't breathe. "I don't know."

"I'll tell you what he'll find. He'll find out about my granddad. When he does, the jig's up."

"Your granddad? What jig? What are you talking about, Ram?" She tried pushing him away. She was struggling now, but he held her pinned behind the trellis.

"Think I just happened to enter your dad's employ?" He laughed. "You're all in for a big surprise."

"Please! What are you talking about?"

"My grandmother died because of your grandfather's medical experiments. My granddad didn't like that too much. He's been planning his revenge for years."

"You're helping him?"

"He's an old fart. He needs my help. See, they let your granddad off the hook because of his position. They didn't want scandal." He eased the pressure of his body against hers. "I am the avenger."

"You're here to hurt my dad?"

"Relax. You don't need him anymore." Ram's cavernous laugh was wicked."

She regarded the beast in horror.

"I'll take care of you from now on—as soon as I avenge my gramma's death. Sins of the fathers. Get it?"

"No."

He stepped away. "You look so much like a woman. I forget you're still a kid. Come on." He grabbed her wrist. "I have other plans for you."

She yanked it away. "No!"

Yanking her away from the wall, he twisted her arm. In agony, she screamed.

"Shut the hell up!" Clamping a hand over her mouth, he marched her toward the dock, his knees prodding her forward.

Footsteps slammed down the walkway beyond the hedgerow. Puny Dakota appeared, wielding a golf club. "Winner, what's...Hey! Hey, what do you think you're doing, Ram? Let go of my sister!" Fiercely, he swung the 9-iron at Ram, but the giant grabbed the club and wrested it from him. In fury, Dakota ran toward Ram as the club skittered across the pool deck.

"You little runt!"

Grasping Ram's meaty forearm, Dakota dug in his nails, and then his teeth, gnashing flesh. Enraged, Ram slammed his face. Flying backwards, the young boy collided with the patio furniture, landing on his back on the outdoor rug. Stunned, he lay inert.

In fury, Winner bit Ram's fingers. Ram throttled her, never taking his ham-like hand from across her mouth.

"You're coming with me, Sleeping Beauty. Keep your trap shut and do as I tell you. You can't save your family any more than your baby brother can save you. You're both fleas on a big dog. I'm the only one who even wants to save your hide.

" 'Cause that's what I intend to do. My grandfather Gabe will never know the difference. You ought to be grateful. You can show me *how* grateful later." He pushed her down to the dock and forced her onto Dakota's moored jet ski.

"You're my pretty baby now," he leered, untying the jet ski and climbing on behind her. All of a sudden, the machine roared out into Naples Bay, sped down Gordon Pass, and emerged into the open Gulf of Mexico. Turning left, Ram headed southwest from the Gulf coast, zooming toward a humongous white yacht drifting on the western horizon, looming closer with each bounce of the waves.

Chapter Forty-Three

"Chantal! Get your fat ass over here and pour me some more coffee," the old man belched. "Get a move on." Toothpick in hand, he picked at his dentures.

Suppressing her rage, Chantal left the cool comfort of the main salon and walked out on deck. Warm wind tousled her wig. Patting her head, she smiled in her typically passive-aggressive manner.

"More creamer, Gabe?" she asked semi-sweetly, pouring thin, tepid brown liquid from its silver pot. "More sweetener?"

He grunted as he gummed a piece of dried toast. That meant "Yes."

"Here you are, Gabe," she said, adding both to his china cup. She kissed the top of his white head, as he sat finishing his breakfast. Hands resting on his bony shoulders, she asked politely, "Gabe, would you mind if I step up on the top deck? I'd like a breath of fresh air."

Sipping his coffee, he grunted again, this time in disapproval. "Needs more creamer." He lowered his cup, placing it in the saucer.

Dutifully, she complied with his wishes and added another teaspoon of creamer. He sipped again. He grunted, satisfied. "Go ahead. But don't go far. I may need you. I'm feeling...restless." He wagged his shaggy, white eyebrows up and down.

"Oh, you!" Playfully, she tapped him on the shoulder. Drawing a scarf from inside her brassiere, she walked out onto the deck of the *Angel Baby* and stood looking at the vast vista of sea and sky. The mega-yacht was speeding southeast now, around The Florida Keys toward the Gulf of Mexico. She took a deep breath and wrapped her blonde beehive with the scarf. She leaned, with her elbows against the ship's railing and watched as the waves churned past.

She hated him. She wasn't sure who she hated worse—Gabe Cade or Poppy Demming. It was a toss-up now.

What was she doing here? On this boat? Sleeping with a man with one foot in the grave? It would be different if he had popped the question, if she had become Mrs. Gabriel Cade. But he hadn't. And she hadn't. The best she could hope for was a palimony suit.

She felt like an hourly employee in fear of losing her job. She'd felt the same way during those awful two years she had worked as a night stock clerk at the big-box store—after she'd been dumped by Rick DuBois. That pig wouldn't marry her either. Maybe it was just men she hated now. *No, I still hate Poppy, too.*

Poppy was the reason she was in the terrible mess: no man, no home, no kids, no job, no life to speak of. Just lonely nights with a repulsive old coot in his floating bed—floating in more ways than one. She smirked, adjusting her scarf. The wind had changed directions. *Poppy Demming is the reason I lost Danny Vega, my one true love. She'll pay. I'll see to it. I'll make her pay. She's going to lose everything she ever had. The old coot and his idiot monster of a grandson Raymond are going to screw you and your lot into the ground, Poppy. I'm the one who's going to end up rich, not you. I'll have the old coot's money if it kills me. If it kills me! I'm not coming out of this with nothing. You are. I've waited eight long years for my revenge on you. Now it's about to happen.*

Would Poppy know? She wanted Poppy to know who she really was. She'd taken Rick's surname—and the name Chantal—when she worked in that strip joint for eight months. The name had stuck. She had stopped being Sasha Bassett the first time she'd performed as a pole dancer. Her mother had disowned her. Who could blame her? Sasha watched as a V-shaped flock of birds sped by overhead. She loved birds. Always had.

She doted on little Gabby, her pet parrot, which had flown away and then returned.

Just like her beloved Danny Vega had flown, only he had never returned. Oh, how she had loved her nights with Danny. What a fool she had been to go after Poppy's stodgy first husband, James Talbot. Who was more repulsive in bed—James or her current bed mate? It didn't matter anymore. Poppy Demming had ruined her life.

Don't worry, Mama Tanya. Our sweet Poppy is going to suffer.

Only one thing she wasn't sure of. Had Heston recognized her that day he saw her in Gabe's office? *What if he tells Poppy?* With a painted fingernail, she tapped her front teeth.

She started as Gabe joined her at the railing, bringing along his bathroom smell. "A penny for your thoughts, Chantal," he grunted, squinting his eyes against the sunlight.

She smiled sweetly as he slid his arm around her shoulders.

It would cost you more than a penny, you old tightwad. Try a hundred million pennies. Then I might blab.

"How about a little mid-morning delight?" he crooned, latching onto her breast.

She remembered the night she had first met Gabe Cade and Raymond. It was at that tiki bar on Marco Island. She'd been their cocktail waitress. Raymond had ordered milk. Gabe had flashed his wealth. She'd overheard them talking about Heston Demming.

"I know Heston Demming," she'd said, hoping for a bigger tip.

"You do?" Gabe had said, giving her the once-over. "Well, now, why don't you just set right down here, little lady, and tell us all about it."

One thing was certain. Gabe was using her, just as much as she was using him. And they both wanted to see the Demmings get what they deserved.

She looked up into Gabe's eyes. She saw the evil there. She looked back at the sea.

She had her answer. She hated Poppy more than Gabe. There was no evil in Poppy Demming's eyes.

Chapter Forty-Four

In hiding near the island cove, Kipp, Beryl, and Shawnee bedded down, camping for the night. A few hours from now, at daybreak, they would try to sail the catamaran. The motorboat had been too low on gas to go far. Danger was all around and growing. Kipp was aware of Beryl's every breath as he lay with Shawnee not two feet from her back.

Lying in tandem on the blanket, hard against the ground, they talked into the night, while Shawnee slumbered between them. Above, clouds obscured the twinkling stars.

"Why did you want the crowd to kill you?"

"I hated the life. I loathed the vulgarity. I felt like a tamed lion. Everyone around me was a phony. Berry, I don't want to be a rock deity. I don't know how it happened. Yes, I do. Lennox seduced me—to be near my dad. But it wasn't her fault. I wanted to be seduced. She wanted me to be a rock star. She introduced me to Gabe Cade. He pumped me full of drugs and worked me like a lackey. Then he stole my fortune."

"I see."

"But it doesn't matter, now, Beryl. I never wanted fame or money. When I was a kid, I wanted to make a real difference in people's lives."

"Haven't you?"

"Not the right kind. I taught them ruthless greed."

"Greed? How?"

"To take whatever they wanted, damn the consequences. I gave them bad advice and took their money for doing it. I hustled them."

"Did you know you were hustling them?"

"No. Not at the time."

"You can't blame yourself for your own naiveté, Kipp. You've only just seen the light yourself."

They fell into silence.

"Listen," he said softly. "The stillness is alive." *Does she feel it, too?*

"Do you ever get lonely?" he asked, contemplating her skin in the moonlight.

"Sometimes, I do. Sometimes, I feel the need for the company of a man. Do you know loneliness?"

"Are you kidding? It's my best bud."

Reaching out, he traced her temple and cheek with his forefinger. His heartbeat quickened as she clasped his finger and, turning, found his eyes in the darkness. He sensed the intensity of her desire. Did she know what she was asking?

"No, don't pull away," he whispered, but she did.

"Shawnee..." she ventured as an explanation—an excuse.

What is she thinking? "Is he teasing me? Will I be another notch on his belt? If I succumb, will I be just another conquest??

He knew the answer—but she didn't. What if he never had another chance to be with her?

"Yeah, okay." He rolled onto his back. *Who could blame her for doubting me?* "Where are your glasses?" he asked, withdrawing his hand.

"In my pocket. If the authorities try to capture us, will you surrender or fight?"

"You know the answer."

"You have a terrible reputation. How many fights have you been in?" she asked, rolling onto her back, too.

Together, they studied the cloudy night sky.

"Don't believe everything you hear. I never start fights, mind you. I defend—me."

"Which was the worst?"

He rubbed his jaw. "I was talking to this girl in a bar on Key Biscayne. Her boyfriend and his friend didn't like it. The friend punched me, and the boyfriend slammed my face into a table."

"Really?" She sat up on one elbow, and stared over at him.

"Uh-huh. I had brain swelling. I was in the emergency room for 24 hours. For days I was in danger of having my brain explode. My face looked like a piece of pounded liver. My eye was purple. The bridge of my nose was diced like bologna. My forehead was swollen."

"Oh, my..." She lay back down on her back. "Poor thing. You know, my cousin was badly beaten once. In hospital, he claimed he could take a punch. My uncle told him, 'Son, the whole idea is NOT to take the punch.' " He saw the gleam of her teeth in the darkness.

"Yeah," he admitted. "That's a good one."

"Very telling," she nodded. Gently, she lifted her small hand and reached out, stroking his grizzled cheek. "Still, I don't like to think of you as hurt."

He clasped her hand, holding to his chest. "Want to kiss it and make it better?" he joked. The taut pliancy of her skin, her tenderness, her *genuineness,* and his own thudding heart, rendered him helpless.

Without a word, she leaned across Shawnee and kissed the bridge of his nose.

"All better," she said. She kissed his forehead. "Better still," she whispered.

Suddenly, he shoved her out of the way. He was on his feet. "What the hell do you think you're doing?"

She sat up. "Nothing! I'm sorry if..."

"Sorry? Save that baby shit for the kid."

Furious, he darted blindly into the night. Searching for the winding footpath, he tore through the dense growth, until, at last he reached the promontory overlooking the sea.

Gasping for breath, he stopped. Bending over, bracing his hands on his knees, he swallowed great gulps of humid, salty air. He glanced behind him. He was well away from her. He would never let her do that to him again. Gradually, he regained his composure.

Resuming his stance, he gazed out at the churning Caribbean. He plunked himself down on gritty rock. His sneakers dangled in space.

His mind roamed, as if on a ship sailing the swelling waves. His thoughts, unfocused and unedited, swirled in his mind, forming and un-forming like the silver surface of the sea shimmering before him, as he allowed his emotions to settle. An occasional thought took shape. Why had he run? Of what had he been so terrified? She was only a small, plain woman who offered him a little kindness...a little *mothering...*

That's what had been so terrifying. He let the thought slip away into the unknown abyss from whence it came. Other thoughts, words, ideas began to coalesce, but he was unmindful of them. He let them arrange themselves as he contemplated the stars appearing in the heavens.

A melody filtered in and wrapped itself around the words. He began to hum the tune. He began to sing the words, working with them, dis-carding those that didn't fit, selecting new ones as they stepped forward in consciousness to fill the vacant slots.

Slowly, the lyrics solidified inside the haunting melody. He sang the lines, tentatively, at first. They were right. They felt straight and true. In a low, clear baritone, he sang the verse aloud into the empty vastness that had given it to him.

Do you love me
As I love you?
A candle's glowing light
Do you love me
As I love you?

A Wild Dream of Love

A far star burning bright
Do you love me
As I love you?
A blazing meteorite
Do you love me
As I love you?
Do you burn for me tonight?

"Yes," whispered a voice behind him. Night had fallen. As he turned to look at her, Beryl emerged shyly, now draped in a white shawl of filmy silk and bathed in pale moonlight. She cuddled Shawnee in her arms, the babe still sleeping soundly.

Her small sandals padded across the rock. Cautiously, she lowered her small body down beside him, seating herself on the ledge. Placing one hand on his shoulder, she stared up at him. He didn't look at her. He couldn't. He gazed out at the ocean and sang a second verse:

Do you love me
As I love you?
A drop of dew in spring
Do you love me
As I love you?
A brook meandering
Do you love me
As I love you?
A cascade thundering
Do you love me
As I love you?
Will you wear my wedding ring?

He stopped singing. "There's a chorus, too. And I have a couple more verses—for the other two elements, air and earth."

"You hustler," she sneered facetiously.

"What?" He was taken aback.

"You're no sleazy striptease artist, no rock'n roll maniac, Kipp. You're a bard, a poet. Egad. You're a closet troubadour."

"Shhh!" he said. "You'll blow my cover."

"Consider it blown."

"Know what's worse. You're my new muse," he said. "I wrote this song for you."

"You're shivering," she chided kindly, enfolding him into her shawl. Tenderly, she grasped his face in her two hands and brought it down to her face and kissed his fevered forehead. He hadn't realized how cold he had become, sitting alone for hours in the rugged sea wind, lost in divine inspiration. The heat of her small, solid body pressed against him was more than comforting. It was erotic.

Rising on a torrent of desire, he met her rapt eyes, their sparkle now rivaling the star light. She wasn't plain. She wasn't pretty. Somehow, she had become beautiful.

His arms went round her, his lips found hers. Forcing her back across the coral rock, he cradled the back of her head in his hand and—as intrepid men have done down through the ages—drove his tongue deep into unexplored territory.

Chapter Forty-Five

An hour later, alone in the universe, Kipp lingered in the overgrown clearing near the mystical old chapel, not far from where Heston had hewn an outdoor theatre from coral rock. Beryl and Shawnee slept nearby, oblivious, in the moments just before daybreak.

Red sky at morning, it was an ominous sign. What did the sign portend? Droplets of tropical moisture drizzled his bare skin. Thunder rumbled on the horizon.

At last, he had found *the woman*—not some elegant stunner with plastic-perfect body work and fashionable homilies dripping from her tongue—but this small, impudent, fussy ball of affection with a fuse as short as his own. He *adored* her.

Another of life's ironies—just when he had found the woman meant to share his life, he no longer had a life to share. But the knowledge of her existence was magical. He felt an exhilaration, a kind of headiness he hadn't felt in years, like the moments before the kickoff in a game. *Something* was about to happen. He just wasn't sure what.

Yet he knew that the outcome depended on him. For the first time in years, he felt in control. A strange euphoria crept from the ozone and settled inside him. The atmosphere around him took on a life of its own, and he was becoming absorbed into it.

The feeling of headiness grew. His consciousness seemed to grow and expand toward the horizon in all directions—north, east, south, west—ballooning as the thin web of skin that comprises a floating jellyfish, a net thrown out farther and farther, until his mind encompassed and captured the whole sea, the whole sky, the whole wind, the whole world, and the great beyond, and it was all he, and he was all it.

He was no more individuation, only one gigantic "everything" of which he also was an integral and ever-changing interaction of particles and processes, a cyclonic dervish dancing on infinite levels, in limitless fields. Now a man, now an animal, now an atom, now a hurricane, now a fish beneath the surface, now the surface itself. Ever changing, ever evolving, *yet* always the same, was he within the enormous grand scale of multilayered, multidimensional existence and nonexistence—now foam cresting the waves, now wind billowing the sails, now clouds roaming the sky, now hot, beaming sunlight, now krill in the belly of the sperm whale sounding his ship.

When seen from the place beyond mind, mind and consciousness were love. And he knew the truth, as surely as he had perceived it only once before, at 19 years of age, that he was at once nothing and everything, that he was insignificant and supremely important, all springing, spiraling, dancing, whirling particles of infinite mind, joy, and pain. And when, at last, his net of consciousness began to reel itself in, he knew he had been given a second glimpse of eternity, of infinity, and that it would have to sustain him until, at last, his spirit would be released and the matter and energy that had once comprised his being were released and absorbed by other blossoming processes.

He had changed. He had become *aware.*

Somehow, his freed spirit settled back into his sneaks, firmly planted.

"Glad you're back," Beryl said, caressing his shoulder. "You were standing still for a very long time."

He shielded his eyes. The sun was mid-way up the morning sky. "Not really," he smiled. "Static nature is an illusion of our limited senses. We feel as though we're standing still, but, in reality, we are hurtling through space on a big rock as it zooms around a massive, burning star in deep space. I've made the trip 27 times—so far. You've done it 30 times, right? We're hanging by the soles of our feet, to boot."

Her pug-like features wrinkled in concern. "You got too much sun yesterday." Reaching up, she pressed her cool palm to his brow. "You should have worn your cap." She kissed his cheek affectionately. He reached for and squeezed her free hand, the one not carrying Shawnee.

"Have you ever wondered," he said, crouching down on a rock, "why so much of life is horrible? Sickness, accidents, death, war, flesh consuming flesh?" He sat.

"Who hasn't?" She stroked his cheek with the back of her knuckles. "The Fall of Man."

He pressed her hand to his cheek. "Maybe it's because it was the only way it would work—to create life, I mean. Maybe divinity made a choice—a hard choice. To give us life at all costs in the only way possible. Fleeting, agonizing life equals consciousness. Awareness. *Love.* Maybe it was an act of love." He brushed her fingertips to his lips. "To give life. Just as we give life by loving, only on an immense scale."

Her soft eyes glowed, backlit by the setting sun. Across the sky, the moon was rising, unseen. Bending down, she kissed his hair. Valiantly, she stood behind him, one hand resting on his shoulder, as he sat and stared into the misty cloudbank hovering on the horizon.

"I don't know what it is, but I feel it. I sense it. It's everywhere."

"Who really knows?" she whispered.

He knew she was thinking about their future together. Within the hour, he would be forced to leave her forever.

He had only one real choice now—prison or disappear. Neither one suited his true purpose. He knew what that was now. He had to share his knowledge with the world. He must grow his knowledge, tend it as a farmer tends food, with no restrictions.

But how? Surely, there must be a way. If there were a way, he would be shown it.

His soul had been revitalized for a reason. His initiation into the mystery was complete. He felt ready now for the fight, for the next phase of his life. He knew now what he must do. He must take his understanding to the whole world. They had heard it before—but not from the lips of a living icon, of a reformed hellish rock and roll reprobate—someone who could *prove* change and growth are possible.

He was no longer alone in the universe. He was now *at one* with it.

"Berry, do you have a pen and paper?"

"Yes," she said, shifting Shawnee and scrounging in her bag.

"Good. There's a message I need to record for posterity—while there's still time."

Chapter Forty-Six

In a sedated stupor, Winner looked out from the observation deck of the mega-yacht *Angel Baby*. All around her was open, rolling seas. She turned to the old man sitting in the chair beside her. He contemplated her with hooded eyes.

"Are you going to kill me?" Winner asked him quietly.

Gabe Cade ruminated. "I'll be doing you a favor, little girl." He stood to stretch his legs. "Growing old is a scary proposition."

"It's part of life."

"Life?" He sputtered. "What do you know about it? Life is like a taking a walk down a long road that leads to a haunted house on a hill. When you first start out walking, you're young. The flowers are in bloom. The fields are ripe; rivers, flowing; forests deep and silent. The haunted house is still far away, hidden up in the mountains. You can't even see it from where you are."

He shot a quick glance, to make sure she was listening. He resumed his seat, settling in.

"When you reach middle age, you notice the foothills. They're a lot bigger, a lot closer than they were before. You can see the haunted house, too. It's sitting up there waiting for you, on the highest peak. Fear overwhelms you, but you got no choice. You can't turn back. Old Man Time won't let you. He has the road blocked behind you."

He was talking to himself now, staring into space. He'd forgotten about her.

"So you trudge forward into old age. The road gets steeper. The journey gets harder. You get tired easier. You're scared all the time. The road gets steep and rocky. You got to climb now, and you're weaker and scared-er. One day you look up. The haunted house is looming over you.

The road leads straight to the front door. You have no choice. You must go in. But now you're terrified because you know your journey is at an end, and you don't know what's waiting for you inside the house. You just know you can never come out."

He jolted in his chair. Swiveling his head, he grunted and plucked a stogie from his shirt pocket. He lit a match on the bottom of his shoe and ignited the stogie; he inhaled and exhaled. He turned to look at her amid a ghostly cloud of smoke.

"I'm so close now, I can see the ghosts and goblins hanging out the windows. There's werewolves and vampires inside, waiting to tear me to shreds." He found her eyes. "You may luck out, little lady," he said. "I may save you the trouble of walking that long road."

"Don't you believe in Heaven?" she asked quietly.

He grunted, peering from beneath bushy brows. "Where'd you hear about Heaven?"

"My counselor," she replied. Her bound wrists and arms ached mercilessly.

He leaned in, too close, nose to nose with her. "Your grandfather, Douglas Demming, stole my wife, and I fixed his wagon. Your father screwed my son Cedric's career. Do you think they're going to Heaven? If old Doug's there, I'll fetch him back and send him straight to Hell, right where I'm sending the rest of you." He leaned back and looked at her. "Dang it, you're a beautiful thing. The curse of the Demmings. Child, you ain't going to Heaven doing racy blue-jeans ads." He cackled and chewed his stogie.

Winner stared at the deck. She was the only one who knew what was about to happen. Somehow, she must warn her father.

Chapter Forty-Seven

In the dim light of Vivian's hospital room, Ezra sat holding her hand. A ray of sunlight shown through the crack in the drawn curtains. Vivian drowsed, but managed to speak.

"Bless you for coming back to me, Ezzie."

"I felt bad." *I'm not back, but I couldn't let you go to your death believing I was scum.* "Ma's going to be okay. The doctor said."

Vivian smiled faintly. "I'm glad." The corners of her mouth turned downward and quivered.

"Vivi—"

She shook his hand weakly. "I need to tell you the whole story, Ezzie. You deserve to know—who I really am."

A nurse came in, and he used her movements as an excuse to release Vivian's hand. He sat somberly, saying nothing as she worked. The nurse went out.

"Ma told me what happened," Ezra said. "You tell me why."

"I'm sorry about your mother. She threatened me. She was going to tell you what was in Lynne's diary. I couldn't let her, Ezzie. I had to stop her."

He felt his blood pulsate. "What was so terrible? Tell me."

She turned her head away, staring at the blank wall. "Twenty years ago, Heston and I were both new to the movie scene. We fell in with the same bad crowd. Lennox's mother, Lynne Cordova, was the ringleader."

"The madam?" he said caustically.

"We didn't do it for money. We did it for kicks. It was just a wild, crazy crowd."

"Were you and Heston lovers?"

"No. Never. We just ran in the same sordid circles. Heston's lover was Lynne herself. Everybody knew he was 'hands off.' Everybody but her own daughter. Lennox didn't care."

"That figures."

"I didn't know until a few days ago—when I overheard Lennox talking to Poppy at the Fontainebleau—that Lynne had kept a diary. I was horrified. She had written it all down."

"Probably with blackmail in mind. But she died first. Go on. What happened? Did you kill Lennox that day? For the diary?"

Breasts heaving, she sobbed. "No."

"Truly?" He stuffed a tissue into her hand.

She wiped her nose. "Truly. I did go to Lennox's penthouse that day. She was surprised to see me, to say the least. But while I was there—someone else buzzed the door. It was Poppy Demming. I didn't want Poppy to know I was there, so Lennox hid me in her secret room."

"Secret room?"

"Yes. It was creepy. It was a secret shrine to Heston—and to Lennox herself, as if they were a couple in real life. It's hard to explain. It was scary. I stayed there for around 45 minutes. Lennox never came back, so I let myself out. And when I walked down the hall into the great room, she was dead. There was nobody else in the apartment. I didn't know about the baby. I swear it, Ezzie. He must have been behind closed doors somewhere. I never would have left him there unattended, with his mother dead."

She sobbed openly, too hard. He stood and leaned over her, wiping her face, pushing back the fair hair clinging to her wet cheeks. "Vivi, stop it. I believe you."

"Ezzie!" She grabbed his sleeve. "I thought Poppy had killed Lennox and taken the diary."

"It was missing then?"

"Yes. It had been sitting on Lennox's desk—and now it was gone, and there were three used wine glasses and an empty wine bottle. I wanted to protect Poppy because she's my friend and because she could be traced back to Heston and the diary—and to me. So I took two of the wine glasses and hid them in my bag. I left Lennox's glass—"

He clasped her wrist. "Three glasses? Who else was there?"

"I don't know. I didn't stop to think—but they both had lipstick. All three glasses did."

"Do you still have the two glasses you swiped?"

"No. I smashed them. Then I tossed the shards into Venetian Bay—off my sea wall."

"You destroyed evidence, Viv—evidence that might have proved Poppy innocent. She's been arrested."

"Oh, no, Ezra!"

"It's okay, Vivi," he heard himself say.

The nurse entered. "Sir, we're going to prepare her for surgery now. You'll have to leave."

Vivian's blue eyes paled in fear. She looked at him.

"I'll pray for you," he said, bending down and kissing her sticky, damp forehead.

"I love you, Ezra," he heard her rasp as she collared him around the neck and pulled him to her in the bed.

He couldn't see the nurse blush at what seemed a passionate embrace, but he heard her step back out of the room, offering them some privacy.

"I didn't want you to leave me, Ezra. That's why I did it. That's why Truett left me. His minions found out the truth, but he hushed it up—and he punished me! If Lynne's diary goes public, he'll kill me. You said you loved me, Ezra. Do you love me now? When I most need your love?"

He clasped her hands, wrenching them from his neck. He towered over her, his rage, a blazing bonfire, as she cringed below him in the bed.

"Do I love you?" he cried. He struggled to keep his voice from alarming the nurse outside the door. "Do I love you? No, I don't love you. I hate you." He grabbed a handful of her hair and twisted it. He seethed, sobbing. "I hate you, you whore. You murderer. I hate you. I hate you. Oh, how I wish I did hate you."

Weeping, too, he fell to his knees. Embracing her, he sobbed as she crawled out of bed. Kneeling before him, she wrapped her arms around him weakly. Trembling, they wept together in mutual despair.

"Get up," he whispered, at last, struggling to stand. On his feet, he helped her into the bed.

"Ezra—"

He walked swiftly from the dim room. The door bumped the back of the policeman stationed in front of it.

"Sorry." Ezra rushed into the brightly lit hospital corridor. Stopping, he braced his hand against the wall and put the other hand over his face. A male nurse came along and led him to a seat in the surgery's waiting room. Returning with a cup of water, the nurse moved on.

Composing himself, Ezra got up and left the hospital. He couldn't spend hours there waiting. He would go crazy. He had to do something useful.

It was either that or sit and stew about what he was going to do if Vivian survived her operation. The past she had revealed was bad enough, despicable, but...

How can I love a woman who assaulted my mother and left her for dead?

Chapter Forty-Eight

The silver Ferrari zoomed down Gulf Shore Boulevard South. Making for home, Heston counted his blessings. He had located Lynne Cordova's diary. It had been right where Vivian had told him it would be—inside the faux footstool in the living area of her bayfront home on Mermaid's Bight. *Hidden in plain sight. Safer than a safe.*

The question remained, however: what was he going to do with it? The bulging booklet was burning a hole in his breast pocket. He could almost feel the scabies, as if the diary itself were a living embodiment of the secrets it contained.

His mobile phone rang. It was Lissette's ring tone.

"Hi, Lissette. I'm on my way home."

"Mr. Heston! Hurry! He has taken Miss Winner! On the jet ski!"

He swerved to the curb and hit the brakes. "Who's taken Winner?"

"Her bodyguard!"

Dakota's voice squeaked on the line. "Ram snatched her, Dad! Just like Berry said could happen. I pounded him with your 9-iron, but he escaped! He stole my jet ski!"

Lissette regained use of the phone. "Mr. Heston, he bloodied your son."

"I've got steak on my eye, Dad!"

"Give me it! Sir, Dack tried to defend his sister. Ram punched him. Please, are you coming home? You should phone the police!"

"I think they already know, Lissette. They're bugging my calls. Stay put. I'll be there in five minutes flat." Reigniting the engine, he flew toward Galleon Drive. *I've been conned by a smooth-talking charlatan?* There must be some kind of connection. *Damn his deceitful hide. My baby girl...*

As he turned west, the phone rang a second time. The ring tone was that of unknown callers. Careening down Gordon Drive in Olde Naples, he used the speaker phone.

"Heston." It was not a question.

"Who's calling, please?"

A weird chuckle scraped his spine.

"In case you don't know, movie star, your trusted bodyguard has absconded with your adolescent princess—while you were off lollygagging. You should be more careful."

"Gabe, you son of a bitch. Where's my daughter?"

"With me. Say 'hi' to Daddy, honey."

He heard a garbled cry. Winner's voice came clearly on. "Daddy, I'm on his yacht."

"Where, Win? Where is the yacht?" he barked in fury. "Are you okay?"

"Oh, Heston. That's all you're going to get from Miss Priss here. She's mine, now."

"What do you want, Gabe? Money?"

"Money? Pshaw!" Gabe's voice sounded offended.

"What, then?"

"What I've always wanted, Heston, my man. To see justice done. To that end, I suggest you meet me—ASAP—at your little chunk of paradise in the Florida Straits."

"On the island?"

"Heart of Fire Key, to be exact. Mighty poetical of you, to be sure."

"You might as well know, Cade. You've lost your advantage. I recently spoke with my attorney in Orlando. I hired private dicks. They've gone through your dirt, old man. I know all about your involvement in my father's downfall."

A moment of silence lingered. "Then you understand why I do what I must."

I understand, all right. But not the way you mean, sucker. "I'll meet you there in three hours. Harm one hair on Winner's head and you are dead meat, Cade." He heard a chuckle and a click and then silence.

"I'll hunt you 'til I die."

He hit speed dial. Ezra answered after several rings. "Hello?"

"Ezra, Gabe's kidnapped Winner. Ram's his accomplice. I'm meeting him at Heart of Fire in three hours. Come with me? I'm launching in ten minutes."

"You serious?" Ezra thought for a moment. "Look, I'm at the Ritz on Vanderbilt Beach, gathering Ma's things. Go without me. I'll take the Lady V—Vivian's cabin cruiser. It's docked behind her place in Park Shore. I should make it onto the island within, say, four hours—on the outside."

"Good. How's Arlene?" Heston remembered to ask.

"Recovering. She'll live."

"I spoke to Vivian before her operation," Heston admitted.

"So did I, again."

"So you know about her past?" Heston asked. "Look, I spoke with her. She said she caught you snooping. You found her photo album. After you left, she shredded the contents.

Silence.

"See you on the island. Oh, and Ezra—"

"Yeah?

"Bring a weapon."

"Does a spear gun count?" Ezra asked, almost joking. "I've been taking dive lessons."

"Anything—as long as it can kill."

"Hey, Heston, wait a minute. I don't know if you heard. Last night. Kipp won a Grammy. I just heard the news."

Chapter Forty-Nine

"How many knots now, Dad?" Dakota yelled, standing on the bouncing prow of the 54-foot sailing yacht as the ship raced south toward The Florida Keys. The gray-green Gulf of Mexico would soon become the Caribbean Sea—but not before they reached Heart of Fire Key.

"He can't hear you," said his younger sister Sage, brown braids whipped by the breeze. "See that cloud?" She pointed skyward. "It looks like Mommy's party dress. Tangerine chiffon."

"Big deal." Dakota rolled his eyes. "See that cloud?" He pointed. "It looks like an army tank!" He made blasting noises and mimed firing a machine gun.

Tegan came alongside them. "Daddy says to come back to the cabin. It's too gusty up here. You'll be blown off."

"No, we won't." Disappointed, Dakota glanced behind him. His father, standing at the wheel, was beckoning them to return.

"Daddy said so."

Using forefingers, Dakota stretched the sides of his mouth and stuck out his tongue at Tegan. "Maah!"

"Meaah!" Tegan returned the favor.

"Dack, don't be such a ninny," Sage said, as the three of them inched their way backwards, holding on tight to anything stationary. "Daddy wants us to be safe."

His safety jacket made Dakota feel clumsy. His sisters didn't seem to mind theirs. Sage was a goody-goody. Tegan was a copycat. Winner was—a damsel in distress.

He and the twins dropped down onto the deck, thud, thud, thud.

"We'll be rounding Cape Florida soon," Dad said. "I want you fed and pottied before we land. Clear?"

He and his sisters nodded. "Why did we have to come with you, Daddy?" pouted Tegan. She was the only one in the family who didn't like sailing or water sports. Sometimes she got seasick, but not today. "Why couldn't we stay with Lissy? When is Mommy coming home?" No one asked about Winner. They were all afraid to. But Dakota guessed they were hot on her trail. And that rat fink, Ram. *He's going to get it.*

He couldn't wait to get another shot at that guy. He punched his palm, relishing the thought of sweet revenge. But he was a little frightened, too, so he had to act like he wasn't—to throw Ram off the scent. Then he would spring!

"Why isn't Berry here?" Perplexed, Sage studied her father in silence.

Dad answered Tegan first. "Lissy has things to do at home. She's not up to caring for you right now."

Dakota watched his father's every move. He was manning the wheel and scanning the sea and talking to them all at once. "What about Berry?" he asked again.

His father cast him a sidelong glance. "I'm taking you to Berry now."

Ah, Dakota thought. *That's why we've been dragged onto the boat without anyone else. Dad's taking us to safe arms.*

"Our nanny is on Heart of Fire Key?" asked Sage, incredulous.

"She is, unless I miss my guess," Dad said. He glanced at his cool, waterproof wrist watch. "We'll be there in half an hour." He pointed a mean finger. "You're to do everything I say, follow me? I don't want any backtalk on this trip. If I say jump, you say how high. Understood?"

"Daddy, I'm cold," Tegan whined, cuddling close to him.

"Dakota, get your windbreaker and put it on your sister," Dad ordered. His brown and gray hair was flying around his head, but it was short, so it didn't stand up much.

Shrugging he removed his windbreaker from the peg. It was no use arguing with Dad. He had tried it before—and always wished he hadn't. He draped it around Teggi's freckled shoulders. *What the whiny baby wants, the whiny baby gets.* Lissette called Tegan her greasy little wheel.

"I can't wait to see Berry," she beamed. "I miss her *terribly.*"

"Yeah, right." He licked his finger to see which way the wind was blowing. Then he remembered to look up at the billowing sails.

"Anyone know anything about this?" Dad held up an old notebook. He stared his worst stare at Tegan. Tegan turned white. Sage stared at the deck. She shuffled her feet. Dakota pushed his palms skyward.

"Not me, Dad," he answered truthfully. But he knew the twins were in for it.

"Sage? Tegan?" Dad waved the book in their faces. No one moved. "Now's not the time. We'll talk about it when we're home safe and sound. But I want you two to think about the fact that two people are in the hospital because you stole this from your mommy's closet."

"Oh, Daddy! I'm so sorry!" Tegan stepped toward Dad, but stopped. She hung her head.

"Sage, I might have expected such mischief from your sister. But I'm surprised at you."

"Sorry, Daddy." She turned away meekly. "Look, dolphins!" she cried, pointing out to sea. He and Teggi ran to her side. Three slick, gray, finned bodies arced in and out of the water alongside the ship. Leaning across the hull, he caught sight of Key West as the island glided by in the distance. He could make out some palm trees and sunbathers along the developed coast. They were that close.

"Land ho!" he yelled proudly. He glanced at his dad for approval. But Dad was wearing his serious face. He wasn't paying attention today. Something was definitely up.

Thrilled, Dakota dropped his jaw. Arms through the wheel spokes, Dad was loading a rifle.

Chapter Fifty

On the island, Beryl, startled by the television news, scooped Shawnee into her arms and rushed down to the shore where Kipp stood lost in reverie, absorbing the wonder of being. Sleepy, the boy rubbed his eyes in rude awakening. He hiccupped as her footsteps pounded the wooden slats along the beach path. Through the fronds of coconut palms, she spied Kipp on the beach.

Approaching him, she stopped short. He hadn't even turned to look at her. He seemed to be praying.

Reaching out, she touched his shoulder. "Kipp?"

"Hello, babe." He touched her hand.

"Kipp, I have news—good and bad."

"Bad first. Get it over with."

"Your mother Poppy has been arrested for Lennox's murder."

"What?" He was suddenly wired. "Have they lost their minds?"

"She's being questioned by the police. I don't think they actually charged her."

"I have to go back," he said.

"No!"

"I have to."

"No. Wait until we know for certain," she begged. "Don't react. Act—after you've had time to think about it."

He swallowed. "It's just not possible that she could do such a heinous thing. She's so sweet. Hell, what's the good news. I need it bad."

"You won!" she yelled, jumping up and down, clapping. Tripping in the sand, she hoisted herself up, clutching Shawnee, and regained her footing. "Kipp! You won! They gave you the Grammy. You won! You won! It's all the talk—"

"I heard you the first time," he said. "I'm sorry to hear it."

"Sorry?" she cried. "How can you say that?"

Leaning down, he kissed her mouth, a caress so sweet she nearly collapsed. As he kissed her, Shawnee latched onto the golden hairs of his beard.

"Ouch, buddy," Kipp smiled. Removing the child's hand from his face, he kissed it tenderly. His eyes met hers in intimate knowledge. Blushing, she studied the sand at her feet. She knew her ears must be the color of the sunrise.

. Golden and wonderful, he squatted down, resting elbows on his knees. Dropping to her knees, she wedged Shawnee between her and Kipp. She tried to understand. She needed to understand. She watched as Kipp toyed with an empty oyster shell.

"Something happened to me, Berry. I've changed."

"Changed? How?"

His eyes met hers. "Can't you tell? Can't you see it?"

She measured her words carefully. "I can see something different in your eyes."

He rose to his feet. "Yes, that's it. It would be the very way."

Scrambling to her feet, she persisted. "Kipp, don't you see? The Recording Academy thinks you're dead or guilty. But they gave you the award for the year's best male vocalist anyway. Oh, how I wish you were there to accept it," she lamented. "What a speech you would give!"

"I don't want the award—not for that. I want it for the work they don't know about yet—the stuff I sent to Mom, and the stuff I'm going to write. I can accept it for that. Hey!" He snapped his fingers lightly. "Is there a video cam at the house?"

She frowned quizzically. "A couple of them. In the game room. Why?"

"Run *get* one," he said, smiling as she cocked her head, not understanding. "I'm going to make a speech, all right. One for the whole world to hear. Someday."

"Oh!"

"Quick!" He glanced down at Shawnee, who, grasping a fistful of sand, watched it pour from his palm. "I'll watch my son. Do it, Berry. Hurry!"

Without another word, she tore back down the path toward the house. Within five minutes, she had returned to Kipp's side, video camera in hand. "I put in new batteries," she panted.

"Good girl," he said, brushing the windblown wisps of his golden mane away from his face. "Video this."

Raising the camera, she found Kipp in the viewfinder, with Shawnee sitting at his feet and playing in the sand. "An acceptance speech?" she asked, squinting. "Maybe someday it will be on the Internet. Your speech will go viral."

"It may be my one shot. I'll give it everything I've got." He thought for a moment. "Hey remind me later. That would make a great song lyric." He smiled, but it was a different smile, not the devilish grin of days past. With the beach as a backdrop, he gazed earnestly into the camera, eyes so sincere and dear that she flashed hot with newly awakened desire for him.

So sweet I may die right here.

This man had been her lover last night. This man was now her whole world.

He stooped down and scooped up a small piece of driftwood from the sand, raising it like a scepter. "I thank you for the honor," he said into the camera as she recorded. "But I renounce my work with Demonsong. I renounce my life up until this very day. Until today, I was not alive. Today I live. I live in the knowledge that the motive power of the universe is love. From today forward, I am love." He pointed his drift-wood scepter. "You are love. Nothing in this world matters but love. Nothing is real, but love. Everything else is an illusion."

"Kipp..." she squinted, not wanting to miss a word. Suddenly, she gasped. Was she seeing what she thought she was seeing?

He kept on. "From now on, I will give, not take. From now on, I will follow in the footsteps of the servant of all."

"Kipp, behind you!" She pointed out to sea. A long, sleek navy-hulled vessel with billowing white sails had appeared, emerging from behind the foliage of the island. "Look!"

He turned to look. He turned back to her. "Now what?" he asked,

"You recognize it?" she cried, shading her eyes with her hand. The yacht could not approach the key directly. The water surrounding the key was too shallow.

"It's Heston. On *Windswept*," he shrugged. "He's found us some-how." He stooped and lifted Shawnee into his strong arms. "C'mon, honey." Taking Beryl by the hand, he stared at the approaching vessel, still far out at sea. "It's time to face the music."

The new family of three watched in anticipation as *Windswept* plowed toward the island dock, a weathered strip of wooden planks stretching 200 feet out to sea. The morning sky was streaked with red. The sea reflected a bloody sun. Beryl pocketed the video camera, Kipp's speech forgotten for the moment.

Chapter Fifty-One

Speeding along in *Lady V,* past the Ten Thousand Islands and beyond Shark Bay, Ezra dodged a low-flying osprey, barely. Preoccupied, he wallowed in his grief for his crumbling love of Vivian and in his remorse for leaving her during her operation.

He felt like a jerk, but he didn't want to be there, either way, after the operation. If Vivian died, it would horrible, of course. But if she lived— He would miss his life with Viv, no question about it. He might even miss her stuck-up cat, Jojo. But there was no option. He had to end it. Vivian attacked Ma and left her for dead.

His mother was on the mend. He had almost forgotten about Winner until the 12-year-old beauty slid into his mind's eye on a sunbeam, as he rounded his boat toward Heart of Fire Key. Ram Kincaid might be a desperado, but sure had good taste in women. *If he harms one flaxen hair on that magnificent girl's head, I'll kill the SOB.*

He was desperate for solace, but not desperate enough to admit to himself that he craved solace from that angelic child. He told himself he needed to stay on Heston's good side to ensure future jobs, so he must ignore Winner. *Ignore her.*

He was troubled. He was starting to feel like James Mason in *Lolita. What the hell is the matter with you, Gold? Why do you relate everything to a movie? Get a life.*

Then he struck a chord. *Heart of Fire.* It was an image from one of great classic films of the ages, *The Red Shoes.*

He laughed to himself beneath the engine's roar. *Heston, you clever boy.* The theme of the *The Red Shoes* is the conflict of the artist—artistic life vs. personal life: which is more important? Should the artist sacrifice all for art?

He knew the story was a based on a tale by Hans Christian Andersen about a dancer who put on a pair of red ballet slippers that wouldn't stop dancing, even when she became exhausted. Her constant dancing wouldn't allow her any rest or personal happiness. It was an age-old question for creative minds. Why work so hard and drive yourself crazy? Like a perfectionist nut case over a work of art no one else cared a fig about—unless they were making a buck off it? Should the drive of the artist be subservient to all other considerations?

As a director, he often faced similar issues. On important films, he worked 25 hours out of every 24. After hours, he was fit for nothing. It was an age-old question, and obviously, one Heston wrestled with daily in the pit of his soul.

Heart of Fire Key, here I come. I should feel right at home—except that Kipp is a loony toon and possibly dangerous. He located his spear gun as, according to his GPS, he approached Heston's private island. He switched off the engines and picked up an oar.

Guiding this boat into the cove, he tied it down and, spear gun in hand, quickly made his way onto solid ground. *Whose seaplane is that?* The atmosphere was tense.

He realized it was his own tension, dense as tropical humidity. Senses on full alert, he crawled, slow and crab-like, along the footpath leading away from the sheltered cove.

Chapter Fifty-Two

Windswept docked at the end of the island's pier. As his younger brothers and sisters followed his father off the vessel and onto the dock, Kipp shook his father's hand—the hand not holding the rifle. His father's eyes hurt him.

"Heston, what are you doing here?" Beryl demanded, hugging him briefly.

"A rendezvous with Gabe Cade. He's got Winner." He tousled Shawnee's locks.

Appalled, Kipp cried out. "He's what? The old man's crazy."

Heston exhaled and spit into the sand. "He's a psychopath. He's trying to destroy our whole family, not just you. Has been for years—anyone who's descended from my father, Douglas Demming. My father probably knew Gabe was insane. He was onto him. Who knows what horror Gabe perpetrated on his innocent young wife, Angela Cady. But it's a long story..."

"Gabe *did* set out to ruin me? I wasn't imagining things?"

His father nodded.

"And now he's kidnapped my kid sister?"

"His grandson—Raymond Cady, alias Ram Kincaid—did. I'm a fool. Do you know who emailed me glowing references for Ram Kincaid, bodyguard extraordinaire? One Ms. Chantal DuBois—Gabe's secretary. That's who."

"Dad, wow." He shook his head in sorrow.

"You don't remember Jill Cady, do you, Kipp?"

"The nanny before me?" asked Beryl, squinting against the sun's glare.

"That's right. Gaunt, ugly girl. Always trying to unzip my pants. Fired her. I didn't want her *near* the family jewels. My instinct was right."

"Oh, Heston!" Beryl colored ruby red.

"She knows what that means now," Kipp noted, to Heston's amusement and Beryl's embarrassment.

"Jill Cady was Gabe's first-attempt to plant a spy in our midst, you see. His daughter. Raymond's sister. Jill sneaked around, conspiring with Maude to torture Win. My PI uncovered Gabe's real name, too—Renfroe Cady, M.D., of down Chicago way."

"I'd have changed it," Beryl observed.

Kipp smiled sardonically. "Now he's an avenging angel?" he marveled. The dots were starting to connect themselves. "Dee-sturbed."

"Gabe hasn't said what he wants yet, by way of ransom—but I think I know. It's part of his plan." He grasped Kipp's shoulder. "I realized it on the way down here. He doesn't want ransom. He wants us all dead." He glanced at the kids. "It's too late now. We're all in danger. But we'll have reinforcements. Ezra's right behind me. And probably the cops."

Fretting, Beryl cradled Shawnee in her arms, even as she stroked the head of each child.

"Stay with me. Don't wander off," his father said to the kids, who hovered around Beryl, hugging her and clinging. He glanced at his Rolex. "I told Gabe three hours. I'm right on time."

"Dad, I—"

"Stop, Kipp. You don't have to explain. I know you didn't kill Lennox. I know who did—and why."

"Tell us!" cried Beryl.

"Is it true Mother's in jail?" Kipp asked.

"Hard to believe, isn't it? If I get Winner back, safe and sound, I'll..."

"When we have Winner back, Dad. That's first. Then you and I will go together."

Heston's eyes darted across the landscape.

Kipp explained. "I just don't want you to think of me the way I was, Dad. I've changed."

His father looked skeptical. "Changed? How?" He shouldered the rifle. "Do you have a weapon? We may need it."

Beryl opened her mouth to speak.

"Wait—" He put out a hand to silence her. "Here on the island— these past few days with Beryl and the kid—I've been reborn spiritually. Now I'd like to be reborn physically—I guess I mean in the eyes of the world. I want to be someone else."

"The man you were meant to be?" his father asked. "I can understand that, Kipp. *Noel.*"

"All your fans know your birth name. From now on, I'm calling you Noel," said Beryl approvingly. "It suits you."

"If I go back with you, Dad, it means prison. I violated probation."

"They say you bought drugs," Heston said.

"I did. To off myself with, not for recreational purposes."

"Oh."

"I never even injected it. I lost it in the surf—the night I ran for Shawnee."

"It won't matter. Only the purchase will. Detective Betancourt wants your hide, son."

"If I go back, he'll get every piece of me. Dad, I need a fresh start." He glanced at Beryl and Shawnee. "We need a fresh start."

His father met his eyes. The silver blues registered his meaning.

"Look there," said Beryl, pointing out to sea. A white ship had appeared in the distance.

Suddenly, the noise of a chopper thundering toward them drowned out their conversation. Winds blew around them with hurricane force as the helicopter settled into the sand of the shore.

"Beryl, take the kids and hide them," Heston commanded.

She looked around. "Where? In the seaplane?"

"First place they'll look," said Heston.

"The ruined chapel," said Kipp. He turned to Beryl. "Go."

"You're coming with us?" she suggested.

"I'm staying here. With Dad. Now go. And not a sound from any of you," he told his siblings.

Dragging Tegan by the hand and toting Shawee on her shoulder, Beryl ran, dogged by Dakota and Sage, into the blowing brush.

Chapter Fifty-Three

Gabe's whirlybird set down on the island. The pilot—his grandson Raymond—was the first one out, then Chantal. Gabe followed behind, grasping on to Winner Demming's slender arm. He held his pistol in the other hand.

There they were—Heston and Kipp, standing like perfect Greek statues, just waiting for him and his precious cargo. Heston, more's the fool, had a rifle in his hands.

He hated these men. They were so young, so handsome, so talented—all to their ruination, just like old Doug Demming. It was to be their downfall, at last, just as it had been his. *Angela, baby, the time has come.* Gabe sighed. He had waited nearly 40 years for this thrill.

"Raymond, take his rifle," he said to his grandson. The boy yanked the rifle from Heston's hand and tossed it into the underbrush.

"Kipp, you've been giving the law a run for its money," he chuckled, pointing his pistol at the Demming girl's head. "Sorry to see you all in one piece. We'll fix that, though. You shouldn't have whacked poor little Lennox."

"I didn't," Kipp said.

"No? Then who did?

"Kipp did it," said Chantal, patting her wig into place. "Don't believe a word he says, Gabe."

"Daddy, please..." His gorgeous hostage whined, scared out of her mind.

She should be. She was about to die. All the Demmings were. The girl's skinny arm was shaky like her voice.

"Kipp didn't kill Lennox," said Heston, eyes glued to his beautiful daughter. "But I know who did—and you won't like it."

Flummoxed, he cast an eye at Raymond. His grandson shrugged. "He's just playing for time, Granddad. He'd say anything to save his wife from the needle."

He was wary of Raymond. Raymond was sweet on the Demming girl. He couldn't be trusted. No one could. He had promised Raymond the girl wouldn't be harmed. But he'd lied.

"Don't move," said a man's voice behind him. It sounded like a New York accent.

"Son of a bitch," moaned Raymond. "Don't move, Granddad. He's got a spear gun drawn and aimed right at your back."

"I thought you were kidding," Heston said to whoever was behind him.

"Drop it, old man," said Kipp, pulling a pistol from his pocket and pointing it at him.

Gabe sighed and let go of the girl, who went flying into Daddy's arms. "So you think you know everything, eh, Heston? Let's hear it." He threw down his weapon.

"Oh, yes, Gabe. I know everything," said Heston, arms around the girl. "And I'll start with who killed Lennox. Ezra, let him have a seat on that piece of coral rock. He's starting to perspire."

"Sweat."

Chapter Fifty-Four

Hugging Winner to his breast, Heston bit back tears. "Are you all right, Ladybug?" He kissed the top of her head. The girl nodded, riveted to him, in the safety of her father's embrace.

Arms encircling his daughter, Heston drew a deep breath and turned to address his audience. Winner stepped back, but he collared his daughter, holding her firmly under his wing. He wasn't going to let her out of his grasp. *Not in this crowd.* Clearing his throat, he began to speak.

"The day Lennox died, I went to see her. I wanted the diary. She laughed at me. I told her I didn't love her and would never love her. She became enraged. She tried to hit me, even spouting nonsense about killing her own mother, Lynne, so that she could get her hands on the diary and blackmail me herself. She screamed, cried, shouted she no longer wanted to live. So she fumbled for a bottle of pills. That was my cue to leave, which I did. Perhaps if I had stayed..."

"Heston, be careful," Ezra said.

Heston spoke evenly, loosening slightly his grip on Winner. "I know I didn't kill her. But I know who did. In the hours leading up to Lennox's death, five other people also paid a visit to her new penthouse. Why? Why did each of them pay a call on Lennox that day?"

Raising one hand aloft, he wiggled his fingers. "Five who get top billing in the cast of suspects—in order of appearance—Arlene Gold, Chantal DuBois, Vivian Champlain, my wife Poppy, and my son Kipp." He indicated those present as he spoke. "For those of you who don't know, my wife is currently being held on suspicion of Lennox's murder."

"Who's surprised?" muttered Chantal under her breath. Gabe smirked unhappily.

Ignoring the gibe, he went on. "Lennox was addicted to painkillers. She died from drinking alcohol after taking an overdose of powerful ones. The bottle of pills spilled beside Lennox's body was her own bottle. The scattered pills, her regular prescription. But Lennox died from a huge overdose—more than could be accounted for by her prescription. Where did this excess medication come from?

"I do believe the dose was self-administered. But I also believe that she was slipped more potent meds than she realized she was taking. Much more potent. A lethal amount."

"According to my wife's attorney, Banks Winston, analysis has shown that the bottle itself bears only two sets of fingerprints—the victim's and my wife Poppy's. I know my wife. She's no fool. Were she the killer, she would have worn gloves or wiped the bottle clean—unless this was a crime of passion, which it was not. This crime was premeditated—by someone else. And yet, paradoxically, it was perpetrated on the spur of the moment."

"Get to the point, Demming." Gabe was quaking sweat in the tropical heat.

"Poppy admits to handling the pill bottle itself—when Lennox stumbled to the bathroom, she was curious. Lennox had already taken some of her own prescription—but Poppy swears Lennox was alive when she left the penthouse, just drowsy after drinking one glass of wine on top of whatever pills she'd already taken. Lennox told Poppy that Shawnee was out with the maid, so Poppy had no idea he was still asleep in the condo."

In his grip, Winner stirred. "Are you okay?" he asked her.

She nodded. "They drugged me, Dad. It's wearing off. I just feel—sleepy."

"She's okay," growled Gabe. "It was a low dose. To keep her quiet for a few hours."

"Dad, I'm okay. Really. Go on with your story."

Uncertain, Heston continued. "Poppy wanted the diary—and she took it and ran when Lennox dozed off. But she didn't murder Lennox."

"It wasn't Ma," said Ezra emphatically, giving Chantal the once-over. "Ma said Lennox hadn't even opened the wine while she was there, but the bottle was there, and a corkscrew."

"No, it wasn't Arlene," Heston agreed. "She went there on business. She could have left the lethally potent pills, but she didn't."

Ezra frowned. "You think Vivian did."

Heston spoke forcefully. "No, I don't. I think Vivian went there that day only to confront Lennox, to demand the diary. But when she arrived and started pleading with Lennox, Poppy arrived. So Lennox hid Vivian in the secret room—the locked shrine she kept to me. Oh, yes. There was such a room. Townsend showed it to me. Vivian waited 45 minutes, but Lennox never returned. Finally, Vivian left the room on her own. Lennox was lying dead on the floor. The pills were scattered around. The wine bottle opened and half empty. Three glasses, all with lipstick on the rim, were visible. The diary was gone. Vivian panicked."

"So panicked she ignored the kid?" Chantal shook her head in disdain. "What a coward."

Ezra bridled. "Vivi didn't know Shawnee was there either, witch. I'll never believe it."

Heston continued. "Vivian panicked. Her first instinct was to destroy any evidence that would implicate Poppy, whom she believed had killed Lennox—because Poppy had come and gone while Vivian had been hiding in the secret room. So she grabbed the two wineglasses—leaving Lennox's on the desk—and threw them in her purse, and fled. She hadn't stopped to think, and never realized, I believe, that the photographs in the secret room would prove her own connection to the Cordova women. She tried to destroy any connection to Poppy—and thus to me."

"Yeah, Vivi's sick—and terrified on top of it," Ezra said. "Her judgment's screwed up."

Heston nodded. "Exactly. But here's the thing: What Vivian also did not realize, is that someone else—other than my wife—also had come and gone while she was hiding in the secret room."

"So you say," Raymond uttered, speaking up for the first time. "Your wife did it."

"Hey, wise ass!" Ezra yelled, pointing a sharp index finger at the bodyguard. "Shut up and listen." Everyone fluttered uneasily. Ezra exchanged glances with Winner, who smiled.

"Easy, Ezra," placated Heston. "Vivian confessed this to me right before life-threatening surgery. I believe she told the truth. Know what else she said? She said that when she went into the secret room, all the doors and windows to the penthouse were closed. When she came out, they were wide open. Know why?"

"Shawnee's guitar," murmured Kipp, snide with the cruelty of it. "On the balcony ledge."

Heston nodded. "Let's suppose that this other person—by the way, there is only one other person it could be—did, in fact, enter the penthouse, give Lennox the lethal pills, have a glass of wine or two with her—really, watched her down a couple glasses, I believe—remember, the wine bottle was empty—and departed—*after* Poppy had fled and *before* Vivian emerged from the secret room.

"Lennox had already been drinking wine and popping pills. It was an easy matter to pump her full of painkillers—lethal doses of Lennox's own prescription. Lennox never knew the tablets hadn't come from her own bottle, but from the killer's bottle. The killer knew all about Lennox's drug habit, had access to her dealer. It was too easy. Lennox was eager to take the drug."

Heston paused, and then said, "Wasn't she, Sasha?"

After a momentary shock, Chantal looked around as though drawing a blank. "Who?"

"What the—" uttered Gabe, gawking at her.

"I believe your original intention was to plant the super-potent pills in Lennox's medicine chest, hoping she would ingest them at a later date. But when you arrived, on some routine business for Gabe, and found her drunk, you seized your opportunity—Sasha."

"Are you referring to me?" Chantal asked haughtily.

"I am. You are unmasked, Ms. Bassett."

"Crap, Heston," Gabe snorted. "Kipp left Lennox those pills and you know it. He's the druggie here. He swallowed roxies like candy."

"Yeah, and you gave them to me, Gabe," said Kipp. "Past tense. Your influence over me is history."

Heston nodded approvingly. "Kipp didn't murder his ex-wife. My son Kipp couldn't even murder himself, much less a wife and son."

"Dad's right. I did not give pills to Lennox," said Kipp. "I have no idea where they came from. Dad says that woman is the culprit. I believe him."

Heston's lip curled in disgust. "I knew you were low, Sasha—after what you did to Poppy years ago. But to entice a child to a 10-story fall? And I thought Lennox was a piece of work. Actually, she was. But she was such a good actress, no one knew. But you're a-a—"

"*Femme fatale,*" said Ezra. "A two-bit floozy with brass knuckles for a heart and a piggy bank for a brain."

Winner was puzzled. "A what?"

"Before your time, cutie," said Ezra sheepishly. He shrugged. "Before my time, too." In his horror, Ezra tightened his grip on Sasha. "Gabe is mentally ill. What's your excuse, dame?"

Kipp spoke up. "I couldn't figure it out. Now it makes sense. Even Lennox wouldn't have put the kid's favorite toy out there."

"Sasha had a motive," said Heston. "The death of Poppy's grandson would have been an unexpected bonus for Sasha Bassett. Never managed to have kids of your own, did you, Sasha? She had an opportunity to twist the blade she'd stuck years ago in Poppy's back. So she twisted it."

"Leave Her to Heaven," quipped Ezra.

"Say what?" asked Kipp.

Ezra glowered. "It's the title of a classic film from 1940s. Jeanne Crain is a murderess. She watches her paralyzed kid brother-in-law drown in a lake without trying to save him. "Leave her to Heaven."

Heston elaborated. "It's a quotation from Shakespeare's *Hamlet.* Hamlet wasn't willing to tackle his mom's guilt in his father the king's death. Ezra means her punishment is out of our league as humans. A higher power will have to handle it."

Sasha piped up. "You can't prove I'm the murderer—because I'm not. It could have been anybody. What if the murdered never visited Lennox's new penthouse at all, that day or any other day? What if the murderer gave the pills to Lennox earlier that day, but in a different location? We know Lennox did go out that morning. You said she met Poppy."

Heston nodded. "Which brings us to another someone else, someone at the Fontainebleau that morning, someone who knew Lennox very well—and secretly—and had for many days. It's possible that the father of Lennox's unborn baby could have given her the pills that killed her.

Lennox was expecting when she died. Did you all know? Gabe knew. But he wasn't the father."

The old man grunted. He seemed to age by the minute.

"Lennox had ended her affair with Gabe. She landed a bigger fish. But you, Sasha, you didn't know that Lennox had found a stronger, faster playmate. You knew Gabe wanted Lennox more than he wanted you. You couldn't take the thought of returning to poverty. You set out to destroy your rival—as I know you've done in the past. And, this time, you succeeded."

"How did you justify killing your rival's unborn baby, too? Figured she was going to kill it anyway? She didn't want it. She didn't want anyone's, but mine or my son's, because it would be my grandchild."

Kipp's face grew florid.

Gabe sat motionless. He seemed a phantom, a pale specter struggling to remain intact. "You're a crackpot, Demming." His words lacked conviction. He cast a withering glance at his personal assistant.

"It's lies, Gabe," she insisted. She looked his way. "You lie, Heston!" Stepping backwards, she clutched her wig in the warm ocean breeze.

"Pipe down, pipsqueak." Ezra ripped off her wig. "Your cover's blown. Deal with it."

At the sight of Sasha's short, dark hair, Heston's lips curved upward.

"You douche bag!" she screamed, dashing down the shore. "How dare you?"

"Hey, look out! She's getting away!" Winner was alert now.

Quickly, Kipp thrust the gun into his Heston's hands. Running after Sasha, he tackled her in the sand. Dragging her back, he held her in a locked grip. "And you hit her."

"And for the record, Gabe," Heston said, summing up, "I now know that you, not my father, killed your young, innocent wife, Angela.

Angela was a patient of my father's, at your insistence. You probably wanted to document that she was incompetent or something—to hide the vicious mind games you played with her." He turned aside. "Gabe himself was once a physician headed for a brilliant academic career, like my father. Did you know that, Ezra?"

"News to me. Charles Boyer did the same thing to Ingrid Bergman in *Gaslight*."

"His wife had mental problems," Heston said. He pointed at Kipp. "He sent her to my father, Douglas Demming—your grandfather—for treatment. And Angela and Douglas Demming had a desperate love affair. When Gabe found out about it, he decided to set them both up for a fall. Revenge has ruled your life, Gabe."

"Go to hell."

"Gabe arranged everything to look as though Doug had conducted secret, illegal drug experiments on his patients. He even murdered two of Doug's other patients to make it look convincing. It did. The scandal ruined my father's reputation. He was never prosecuted because the institution hushed things up at the request of the other victims' wealthy families. Mental illness was taboo back then, considered bad taste. But my father was drummed out of his profession. He never recovered. And I don't think he ever knew what actually happened to him. He was terrified all the time."

Gabe laughed. "Yeah. He hanged himself." He kept laughing, unable to stop.

"Are you suggesting he didn't actually hang himself?" asked Heston.

"I am suggesting," snickered Gabe, "that he had some help."

"Why, you!" Heston lunged for the old devil. Kipp stopped him.

"He's old and crazy," said Kipp. "Let him be. Whatever he did, it's too late now. He's to be pitied, pour soul. Think what a hell his whole life has been. I forgive him."

"You what?" asked Heston. He eyed his son. "You have changed."

"That's all well and good," said Ezra. "But what about the diary? Where is it now?"

Reaching inside his jacket, Heston pulled out the frayed, old journal and waved it tauntingly in the air.

"You mean this?"

"That's mine by legal right," growled Gabe, standing up and hobbling forward. "I own Lennox's Life Rights. It's mine to publish or not. Give it to me."

"Granddad!" Ram ran after the tottering old man, who panted from heat exhaustion.

"Stay back!" Heston shouted.

But it was too late. Gabe teetered forward, lashing out for the diary, flailing at Heston. Heston tossed the book to Ezra. In his fury, Ram latched onto Winner, who screamed. He encircled Winner's throat with a meaty, muscular arm and stood behind her, threatening her life.

"Weapons down," he said to Kipp and Ezra. "Or I'll break this beauteous neck."

"Like a wishbone," guffawed Gabe, who collapsed into a sitting position on the sand.

"Old man, you got us into a hell of a mess this time," said Ram. "And don't give me any lip about Laurel and Hardy," he said to Ezra, who shrugged resignedly and jammed his spear gun into the sand.

"Go on," Ram told Kipp, who, hesitantly, did as instructed. His questioning eyes flew to Heston. "Now, you three gents—lie down. Face down, on the ground."

"The diary..." Gabe wheezed, but his grandson ignored him. He struggled to one knee. He stretched his arm toward Kipp's discarded gun. His fingers reached it...

"The diary is your concern," said Ram, backing away, his massive bicep choking Winner's throat. Her blue eyes bulged. Her jaw was drawn. Her limbs flopped like sea grass in the wind. "Do it! I mean it! Or this beautiful girl dies, cracked in half like a pretzel. And that will piss me off even more because I had plans of my own for Winner. I'm in love with her."

"You can't be!" shouted Ezra. "She's only twelve years old!"

"She won't always be twelve, you moron!" Ram retorted. "Shit. You're too stupid to live." He tightened his choke-hold on Winner. "On the ground, all three of you."

Firing lightening quick glances at one another, Heston, Kipp, and Ezra dropped to their knees and fell prone on the ground. Heston knew he had to something quickly, or his daughter would be killed—or worse. He could hear her piteous squeals as the brute choked her.

"Dakota, no!" screamed Beryl from the brush. But she was too late.

His youngest son appeared from beneath the branches of a tall Australian pine. Dakota brandished a rifle—the one Gabe had discarded for him. Securing the rifle butt against his small shoulder, the boy aimed the gun at Ram. His eye found the rifle sight. He squinted, taking aim.

"Let go of my sister, you creep," Dakota said evenly to Ram.

"You, again? Shit." Ram almost laughed. He shook his head at the foolishness. But he didn't fool Heston. *Not this time.* Ram was scared. Dakota was a loose cannon with a lit fuse.

On the ground, Gabe, chortling at the sight of the small boy armed to the hilt, had secured Kipp's pistol in his claw. He turned the gun, pointing it at Dakota.

"Put it down, son, or I'll blow your puny brains out," Gabe wheezed, cocking the pistol.

Dakota swung the rifle back and forth between Ram and Gabe. Which to shoot? Heston could see his son was desperately torn and unsure. He looked at his daughter. He would die in her stead. What should he do? What was possible? Which child should he save? Which to sacrifice?

Suddenly, Kipp was crawling toward Gabe. He was up on his knees. Gabe trained his gun on Kipp. "Gabe, you don't want to do this, believe me. You're better than this." Kipp reached out an open hand to Gabe.

Heston knew Kipp was distracting the old man from the boy.

"You're going first, Kippy," Gabe said hoarsely. "Because I like you least of all. You are sexual vermin, just like your grandfather. A plague on this earth."

"If that's the best you've got—but I forgive you," Kipp said simply.

Heston watched Dakota's eyes. The boy had made a decision. Slowly, Dack turned his sights on Raymond, pointing the rifle directly at the former bodyguard's head, not fifteen feet away.

"You forgive me?" Gabe snarled at Kipp, his strength waning as the sun beat down.

"You've made mistakes. So have we all."

"You made some whoppers," the old man snapped.

"Yes, I did. But haven't you heard? 'The ones who are the hardest to love are the ones who need it the most.' I was hard to love. I hated myself, just as you hate yourself, for not being perfect, for doing things that were wrong—very wrong. Yet I forgave myself. You should forgive yourself, Gabe." Kipp held out his hand to the old scoundrel. "Revenge won't bring back her love, Gabe. No death—mine, my father's, my sister's, my brother's—can help you find her love again. That's going in the wrong direction."

"So is prison, Kipp," observed Ezra snidely, standing guard. "I don't think you need it."

"Take my hand, Gabe. Come on." Kipp extended his arm and wiggled his fingers. "Give it up. I love you, man." Moving forward in the sand, Kipp helped the wavering old man sit on the ground.

Eagle-eyed, Dakota trained his sight on Ram, who instantly released his choke-hold on Winner and tore off running toward the ocean waves.

Gabe and Kipp gazed into one another's eyes. Slowly, Gabe surrendered his weapon, letting it fall into Kipp's grasp. Kipp knelt down beside the old man.

A split-second later, Dakota fired his rifle at Ram. The tissue burst from the bodyguard's triceps in a rainstorm of spurting blood. Plunging into the crashing surf, Raymond Cady swam out to sea and, in moments, had disappeared. Grabbing Kipp's gun, Heston ran across the sand firing shots, but all missed the mark, as far as he could tell. He had aimed at Ram's bobbing bald head.

Screaming, Sasha ran toward the house, but Ezra tackled her enthusiastically. "I should have played football, Kipp. *The Male Animal* is one my *favorite* films," he wheezed, wrestling her to the ground. "Jack Carson and Henry Fonda. Olivia de Haviland."

Sasha seethed, struggling in the sand. Heston watched in fascination as he cradled Winner in his arms. Knowing Ezra, he enjoyed the feel of Sasha's voluminous breasts, the only real thing about the vixen who had materialized out of the distant past.

Chapter Fifty-Five

After an extensive dive search, Kipp swam back to shore empty handed. Ezra stood watch over Sasha Bassett—and the deflated ego of Renfroe Cady, alias Gabriel Cade—while the others regained their equilibrium.

"No luck?" Ezra asked Kipp.

Kipp shook his head, flinging water from his hair and body. Ram had disappeared, swallowed by the sea—a lost cause, at least for the time being.

"Thank you, bro," Kipp said to Dakota, extending a wet hand.

Dakota shook his hand, a look of astonishment on his face. "You're my idol. I couldn't let the old guy and the wig lady mess with my idol, now could I?"

"Heck, no." Kipp hugged the too-calm boy. He was worried. He knew Dakota's reaction would come later. "I owe you one, Dakota Demming."

"Other way around," Dakota nodded conclusively. But he didn't push Kipp away when he embraced him. He believed the boy was shuddering inside.

"Don't idolize me, man. Idolize some guy who does something good in the world."

"You're good. You're the best."

"Nah. Not where it counts. But maybe someday I will be. I'd like to be worthy of your admiration, little bro." He released the shattered child, adding, "I'll give it my utmost attention."

Short and tall, the two brothers high-fived. Hearing a noise, they looked up. Out of the northeastern sky, another helicopter was approaching—a helicopter emblazoned with the letters 'FBI.'

"Come on, Berry," cried Kipp. "We're getting out of here." He grasped her hand.

Grabbing her arm brusquely, Heston said, "Beryl, ditch the plane." Both she and he understood his meaning. Grinning fondly, she placed the video camera in his hand and nodded. Awkwardly, Kipp shook his hand. Heston pulled him close in an embrace, slapping his back, and releasing him.

"Son, I must tell you. I visited Lennox the morning of her death demanding the diary."

"Why—"

"Listen up. Lennox confided how she lied to you about Shawnee's paternity. She laughed in my face. Son, I swear to you. You are that boy's father, not I. It's not possible that I could be his father. There was nothing between Lennox and me—except for one night of mistaken identity 23 years ago. It's a long story, but—"

Kipp looked at the descending FBI chopper. "Okay, Dad. I believe you," he mumbled quickly, glancing at Beryl and Shawnee. Beryl was aglow with excitement. Shawnee looked dazed.

"I love you, son," Heston whispered. "And grandson." He kissed Shawnee's chubby cheek and pushed Kipp towards the far end of the key. "Go!"

"Dad," Kipp said, doubling back. "Give a scoop to Cecily Hodges— the reporter. She was the only friend I had left." Quickly, he kissed Heston's cheek. "That's for Mom."

"Okay, go!"

Sprinting, Kipp extracted Shawnee from Beryl's arms, and the trio disappeared down the shore, presumably headed to the cove, and waded out to the seaplane, climbing aboard. In the pilot's seat, Beryl taxied out into the ocean, built up speed, and took off over the heads of the people spilling out of the FBI chopper and the sudden appearance of a collective media onslaught at sea. Airborne over the anchored *Angel Baby,* Beryl gave the world one last wave of her wings. The seaplane—carrying his generation's most provocative rock star—disappeared over the northeastern horizon. Beryl was flying right smack into the Bermuda Triangle.

Chapter Fifty-Six

"Can you see anything?" Facing the window, Poppy leaned across Banks as the FBI helicopter set down in the sugary beach sand of Heart of Fire Key.

"I see people," Banks responded, long neck craning as he discerned images outside the window. "A man and woman running up the beach—with babe in arms."

"Do you see Heston?" she asked, nearly on top of him. "Kipp?"

Suddenly, they were on the ground. Unbuckling her belt, she climbed out over Banks and accompanied officers into the clearing around their landing spot. They were on the far side of the island, away from the house. She had been able to identify the island for Agent Townsend and Detective Betancourt, as they had requested. Banks had arranged for her to accompany the officers, but only if he were allowed to be present.

But she knew that legal representation wasn't the only reason he had accompanied her. Banks had fallen hard for her. She knew the signs, and this man wanted her. Did she want him?

Maybe.

Even though Heston is the love of my life?

Heston was a rogue. He couldn't be trusted. He had proven it with his lies and deceit. He was self-centered. He was irritable. He was quick tempered. He was thoughtless. He had been with more women than he could count.

But he knew the entire erogenous landscape of her body. It wasn't even her body anymore. It had become his. Could she live without his touch, his scent, the feel of him? Even when she hated him, he was the life and breath of her.

Starlight on salt water... Their nights of love had produced four living human beings.

Could this wooden, affected, cosmetically tanned attorney ever be all that to her? She had to be frank with herself. The most attractive thing about Banks was his bankroll. His famous way with the ladies was unquestionably due to his wealth and manners, not his masculine prowess.

Heston had *prowess*. But he had lied about his past. He could lie again.

She knew it wasn't the first time an attorney had fallen in love with a client. *Probably happens all the time.* Like movie stars falling for their leading ladies, changing their minds with each new picture. Even she had not yet been able to acknowledge the depth of her hurt. Too much had been happening...

"Where is everybody?" she asked Detective Betancourt. She seemed to be drifting nowhere, nonsensically.

"Over there. By the pines." He pointed. "Mint?"

"Mommy! Mommy!" To her utter astonishment, her children ran into her arms. Even Winner, who had been acting so grown up and aloof, ran to her and encircled her along with Tegan and Sage. Dakota, however, she could see still standing in the distance. He dashed away as Heston approached him.

"Dack shot Ram, Mommy," Winner whispered automaton-like, hand caressing her own throat. "To save me. I was a fool..."

"Where is he?" She didn't know which way to turn. "Are you all right, Winner? We came here after you. Did they hurt you?"

"I'm fine. Thanks to Dakota, and Dad and Kipp and—" She cast a glance back toward the beach, where Banks and Townsend were getting the lowdown from Ezra, who stood watch, spear gun in hand, over a short, buxom woman who seemed oddly familiar.

"Who is that?" she asked Winner, as the twins yanked on her arms and danced her around happily. The woman had caught sight of her. If looks could kill, she would be a dead woman. It was Sasha Bassett, all right. She returned Sasha's evil glare, until Winner blocked her view.

"She's Mr. Cade's secretary. Dad said she was jealous. That's why she killed Lennox."

Poppy gasped. She whirled around. "Where's your father? I saw him a minute ago. Where's Kipp? Detective, will you watch my children for a moment, please? I n-need to speak to my s-son—and my husband. I need to make s-sure..."

"Sure thing. Say, Mrs. Demming. But your older son's flown the co-op. Did you see this?" He held up his mobile. The headline screamed: GRAMMY WINNER ALIVE IN FLORIDA KEYS?

"That's why these boats are showing up around here," she observed, hand shading her eyes as she looked out to sea. "Was Kipp here?" She had been afraid of something like this.

"Yep," said Ezra, approaching her. The woman he had been guarding was now in police custody. "He and Berry and Shawnee took off a few minutes ago."

"T-Took off for where?"

He shrugged. "The wild blue yonder."

She didn't know what to think. She watched as Detective Betancourt brought out his roll of spearmints and passed out samples to the kids.

"Like one?" he asked her, ready with his finger to pop a mint from the open roll.

"S-Sure. Thanks," she said, taking the mint he popped out for her. She might not want to be married to Heston anymore, but, for some odd reason, she still wanted him to find her desirable—some feat after she'd spent the past 24 hours in the clink. *Oh, why does he matter so much to me?*

She would have to speak to him. He had spotted her—and he was talking to Banks.

Chapter Fifty-Seven

"Sorry, old son," Banks said, taking Heston aside. "But obviously, after her release, Poppy will be coming with me. Life goes on and whatnot."

Anxiously, Heston's eyes sought for and found the slender figure of his middle-aged wife. To him, she was as desirable as ever. He had never loved another human more. She didn't seem to notice him. She was busy listening to Betancourt pontificate.

Winner ran back to his side. He caught her in his arms. Her head tucked beneath his chin, he squeezed his daughter tightly as an octopus massaging its dinner. "My Ladybug."

"Ow, Daddy." But she stayed close to him, hand on his biceps. "Dad, look at Dack," she said, pointing to the forlorn little boy meandering aimlessly.

"I'll be right back, " he assured the girl, releasing her and ambling nonchalantly toward Dakota, who was leaning against a swaying coconut palm, toying with a downed pod.

"It's cool, Dad. I get it." Winner receded inside herself.

He didn't know what to say to his son. *What do you say to a young boy who just winged a man with a firearm, a man who apparently drowned as a result?*

"Where did all the press come from?" He wondered aloud, hands on his hips. He tried to behave so as not to alarm the already traumatized boy. He placed a hand on Dakota's bony shoulder.

Dakota tugged at his shirttail. The boy held a mobile aloft for him to see. "I think I did it, Dad," he confessed. "This is yours. I sent Felicia a text message—that we found Kipp. She posted it on her social networking page. See?"

"Damnation." He squatted before his young son, taking him by the shoulders. "Are you all right, son?" Gently, he touched the boy's shiner. He put his arm around the boy's shoulder.

Wincing slightly, Dakota nodded. He smiled, a gap opening up.

"You lost a tooth." He said softly, heart breaking like swells in a thunderstorm.

"A baby tooth," Dakota confessed. He drew the tooth from the pocket of his shorts. "I saved it for the Tooth Fairy."

"Good man," he said, squeezing the boy's shoulders. Abruptly, he drew him near in a tight embrace. "I'm proud of you, Dakota." *Winner's counselor, Dr. Fishburne, will welcome a new patient next week.*

Rising, he stepped away and stood beside his youngest son, staring toward the eastern horizon. Dakota slipped a hand into his and stared with him.

What would become of his eldest son?

"Hi, guys." Poppy sauntered up behind them.

He and Dakota turned.

"I hear you're a big hero."

Abashed, Dakota slinked away into the shadows. Quietly, Poppy followed and slipped her arm around his shoulder and kissed the top of his red head. "You saved their lives, Dakota. You're a hero," she observed, shaking him affectionately. She hugged him to her bosom. "Oh, thank Heaven you weren't killed."

Forgotten for the moment, Banks looked toward Heston, and then started for the police chopper.

Accepting the challenge, he loped to the lawyer's side, blocking his departure. "I'm no logician, Banks. It's true. I only know it makes sense. You fathered Lennox's unborn child. You were her new sugar daddy—you, the missing X who told her where to find Poppy."

"What's this?" said Poppy meekly, approaching them, holding Dakota by the hand.

"Poppy, how did Lennox know you were going to be in Miami?" Heston asked. "At the Fontainebleau?"

Poppy cocked her red head. She looked askance. "I don't know. No one else knew, except Winner—and you and Lissette. We didn't even tell Ram until the morning of the drive over."

He pointed to the man at her side. "There is only one other person who did know."

"Banks!" Turning, Poppy gaped in astonishment at her attorney.

Heston nodded. "Gabe Cade was Lennox's lover, all right—her *old* lover, her discarded sugar daddy, the gullible fool who had footed the bill for her excesses in recent months, but not for her elegant new penthouse. Banks sprang for it."

Poppy stared. "You mean Banks..."

"Does not have your best interests at heart." He turned to Banks. "Does the term 'conflict of interest' ring any bells with you, Lawyer Winston?"

"Now, see here," Banks whined, taking offense as he backed away slightly.

"What Gabe didn't realize—or didn't face—was that Lennox was in love with, had always been in love with, and would always be infatuated with me. She would never love him or anyone else. But she was willing to use anyone for her own gain."

"You're an arrogant prick," Banks scoffed. "My sister Maude is right about you. Your ego is insufferable."

Anger piqued, Heston pointed an accusing finger at the upper-crust snob. "When Lennox told you she was pregnant with your child, you were done with her. When she told you, later, she planned to have the child aborted, you were glad, but done, nevertheless. No, Banks, you didn't kill Lennox. You dumped her that morning. Why else would she be drinking midday?"

Turning to Poppy, he reached out for her hand. She withheld it coldly. "I want to know only one thing from you, Heston. Is it true? Did Sasha Bassett kill Lennox?"

"Yes, my love. You are absolved."

"Why did she do it? She wasn't mentioned in the diary."

"Lennox's death had nothing to do with the diary. It was a coincidence. Can we go home now? I'll speak to Townsend about your release."

But, to his utter shock, she walked away without a word, taking his children, his whole life, with her. Following, he wheeled his wife around. He searched her eyes. It was no go.

"Drop it for now, Heston. Please. Whatever Banks did, whatever Sasha did, it doesn't change anything between you and me. You lied to me—by commission and omission. I can't trust you. I'll never be able to trust you again—and I don't know if I can live with that." She walked away, leaving him senseless and Banks trailing speechless in her aftermath.

Sad-eyed, Townsend approached him. "We're taking your kids with us—for their own protection. It was your wife's idea. Okay with you?"

Reluctantly, he nodded. Every part of his being wanted to argue, except for the one small kernel of truth at his core. His kids were better off without him.

"Maybe after all this blows over, we can take that fishing trip together," Townsend suggested with affable compassion.

"Sounds like a plan. But you'll be busy booking Dr. Renfroe Cady for a while. His old sins cast a longer, deeper shadow than mine." He turned away. "If such a thing is possible."

Chapter Fifty-Eight

Three weeks later, Heston commanded center stage in the jam-packed main concert hall of The Naples Philharmonic. His charity event to benefit The Franco Demming Trust, "An Evening with Heston Demming," had evolved into a memorial service and musical tribute to his son, Kipp, and those who had disappeared with him in the plane crash. The event had become a world-class, SRO sell-out, with Kipp's legion of adoring fans—many carrying posters of Kipp and funereal floral offerings—congregated outside on the grounds and spilling over onto the upscale Pelican Bay Boulevard. Police and security officers had been called to rein them in. Satellite dishes on trucks lined the street in both directions. Reporter with mics and cameramen abounded, as did paparazzi. He was pleased with the turnout.

Although Heston was the star of the show inside the hall, he was not alone on stage. Back-up singers, including Lissette's daughter Felicia—his own discovery—lined up behind him, swaying to the music as they sang. Heston knew he was launching the girl's career as a professional singer. She had received her Equity card, thanks to him, because it was her first professional appearance. He believed she had a real future in the music industry, as did Arlene Gold, who had taken her on—as a favor to him—as her client.

In the audience, a wheelchair-bound Arlene, her son Ezra, his own four kids, and, amazingly enough, Poppy were seated in the second row of the audience. He was stunned to see his wife. He hadn't seen her in three weeks, not since the plane crash and the ruckus on Heart of Fire Key. She and the kids had been living at the Ritz-Carlton. She appeared to be escort-free, a fact which gave him a glimmer of hope as his song ended, and the orchestra prepared for the grand finale.

Bowing, he addressed the audience. "I want to thank you all for coming tonight, to share this time with me and my family as we honor our lost sons—most recently, Kipp, as well as our grandson Shawnee, and our beloved family faithful, Nanny Beryl Northgate." Quickly, he cast a glance into third row center, where Beryl's British mum and dad wept openly as they listened to him. "As you know, my young son, Franco, was lost in a tragic car accident eight years ago. He would be 20 years old, were he still alive. My son, Kipp, along with Beryl, and Shawnee were lost in a plane crash three weeks ago off Key Largo. By the time the rescue workers reached the plane, it had sunk into the sea. No bodies were recovered, a fact most difficult for us all to bear. With no final resting place, we can only hope to keep their memories alive through the generosity of your spirits—and through Kipp's great gifts of music and love." Here the audience applauded warmly.

His jaw clenched. "Of course, we will miss the unforgettable Lennox Cordova. Words cannot express my feelings for her." He clutched the handkerchief in his pocket, but did not remove it. "All evening my friends and I have performed songs for you from the catalogue of material Kipp left for his mother and me. I'm going to end with a final selection, one I find to be lovely and, I believe, indicative of the strong feeling Kipp had developed for Berry before their untimely—er, loss.

"But, first, I ask you all to watch this video, the one Beryl shot of Kipp and Shawnee only hours before the crash. It was Kipp's acceptance speech, for he had just been informed by Beryl that he had won the Grammy Award for the year's best male vocalist. Only hours before, he had undergone a major change of consciousness—and he wanted to share it with you and with the world."

A large screen revealed itself on stage. The house lights dimmed. Suddenly, Kipp's larger than life image appeared. As Kipp's words flowed over the audience, sobs could be heard, coughs and uncontrolled weeping. The video faded quietly away. Heston stepped back onto the stage, now dark except for his sole spotlight. Microphone in hand, he nodded, and the orchestra began to play

"So here it is, Kipp's song for Beryl." Away from the mic, he cleared his throat. On cue, the words poured forth. For some reason, his eyes sought out his wife, sitting small, alone, and achingly lovely in an aisle seat on Row Two center.

Do you love me
As I love you?
A baby's tender sigh
Do you love me
As I love you?
A balmy summer sky
Do you love me
As I love you?
A hurricane's great eye
Do you love me
As I love you?
Cupid, let your arrow fly
Is the love I offer you
The love you're dreaming of
Or is my lonely reverie
A wild dream of love?

Singing, he reached out to embrace his audience only to once again glimpse his wife as she buried her face in her hands. Crossing downstage right, he stood at the foot of the stage. Dropping onto one knee, he sang directly to her.

Do you love me
As I love you?
A candle's glowing light
Do you love me
As I love you?
A far star burning bright
Do you love me
As I love you?
A blazing meteorite

Rising, he walked down the steps at the edge of the stage. The spotlight followed him. Entering the aisle, he stood before his wife, who was seated in the aisle seat. On impulse, he knelt and sang the final verse to her amid a hushed crowd of onlookers.

Do you love me
As I love you?
A drop of dew in spring
Do you love me
As I love you?
A brook meandering
Do you love me
As I love you?
A cascade thundering
Do you love me
As I love you?
Will you wear my wedding ring?

In the glare of the spotlight, Poppy sprang to her feet and rushed up the aisle toward the exit doors. Along with the craning audience, he watched her receding figure disappear through the lobby doors. The music died. A terrible longing—pain and embarrassment—hung in the air of the packed hall. The audience watched him. What would he do now? He wanted to die.

Maybe I already have. Backing away, he groped the wall. *Dignity, man.*

Somehow, he regained his footing. "Well, there you have it, ladies and gentlemen," he croaked into the microphone. Awkwardly, he retraced his steps up onto the stage. "The Bard said it best, did he not? The course of true love ne'er did run smooth.' " He panned the hall, a tempered smile pasted on. "Good night," he said, voice breaking. "Thank you for coming to honor our beloved...darlings."

He broke down. Rushing forward, Felicia caught him in her arms and led him into the wings. The audience rose in a solemn standing ovation.

Chapter Fifty-Nine

The following day dawned gray and overcast. Alone inside the exhibition gallery of The Naples Philharmonic, Heston contemplated with contempt the self-portrait on which he had labored so painstakingly in the past. The local art critics had been lukewarm. They hadn't sliced and diced him, but he was no Paul Gauguin. *Not yet.* He watched two workers remove his self-portrait from the wall and wrap it for transport.

"Careful," he said brusquely. "It's been sold. They all have."

Obeying, the workers disassembled the rest of his exhibition. Drifting, he stood watching, hands in his pants pockets. He felt the letter, safe and secure. Drawing it out, he unfolded the piece of stationery. For what seemed the hundredth time, he read Marissa's precious letter. He had received it three days ago.

Dear Mr. Demming,

Thank you for your discrete support of our new school and clinic in the Dominican Republic. Thanks to The Franco Demming Trust, 40 children of the slums are now being educated and fed two meals a day. They are receiving quality medical care.

I cannot overstate the importance of your generous financial gift to the lives of these children. Believe me, nothing is wasted. When each meal ends, we find not one, single grain of rice left on any plate. Someday, when you give permission, we will disclose your identity to our boys and girls. I know they would wish me to send their love.

Happily, we now have new helpers here at our remote facility. One is a handsome, young bearded man who assists my husband, Dr. Perfecto Logue, with the running of the clinic. The man's new bride is a short, bossy woman who is wonderful with the children. The man has a small son from a previous marriage. I am happy to report that the boy grows taller and more sturdy with each passing day. The child is good with fig-ures. As soon as he is old enough, he will enter our school. This family has become indispensable to our work. They are, I be-lieve, very happy here.

On a personal note, Perfecto's and my baby, a girl, will be born soon. We will call her Chloe. Looking forward to our con-tinued association, I am

Yours Most Sincerely,

Marissa Neville Logue, Ob. Gyn.

Santo Domingo

Reassured, he refolded and replaced the letter in his pocket. Last night, he had given the performance of his life. He had lied for love—perhaps not the most ethical of acts, but he had never been known for his stellar moral choices. It was enough to know his loved ones were safe—for the time being. But what of his own future?

His phone chirped. He viewed the text message. "I'm flying the chil-dren to The Hamptons. Poppy." Numbly, he replied to her message. "Be careful."

"Nice work, Mr. Demming," a timid worker offered, studying him closely.

"Thank you." He looked up and nodded. *He knows.* Inadvertently, he touched his lapel.

He looked around. His old self-portrait had disappeared, just as had his old self. In the twinkling of a fading star, reality had changed. His eldest son was his own man. His own poor father had been exonerated.

His children were out of harm's way, although Ram was still a wild card. The restraining order was only a band-aid. No one knew whether Raymond Cady was alive or dead.

It was his job to protect his kids. But who had faith in him now? Poppy had left him. She had taken his children with her. Should he follow them to The Hamptons? Demand to take his place at the head of the table? He had made such a mess of things. *Poor little Ladybug.* He had failed her twice, when she needed him most. He needed to make things right.

He sent a second reply. "Shall I join you?" Instantly, the reply came. "No." Moments later, a second reply, more polite. "Give me time. Please." He didn't reply. Restlessly, he tossed his phone repeatedly, catching it like a one-armed juggler.

Paul Gauguin was right. Heart of Fire Key was beckoning. Alone with the elements, he could do what he liked, live as he wanted, without asking permission from anyone, not even his public. He could be alone to create—*what?*

Townsend said a man either creates or destroys himself. Which would it be? He must paint a new self-portrait in years to come. A man is the artist of his own life. He fingered the small silver flask in his lapel pocket. Removing the flask, he unscrewed the lid and drank.

All gone.

He looked around the deserted exhibition hall. He was the only living soul in a castle fortress with empty walls. He chucked his phone into the nearest ceramic vase and headed for the lobby and his Ferrari. He needed to find the nearest liquor dispensary. Last night he had taken his first sip of Scotch in eight years of sobriety. His fingers trembled as he ignited the engine. The Ferrari squealed toward The Waterside Shops and the Starfish Grille.

No way I can live without Poppy—unless I'm drunk off my ass.

Chapter Sixty

Cradled in Kipp's arms, Beryl lay spent in afterglow, her cheek pressed to her husband's bare chest. She stared in the low embers in the grate.

"I love you, Mrs. Kendrick," he said, his voice a slow trickle. Musing, he stroked her naked back and shoulders. She glanced round. He was staring into space.

She heard a humming sound. A new tune resonated deep within his breast. He hummed the melody louder. She glanced at the guitar standing in the corner of the tiny bedroom.

"While you're up, babe, hand me that guitar, will you?" He grinned, popping her playfully.

Sighing prettily, eyes rolling, she rose, naked, and retrieved the guitar. Handing it to him, she kneeled on the bed and sat back on her haunches. He took it, pulling the bed sheet over his lower extremities. "I feel a song coming on," he explained, strumming a G-chord.

She leaned in, watching him and listening, distracting him. His eyes caressed her body. His hand ceased strumming. His fret hand fondled her engorged nipple.

"I'm still not accustomed to all this, you know," she said, flushing. "I'm afraid I'll slip. Call you Kipp by mistake."

Unconcerned, he smiled lazily at her, stroking her forearm. Quickly, he dropped the guitar onto the floor, propping its neck against the mattress. "Won't happen, Mavis," he said. Rolling onto his side, he placed his elbow on the pillow and propped his shaggy, golden head in his hand. Deftly, he slid a hand between her legs. "So, tell me, ma'am. How do you like married life?"

"I like it just fine, thank you." She giggled. She gasped in pleasure.

"Anything about it you don't like?" he asked playfully.

"Absolutely nothing," she said, her breath catching. "I am a fortunate woman. My husband is the world's greatest lover."

"Ah," said Kipp. "Your husband is the world's luckiest man."

"Indeed? How so?" she asked, as he drew her on top of him, his lips grazing hers repeatedly. His hands clenched her buttocks. He entered her. It was a pleasure unimaginable in her wildest dreams. Kipp's body began to undulate.

"Because—even if he weren't—the world's greatest lover—which he is—his bossy, little British wife—wouldn't—know—the difference."

Her giggles were lost in the storm of ecstasy that followed as the resonating guitar went spinning across the concrete floor of the hut. In the crib in the front room, Shawnee, oblivious, slumbered soundly into the night. Outside their window, a full moon shone down brightly over the remote enclave on the eastern shore of the Dominican Republic.

About the Author

Tina Murray is the acclaimed author of a captivating series of glitzy, suspense-filled romance novels, the Heston Demming series. Murray's steamy, yet spiritual saga chronicles the life and loves of handsome movie-superstar, Heston Demming. In Murray's stories, the sexy actor struggles to tame his passions and torments. While he copes with fame and fortune, he searches for his lost soul, amid the hidden ruins of a secret past. Although he travels the world, Heston's home base is upscale Naples, Florida, where author Murray has lived, intermittently, since her teen years, and knows well. An actress and artist, she also lived in New York and Los Angeles. Returning to college as an adult, she earned both her bachelor's degree and master's degree from the University of Miami. After a tour in real estate, she returned to graduate school. She now holds a doctorate in art education from The Florida State University. Her hobbies include genealogy and songwriting.

She belongs to the Romance Writers of America and the Florida Writers Association.

Coming Soon!

A BIG FAN OF YOURS|
BY
TINA MURRAY

"Complicated relationships add an undercurrent of complexity to Tina Murray's latest novel, a sun-drenched Florida romp filled with movie star glitz, a handful of attempted murders, and plenty of romance."
— Jaden Terrell, Author of the internationally published Jared McKean mysteries

For more information
visit: www.SpeakingVolumes.us

On Sale Now!

BETH GROUNDWATER
CLAIRE HANOVER MYSTERIES